John Banville's Narcissistic Fictions

John Banville's Narcissistic Fictions

Mark O'Connell
Trinity College Dublin, Ireland

First published 2013 by
PALGRAVE MACMILLAN

Palgrave Macmillan in the UK is an imprint of Macmillan Publishers
Limited, registered in England, company number 785998, of Houndmills,
Basingstoke, Hampshire RG21 6XS.

Palgrave Macmillan in the US is a division of St Martin's Press LLC,
175 Fifth Avenue, New York, NY 10010.

Palgrave Macmillan is the global academic imprint of the above companies
and has companies and representatives throughout the world.

Palgrave® and Macmillan® are registered trademarks in the United States,
the United Kingdom, Europe and other countries.

ISBN 978-1-349-34834-3   ISBN 978-1-137-36524-8 (eBook)
DOI 10.1007/978-1-137-36524-8

This book is printed on paper suitable for recycling and made from fully
managed and sustained forest sources. Logging, pulping and manufacturing
processes are expected to conform to the environmental regulations of the
country of origin.

A catalogue record for this book is available from the British Library.

A catalog record for this book is available from the Library of Congress.

Typeset by MPS Limited, Chennai, India.

Contents

Acknowledgements

This book is the result not just of my own work, but also of the financial, intellectual and moral support of a number of others. I want firstly to thank Paul Delaney for his enthusiasm for my research and for his generosity with his time and ideas. His keen eye as an editor has been invaluable, as has his guiding hand as supervisor of the Ph.D. thesis in which this book originated. I never once walked out of his office without feeling in some way wiser than when I walked in. My gratitude is also due to Nicholas Grene for his support in the early stages of this project, and for suggesting John Banville's work as a research topic. I have benefited greatly from the support and advice of Patricia Waugh and Eve Patten, both of whom were extremely helpful in the later stages of the project. I am grateful for the input of Joseph McMinn, with whom I had a number of very helpful conversations when I was formulating my ideas. Friends and colleagues at Trinity College Dublin have been an indispensable source of support and stimulation over the last few years. In particular, I want to thank Lisa Coen, Dorothea Depner, Ute Mittermaier and Simon Workman for all the lunchtime conversations of ambitious length and range. Adam Kelly has also been a tremendous source of support, constructive criticism, encouragement and inspiration. I owe a huge debt of gratitude to the Irish Research Council for the Humanities and Social Sciences, who funded this project firstly through a Postgraduate Scholarship and finally through a Postdoctoral Research Fellowship, and to the School of English at Trinity College Dublin for supporting my work in its postgraduate and postdoctoral stages. I also thank my wife, Amy Smith, and my parents, Michael and Deirdre O'Connell. Without their love, generosity and goodwill I could not have completed this book, nor would I ever have been in a position to begin it.

Parts of this book have previously appeared, in altered forms, as articles in journals. These original publications are as follows: 'The Weight of Emptiness: Narcissism and the Search for the Missing Twin in John Banville's *Mefisto* and *Shroud*,' *Irish University Review*, 40.2 (2010), pp. 129–47; 'On Not Being Found: a Winnicottian Reading of John Banville's *Ghosts* and *Athena*,' *Studies in the Novel* 43.3 (Fall 2011), pp. 328–42; and 'The Empathic Paradox: Third-Person Narration in John Banville's First-Person Narratives,' *Orbis Litterarum: International Review of Literary Studies* 66.6 (December 2011), pp. 427–47. I am grateful to these journals for granting permission to reprint that material.

1
Introduction

Despite the vivid elegance of his prose and the surface of sophisticated allusion with which he textures it, there is a sense in which John Banville's writing remains fundamentally insular. With the exception of *Doctor Copernicus* (1976) and *Kepler* (1981), all of his novels have been written in the first-person confessional form, a narrative mode that attempts – or seems to attempt – the communication of an essence which is, at its core, incommunicable. In the typical Banville novel we are presented with a troubled male narrator's effort to give a written account of himself, to explain himself to himself. The reader of these documents, these books of evidence, is always external or incidental to this process, as though he or she had simply stumbled across the diary of a perfect stranger and begun to turn the pages.

The reader is not the object of the documents; they are, within the internal logic of the novels, entirely self-directed. Even when the narratives are nominally 'addressed' to implied readers – the 'Clio' of *The Newton Letter* (1982), for instance, or the 'My Lord' of *The Book of Evidence* (1989a) – these are really just imagined surrogates for the narrator's own self, the authority to whom he must ultimately answer. These are textual self-portraits for which the narrators are objects as well as subjects. They do not attempt depictions of themselves in order to show their faces to the world, but to themselves. As he sets about writing an account of his life as a double agent in *The Untouchable* (1997), Victor Maskell characterises his task as one of self-revelation: 'I shall strip away layer after layer of grime – the toffee-coloured varnish and caked soot left by a lifetime of dissembling – until I come to the very thing itself and know it for what it is. My soul. My self' (Banville, 1997: 15). The text is a mirror – more often than not a distorted one – in which an image of the self is conjured.

In Seamus Heaney's 'Personal Helicon', the poet ('big-eyed Narcissus') refers to his art as a kind of active, creative form of reflection-gazing: 'I rhyme/To see myself, to set the darkness echoing' (Heaney, 1998: 15). A similar impulse drives Banville's narrators: they create their narratives in order to see themselves. They are, almost without exception, narcissists of one sort or another. In *Birchwood* (1973), Gabriel Godkin embarks on a picaresque odyssey to find his own imagined twin sister, his journey a quest for union with an illusory vision of himself. Similarly, his namesake Gabriel Swan in *Mefisto* (1986a), traumatised by the loss of a twin brother at birth, is motivated by a desire to attain a state of wholeness, to become 'real'. Freddie Montgomery, the narrator of the trilogy comprised of *The Book of Evidence* (1989a), *Ghosts* (1993a) and *Athena* (1995), murders a young woman, as he sees it, because of his inability to see beyond himself. The 'sin for which there will be no forgiveness', he declares, is that he 'never imagined her vividly enough, that I never made her be there sufficiently, that I did not make her live. I could kill her because for me she was not alive' (Banville, 1989a: 215). In *The Untouchable*, Victor Maskell betrays his family and commits high treason in order to bring to life an ideal vision of himself. Like Wilde's Dorian Gray, he narcissistically projects his own identity into a work of art (a fictional Poussin painting entitled *The Death of Seneca*), to the point where there is more at stake in his relationship with the painting than there is in any of his interpersonal connections. In *Eclipse* (2000a), the singularly self-obsessed actor Alexander Cleave suffers a kind of ontological crisis on stage and, turning his back on the world, retreats to the house of his birth in order to reintegrate with his fractured self. Axel Vander, his counterpart in *Eclipse*'s companion novel *Shroud* (2002), and perhaps Banville's most supremely narcissistic protagonist, is a self-hating Jew who steals the identity of an ostensibly Gentile friend after his sudden disappearance. Vander is an unrepentant misanthrope, an anti-humanist deconstructionist who disavows the existence of truth and the reality of the self, but cannot see past his own problematic identity to the world of others. *Ancient Light* (2012) (which forms the third volume of a trilogy with *Eclipse* and *Shroud*) is similarly concerned with a kind of narcissistic blindness toward the lives of others. Here, Cleave looks back at an affair he had at the age of 15 with the mother of his best friend, and in whom he never takes sufficient interest to notice her terminal illness.

In each of these novels the narrative is, paradoxically, both a means by which the narrator's narcissism is indulged and, as we shall see, a means by which an attempt is made to transcend it. In giving a narrative account of himself, the typical narrator of a Banville novel attempts to create a coherent identity and attain a unity with that identity.[1] Banville's protagonists are always self-made men: they create themselves not merely through the way in which they live their lives, but also the way in which they narrate those lives. They are artists whose material is the impalpable substance of the self.

Given both the concept's centrality to Banville's work and its tendency to resist straightforward, stable definition, it will be useful at this point to outline the various interpretations of the notion of narcissism. There is, it should be stated, no one accepted definition of the term. Although it is one of the most important concepts within psychoanalytic theory, it is also among the most problematic. In order to elucidate the various interpretations of narcissism, it is best to begin with the classical myth of Narcissus, as it is in this story that all understandings of the term have their roots. In the Roman poet Ovid's version of the myth, the naiad Liriope is raped by the river god Cephisus. When her son Narcissus, an unusually beautiful young boy, turns 15, she takes him to the seer Tiresias and asks if he will live a long life. Tiresias's reply is affirmative, but comes with a seemingly enigmatic caveat: 'If he shall himself not know'. Thus Narcissus's fate is linked implicitly to the question of self-knowledge. As Narcissus becomes a man, he is approached by many admirers of both sexes, but spurns all advances: 'hard pride/Ruled in that delicate frame, and never a youth/And never a girl could touch his haughty heart' (Ovid, 1986: 61). One day he becomes lost whilst hunting in the woods with his friends. The wood nymph Echo – whose mother, Juno, has punished her for her volubility by denying her the power to speak anything but repetition of what has just been said to her – catches sight of him and becomes instantly smitten. Narcissus calls out to his friends and is answered by Echo, who throws herself upon him. Utterly uninterested, Narcissus pushes her away, and tells her 'be off! I'll die before I yield to you', to which she replies, 'I yield to you'.

Narcissus's rejection of Echo causes her to suffer a breakdown, in the fullest sense of that term: 'her body shrivels, all its moisture dries;/Only her voice and bones are left; at last/Only her voice, her bones are turned to stone'. Narcissus continues scorning all admirers until one rejected youth prays for justice ('So may *he* love – and never win his love!') to the goddess Nemesis. Nemesis, the divine agent of retribution for hubris and iniquity, endorses the appeal and ensures that Narcissus falls instantly and desperately in love with his own image – his own 'false face' – in a 'limpid and silvery' pool: 'All he admires that all admire in him,/Himself he longs for, longs unwittingly,/Praising is praised, desiring is desired,/And love he kindles while with love he burns' (63). 'You simple boy', admonishes Ovid's narrator:

> why strive in vain to catch
> A fleeting image? What you see is nowhere;
> And what you love – but turn away – you lose!
> You see a phantom of a mirrored shape;
> Nothing itself; with you it came and stays;
> With you it too will go, if you can go! (1986: 64)

The harder he tries to embrace himself – to attain unity with his own 'false phantom' – the more his infatuation is frustrated. Realising finally that it is in fact himself he has fallen in love with, he wastes away, like Echo before him, of a broken heart: 'by love wasted, slowly he dissolves/By hidden fire consumed' (64). Tiresias's cryptic prophecy is borne out, with Narcissus dying a premature death because of his coming to 'know himself'. More specifically, he dies as a result of having invested himself so completely in himself – all his attention, all his energy and passion – at the expense of all others. Narcissus's crime is, like Freddie Montgomery's, essentially one of negligence: a catastrophic inability or unwillingness to see beyond himself. He starves to death, both literally and figuratively; he dies because he cannot take in the world outside of himself.

The Victorian sexologist Havelock Ellis, who coined the term 'narcissism', used the myth to explain what was then considered the pathology of homosexuality. Ellis saw homosexuality as a perverse form of self-love, whereby a man or woman is attracted to an image of him- or herself (i.e., a person of the same sex). In 1911,

Freud's colleague Otto Rank wrote the first psychoanalytic paper on narcissism, 'Ein Beitrag zum Narcissismus' ('A Contribution to Narcissism'), in which he discusses the case of a woman who cannot love a man unless she is first assured of his love for her. Rank presents female narcissistic self-love as a kind of neurotic defence mechanism. Ultimately, he makes a case for considering narcissism as integral to normal sexual development.

It was Freud, however, who first constructed a substantial theory around narcissism as a significant psychological phenomenon in itself. In his 1914 paper 'On Narcissism: An Introduction', he distinguishes between what he terms 'primary' and 'secondary' narcissism. Primary narcissism was, for Freud, a stage through which all children go in early infancy before they begin to see themselves as existing separately and independently from the world – most crucially the mother. It is not so much that the infant sees itself as being the centre of the world, as that it has not yet come to differentiate between itself and the world. A normal child will transcend this state of primary narcissism, becoming increasingly aware of its mother as a distinct entity, and therefore as someone who can be loved, or, to use Freud's term, 'libidinally cathected'. Whereas primary narcissism is, in Freud's schema, a normal and healthy stage of human development, secondary narcissism is a pathological condition. In certain cases a person will regress toward a condition of secondary narcissism, where he or she withdraws libido from the outside world and focuses it inwardly upon the self. Characteristically, Freud lays a great deal of stress on the sexual aspect of narcissism.[2] The narcissist turns his sexual attention towards himself; he falls in love, as it were, with his own 'mirrored shape'. Homosexuality was for Freud a form of narcissism brought on by a disturbed 'libidinal development':

> We have discovered, especially clearly in people whose libidinal development has suffered some disturbance, such as perverts and homosexuals, that in their later choice of love-objects they have taken as a model not their mother but their own selves. They are plainly seeking *themselves* as a love-object, and are exhibiting a type of object-choice which must be termed 'narcissistic'. In this observation we have the strongest of the reasons which have led us to adopt the hypothesis of narcissism. (Freud, 1986: 30 [emphasis in original])

Freud saw the reflection of Narcissus not just in homosexuals, but also in hysterics, hypochondriacs, schizophrenics and psychotics. Narcissism was, in his view, a characteristic of any disorder in which the libido is turned away from the outside world and towards the ego.

From its very inception, the concept of narcissism has, perhaps appropriately, been bedevilled by problems of definition, by irreconcilable versions of itself. Even in the years immediately after Freud's publication of 'On Narcissism', it was being used to denote a bewildering array of conditions. 'Few concepts in psychiatry,' as Arnold M. Cooper put it, 'have undergone as many changes in meaning as has narcissism. Perhaps the single consistent element in these changes is the reference to some aspect of concern with the self and its disturbances' (Cooper, 1986: 112). Such a definition, which all but reduces the term to a synonym for psychoanalysis itself, is undoubtedly too broad, but it does give some impression of the considerable ambiguity of the concept within psychoanalytic theory.

In the 1950s Annie Reich returned to the idea Freud had more or less abandoned four decades previously. Her paper 'Pathologic Forms of Self-Esteem Regulation' marks a progression from Freud's view of narcissistic pathology as restricted to psychosis, disputing the 'usefulness of a too narrowly circumscribed nosology' (Reich, 1986: 44). Narcissism, in her view, is a normal condition that only becomes pathologic under certain specific conditions, such as in 'states of quantitative imbalance; e.g. when the balance between object cathexis and self-cathexis has become disturbed', and 'in infantile forms of narcissism, which are frequently [...] present in the states of quantitative imbalance' (44). Her concept of 'pathologic self-esteem regulation', resulting in an excess of worldly ambition, relates specifically to the male psyche, beset in her view by the desire for phallic reassurance and anxieties about castration. Narcissistic self-inflation is, in Reich's analysis, a form of compensation or mitigation of these peculiarly male disquietudes. Thus the obverse side of the coin of narcissism bears the indelible imprint of painful self-consciousness – a theoretical thread which would be taken up by later theorists. Narcissists are those, she maintains, who vacillate between excessive self-aggrandisement and feelings of utter worthlessness and meaninglessness. If a traumatic situation occurs at a very early stage of the child's development, it can warp the maturation of the ego. In such instances, the affected child withdraws its attentions from the outside world and focuses them inward upon itself, like a turtle retreating into its shell: 'Under the conditions of too frequently repeated early traumatizations, the narcissistic withdrawal of libido from the objects to the endangered self tends to remain permanent' (49).

In this way, she conceives of what she calls 'narcissistic imbalance' as a defensive and an essentially negative position. That is to say, it is not so much about what the narcissist is as what he is not. 'Magical denial' is her term for this defensive mode: '"It is not so",' she imagines the narcissist saying, '"I am not helpless, bleeding, destroyed. On the contrary, I am bigger and better than anyone else. I am the greatest, the most grandiose."' (49) In Reich's version of the narcissistic mind, the phallus is 'overvalued' due to perceived castration threats – the most conspicuous form of what she calls 'narcissistic traumata' – and it is the female organs which are conceived of as being 'destroyed, bleeding, dirty, etc.' (51). In this context, the narcissist's entire body is 'equated' with a phallus. Interest is withdrawn from the outside world and the distinction between grandiose fantasy and reality becomes blurred in a way that is characteristic more of infants than of adults. 'Thus the fantasy is not only a yardstick', as she puts it, 'but is also experienced as magically fulfilled' (50).

In Banville's work, this blurring of the distinction between the 'real self' (such terms, in any discussion of this writer, must always be treated with circumspection) and the phallic ideal of the self is a recurring motif. In *Ghosts*, Freddie Montgomery speaks approvingly of Diderot's principle that we become 'sculptors of the self' through 'cutting and shaping the material of which we are made, the intransigent stone of self-hood, and erecting an idealised effigy of ourselves in our own minds and in the minds of those around us' (Banville, 1993a: 196). In *The Untouchable*, Victor Maskell echoes not just Freddie's sentiment but also his phallically charged language:

> Diderot said that what we do is, we erect a statue in our own image inside ourselves – idealised, you know, but still recognisable – and then spend our lives engaged in the effort to make ourselves into its likeness. This is the moral imperative. I think it's awfully clever, don't you? I know that's how *I* feel. Only there are times when I can't tell which is the statue and which is me. (1997b: 86 [emphasis in original])

Likewise in *Eclipse*, Alexander Cleave, in describing his onstage 'death' (he comes unstuck on a line from Kleist's *Amphitryon*), uses the metaphor of 'a giant statue toppling off its pedestal and smashing into rubble on the stage' (2000a: 87). And in *Shroud*, Cass Cleave describes Axel Vander (or rather Vander describes himself through her ventriloquised narrative voice) as he 'heaved himself on top of her' in bed as being like 'one of those huge statues of dictators that were being pulled down all over eastern Europe' (2002: 75–6). These conspicuously phallic images reflect Reich's notion that the 'grandiose body-phallus fantasy – for instance, "standing out high above everybody else, like an obelisk" – turns *suddenly* into one of total castration [...] as though the original castration fear had extended from the penis to the whole body' (Reich, 1986: 53 [emphasis in original]). Narcissism is, for Reich, defined every bit as much by vulnerability as it is by grandiosity, with the latter a form of compensation for the former.

Reich's ideas are often seen as a crucial influence on Heinz Kohut and the school of self psychology which he founded. Kohut, one of the most important post-Freudian theorists of narcissism, has done more than perhaps any other psychoanalyst (including Freud himself) to define this nebulous concept. In *The Analysis of the Self* (1971), he argues for an understanding of narcissism as a necessary characteristic of any healthy psyche. His departure from Freudian convention is a fairly radical one, in that he emphasises interpersonal relationships over Freud's theory of instincts. He uses the word 'selfobject' to point to the way in which the ego incorporates elements of alterity within itself – 'objects', as he puts it, 'which are not experienced as separate and independent from the self' (Kohut, 1971: 3). A young child's parents are, in Kohut's view, 'selfobjects' in the sense that he or she experiences them 'narcissistically', supposing a degree of control which 'is closer to the concept which a grownup has of himself and of the control which he expects over his own body and mind than to the grownup's experience of others and of his control over them' (33). Kohut insists that narcissism is something which must be firmly established and accommodated in order to reach a mature and stable psychological state. Narcissism, properly negotiated, gives rise to such noble human attributes as creativity, empathy and humour – attributes which Kohut views as mature forms of narcissism. The child's sense of what he terms the 'grandiose self' – the typical toddler's formidable self-importance and assumed omnipotence – must be mitigated by the gradual imposition of reality, or 'optimal frustration'. 'If the child is spoiled (not optimally frustrated),' explains Kohut, 'it retains an unusual amount of narcissism or omnipotence; and at the same time because it lacks actual skills, feels inferior. Similarly, overly frustrating experiences [...] lead to retention of omnipotence fantasies' (Kohut and Seitz, 1963: 20). Kohut – who takes his cue in this instance from Freud's Oedipal hypotheses – sees the responsibility for optimal frustration falling squarely upon the shoulders of the father. The father must temper the mother's indulgence of the child's narcissism through the progressive imposition of reality. The ultimate optimal frustration is, he maintains, the realisation of one's own mortality.

Narcissistic disturbance occurs, Kohut tells us, when this kind of healthy selfobject development is somehow obstructed by, for instance, a childhood trauma or a shortfall of optimal frustration. The infant has a need to idealise the parent, to sustain the original sense of omnipotence 'by imbuing the rudimentary you, the adult, with absolute perfection and power'. This results in the formation of what Kohut calls the 'idealised parent imago' (Kohut, 1966: 64). When the child finds out that he cannot depend on the parent's idealised strength – when the parent is for whatever reason not reliable or reliably present – it comes to perceive that it must rely upon itself alone. In the absence, in other words, of an idealised selfobject, the self becomes its own idealised selfobject (64). In such instances, there is a lack of a strong, cohesive self-image. The 'preconscious center from which these characterological disturbances emanate is the sense of an incomplete reality of the self and, secondarily, of the external world' (Kohut, 1971: 210). In analysis, the patient is likely to let the analyst know of his 'impression that he is not fully real, or at least that his emotions are dulled' (16). Kohut's understanding of narcissism as a disorder, therefore, rests somewhat uneasily upon an apparent contradiction, in that it is rooted in a defective sense of self.

Narcissus's tragedy – or, what amounts to the same thing, his madness – is that he cannot attain a unity with himself. Each time he tries to grasp himself, he seems to cease being there. His inability to look away from himself is partly motivated by the fear that, were he to do so, he would disappear completely. He is indeed obsessed with himself, but that obsession does not contain any assurance that its object has any solidity.

Otto Kernberg, a leading theorist of narcissistic disorders, accentuates the destructive elements of narcissism. Like Kohut and Reich before him, he employs the concept of the 'grandiose self'. However, in his insistence upon narcissism as the result of a pathological development in which aggression plays a central part, he conforms closer than either to Freudian orthodoxy, with its emphasis on conflicting drives. For Kernberg, the grandiose self is 'a fusion of the real self, ideal self and ideal object' and results in 'an idealised self-sufficiency, making the subject impervious to intimate relationships, including analysis'. Kernberg claims that narcissistic personalities are distinguished amongst psychological disorders by their 'relatively good social functioning' and their 'capacity for active, consistent work in some areas which permits them partially to fulfil their ambitions of greatness and of obtaining admiration from others' (Kernberg, 1986: 215). The narcissist's grandeur, in other words, is not always wholly delusional, but is often superficial:

> Highly intelligent patients with this personality structure may appear as quite creative in their fields: narcissistic personalities can often be found as leaders in industrial organizations or academic institutions; they may also be outstanding performers in some artistic domain. Careful observation, however, of their productivity over a long period of time will give evidence of superficiality and flightiness in their work, a lack of depth which eventually reveals the emptiness behind the glitter. (1986: 215)

Banville's protagonists, though they are often charismatic, dominant figures, are typically haunted by a sense of their own essential fraudulence. In *Shroud*, the celebrated academic Axel Vander confesses to being driven by 'fury, fury and fear [...] fury at being what I am not, fear of being found out for what I am' (Banville, 2002: 67). His 'poised' prose style with its 'high patrician burnish and flashes of covert wit' serves as a cover for the essential shoddiness and unoriginality of his scholarship (137). He admits, in fact, to not having read many of the writers upon whose deconstructed rubble he builds his own fame. Vander, like so many of Banville's narcissists, is 'a thing made up wholly of poses' – an emptiness, in Kernberg's phrase, concealed by glitter (Kernberg, 1986: 210).

Kernberg imagines the narcissist as communicating the following message to the world: 'I do not need to fear that I will be rejected for not living up to the ideal of myself which alone makes it possible for me to be loved by the ideal person I imagine would love me. That ideal person and my ideal image of that person and my real self are all one and better than the ideal person whom I wanted to love me, so that I do not need anybody else any more' (217). This seems almost a translation into prose of Narcissus's refusal to yield to Echo. Why should one put oneself in the way of the confusion and pain that comes with engagement with others when the ideal object is one's own reflected image – even if that image is merely a 'false phantom'? The narcissist strives, as Jeremy Holmes puts it, 'to think of himself as a "self-made man"' (Holmes, 2001: 47). One might pick a Banville narrator almost at random and be confident that he would fit this description. There is, as we shall see, a dominant emotional note of shame running through the entire *oeuvre* – specifically the narcissistic shame of one's origins – which is intimately connected with this ideal of self-creation. Its presence is obvious in *The Untouchable*'s Victor Maskell, the 'tricky question' of whose unsophisticated Ulster provenance is characterised as 'that constant drone note in the bagpipe music of my life' (Banville, 1997b: 47). The young Alexander Cleave in *Eclipse* is fixated on this narcissistic vision of himself as a kind of demigod who transcends his mundane origins:

> As a child I took it that when the time came for me to leave they would stand back, two humble caryatids holding up the portal to my future, watching patiently, in uncomplaining puzzlement, as I strode away from them with hardly a backward glance, each league that I covered making me not smaller but steadily more vast, their overgrown, incomprehensible son. (2000a: 49)

This is a pattern that recurs continually throughout Banville's work, the narrator who conceives of himself as infinitely more complex, more sophisticated, more worthy of regard, than his plain and unremarkable parents. The family is never a solid base, a grounding in coherence and stability, but invariably either a kind of calamity from which the protagonist must escape or a base provenance he must rise above. Thus the young Max Morden in *The Sea* (2005c) effectively abandons his lower-middle-class parents – of whom he is obscurely, acutely ashamed – for the sophisticated and cosmopolitan Grace family. Gabriel Godkin in *Birchwood* knows all along, but cannot admit to himself, that he is the product of an incestuous union between his father and aunt, and abandons his disintegrating family, embarking upon a quest (both narcissistic and, as we shall see, enigmatically incestuous) to find an illusory twin sister. Freddie Montgomery's relationship with his parents – in particular his mother – is fraught with obscure and seemingly preconscious rage and resentment. Axel Vander in *Shroud* denies his origins in the most extreme fashion imaginable, creates an entirely false identity, and seems utterly incapable of genuine, non-narcissistic love. He is, in his own words, 'a thing made wholly of poses' (2002: 210). Like so many of Banville's egocentric protagonists, what Vander seeks primarily in others is his own reflection. Though he claims here and there throughout his 'confession' to love Cass Cleave, his interest in her, he ultimately reveals, is a self-reflective one: 'The object of my true regard was not her, the so-called loved one, but myself, the one who loved, so-called. Is it not always thus? Is not love the mirror of burnished gold in which we contemplate our shining selves?' (210).

Alexander Cleave, too, takes a characteristically narcissistic view of his relationship with his wife Lydia whom he sees, he says, as 'the one capable of concentrating sufficient attention on me to make me shine out into the world with a flickering intensity such that even I might believe I was real' (2000a: 32). This idea of the narcissist as one who lacks independence – whose very sense of self must be sustained by the regard of others – is delineated by Christopher Lasch in his book *The Culture of Narcissism*:

> Notwithstanding his occasional illusions of omnipotence, the narcissist depends on others to validate his self-esteem. He cannot live without an admiring audience. His apparent freedom from family ties and institutional constraints does not free him to stand alone or to glory in his individuality. On the contrary, it contributes to his insecurity, which he can overcome only by seeing his 'grandiose self' reflected in the attentions of others, or by attaching himself to those who radiate celebrity, power and charisma. For the narcissist, the world is a mirror. (Lasch, 1980: 10)

Banville's narcissistic narrators are both desperately unsure of themselves – sceptical as to the very reality of their own selves – and utterly captivated by themselves, often at the expense of interpersonal relationships. They cannot quite bring themselves to believe in their own reality as coherent individuals. Whether this lack of a sense of full and intelligible selfhood stems from the fact of their being liars (and they are all liars in one way or another) or whether the case is the exact reverse is one of the many questions posed by Banville's work. It is this friction between, on the one hand, the desire for self-knowledge and, on the other, a rigorous scepticism about the very notion of selfhood which constitutes one of the most fascinating elements of these novels.

Narcissism can be viewed as originating in a profound sense of doubt as to the reality of the self, its coherence and stability. Narcissus, the bastard child of a water nymph and a river god, is conceived in the violence of rape and is defined – or, more accurately, not defined at all – by a fluid identity. His traumatic origin and his tragic end are in water; with his liquid nature, he is bound to have a problematic, perilously fragile sense of his own selfhood.

Banville's narcissists are similarly unsure of themselves, and similarly obsessed with themselves. These novels are, amongst other things, a meeting place of self-absorption and self-doubt. In *Eclipse*, Alexander Cleave retreats in the wake of his breakdown to the childhood home he shared with his mother, where he undergoes a psychological rebirth process which results in an almost infantile self-obsession, a regression to something very like Freud's primary narcissism. 'I feel at once newborn and immensely old [...] in my clumsy groping after things that keep evading my grasp I am as helpless as an infant. I have fallen into thrall with myself. I marvel at the matter my body produces, the stools, the crusts of snot, the infinitesimal creep of fingernails and hair' (Banville, 2000a: 50–1). The choice of the word 'thrall' here is significant – it is as though Cleave, like Narcissus, has fallen under a kind of spell that forces him into an endless contemplation of his own surfaces and depths. Similarly in *The Sea*, the recently widowed Morden returns to the coastal village in which he spent his childhood holidays in order to immerse himself completely, through the process of narration, in his own past. Narrative here, as in so many of Banville's novels, is a method of intense self-scrutiny. There are indeed moments in the novel in which it seems as though he is not so much devastated by the loss of his beloved wife as he is gripped by narcissistic rage over having been deprived of a way of seeing himself, of a means of self-definition. 'You cunt', he spits at one point, his fury breaking through the still surface of the narrative, 'you fucking cunt, how could you go and leave me like this, floundering in my own foulness, with no one to save me from myself?' (2005c: 196). As Otto Kernberg writes of narcissistic personalities: 'When abandoned or disappointed by other people they may show what on the surface looks like depression, but which on further examination emerges as anger and resentment, loaded with revengeful wishes, rather than real sadness for the loss of a person whom they appreciated' (Kernberg, 1986: 214).

For Morden it is the abandonment which stings above all else. There seems, on the face of it, to be an interesting contradiction in the idea of an utterly self-centred man who is traumatised by being left utterly by himself. But Morden, like all of Banville's narcissists, needs the presence of others to be reassured of his own reality. Banville's protagonists are always looking for ways of seeing themselves. Very often the regard of another takes precedence over the other doing the regarding, offering the protagonist an indirect perspective on themselves. Narrative serves a similar reflective purpose. The regard, the reflection, is what matters.

The aim of this book is not simply to offer a reading of a single, isolated aspect of Banville's work, but rather to present narcissism as the key to understanding this writer, and as a way of bringing together the various disparate strands – thematic, stylistic and formal – of his complex and enigmatic fiction. As befits a body of work so characterised by and preoccupied with narcissism, it is one which is endlessly in commune with itself, endlessly attentive to its own internal reflections and echoes. The continuity of thematic elements and the persistence of narrative tone across the *oeuvre* are such that it can be viewed as though it were a single project, a novel of many volumes. The names of the narrators change, as do the particulars of their situations, but they speak of the same fixations and anxieties, and they do so in a single voice. Each chapter of this book deals, therefore, not with a specific text but rather with a particular aspect of narcissism as a distinct means of approach to Banville's work. In this sense, its structure is such that, over six chapters, it presents a comprehensive exploration of Banville's work – from the point of view of narcissistically related themes – as opposed to simply exploring narcissism per se in each of the works under discussion.

Although it is my contention that narcissism, understood as an aspect of character and of the narratives themselves, is a thread that binds Banville's *oeuvre* together, it is necessary to focus on some of the works more intently than others. Whilst references are made to each of the novels, a number of them are turned to less often in support of larger arguments. The author's debut novel *Nightspawn* (1971) – while it certainly contains elements that might be considered narcissistic – is his least accomplished and in many ways his least interesting work. Although it contains many of Banville's lifelong preoccupations in germinal form, they are all of them more expertly and interestingly explored in the later fiction. The same holds for the early short story collection *Long Lankin* (1970) with its accompanying (and subsequently excised) novella *The Possessed*. The series of popular detective novels published under the pseudonym Benjamin Black (currently comprising *Christine Falls* (2006), *The Silver Swan* (2007), *The Lemur* (2008), *Elegy for April* (2010) and *A Death in Summer* (2011)) also lie beyond the scope of this study.

Chapter 1 examines the presence and significance of narcissistic personality traits in Banville's narrators. The characters with which the chapter is specifically concerned are Freddie Montgomery in the Art Trilogy (*The Book of Evidence, Ghosts* and *Athena*), Alexander Cleave in *Eclipse* and *Ancient Light*, and Axel Vander in *Shroud*. Although the majority of Banville protagonists fit the description of narcissist to some degree, it is in these three characters that the complexities of the narcissistic personality are most thoroughly explored. The chapter provides a useful general introduction to theories of narcissistic personality, and also lays down a strong foundation for more specific areas of focus later in the book.

Chapter 2 examines Banville's use of doubles and twins in his work from the point of view of psychoanalytic theories of narcissism. The chapter argues for an understanding of *Birchwood* and *Mefisto* – both of which are concerned with lost twins – as quest narrative, the ultimate aim of which is a narcissistic unity of self with self. The searches for missing twins in each of the books are seen as a kind of psychological McGuffin, a device that serves a catalyst for the more fundamental 'plot' of the search for wholeness and personal cohesion.

Chapter 3 looks at *Ghosts, Athena* and *Shroud*, examining the prevalence of false identities in Banville's fiction. The British psychoanalyst D. W. Winnicott's notion of the 'False Self' is explored in its relation to the idea of narcissism, and his theories about the ways in which people fabricate fictitious selves as a protection against the world are used as a means of interpreting the fraudulence of the narrators. The chapter ultimately argues for an understanding of these novels, with their representation of relationships as based more on concealment and suppression than on openness and communication, as sharing a profound affinity with Winnicott's view of fraudulence and authenticity.

The connection between narcissism and shame is explored in Chapter 4. Many of Banville's self-made narcissists, though they attempt to construct themselves as Nietzschean *Übermensch* through their actions and their narratives, exhibit an acute sense of shame at their humble origins. This shame and humiliation – a kind of opprobrium of the unremarkable, intimately linked with narcissism – is examined as a particular feature of *The Untouchable, Shroud* and *The Sea*. Ultimately, through an analysis of these novels, the chapter establishes the shame experienced by these narrators as inseparable from their narcissism, and from their grandiose egos.

Chapter 5 focuses on narcissism as an aspect of form and style, exploring the ways in which Banville reflects his narrators' narcissism in the narratives themselves. Here, the allusive and self-reflective nature of Banville's writing is presented as a form of textual narcissism that is of a piece with, and proceeds from, the narcissism of his narrators. This is achieved through analyses of three of Banville's most explicitly metafictional texts: *Doctor Copernicus, Kepler* and *The Newton Letter*. The chapter also explores Banville's use of *mise en abyme* in his work, in particular *Ghosts, Athena* and *Ancient Light*, and links this self-reflexive strategy to the overall theme of narcissism.

The book's sixth and final chapter examines the relationship between empathy and narcissism, and the role played by narrative in the negotiation of that relationship in Banville's work. A recurring pattern in the fiction is that of the self-centred, egotistical narrator who works through his narcissism and is brought back at least some of the way to a position of relatedness to the larger world. Freddie Montgomery's faltering progression in the *Trilogy* from abject solipsism and malignant narcissism to a more outward-looking attitude – in particular his intensely felt moral imperative of 'resurrecting' his murder victim Josie Bell through his narrative – is examined. Freddie's adoption of other characters' points of view in his narration of *Ghosts* – his authorial stance as 'little god' – and, in *Shroud*, Axel Vander's problematic co-option of Cass Cleave's voice for large portions of his narration are of particular significance here (Banville, 2002: 4). *The Infinities* (2009) is also discussed in relation to its explorations of the relationship between empathy and narrative. The chapter ultimately presents third-person narration as an undertaking that can become a means of tentatively transcending narcissism, and of entering into an empathic engagement with the world.

In a short piece published in April 2007 to promote the American publication of *Christine Falls*, Banville performs a trick that might be described as a kind of Borgesian publicity stunt: he interviews himself. More accurately, John Banville interviews Benjamin Black about his new novel. He finds Black living in 'an anonymous apartment building just across the river from Temple Bar, that God's little acre laughingly known as Dublin's Latin Quarter'. As they begin the interview, Black walks to the window and turns his back to Banville, who remarks that 'he seems to me peculiarly blurred. He is less himself than the shadow of someone else. Does this explain the unease I sense in him? He avoids my eye; I suspect he avoids everyone's eye' (Banville, 2007). Banville can't get a clear look at Black; he can't seem to get to grips with him. As this comically stilted conversation between the man and his own literary shadow draws to a close, it threatens to erupt into hostility. Black passive-aggressively suggests that Banville is less than interested in his own characters as humans; that, whilst they are 'humanish', their humanity is 'not their point'. When Banville protests that he has come to talk about *Christine Falls*, Black shakes his head:

'No, you didn't.'
'Oh?'
'You came here to talk to yourself. You've done a grand job of it. Now, how about a drink?' (Banville, 2007)

The conceit is a light-hearted one, a wry nod to the author's own reputation as a coldly intellectual formalist more concerned with the austere beauty of his own prose than with the humanity of his characters. But for all its throwaway jokiness, it demonstrates Banville's recognition of an overwhelming tendency toward self-regard in his work. He is obviously keenly aware that a major characteristic of his fiction is its obsession with itself and, more importantly, with the ways in which we are all obsessed with ourselves. It is this crucial characteristic of the fiction with which this book is concerned.

2
Banville's Narcissists

There is a common misapprehension of narcissism that interprets it as little more than psychologically entrenched vanity or self-love, as an acute form of smugness. It would be much closer to the truth, however, to describe it as an exhaustive anxiety, or cluster of anxieties, about the self. In most post-Freudian psychoanalytic writing about the condition, it is seen as a way of looking at the world and one's place in it that is ultimately diminishing, even degrading. There is a sense in which narcissism, as an affliction, is a kind of psychic double bind, whereby the narcissist is wholly consumed with finding some fundamental truth about himself and yet prevented from ever reaching such knowledge by his or her own self-absorption. The thing sought and the overwhelming desire to find it become, that is to say, irreconcilable.

To put it in terms of Ovid's version of the myth, as long as Narcissus fixes all his attention upon his reflected image, he denies himself satisfaction and self-knowledge and, in refusing to look away from himself towards the world, ultimately destroys himself. Depending on which version of the myth one reads, he either wastes away or is drowned in his own reflection. Narcissism, then, is not nearly so much about self-love – about complacency or egotism – as it is about self-absorption. Though it may frequently seem to take the form of grandiose self-satisfaction and smugness, it is, at bottom, a matter of endless lack and psychological privation. Narcissus never takes possession of the object of his desire, because that object is literally a false impression, the optical illusion created by light rays striking and reflecting off the water's surface. What is real is the world itself, and Narcissus perishes because of his neglect of that reality. Like all obsessions, then, narcissism is dangerous for two principal reasons: it drastically distorts one's view of reality, and it inevitably leads to self-diminishment, even to self-destruction.

The sociologist Richard Sennett, in his book *The Fall of Public Man*, provides an eloquent distinction between the misconception of narcissism as self-love and its proper definition as a perilous disengagement with the outside world:

> As a character disorder, narcissism is the very opposite of strong self-love. Self-absorption does not produce gratification, it produces injury to the self; erasing the line between self and other means that nothing new, nothing 'other', ever enters the self; it is devoured and transformed until one thinks one can see oneself in the other – and then it becomes meaningless [...] The narcissist is not hungry for experiences, he is hungry for Experience. Looking always for an expression or reflection of himself in Experience, he devalues each particular interaction or scene, because it is never enough to encompass who he is. The myth of Narcissus neatly captures this: one drowns in the self – it is an entropic state. (Sennett, 1977: 324–5)

Banville's novels are consistently concerned with states of entropy. Even the youthful narrators of the early fiction – specifically *Nightspawn*'s Ben White and *Birchwood*'s Gabriel Godkin – are already entering states of decline, of self-absorbed disintegration which mirror and are mirrored by the disintegrations of the outside world (the famine and uprisings of the latter and the military *coup d'état* of the former). By the later work – the novels, that is to say, from *The Book of Evidence* onwards – this entropy has become a defining quality of the fiction. *The Book of Evidence*'s Freddie Montgomery, *Eclipse*'s Alexander Cleave and *Shroud*'s Axel Vander are men in respectively advancing stages of middle age; we find all three of them, when their stories begin, at their nadirs of self-absorption and disintegration. They may frequently be arrogant and self-admiring, but their narcissism is not a source of gratification to them. It is, in all three cases, what brings them to the miserable circumstances from which they begin to narrate. Frequently, the act of narration is itself an attempt to impose a kind of conceptual coherence upon the impenetrable confusion of their experiences of themselves.

Sennett's characterisation of the narcissist as the person who is hungry, not for 'experiences', but for 'Experience' seems to disclose something essential about these three characters. Their consciousnesses are turned almost completely away from the world of experiences. To the extent that they are attentive to it at all, they are focused not on its depths but on the specular sheen of its surfaces. As Freddie Montgomery says of his wife in *The Book of Evidence*, 'I was only interested really in what she was on the surface [...] This is the only way another creature can be known: on the surface, that's where there is depth' (Banville, 1989a: 72).[1] What these characters are in search of is some unifying vision of themselves – an 'Experience', in Sennett's capitalised, singular sense – and this is precisely what their narcissistic condition will not grant them. The more they reflect upon themselves, the further they appear to drift from any kind of solid notion of who it is they are. The more absorbed they become in their own inner lives, the more tentative their senses of self become. An analysis of these three characters will throw some light upon what narcissism means, and what it might bring to a reading of Banville's work. As we shall see, almost all of his protagonists are narcissists in one sense or another. It is these three, however – Cleave, Vander and Montgomery – who provide the most elucidating case studies of the narcissistic character in all its contradictions, its involuted contours and recesses.

In Heinrich von Kleist's 1810 essay 'The Puppet Theatre', the author relates a chance encounter in a public park with an acquaintance of his, Herr C., who is a renowned male ballet dancer. He mentions to Herr C. how surprised he is to have seen him frequenting a local marionette theatre, to which C. replies that a dancer wishing to gain mastery of his art might learn a great deal from the puppet theatre. The puppet, he claims, can attain a degree of grace in its movements that the human dancer cannot, a grace which is due to the puppet's movements being purely mechanical and therefore entirely devoid of affectation and artificiality. This apparent paradox is explained as follows: 'For affectation occurs, as you know, whenever the soul [...] is situated in a place other than a movement's centre of gravity. Since the puppeteer, handling the wire or the string, can have no point except that one under his control all the other limbs are what they should be: dead, mere pendula, and simply obey the law of gravity; an excellent attribute which you will look for in vain among the majority of our dancers' (Kleist, 1997: 413).

The human dancer, by comparison with the wooden marionette, is necessarily pretentious and graceless by virtue of his or her consciously striving *toward* grace. Such imperfection has been unavoidable, according to C., 'ever since we ate from the Tree of Knowledge' (413). Here Kleist invokes the myth of Genesis to explain why such grace is attainable only to gods and objects. Mankind, in becoming the animal that is conscious of itself, the animal that is at a remove from its own centre of gravity, effected its own fall from grace. The author responds by recalling an incident that occurred three years previously when he went swimming with a friend of his, a handsome and charming 16-year-old boy in whom the first traces of vanity were only just beginning to become apparent. After the swim, Kleist's young friend catches sight of himself in a large mirror as he places his foot on a stool to dry it, and is instantly reminded of the famous Greco-Roman 'Spinario' sculpture of a boy removing a thorn from his sole. Kleist says that he himself notes the similarity but, not wanting to fortify his friend's vanity, tells him he is imagining things. The boy tries and fails to repeat the movement again and again, becoming progressively more self-conscious and awkward, to the point where Kleist can barely keep from laughing. The incident has a profound effect on the youth. 'From that day, or from that very moment, the young man underwent an unbelievable transformation,' writes Kleist. 'He began spending days in front of the mirror; and one after the other all his charms deserted him. An invisible and incomprehensible power seemed to settle like an iron net over the free play of his manners and a year later there was not a trace left in him of those qualities that had in the past so delighted the eyes of people around him' (415).

Kleist's implicit point here has to do with the mutual exclusivity of self-consciousness and grace. The youth forfeits his elegance at the very moment he becomes conscious of it; the marionette, because it is a mere unconscious *thing*, is possessed of a grace that is otherwise the preserve of gods.

The idea of the youth who is transfixed and slowly corrupted by his own reflected image is one that recurs continually throughout the history of western culture, from Ovid to Wilde, from Freud to Salvador Dalí. A special place in the history of the idea of narcissism, however, can be made for Kleist's essay because of its influence on Heinz Kohut in the development of his theories. In his 1972 paper

'Thoughts on Narcissism and Narcissistic Rage', Kohut claims that his fascination with the short prose piece had a 'specific significance' for his intellectual development in that 'it marks the first time that I felt drawn to the topic that has now absorbed my scientific interests for several years' (Kohut, 1972: 361). Kohut identifies in it the presence of most of the thematic threads he would later weave together to form the material for his theory of narcissism:

> Apprehensions about the aliveness of self and body, and the repudiation of these fears by the assertion that the inanimate can yet be graceful, even perfect. The topics of homosexuality [...]; of poise and of exhibitionism; of blushing and self-consciousness are alluded to; and so is the theme of grandiosity in the fantasy of flying – the notion of 'antigravity' – and that of merger with an omnipotent environment by which one is controlled – the puppeteer. Finally, there is the description of a profound change in a young man, ushered in by the ominous symptom of gazing at himself for days in the mirror. (1972: 361–2)

John Banville hints at a similar reading of the text in *Eclipse*, a novel in which Kleist is a recurring presence. The plot centres on the actor Alexander Cleave, whose performance as Amphitryon in an unspecified adaptation of the legend is brought to an ignominious end when he 'corpses' onstage, coming unstuck on the line '*Who if not I, then, is Amphitryon?*' (Banville, 2000a: 88 [emphasis in original]). Cleave, a self-obsessed narcissist wracked by doubts as to the solidity of his own identity, retreats to his childhood home, essentially abandoning his wife in order to spend time alone to commune with himself. Though it is not specified whether it is Kleist's 1808 version of *Amphitryon* that constitutes Cleave's disastrous final performance, it seems reasonable to assume that Banville had it in mind, given that around the time he was writing *Eclipse* he was also engaged in writing the play *God's Gift*, a version of Kleist's comedy *Amphitryon* set in his native Wexford during the 1798 rebellions.[2] Cleave mentions, too, that his daughter Cass has embarked on a research project centring on the final hours of Kleist's life before his suicide. He also states that, as part of an autodidactic course of self-improvement, he read 'Kleist on the puppet theatre'. 'I was,' he says, 'after nothing less than a total transformation, a make-over of all I was into a miraculous, bright new being. But it was impossible. What I desired only a god could manage – a god, or a marionette' (35–6). Cleave's strange 'malady of selfness' takes a form similar to that of Kleist's teenage Narcissus (2000a: 88). He becomes the object of his own almost unbearably intense scrutiny, and this self-obsession has a curiously diminishing and debilitating influence upon him:

> For months I had been beset by bouts of crippling self-consciousness. I would involuntarily fix on a bit of myself, a finger, a foot, and gape at it in a kind of horror, paralysed, unable to understand how it made its movements, what force was guiding it. In the street I would catch sight of my reflection in a shop window, skulking along with head down and shoulders up and my elbows pressed into my sides, like a felon bearing a body away, overwhelmed by the inescapable predicament of being what I was. (2000a: 87)

'Overwhelmed' is a powerfully significant word in this passage and in the novel as a whole, presenting a key to an understanding of Cleave's peculiar complaint.

The psychotherapist he consults in the aftermath of his onstage 'collapse' tells him that he 'seemed to him to be overwhelmed – that was the word he used' (92). When he writes to Cass to tell her about his taking his place 'shamefacedly in the lower ranks of the high consistory of which she was an adept of long standing' (the high consistory, that is, of subjects of the mental health profession), he signs himself 'The Overwhelmed' (92). The word has connotations of flooding and of drowning; the *Oxford English Dictionary* offers us the definition of 'bury or drown beneath a huge mass'. If Cleave is being engulfed by or drowned in something, that something is surely himself. (It is worth bearing in mind here that in certain Greek versions of the Narcissus myth, the youth actually drowns in the attempt to embrace his reflection – becomes, that is to say, overwhelmed by and *in* himself.) Cleave's awareness of himself has become more than he can bear – what leads to his collapse is what he calls 'this insupportable excess of self' (87). Reflective surfaces play a particularly central role in his self-mesmerisation. Like Kleist's young friend, Cleave suffers a kind of paralysis when confronted with the spectacle of his own image. On stage, as he freezes while playing the part of a man whose own identity has been usurped, he sees himself in the eyes of 'the young fellow playing Mercury [...] doubly reflected, two tiny, bulbous Amphitryons, both struck speechless' (88). 'Mercury' refers not just to the Roman messenger god, but also to the substance that turns transparent glass into reflective mirror. He sees himself, becomes self-conscious, and falls irrecoverably from grace. Kleist's ideas about the relationship between grace and unselfconsciousness are again alluded to when Cleave tells of his furtive observation of a young woman from the bathroom window of his former flat as she dresses in a neighbouring house. In her obliviousness to the fact of Cleave's gaze – to her status as object – she attains something like the grace of a god or a marionette:

> Without knowing, in perfect self-absorption, she achieved at the start of each day there in her mean room an apotheosis of grace and suavity. The unadorned grave beauty of her movements was, it pained the performer in me to acknowledge, inimitable: even if I spent a lifetime in rehearsal I could not hope to aspire to the thoughtless elegance of this girl's most trivial gesture. Of course, all was dependent precisely on there being no thought attached to what she was doing, no awareness. One glimpse of my eager eye at the bathroom window, watching her, and she would have scrambled to hide her nakedness with all the grace of a collapsing deck chair or, worse, would have slipped into the travesty of self-conscious display. Innocent of being watched, she was naked; aware of my eye on her, she would have turned into a nude. (2000a: 99)

This girl is momentarily elevated to a divine status – reaches 'an apotheosis of grace' – by her complete lack of self-consciousness. Because she is not thinking about what she is doing, what she does, in its quotidian triviality, becomes 'a kind of art' (99). This reflects Kleist's notion, outlined in 'The Puppet Theatre', that the Christian myth of the Fall is really about our fall from prelapsarian unselfconsciousness into the human states of narcissism and shame. (Jean Paul Sartre neatly expresses this notion in his assertion that 'My original fall is the existence of the Other' (Sartre, 1943: 263)).

It is, Banville suggests, in these unguarded moments of unconscious grace, that we are most indivisibly ourselves. 'It is this forgetfulness, this loss of creaturely attendance, that I find fascinating,' Cleave tells us. 'In watching someone who is unaware of being watched one glimpses a state of being that is beyond, or behind, what we think of as the human; it is to behold, however ungraspably, the unmasked self itself' (Banville, 2000a: 100).

Alexander Cleave's narcissism, then, is presented as the precise opposite of this 'forgetfulness'. He has lost the ability to overlook himself; he is always the object of his own regard – is in fact *over-whelmed* by himself. Like the youth in Kleist's essay, some force has seized like a net 'over the free play of his manners' and his every physical and mental manoeuvre becomes the focus of intense, debilitating scrutiny. The strangeness of his predicament is that, while he can no longer perform onstage, he can no longer ignore the fact that he is only ever performing in life. His wife Lydia, during an argument, makes this point explicitly: *'You're never off the stage, we're just the audience'* (2000a: 138 [emphasis in original]). He is, like so many of Banville's protagonists, painfully aware of his own preening fraudulence. From the moment he introduces himself at the beginning of *Eclipse* it becomes apparent that we are in the presence of – in his wife's words – 'a monster of self regard' (150). The comical swagger and vainglory of his tone at this early point will gradually be revealed as a sham, as a stylistic feint by a narrator not nearly as sure of himself as he at first seems. The urbane poise and arrogance with which he introduces himself, however, is reminiscent of Humbert Humbert's comic conceit in *Lolita*. He sketches his elegantly handsome features for the benefit of his readers (an awkward notion in itself: for whom is Cleave writing if not for himself alone?). 'Think,' he suggests, 'of your ideal Hamlet and you have me: the blond straight hair [...] the transparent, pale-blue eyes, the Nordic cheekbones, and that outthrust jaw, sensitive, and yet hinting at depths of refined brutality' (8). This is the narrator posing before the reflective surface of his own narrative, painting himself in his own words, and being very much taken by what he sees.[3] Cleave is perfectly aware that the stage is the ideal place for a narcissist such as himself: 'I do not find my fellow man particularly lovable, only I must be part of a cast' (9). He cares for others, by and large, only insofar as they provide him with the regard he needs in order to sustain his fragile sense of self. The theatre becomes, in this way, a rich, Shakespearean metaphor for Banville's notion of human relationships, and of the narcissistic condition. 'In our box of light we players strut and declaim, laughing and weeping,' says Cleave, 'while out in the furry gloom before us that vague, many-eyed mass hangs on our every bellowed word, gasps at our every overblown gesture' (10). Acting is, for Cleave, a way of being whereby significance is given to every step, every action, by the attention of others. Being the object of the world's regard, in his own mind – which is after all the only reality that truly counts – elevates the narcissist above the merely human:

> Acting was inevitable. From earliest days life for me was a perpetual state of being watched. Even when alone I carried myself with covert circumspection, keeping up a front, putting on a performance. This is the actor's hubris, to imagine the world possessed of a single, avid eye fixed solely and always on him. And he, of course, acting, thinks himself the only real one, the most substantial shadow in a world of shades. (2000a: 10)

Cleave's profession allows him to indulge his grandiose tendencies while foregrounding his profound existential doubts as to the solidity and reality of his own identity. Narcissus was, after all, a Thespian – a citizen, according to the legend, of Thespiae. Like Narcissus, Cleave is an undeserving object of the desires of the opposite sex, and hints at having had a number of affairs with leading ladies. Others want to be close to him, but he cares little for them. Having more than adequately established, for the benefit of his readers, his striking physical attractiveness, Cleave goes on to ponder the reasons for his appeal toward the opposite sex:

> I mention the matter only because I am wondering to what extent my histrionic looks might explain the indulgence, the tenderness, the unfailing and largely undeserved loving kindness, shown me by the many – well, not *many*, not what even the most loyal Leporello would call *many* – women who have been drawn into the orbit of my life over the years. (2000a: 8 [emphasis in original])

What is particularly telling here is not so much the hasty parenthetical retreat ('well, not *many*') Cleave beats toward the safety of feigned diffidence, as the choice of the word 'orbit'. Few words could more comprehensively betray the narrator's utter self-centredness: he is the star at the centre of his own solar system and, though some people may be closer to him than others, none of them are any more than satellites. The words Banville places in his narrator's mouth continually betray the essential narcissism of his outlook. The Shakespearean world-as-stage metaphor goes to the heart of *Eclipse*: Cleave is the central player in his own drama, the rest of the world merely a 'vague, many-eyed mass' that watches from the comparative gloom of the auditorium. In much of the psychoanalytical theory on narcissism (including that of Kohut), the narcissist is defined as lacking a coherent and solidly anchored sense of self. Cleave, having no clear idea of who or what he is, fits this profile. Both onstage and off he is perpetually playing a role:

> I would be anyone but myself. Thus it continued year on year, the intense, unending rehearsal. But what was it I was rehearsing for? When I searched inside myself I found nothing finished, only a permanent potential, a waiting to go on. At the site of what was supposed to be my self was only a vacancy, an ecstatic hollow. And things rushed into this vacuum where the self should be. Women, for instance. They fell into me, thinking to fill me with all they had to give. (2000a: 32)

In having Cleave draw attention to his own 'vacancy', Banville is not merely reminding us that his character is 'just' a character. There is a real and important distinction to be made here. Cleave's hollowness is no metafictional in-joke, no blithe allusion to his ontological status as nothing more than ink on paper. It is a real sense of lack and insubstantiality – something that has far more to do with a complex flesh-and-blood humanity than any recognition of his own fictionality. It is, perhaps, this lack of a stable sense of self which ultimately causes his professional downfall, in that he cannot invest himself in the portrayal of a character for fear that he will lose himself entirely. Kohut's conception of the relationship between the theatre and analysis as analogous 'art forms' would seem to substantiate this. To abandon oneself to 'the artistic experience' of the theatre and to abandon oneself to the 'quasi-artistic, indirect reality' of a psychoanalysis, writes Kohut, one must be relatively secure in one's sense of self and of reality:

> If we are sure of the reality of ourselves, we can temporarily turn away from ourselves and can suffer with the tragic hero on the

stage, without being in danger of confusing the reality of our participating emotions with the reality of our everyday lives. People whose reality sense is insecure, however, may not be able to abandon themselves easily to the artistic experience. (Kohut, 1971: 210)

It is perhaps because Cleave is so unsure of his own reality that he cannot 'abandon' himself to the portrayal of a character. His self-consciousness – what Kleist would see as his 'fall from grace' – and his sense of the unreality of that self are, in this sense, constituent elements of his narcissistic condition. His withdrawal into himself, his abandonment of his wife as he retreats to his childhood home and his creation of the strange, introspective journal that constitutes *Eclipse*, are elements of an attempt to find something real and solid in the 'ecstatic hollow' of his core. His writing is a form of intense self-focus, the aim of which is the reification of the object of perception. Surrounded by the ghosts of the past and the future, and by the only slightly more solid phantoms of real and living others, Cleave's undertaking is oddly suggestive of a psychoanalysis. He is not so much telling a story as he is trying to bring himself into focus through narrative: *Eclipse* is, in the fullest sense of the term, his attempt at self-composition. Ostensibly alone in the house where he grew up amongst transient lodgers, haunted by visions of what seems to be a ghost-mother and her child, Cleave realises that he was 'never fully at home here' – an admission which surely bears a weight of existential significance. His childhood was populated by ghosts, he reflects, in the form of the fleeting, never-wholly-present presences of the lodgers his parents kept:

Doubtless there is a reason why the apparitions do not frighten me, that the place was always haunted. I spent my childhood among alien presences, ghostly figures. How meek they were, our lodgers, how self-effacing, blurring themselves to a sort of murmur in the house. I would meet them on the stairs, squirming sideways as they edged past me and smiling their fixed smiles of pained politeness [...] At night I would seem to hear their presence all around me, a tossing, a shifting, a low, restless sighing. Now here I am, a lodger myself, no more real than the phantoms that appear to me, a shadow among insubstantial shadows. (2000a: 48)

A childhood spent among these hazy and ephemeral presences, aside from inoculating him somewhat against actual hauntings, seems also to set the tone for Cleave's attitude towards himself and others. The world he inhabits is one in which everything, himself included, seems forever on the brink of becoming nothing at all. He has, he writes, 'come to distrust even the solidest objects, uncertain if they are not merely representations of themselves that might in a moment flicker and fade [...] Everything is poised for dissolution' (47). Aside from (or perhaps in parallel with) the obvious metafictional insinuations, Cleave's sense of his own near-absence and that of the larger world resonates distinctly with Kohut's idea of narcissistic disturbance. Such disturbances, in Kohut's view, emanate from 'the sense of an incomplete reality of the self and, secondarily, of the external world' (Kohut, 1971: 210).

The two elements that most define Cleave's character – his narcissism and his sense of internal division and disintegration – are present in his very name: 'Alexander' marks the grandiose, conquering side of his personality, whereas 'Cleave' suggests the fragility and brokenness that constantly undercuts it. In retreating into himself and contemplating himself in the mirror of his narrative, what he is doing is attempting to piece his fragmenting world back together from the inside out. Her capacity to offset this lack of cohesion in his sense of self accounts for a large part of his wife's appeal to him. She is 'the one capable of concentrating sufficient attention on me to make me shine out into the world with a flickering intensity such that even I might believe I was real' (Banville, 2000a: 32). She is a mirroring presence in his life; she fixes him and reifies him through her regard. In this sense, she is experienced by Cleave as what Kohut refers to as a 'selfobject' – the mirroring other upon whom the formation of a coherent self depends. Here is how Phil Mollon describes the psychological function of such objects: 'The prime roles of selfobjects are in terms of their mirroring (empathic responsive) functions, and their availability for idealization [...] we never outgrow the need for selfobjects, although their form changes' (Mollon, 1993: 57). Robert D. Stolorow defines a narcissistic object relationship as 'one whose function is to maintain the cohesiveness, stability and positive affective colouring of the self-representation' (Stolorow, 1986: 201). In such relationships, he argues, 'archaic narcissistic configurations are mobilized (e.g. in which the individual requires continuous mirroring of his grandiose fantasies or merger with an aggrandized omnipotent mirroring object) in order to solidify a fragile and precarious sense of self-cohesion and self-esteem' (200).

Cleave, it seems, falls in love not so much with Lydia herself as with a romanticised, idealised version of her which he constructs in order to fulfil his own grandiose yearnings. Simone de Beauvoir sees this narcissism as a fundamental characteristic of the way in which men interact with women. A man's relationship with a woman, as she sees it, is largely a way of relating to himself. Her reading of this narcissistic archetype amounts to a powerful and provocative statement about heterosexual relationships:

> Woman is often compared to water because, among other reasons, she is the mirror in which the male, Narcissus-like, contemplates himself: he bends over her in good or bad faith. But in any case what he really asks of her is to be, outside of him, all that which he cannot grasp inside himself, because the inwardness of the existent is only nothingness and because he must project himself into an object in order to reach himself. (De Beauvoir, 1997: 173)

Cleave is the quintessential Banville character in that he cannot accept the shameful ordinariness of his own origins, and feels he must expunge that background in order to fully foreground his own grandiose self-image. In de Beauvoir's terms, his wife is the object onto whom he projects himself in order to reach himself. He is a self-made man, but would give anything to have been born into a condition of elegance and grace. 'The fact is,' he admits, 'I would happily have exchanged everything I had made myself into for a modicum of inherited grace, something not of my own invention, and which I had done nothing to deserve' (Banville, 2000a: 35). In this respect, Lydia fulfils the need for an idealised selfobject in that she presents an exotic, indistinctly Eastern figure. She was, Cleave tells us, 'an object of keen speculation' for him before he ever knew who she was. He would secretly watch her coming and going from the quayside hotel owned by her family, he says, 'got up in outlandish confections of cheesecloth and velvet and beads [...] an exotic, a daughter of the desert' (32–3). He 'made up lives for her', he claims: 'She was foreign, of course, the runaway daughter of an aristocratic family of fabulous pedigree; she was a rich man's former mistress, in hiding from his agents here in this backwater; certainly, she must have something in her past, I was convinced of it, some loss, some secret burden, some crime, even' (33).

He constructs Lydia as an ideal and exoticised other; she appears to be of Jewish or perhaps Arab origin, although her ethnicity is, like so many identifiers in Banville's work, never actually identified. His idealisation of her, in fact, has a distinctly Orientalist tone to it: her 'Levantine' looks, 'the hothouse pallor and stark black brows and faintly shadowed upper lip' are a 'powerful attraction' to the young courting Cleave. 'Even her name,' he says, 'bespoke for me a physical opulence. She was my big sleek helpless princess [...] I basked in her' (2000a: 33–4).[4] The hotel, too, is imagined as an enclave of Semitic mystery in the centre of dreary Dublin. 'The Hotel Halcyon, writes Cleave, 'took on for me the air of an oasis; before I entered there I imagined behind that revolving door a secret world of greenery and plashing water and sultry murmurings; I could almost taste the sherbet, smell the sandalwood' (33). Having found his princess, Alexander wishes to establish himself, like his namesake, as conqueror of this imagined Orient. She affords him, by association with her 'dauntingly exotic world', that modicum of inherited grace he so richly desires: 'I had come from nowhere, and now at last, through Lydia, I had arrived at the centre of what seemed to me to be somewhere' (36).

Both Cleave's relationship with Lydia and his career on stage, then, enable him to construct – to forge, in both senses of the word – an identity for himself out of the incoherence and absence of his inner life. Just as he is attracted to his wife initially for the air of aristocratic exoticism she exudes and – what is more important – lends to him, he is attracted to the stage because it allows him to try on identities. He becomes an actor, he says, 'to give myself a cast of characters to inhabit who would be bigger, grander, of more weight and moment than I could ever hope to be' (35). What he wants from both endeavours – from his 'miscegenous' marriage and his 'role of being others' – is to create himself anew, 'to achieve my authentic self' (35; 36). That both career and marriage collapse at more or less the same time is, it seems, an important detail: he loses the two crucial sources of mirroring in his life in one catastrophic episode. It is the sudden death of his career and the slower death of his marriage that generate his compulsion to be alone and to take stock of himself.

Crucially, it is Cleave's own narcissistic self-absorption that actually causes both events. Before the on-stage 'collapse', as we have seen, he had been 'beset by bouts of crippling self-consciousness' (87). He cannot continue acting because of what he calls 'my malady of selfness' – a quintessentially Banvillean turn of phrase for the kind of destructive self-obsession that beleaguers so many of his characters (89).

Cleave abandons the wreckage of his life to go and live in the now-dilapidated home where he was raised. He does this in an attempt to find some kind of answer to the question posed by his existence. 'Perhaps,' he reflects, 'this is what I need to do, finally give it all up, home, wife, possessions, renounce it all for good, rid myself of every last thing and come and live in some such unconsidered spot as this' (2000a: 70). What he is doing is clearing away the clutter from his life – the clutter of other people – in order to see himself more clearly. He is, in a sense, like Descartes in his *Meditations*, clearing away the rubble of untenable assumptions in order to get to the core of what he might finally know about himself. The language with which Cleave frames these intentions is one of confrontation and reconciliation: he plans to come face-to-face with himself and, like Narcissus leaning closer and closer to the pool, 'reunite' with himself. It is a language that is at once both profoundly self-alienated and utterly narcissistic:

> Free then of all encumbrance, all distraction, I might be able at last to confront myself without shock or shrinking. For is this not what I am after, the pure conjunction, the union of self with sundered self? I am weary of division, of being always torn. (Banville, 2000a: 70)

A more concise depiction of the narcissist's complex nexus of drives and desires can scarcely be imagined than 'the union of self with sundered self'. Like Narcissus, he is estranged from himself – cannot recognise his own reflection when he sees it – and yet disastrously preoccupied with himself.

In *Ancient Light* (2012), set 10 years after the events of *Eclipse*, Cleave looks back on a brief affair, at age 15, with the mother of his closest childhood friend Billy Gray. This affair is one of Banville's most thorough engagements with the narcissistic nature of sexual relationships. The young Alexander believes himself to be in love with Mrs Gray (to whom he almost never refers by her first name), but his attachment to her is an extraordinarily selfish one. At the end of the novel, Cleave – the middle-aged Cleave who narrates the story – finds out that she was in fact terminally ill at the time of their affair. From his first glimpse of her, he fabricates an idealised version of her as a kind of sexualised maternal figure ('my Venus Domestica'), a composite embodiment of feminine ideals (Banville, 2012: 6). Throughout the novel, the young Cleave is guilty of a failure to even try to see her for what she is; he is engaging not with a person per se, but with his own desire as it is manifested in that person. This is something that the older Cleave has come to recognise, and his narrative is weighted with a sense of guilt about his inattention to her as anything other than an object of desire (although it is an incomplete guilt, as he does not become aware of her illness until the end of the novel). His experience of Mrs Gray is an experience, first and foremost, of self-discovery; she is the other through which he comes to know himself. As a consequence, he has no sense that she might feel anything like love for him: 'Engrossed in what I felt for myself, I had no measure against which to match what she might feel for me. That was how it was at the start, and how it went on, to the end. That is how it is when one discovers oneself through another' (42).

Throughout the novel, the young Cleave's conception of his lover is presented as glaringly Oedipal. She is forever tousling his hair, scolding him and comforting him, and he is prone to sulking and weeping in her presence, clinging to her as a young child clings to its mother. 'Mothers were put on earth to love sons,' he reasons, 'and although I was not her son Mrs Gray was a mother, so how would she deny me anything, even the innermost secrets of her flesh?' The Oedipal dimension of the relationship is not so much subtext as supratext – at one point he happens, by chance, to look at her face during sex as she smiles down at him with a 'maternal' benevolence – and it envelops Cleave's narrative, threatening to sink it beneath the weight of its faintly ludicrous overdetermination (2012: 125). But it isn't so much the incestuous implications of this reasoning that make it so disturbing as the creepy lyricism of the phrase 'innermost secrets of her flesh.' It's as though this woman is less a person than a thing – a location – to which access is sought and granted as something like a natural right. What he requires of her is the gratification of his own desire (a desire which is suspended, troublingly and yet somehow comically, between a mature heterosexual impulse and the urgent need of an infant for its mother). He takes no interest in her inner life:

> In all of the time we were together I never knew what was going on in her head, not in any real or empathic way, and hardly bothered to try to find out [...] Her ramblings and ruminations and the odd breathless flight of wonderment I regarded as no more than the preliminaries I had to put up with before getting her into the back seat of that pachydermous old station wagon or on to the lumpy mattress on Cotter's littered floor. (Banville, 2012: 110)

It is occasionally apparent that her 'ramblings and ruminations' are stimulated by the knowledge that she will soon die. At one point, as he is attempting to make love to her in the car, she stares out the window and remarks on the strangeness of mortality, on 'how permanent people seem [...] as if they'll always be here, the same ones, walking up and down' (2012: 110–11). He pays no notice, concerned as he is only with the question of whether there is enough time left for her to let him 'assuage for a little while longer my so fierce, tender and inveterate need of her and her inexhaustibly desirable flesh' (111). The word 'flesh' here is perilously overloaded with significance; it bears the entire weight of the sad irony at the centre of the novel. For Cleave, the word seems to have a purely carnal significance, but it's powerful here because of the shadow of death it throws – despite Cleave's intentions – across the description of his lust. Thus the selfishness of his desire (of all sexual desire) becomes complicated by the fact of the desired person's mortality, which is, in Banville's writing, inseparable from the fact of their otherness, their autonomous individuality. The young Cleave may think Mrs Gray's flesh is inexhaustibly desirable, but the shadowed significance of this poetic invocation of youthful sexuality is the prosaic exhaustibility of that flesh. She is going to die very soon, but he has no notion that this is the case because he has no interest in her internal life – no real concern for her at all beyond the erotic (and curiously infantile) desire for her flesh.

The self-directed nature of love is a major theme of Banville's work, and it is one that is linked with the profound difficulty of making real and empathic connections with others. Cleave is a particularly

Banvillean figure in this sense, and his affair with Mrs Gray sets the tone for his adult relationships. Lydia is a minor figure in *Ancient Light* (even more minor than she is in *Eclipse*), and when Cleave does speak about her, it is often in regard to the essential strangeness of this most familiar person. 'It occurs to me,' he tells us, 'that of all the women I have known in my life I know Lydia the least.' He refers to her as 'an enigma of my making', and remarks upon the fact that he 'can no longer see her properly.' He then comes to the realisation that this is because 'she has become a part of me, a part of what is the greatest of all my enigmas, namely, myself' (2012: 139). There is an emotional contradiction here: the strength of his identification with Lydia has led to a kind of obliteration of his sense of her otherness, which is a peculiar kind of solipsism (this question of the paradox of empathy in Banville's work is dealt with in much greater detail in Chapter 7).

In *The Fragile Self*, Phil Mollon identifies as one of the varieties of self-consciousness what he refers to as 'a compulsive, and hypochondriacal preoccupation with the self' – a condition characterised by 'a compelling need to look in mirrors and to evoke mirroring responses from others' (Mollon, 1993: 54). To illustrate this narcissistic affect, he provides a psychoanalytic case study. The analysand is Miss J., an art photographer. She seeks therapy in the wake of a period of professional and personal upheaval – she has had a relationship break-up and has had to leave a studio she has worked in for many years 'and which she clearly experienced as part of her'. The episode arouses feelings of 'panic and depersonalisation' (63). During this period, writes Mollon, 'she felt old and ugly and found herself compulsively looking in mirrors and in shop windows' and 'felt continually compelled to take photos of herself', fearing that 'she might not be seen, that she might become invisible' (62). Mollon's claim is that both her job and her relationship served as 'mirroring' environments: 'In both instances [...] she felt wrenched from an environment or person in which she had felt embedded. She then found herself lost and alone in an alien context which did not mirror her in a familiar way. Her sense of self was then considerably disturbed' (63). The compulsion to seek one's reflection and the sense of disintegration of one's self are, for Mollon – and for most other theorists of narcissism – intimately connected:

> In the case of Miss J., the loss of her previous relationship, functioning as a selfobject background, had led to the emergence

of a grandiose self, shoring up a disintegrating self-representation, and combined with an imperious demand for mirroring. In the absence of a human mirroring partner, she had turned to actual mirrors and to photographing herself. The use of mirrors to restore the sense of self in lieu of a human mirroring response seems very common. Mrs L. [the analysand in another of Mollon's case studies], for example [...] explained that when she felt chaotic internally she would look in a mirror and feel both amazed and reassured that her outer appearance was still organised. (Mollon, 1993: 64)

The idea of the mirror image as imposing a superficial coherence upon internal disorder is an important idea in psychoanalysis. In his seminal 1949 paper, 'The Mirror Stage as Formative of the *I* Function as Revealed in Psychoanalytic Experience', Jacques Lacan claims that the infant only begins to get a sense of itself as a cohesive, integrated subject when it recognises its own reflection. Met with this *imago*, the infant begins to think of itself as something more real than a diffusion of disconnected phenomena, as something more solid than a chaos of limbs and extremities, fears and desires. In Lacan's deeply anti-humanist view of human psychology, it is in the apprehension of one's reflected image that the misapprehension of subjectivity, the illusion of the self, has its origin. Kohut envisages 'the gleam in the mother's eye' at the child's 'exhibitionistic display' as serving the same sort of mirroring and unifying function as Lacan's mirror (Kohut, 1971: 116). In Kohut's developmental model it is the mother's regard, with its confirming and approving gaze, that facilitates the crucial shift from 'the stage of the fragmented self [...] to the stage of the cohesive self – i.e., the growth of the self experience as a physical and mental unit which has cohesiveness in space and continuity in time' (118).

What Kohut's child, Lacan's *infans*, Mollon's Miss J. and Mrs. L., and Banville's Alexander Cleave have in common is the need for mirroring surfaces, human and otherwise, to reinstate a sense of self. The unifying idea is that self-cohesion is not generated primarily from within, but is a product of the self's relationship with the world, and is contingent upon images received from outside. Cleave feels his self to be cloven; to be, as he puts it, 'sundered' and 'torn'. Like Banville's other great masqueraders, Axel Vander and Victor Maskell, Cleave has spent so long in trying to pass for other people, he is no longer sure whether he has a 'real' self. In *Eclipse,* what he strives for, in the creation of his narrative – his story of self – is the construction of a cohesive identity. In this sense, his narrative is his mirroring surface. The clearing away of the clutter, however, proves so difficult that he begins to doubt whether there is anything more to him than a tangle of fabrications and self-deceptions. 'I thought that by coming here I would find a perspective on things, a standpoint from which to survey my life,' Cleave tells us, 'but when I look back now to what I have left behind me I am afflicted by a disabling wonderment: how did I manage to accumulate so much of life's clutter, apparently without effort, or even full consciousness? – so much, that under the weight of it I cannot begin to locate that singular essential self, the one I came here to find, that must be in hiding, somewhere, under the jumble of discarded masks' (Banville, 2000a: 50).

Cleave's project of self-revelation is closely aligned with that of the art historian Maskell who, in the opening pages of *The Untouchable,* characterises his task in terms that reflect those of his profession, as one of 'attribution, verification, restoration.' He intends, he claims, 'to strip away layer after layer of grime – the toffee-coloured varnish and caked soot left by a lifetime of dissembling – until I come to the very thing itself and know it for what it is. My soul. My self' (Banville, 1997b: 7). Such a project can be viewed as a kind of critical endeavour: Cleave and Maskell seek to penetrate the unyielding and multifarious strata of style that seem to cocoon them in order to reach whatever substance, whatever self, may lie within.

Like Mollon's patient Miss J., who falls into the self-mirroring routine of habitually taking photographs of herself, Cleave develops an idle, curiously infantile fixation with his own person. He falls, as he puts it, 'into thrall with' himself, marvelling at the brute phenomena of his own physicality – 'the stools, the crusts of snot, the infinitesimal creep of fingernails and hair' (Banville, 2000a: 50). He scrutinises himself with the kind of intensity one would ordinarily direct at a work of art or an object of lust. When he cuts his hand gardening and develops a septic palm, these two modes of observation – the aesthetic and the sensual – appear to merge in his experience of himself:

> ... I would stand motionless and rapt at the window with my hand held up to the daylight, studying the swelling with its shiny

meniscus of purplish skin, taut and translucent as the stuff of an insect's wing; at night, when I woke in the dark, the hand would seem a separate, living thing throbbing beside me. The dull hot pain of it was almost voluptuous. Then one morning when I was getting myself out of bed I stumbled and caught my hand on something sharp, and a tattoo of pain drummed up my arm and the swelling burst and the splinter popped out in a blob of pus. I sank back on the bed clutching my wrist and whimpering, but whether from pain or pleasure I could not exactly say. (Banville, 2000a: 51)

The sustained excitability of the language here, and in particular the quadruple rolling conjunctions of its climactic sentence ('Then one morning ... and ... and ... and ... and ...'), reflects the enigmatic eroticism of its subject matter. Banville's prose is working itself up into a state of high arousal.

Inevitably, Cleave's narcissistic quest for 'the union of self with sundered self' has a more grubbily literal dimension, too. He spends much of his time in erotic congress with himself, and the descriptions he offers of his 'shameful pleasures' are comically suggestive of the transcendent bliss of consummated love. Reclining in 'guilty heat' on his plumped up pillows with a cherished collection of reproductions of Victorian erotic paintings, he sinks back 'with a hoarse sigh into my own vigorous embrace'. There are, he admits, 'rare and precious' occasions when 'having brought myself to the last hiccupy scamper [...] I will experience a moment of desolating rapture that has nothing to do with what is happening in my lap but seems a distillation of all the tenderness and intensity that life can promise' (Banville, 2000a: 51–2). On one such occasion, in prose as tumescent as the act it describes, he tells us that 'as I lay gasping with my chin on my breast, I heard faintly through the stillness of afternoon the ragged sound of a children's choir in the convent across the way, and it might have been the seraphs singing' (52). There is undoubtedly a self-ironising impulse in operation here, though whether the impulse is Cleave's or his creator's is unclear. Surely, however, only a Banville character could get quite so worked up over a collection of nineteenth-century 'hand-tinted' erotica ('postcard-sized but rich in detail, all creams and crimsons and rose-petal pinks'). There is something absurdly affected about a middle-aged man masturbating over such a tastefully titillating collection of 'mostly oriental scenes' (52). Doubtless, the treasury of antique exotica is not the focus of his arousal, but rather its catalyst. If Cleave is not strictly speaking, in the classically Freudian sense of narcissism, the object of his own desire, there is certainly no immediate object outside of himself for that desire.

This moment might be said to constitute a defining image in Banville's oeuvre, containing as it does an aggregation of themes: self-absorption, isolation, the enigmatic overlap of sex and aesthetics. It is, finally, a grotesquely comic vision of the abjectness and pomposity of Banville's model of masculinity. There is a trace of the mock-heroic, surely, in Cleave's rapt invocation of a choir of singing seraphs to mark the less than momentous occasion of his own self-induced orgasm. What is particularly apparent here (and is never very far from being manifest throughout *Eclipse*) is that Cleave is always, even in his most private moments, playing a role. He is inauthentic to his hollow core. A ham in every aspect of his being, he even manages to render grandiloquent the bluntly prosaic business of masturbation. In the ongoing masquerade that is his life – the lengthy run of his performance as himself – Cleave's self-portrayals are, he understands, little more than an unsatisfactory series of simulacra. In this respect, his existential predicament seems to reflect two opposed senses of the word 'character', which is to say that his distinctive nature is to be found in the playing of roles. As Adam Phillips puts it in *Terrors and Experts*:

> If, as Freud suggests in *The Ego and the Id*, character is constituted by identification – the ego likening itself to what it once loved – then character is close to caricature, an imitation of an imitation. Like the critics Plato wanted to ban, we are making copies of copies, but unlike Plato's critics, we have no original, only an infinite succession of likenesses to someone who, to all intents and purposes, does not exist. (Phillips, 1995: 77)

This is a major recurring predicament – perhaps *the* predicament – in Banville's fiction. The insurmountable obstacle to the pursuit of authenticity is the fact that the object of the pursuit does not, in all probability, exist in any kind of stable form. This search for what cannot be found – for what Richard Sennett refers to as 'Experience' – is not merely a futile search, but one which inevitably has a depleting effect on that which is sought. The more Alexander Cleave allows himself to fall 'into thrall with himself', the less there is of that self, real or illusory, to be contemplated. A 'caricature' is a mere impression, and a distorted one at that. It bears only a notional relation to that which it claims to represent. It is this idea of the self as a slender simulacrum which motivates so much of the ontological unease of Banville's narcissistic narrators. It is in *Shroud*, however, that such anxieties reach their culmination.

The notion of character as 'an imitation of an imitation' is a central one in *Eclipse*'s companion novel, *Shroud*. *Shroud* is the story of Axel Vander, a world-renowned academic with a disgraceful past to conceal. Amongst his worst sins are the shamefully self-interested euthanising of his senile wife and the series of explicitly anti-Semitic articles he supposedly authored during the war. The latter, in their claim that 'nothing of consequence would be lost to the cultural and intellectual life of Europe [...] if certain supposedly assimilated elements were to be removed and settled somewhere far away', unequivocally endorse the Nazi party's overall conception of the Jewish problem, if not the sickening specifics of its solution to it (Banville, 2002: 137).[5] The novel opens with Vander receiving a letter from Cass Cleave, a young Irish academic (and daughter of *Eclipse*'s Alexander) who has unearthed his wartime journalism and seems to be preparing to expose him. In an apparent act of fatalism, Vander agrees to meet with her at an academic conference in Turin. He initially conceives of Cass Cleave as his 'mysterious nemesis' (21), and the term's myriad definitions reverberate throughout the novel. She is his nemesis, as he sees it, in the sense of her being the agent of his imminent downfall, and she is also perceived as the (unwitting) personification of some indistinct but powerful force of retributive justice, some requital he has had coming for most of his life. But she is also a version of Nemesis, the Greek goddess of fate usually portrayed in mythology as the spirit of divine vengeance against those who have succumbed to hubris. As the possessor of the incriminating wartime articles, she is the emissary of his destiny: 'She held his fate in her hands, his future; she had found him out' (21). In Ovid's *Metamorphoses*, it will be remembered, it is Nemesis who punishes Narcissus for his self-absorption by condemning him to fall in love with his own reflected image. Likewise, in *Shroud*, it is Cass Cleave who forces Vander to come face to face with himself, who precipitates his narrative descent into the 'primordial darkness' of his own past (3).

Axel Vander is perhaps the most fascinatingly complex and repellently narcissistic of Banville's fictional creations. He is violently egotistical to a degree that makes the novelist's other self-obsessed misanthropes – even Freddie Montgomery – seem relatively agreeable by comparison. He is also an alcoholic (a hallmark attribute of Banville's narrators). Even at the level of the physical he is monstrous – outlandishly tall with one cyclopean eye and a wooden leg that afflicts him with a lurch. He is, as he puts it, 'a bad fit with the world, an awkward fit; I am too high, too wide, too heavy for the common scale of things' (Banville, 2002: 25). He is also, like Victor Frankenstein, the creator of his own monstrous version of himself – he envisions himself walking 'out of the fire and furnace smoke of the European catastrophe, like Frankenstein's monster staggering out of the burning mill' (38). Like Victor Maskell in *The Untouchable* and Freddie Montgomery in *Ghosts*, who imagine themselves as sculpting grand monuments in their own images, Vander depicts his self-construction in the language of artistic creation. Even his chosen tipple is a stylistic affectation: though he dislikes the taste of bourbon he chose it early on as his regular drink, 'as part of my strategy of difference, another way of being on guard, as an actor puts a pebble in his shoe to remind him that the character he is playing has a limp'. He boasts that 'had it been a work of art I was fashioning they would have applauded my mastery' (7). This representation of Vander as a gifted performer of his own ideal identity subtly links him with Cleave, his counterpart in *Eclipse*.

Like *The Untouchable*, *Shroud* opens with an exposure. Just as Victor Maskell's narrative begins with the public revelation of his past as a Soviet double agent, Vander's descent into the 'primordial darkness' of his biography is expedited by the threat of exposure. The language with which he conveys his disquiet at the return of his past is permeated with a palpable sense of self-loathing: 'I had thought I had shaken off the pelt of my far past yet here was evidence that it would not be entirely sloughed, but was dragging along behind me, still attached by a thread or two of dried slime' (2002: 7). Here the languages of transformation and disgrace are synthesised into a single mode of expression: Vander's own idiolect of shame. The metamorphic imagery recalls Victor Maskell's peculiar self-portrayals in *The Untouchable*, in which Maskell imagines himself as having undergone 'the exquisite agony of the caterpillar turning itself into a butterfly, pushing out eye-stalks, pounding its fat-cells into iridescent wing-dust, at last cracking the mother-of-pearl sheath and staggering upright on sticky, hair's-breadth legs, drunken, gasping, dazed by the light' (1997b: 63).

What must be confronted by both men is what the narcissist wishes never to have to face, but inevitably must: the largely repressed *other* self which he imagines himself to have transcended through careful self-sculpting, but which invariably returns in the form of shame. For Vander, this return of the repressed is an almost unbearable imposition: 'What could I find to say, at such a distance of time, to this discarded version of myself?' (2002: 5). It is as though he himself is a figure from his own distant past with whom he no longer has anything in common. This break with the facts of his biography – this shedding of the 'pelt' of his own history – is what defines Vander's ruptured, self-estranged identity. He exists in self-imposed banishment not just from his country and from his people, but ultimately from himself. The name 'Vander' is itself emblematic in this regard: in the Dutch language (Vander is originally from Flanders), his name literally means 'from the'. Like Cleave's, which hints at the split nature of his character, and Maskell's, which suggests his self-concealment, Vander's name expresses his expurgated identity. It is as though a final syllable or syllables have been hacked off, and a ghostly question mark remains at the end of his name, a phantom limb of signification. 'Vander' is also very close to the Dutch word 'ander', which means 'other' or, in certain usages, literally 'another man'. This matter of nomenclature can be viewed as addressing two of the novel's major issues in miniaturised form: the question of identity and the essential treachery of the text as a means of conveying truth or meaning. The word Vander – as marker of identity and as written communication – is significant less for what it discloses than for what it refuses to disclose. It is not so much a name as the denial of a name.

The novel is in many respects Banville's most resolute engagement with the postmodernist ideas he has dealt in for most of his career. Vander is a deconstructionist critic in the mould of de Man, his academic métier being, rather appropriately, the denial of the existence of the self. As he puts it:

I spent the best part of what I suppose I must call my career trying to drum into those who would listen among the general mob of resistant sentimentalists surrounding me the simple lesson that there is no self: no ego, no precious individual spark breathed into each one of us by a bearded patriarch in the sky, who does not exist either. (Banville, 2002: 18)

Like his antecedent and fellow academic Victor Maskell, Vander's philosophical position amounts to little more than 'a cluster of fiercely held denials' (1997b: 327). His professed disbelief in the existence of truth and of the essential self – a convenient credo, to be sure, for a man whose truths, were he to acknowledge truth as a legitimate category, would include murder, identity theft and Nazi collaboration. Indeed, there is a larger issue, a larger wrong and a larger repudiation, which Banville appears to hint at through Vander's deconstructionist denials. A popular 'slippery slope' argument against such denials is that they lead, with depressing inevitability, to the moral and intellectual abomination of Holocaust denial. When Vander dismisses history as 'a hotchpotch of anecdotes, neither true nor false' and asks what difference it makes 'where it is supposed to have taken place', the spectre of Auschwitz – a spectre which haunts the margins of the narrative throughout – seems to rise up and overshadow his words (2002: 32). Vander's entire family have been consumed in the blaze of the Holocaust, and it is only by the narrowest of margins that he has escaped it himself. His trivialising of history as a kind of worthless miscellany of meaningless yarns, therefore, sounds a strange and hauntingly ironic note.

His rejections of the concept of self are equally problematic. Despite his more or less orthodox postmodernist stance on such matters, he cannot quite bring himself to disbelieve in the existence of an essential self (he is, perhaps, finally too self-obsessed to do so). His 'secret shame', he admits, is that he 'cannot entirely rid myself of the conviction of an enduring core of selfhood amid the welter of the world' (18). Though he cannot rid himself of this idea, neither can he reach this notional core. It is a particular facet of his narcissism, however, that he continually searches for it whilst doubting its existence. Crucially, such scepticisms are wholly commensurate with the narcissist's approach to experience. For Kohut, as we have seen, narcissistic personality disorders are characterised by 'the sense of an incomplete reality of the self and, secondarily, of the external world' (Kohut, 1971: 210). The opening words of *Shroud* – 'Who speaks?' – immediately foreground this postmodern concern with the nature of the self and with the ontological status of fictional narrative. We can take the question, perhaps, as a sly citation of Roland Barthes' question about the narrative voice of Balzac's story 'Sarrasine': 'who is speaking thus?' Barthes answers his own question by resoundingly dismissing it along with all such others:

> We shall never know, for the good reason that writing is the destruction of every voice, of every point of origin. Writing is that neutral, composite, oblique space where our subject slips away, the negative where all identity is lost, starting with the very identity of the body writing. (Barthes, 1977: 142)

The crucial consideration with *Shroud* is the way in which Vander uses these critical abstractions as a smokescreen behind which to hide. There is a curious contradiction at work here, in that if writing is the process by which 'identity is lost', it is also the process by which he attempts – or appears to attempt – to retrieve it. There is a faint echo, too, of the opening words of *Hamlet* ('Who's there?'), resonating with Vander's search for a definitive authentic version of himself, the 'who' which can be finally designated as speaking, as being *there*. There is no final answer to this question – or rather, too many answers for the question to be satisfiable. It is Vander who speaks, in his many guises. It is Cass who speaks through Vander and vice versa. It is also, and perhaps most pertinently, John Banville who speaks through each of them. In this way, *Shroud* sets out its stall of themes and paradoxes from its very first words. Crucially, it begins with an act or invocation of self-examination, with Vander examining himself and the novel examining itself whilst inviting the reader to do likewise. As such, it begins as it means to go on.

Shroud is, like *Eclipse*, a novel filled with reflected images of its protagonist, both real and imagined. From the very first page, Vander sees himself through the eyes of others, imagining what he must look like to the nameless hordes – 'the baker and the butcher and the fellow at the vegetable stall, and their customers, too' – as he hauls himself through the streets of Turin. 'Clearly I interest them', he suggests. 'Perhaps what appeals to them is the suggestion of the commedia dell'arte in my appearance, the one-eyed glare and comically spavined gait, the stick and hat in place of Harlequin's club and mask' (Banville, 2002: 3).[6] This is perhaps the first indication we are given that Vander is not to be taken at his word. The extreme subjectivity of his narrative and the drastic narcissism of his worldview are more or less laid out at this early stage. It is, the reader suspects, highly unlikely that the bakers, butchers and greengrocers of Turin are marvelling at this elderly man's aura of the *commedia dell'arte*, or even that they are paying him much attention to begin with.

Axel Vander is obsessed with perceptions of himself, both his own and others'. At one point, he emerges from his hotel room's bath and considers his reflection in the floor-length mirror before wandering into the bedroom to stand naked before the window. A woman selling flowers looks upward and seems, despite the position of his hotel room several storeys from street level, to see him. He marvels at the idea of being perceived: 'What a sight I would have been, suspended up there behind a glass, a grotesque seraph, vast, naked, ancient'. Moments later he glances downward and catches sight of 'yet another, dim reflection of myself [...] like that bronzen portrait of the dead Christ by what's-his-name, first the feet and then the shins, the knees, and dangling genitals, and belly and big chest, and topping it all the aura of wild hair and the featureless face looking down' (2002: 25). The language of both of these self-images seems to betray the strange admixture of awe and aversion with which the narcissist regards him- or herself. In both instances, Vander represents himself as not just a monument, but a monument of a divine figure – an angel of light and a messiah. But he is a 'grotesque' seraph and a dead Christ with exposed genitalia and 'featureless' face.

There is a suggestion of Lucifer in that image of the ancient, grotesque seraph. The association is strengthened when a variation of the same image reoccurs later: 'I imagined again how I would seem to someone looking up from the streets below, an airborne figure [...] about to plummet, a decrepit, lost archangel' (45). These are visions of forbidding grandiosity: Lucifer, the archetypal fallen angel who is flung from heaven for the sin of pride; Christ the redeemer of sins. This is evidently a person who conceives of himself in mythopoetic terms. He is also, these images suggest, equally captivated and mortified by himself. In *The Analysis of the Self*, Kohut writes of the narcissistic personality: '[V]arious – and frequently inconsistent – self representations are present not only in the id, the ego and the superego, but also within a single agency of the mind. There may, for example, exist contradictory conscious and preconscious self representations – e.g., of grandiosity and inferiority – side by side' (Kohut, 1971: xv).

Throughout the novel, there are repeated allusions to the death of Christ and the mythology and iconography which surround it, with Vander continually portraying himself in the light of these associations. These Christ references are sufficiently frequent (and sufficiently strange) to merit some closer scrutiny, particularly with respect to the access-points they provide to the enigmatic and extreme narcissism of Vander's psyche. There is, patently, an astringent irony to these self-representations: Vander knows well enough that he is more Judas Iscariot than Jesus Christ. He has betrayed everyone and everything it has ever been in his interest to betray, and he cannot bring himself to overlook the fact of his own personal and professional fraudulence. As he admits to Cass, '"My dear [...] I have turned my coat so often that it has grown threadbare"' (Banville, 2002: 65). And yet Banville continually invites the reader to cross-reference Vander against Christ. His wife's name, Magda, creates an implicit link, for example, with the figure of Mary Magdalene, the biblical paradigm of the penitent sinner who devoted herself utterly to Christ. At one point, Vander is asked by his academic colleague Kristina Kovacs (with whom he once had a brief affair) whether he has seen the Shroud of Turin. '"They say it is the first self-portrait. I always think it was the Magdalene who held the cloth, not Veronica. But Magdalene was hair, is that not so?"' (100). This mention of the biblical Magdalene holding Christ's hair brings to Vander's mind a memory of his own washing of Magda's hair. The passage has an oddly distracted, almost Joycean stream-of-consciousness quality that is atypical of Banville's normally calculating and calculated prose:

> Long thick brown tresses streaming like water weed in the yellow lamplight, the water sluicing from the white jug. She would kneel beside the bathtub, a votary before the sacred fount, broad shoulders bowed, her white neck bared. Feel of her big skull frail as an egg under my kneading fingers. Where? Newyorpennindianabraska. (Banville, 2002: 100)

There is a ritual aspect to this act of washing, or at least to Vander's narration of it. Magda is a kneeling 'votary before the sacred fount', and her 'white neck bared' suggests a kind of ceremonial gesture of submission or penitence. There is a great sweep of associations to this image, most prominent of which are those of Christ's washing of his disciples' feet and Mary Magdalene's washing of Christ's feet with her hair. But Vander is no redeemer: after a long marriage in which he pays her little heed, Magda develops Alzheimer's disease, and Vander poisons her with an overdose of her medication, a deed which is an act of mercy as much upon himself as upon her. One morning, he witnesses her walk into the kitchen 'leaving behind her a trail of little turds as flat as fishes' and decides on the instant that 'the time had come when she must go' (59).

After her death, he realises that he did not know her at all; that he had no real interest in her outside of the purposes she served for his own self-image. He has alternately neglected and abused her, taking advantage of her docile nature. He has made disparaging 'dry asides' at her expense in company, something which she seemed to accept with stoic resignation and submissiveness. If he did indeed love his wife, it was a peculiar kind of love, characterised by distance and detachment. They may have lived together, but they have not shared a life in any meaningful sense. 'My life with her,' as he puts it at one point, 'was a special way of being alone', their relationship 'a state of mutual incomprehension' (39). She too was a survivor of the Holocaust, having lost her entire family to the camps like Vander, and there is a suggestion that his attachment to her may have had some basis in the horrific experiences they shared. But Vander was never fully honest with her about his past – never revealed to her that he was not in fact Axel Vander, but had stolen the identity of a childhood friend of that name, and had created a version of himself for and *through* her that became somehow real for him via her acceptance of it. In this sense, his connection with her was a profoundly narcissistic one. Because she did not truly want to know the ugliness of his 'real' self, she permitted him to create a self that was more to both of their liking, becoming, as it were, a warped mirror in which he saw a distorted, but conveniently flattering, image of himself: 'I could not but admire my own performance. What a fabulist I was; what an artist! And I never did tell her the real, the whole, the tawdry truth' (42–3). Vander is a man living a fiction, a man who has become the embodiment of his own lies.

His relationship with Cass is similarly narcissistic. Though he claims to have loved her, Vander is quite ruthless in exposing the fundamentally self-directed nature of that love. There is, on the surface, what might be called the normal narcissism of infatuation ('I wanted her to admire me [...] to deliquesce in my arms, helpless with astonished desire and adoration'), but running beneath that surface is a vein of cold-blooded solipsism (209). This is acknowledged in terms of self-recrimination – arguably the dominant tone of the book as a whole – in the wake of Cass's suicide. There was, Vander acknowledges in retrospect, something horribly chilly about his need for her:

> [H]ad I harboured any real, honest, human feelings for her I would have protected her and not let her drop from my safe-keeping like a drunk man dropping a brimming glass [...] It was plain inattention. The object of my true regard was not her, the so-called loved one, but myself, the one who loved, so-called. Is it not always thus? Is not love the mirror of burnished gold in which we contemplate our shining selves? (Banville, 2002: 210)

His love for her, such as it is, is really a form of *amour propre*; she provides him with the mirror in which he may contemplate his shining self. He performs himself for her, striking poses before her. At one point, he becomes involved in a dinner table argument with a fellow academic about the work of 'some fashionable scribbler', and Cass's gaze, he notes, is 'fixed on me with what I took to be an almost ecstatic intensity'. His performance is staged more for his own benefit than for hers: 'How I swirled and skirled for her, flashing my blade, captivated by my own ferocity and fighting skill' (222). In this respect, the configuration of their relationship is markedly similar to that of Cass's parents, Alexander and Lydia Cleave.[7] His psycho-sexual attachment to her and his narrative expropriation of her identity are presented as being inseparable, and as irretrievably narcissistic and fraudulent. 'There is not a sincere bone,' he tells us, 'in the entire body of my text. I have manufactured a voice, as I once manufactured a reputation, from material filched from others.' As is the way of narcissists, he uses her as a guarantor of his own cohesiveness, as a means of piecing himself together. 'I used Cass Cleave,' as he puts it, 'as a test of my authentic being [...] I seized on her to be my authenticity itself. That was what I was rooting in her for, not pleasure or youth or the last few crumbs of life's grand feast, nothing so frivolous; she was my last chance to be me' (210).

The brutal aspect of the language – 'used', 'seized', 'rooted in her' – seems to capture the way in which the narcissist tends to approach relationships with others. There is something shockingly utilitarian and opportunistic about such an approach. Whilst being wholly 'inattentive' to her in a crucial respect, he uses her to reflect a desired image of himself, an idealised vision of a coherent Axel Vander. The American Psychiatric Association's *Diagnostic and Statistical Manual of Mental Disorders* stresses precisely this exploitative quality of the narcissistic personality's interaction with others, which it characterises as lacking 'sustained, positive regard': 'Interpersonal exploitativeness, in which others are taken advantage of in order to indulge one's own desires or for self-aggrandisement, is common; and the personal integrity and rights of others are disregarded'. Interestingly, the manual gives as an example of such behaviour the possibility that 'a writer might plagiarize the ideas of someone befriended for that purpose' (American Psychiatric Association, 1980: 317).

If Vander is not literally a plagiarist – his academic work, though hollow and, by his own admission, frequently based on texts he has not bothered to read, is at least of his own creation – he is something at once very similar and a great deal worse. He is, in the case of his theft of his friend the original Axel Vander's identity, a usurper not just of ideas, but of entire characters. There is, too, a sense in which his expropriation of Cass's identity for the creation of 'her' narrative can be seen as a kind of emotional and psychological, as opposed to intellectual, plagiarism. He takes Cass, inhabits her, and uses her for his own ends.

Richard Sennett, who argues in *The Fall of Public Man* that an isolated and narcissistic existence is the norm in wealthy and atomised Western societies, sees this kind of inability to remove other people from the context of what they mean to oneself as the essence of narcissism:

> This question about the personal relevance of other people and outside acts is posed so repetitively that a clear perception of those persons and events in themselves is obscured. This absorption in self, oddly enough, prevents gratification of self needs; it makes the person at the moment of attaining an end of connecting with another person feel that 'this isn't what I wanted.' Narcissism thus

has the double quality of being a voracious absorption in self needs and the block to their fulfilment. (Sennett, 1977: 8)

The search for authenticity is, for Sennett, ultimately a narcissistic one. Vander uses Cass, by his own admission, 'as a test of my authentic being' and as his 'last chance to be me'. It is this voracious absorption in himself that blocks, finally, the fulfilment of this desire to be himself authentically. Like Cleave and, as we shall see, like Freddie Montgomery in particular, Vander's profound unhappiness is largely a result of his incapacity to see other people as anything but adjuncts to his own ego. That he remains, by the end of the novel, seemingly as unknown to himself as he does to the reader is a function, paradoxically, of his narcissistic obsession with translating himself into language. For Vander, fraudulence and self-definition are, for all their irreconcilability, finally inseparable. Both are components of the malign and demeaning narcissism that defines his character.

Freddie Montgomery, the narrator of *The Book of Evidence* (as well as of *Ghosts* and *Athena*, the two novels which followed it), has a great deal in common with Axel Vander. Both are academics (Freddie is a once-promising mathematician who has since eased himself into premature retirement); both are almost absurdly misanthropic; both have killed a woman and both are, most prominently, narcissists of a particularly malignant type. What distinguishes Freddie from both Vander and Cleave, however, is that he is a more or less unqualified failure: his story is signally one of defeat and disappointment. Whilst the latter two characters eventually plummet from the apexes of their successes, Freddie never really gets off the ground in the first place. After an abandoned academic career he is, in his late thirties, little more than a privileged layabout, living off an inheritance on an unnamed Mediterranean island with his equally self-obsessed wife and their mentally handicapped child, to whom neither he nor his wife pay very much heed.

Freddie begins his story on the island where he and his wife Daphne spend their days in bored, drunken oblivion. In a bungled attempt to blackmail a petty drug dealer named Randolph, Freddie ends up owing a large sum of money to one Señor Aguirre, a dangerous Spanish crime lord. Agreeing (without any apparent qualms) to leave his wife and child behind as human collateral, he travels home to Ireland where he hopes to raise the money to pay off Aguirre. Having arrived in Dun Laoghaire, he continues on immediately to Coolgrange, his grandly dilapidated family home, where he finds that his mother, whom he has not seen in many years, has already sold off to the extremely wealthy neighbouring Behrens family the paintings he had hoped would finance his debt. Enraged, Freddie pays a visit to the Behrens estate at Whitewater House, where he becomes captivated by a seventeenth-century Dutch portrait of a middle-aged woman entitled 'Portrait of a Woman with Gloves'.

The following day, he returns to Whitewater, where, in a badly botched attempt at stealing the painting, he is interrupted by a servant, Josie Bell, whom he bundles into his rented car and batters to death with a hammer. Freddie dumps her body in a ditch along with the painting and seeks out Charlie French, an old family friend and, it turns out, probable former paramour of his mother. Charlie agrees to put him up in his home, aware only that he has gotten himself into some pecuniary scrape or other. For a number of days, Freddie evades capture whilst following the coverage of the murder eagerly in the national press and getting morbidly drunk on the contents of Charlie's drinks cabinet. Eventually the police catch up with him and he is jailed. It is at this point that he begins to write his book of evidence.

Though the plot is brisk and straightforward by Banville's standards, its movement often seems incidental to the retrospective reflections it prompts, the greater part of Freddie's narrative being given over to relentless introspection and self-examination. Perhaps more than any other of Banville's protagonists, he is given to alternate extremes of narcissism and shame. His rather grandiose image of himself is repeatedly undercut, often in the most visceral of language, by his sense of self-loathing. The shortfall between his idealised self-image as a cultured and suave sophisticate and his underlying – and often overwhelming – sense of disgust at himself is a constant source of tension and agitation in the novel. Like so many of Banville's narcissistic protagonists, Freddie claims to possess a Platonic ideal of himself which he longs to make a reality:

> Indeed, when I was young I saw myself as a masterbuilder who would one day assemble a marvellous edifice around myself, a kind of grand pavilion, airy and light, which would contain me

utterly and yet wherein I would be free. Look, they would say, distinguishing this eminence from afar, look how sound it is, how solid: it's him alright, yes, no doubt about it, the man himself. (Banville, 1989a: 16)

This desired solidity, however, is something which continually eludes him, and he admits to feeling 'a sense of myself as something without weight, without moorings, a floating phantom', to lacking 'a density, a thereness' which other people seem to have (16). In certain respects, notwithstanding the terrible weight of his crime, Freddie seems defined more than anything else by a kind of inconsequentiality. He has, despite the self-aggrandising representations in which he indulges himself, made little impact upon the world, having taken seemingly no decisive action in his life. (In this respect, Freddie's pedigree as a perverse and misanthropic wastrel is a strong one – his literary lineage can be traced back to Camus' Meursault and Dostoevsky's Raskolnikov and Underground Man.)

His life has been characterised by what he calls 'drift'. 'My journey', as he puts it, 'had not been a thing of signposts and decisive marching, but drift only, a kind of slow subsidence, my shoulders bowing down under the gradual accumulation of all the things I had not done' (37–8). This notion of 'drift' seems a pivotal one in Freddie's view of his own life, particularly given the term's strange ambiguity, conveying as it does an aimless movement and a lack of resolution, whilst also hinting at a sense of fatalism, of drifting *towards* something, of being borne along with slow inexorability by a current or a force. His moral view of the universe seems a distinctly contradictory one, characterised by a compound of chaos and determinism. He imagines life as 'a prison in which all actions are determined according to a random pattern thrown down by an unknown and insensate authority', and he discovers in science 'a vision of an unpredictable, seething world that was eerily familiar to me, to whom matter had always seemed a swirl of chance collisions' (16; 18). This evocation of an 'unknown and insensate authority' creating a 'random pattern' might be seen as hinting at a kind of quasi-deist belief in a cold, aloof God who takes no compassionate interest in human affairs. It can equally be read, however, as a self-reflective portrayal of the relationship between the novelist and his protagonist. This odd tension between chance and control is characteristic, in a sense, of both a vision of the workings of the universe and of the workings of the creative literary imagination. It strikes a chord, certainly, with Banville's distinctly Nabokovian pronouncements about the purely functional nature of characters as marionettes created to do the author-puppeteer's bidding:

> When I hear a writer talking earnestly of how the characters in his latest book 'took over the action' I am inclined to laugh [...] Fictional characters are made of words, not flesh; they do not have free will, they do not exercise volition. They are easily born, and as easily killed off. They have their flickering lives, and die on cue, for us, giving up their little paragraphs of pathos. They are at once less and more than what they seem. (Banville, 1993c: 107–8)

Metaphysics and metafiction aside, Freddie's professed disbelief in free will can be seen as having a more practical, worldly aim: the deflection of guilt, of responsibility. As he puts it:

> I used to believe, like everyone else, that I was determining the course of my own life, according to my own decisions, but gradually, as I accumulated more and more past to look back on, I realised that I had done the things I did because I could do no other. Please do not imagine, my lord, I hasten to say it, do not imagine that you detect here the insinuation of an apologia, or even of a defence. I wish to claim full responsibility for my actions – after all, they are the only things I can call my own – and I declare in advance that I shall accept without demur the verdict of the court. I am merely asking, with all respect, whether it is feasible to hold on to the principle of moral culpability once the notion of free will has been abandoned. (Banville, 1989a: 15–16)

This kind of rhetorical misdirection is fairly typical of Freddie's manipulative style as a narrator. He effectively denies responsibility, then denies that he is denying it, before going on to deny the very possibility of responsibility. We are, as ever in Banville's work, being led through morally and epistemologically uncertain territory, and Freddie is clearly a flagrantly untrustworthy guide, always with one eye on the reaction of his 'readership'. He has a habit of second-guessing our perception of him, of seeing himself through our eyes and then taking steps to address that perception, to reorder it. He is endlessly alert to how he appears to others, to real and imagined images of himself. In certain respects, the novel is about nothing more or less than perception itself: how Freddie perceives the world and himself in it, and how he perceives others perceiving him. Joseph McMinn recognises the importance of this concept to *The Book of Evidence*, defining it as 'an ingenious parable of perception' (McMinn, 1999: 123).

This narcissistic hyperawareness of how he is perceived – which is in equal parts overweening vanity and overbearing shame – is apparent from the very first words of his story and permeates from its stylistic surface to its psychological core. Ruthlessly dispensing with any kind of prefatory small talk, he commences his narrative with an image of himself as a caged man-beast at whom the general public will gladly pay money to gape:

> I am kept locked up here like some exotic animal, last survivor of a species they had thought extinct. They should let in people to view me, the girl-eater, svelte and dangerous, padding to and fro in my cage, my terrible green glance flickering past the bars, give them something to dream about, tucked up cosy in their beds of a night. After my capture they clawed at each other to get a look at me. They would have paid money for the privilege, I believe. (Banville, 1989a: 3)

It is an extraordinary opening, setting us straight down into the hall of warped mirrors that is Freddie's inner world. His perception of himself and his perception of others' perceptions of him are both elements of one profoundly narcissistic act of consciousness. It is worth bearing in mind, too, given the way in which he seduces the reader over the course of the novel into imagining that he is intent on transcending his self-obsession, that it is the post-murder Freddie who is writing here, the supposedly repentant Freddie who wishes to atone for the actions to which his narcissism has led him.

The opening pages of the novel launch a sustained deluge of narcissistic self-portrayals. Seeing the members of the public who have gathered to shout their abuse at him as 'film extras', he is clearly entranced with his own starring performance (3). 'What an interesting figure I must have cut,' he muses, 'glimpsed there, sitting up in the back like a sort of mummy, as the car sped through the wet, sunlit streets, bleating importantly' (4). There is, at this early stage, something at once irresistibly funny and intensely disquieting about this self-regarding narrative voice – a voice about which at this point the reader knows next to nothing, apart from that it issues from someone who has committed some terrible transgression and who is evidently quite impressed with himself. When he informs us that there is a television in his cell which he tends not to watch because his case is '*sub judice* and there is nothing about me on the news', we get the sense that if he could enjoy the spectacle of himself in the media, he perhaps wouldn't need to write about himself (4).

There is, unmistakably, a fair amount of self-derision in Freddie's exposition of his own narcissism, but that he is aware of the comic aspects of his self-absorption does not make that self-absorption any less thoroughgoing. He confesses, for instance, to harbouring 'hopelessly romantic expectations' of how it would be for him in prison, having pictured himself as 'a sort of celebrity, kept apart from the other prisoners in a special wing, where I would receive parties of grave, important people and hold forth to them about the great issues of the day, impressing the men and charming the ladies'. It is difficult to know whether he is inviting us to laugh at his delusions or to join him in beholding this image of himself, as real as any other. 'And there am I,' he declares in his serio-comic tone, 'striking an elegant pose, my ascetic profile lifted to the light in the barred window, fingering a scented handkerchief and faintly smirking, Jean-Jacques the cultured killer' (5).

Freddie's recollections, throughout the early part of the novel, of his life on the island reinforce this impression of his existence as one of utter self-absorption. Though he and his wife live together with their young son, Van, they both seem entirely self-consumed. He introduces Daphne as 'my lady of the laurels, reclining in a sun-dazed glade [...] while some minor god in the shape of a faun, with a reed pipe, prances and capers vainly playing his heart out for her' (7). She is a cold and detached figure, whom Freddie seems to admire precisely because she is lacking in warmth, seeing her as a kind of human idol, 'beautifully balanced' but hard and chilly as marble. When he sees her naked, he confesses to an urge to caress her 'as I would a piece of sculpture, hefting the curves in the hollow of my hand, running a thumb down the long smooth lines, feeling the coolness, the velvet texture of the stone' (8). Like a goddess or a statue, she is also blithely heedless of the needs of her son. In one of the novel's more shocking asides, Freddie touches upon Daphne's appalling maternal deficiencies:

> There were things she could not be bothered to do, no matter what imperatives propelled them to her jaded attention. She neglected our son, not because she was not fond of him, in her way, but simply because his needs did not really interest her. I would catch her, sitting on a chair, looking at him with a remote expression in her eyes as if she were trying to remember who or what precisely he was, and how he had come to be there, rolling on the floor at her feet in one of his own many messes. (Banville, 1989a: 7–8)

What is most disturbing about this passage is not what it actually describes – Daphne's complete disregard for her son (who, it turns out, is severely mentally handicapped, though his affliction seems not greatly to concern either of them) – but the way in which it describes it. There is a conspicuous absence of moral judgement here; even, it seems, a hint of admiration for the uncompromising rigour of her indifference. There is a distinct note of identification, too, in Freddie's assertion that Daphne's neglect of their son is due to the fact his needs 'did not really interest her'; and also, perhaps, one of understanding. Freddie's own neglect of his son is passed over in silence; it scarcely requires mention, being merely one aspect of his larger failure to take notice of the world as a whole. 'She was not nice,' he tells us, 'she was not good. She suited me'. It was, he claims, her 'abstracted, mildly dissatisfied air' that first drew him to her; he recognises in her 'one of my own kind' (7).

Just as he admits to imagining himself in prison as 'a sort of celebrity', Freddie sees himself and Daphne on the island as presenting a regal spectacle amid the motley courtiers and supporting players of their 'set', few of whose names they ever went so far as to find out, being content to call them 'pal, chum, captain, darling' (10). They presided, as he puts it, 'among this rabble [...] with a kind of grand detachment, like an exiled king and queen'. He notes the slightly fearful regard in which they were held by these attendants, their 'motley court', and ponders the reasons for this:

> What was it in us – or rather, what was it *about* us – that impressed them? Oh, we are large, well-made, I am handsome, Daphne is beautiful, but that cannot have been the whole of it. No, after

much thought the conclusion I have come to is this, that they imagined they recognised in us a coherence and wholeness, an essential authenticity, which they lacked, and of which they felt they were not entirely worthy. We were – well, yes, we were heroes. (Banville, 1989a: 11)

As is more often than not the case with narcissists, such arrogance and self-regard is accompanied by a glaring contempt for others. Other people are there simply to provide favourable reflections for the narcissist, and are thus not granted respect as individuals in their own rights. Freddie illustrates the patrician disdain in which he holds his supposed inferiors by describing the 'special, faint little smile I had, calm, tolerant, with just the tiniest touch of contempt' which he reserves especially for the 'poor fools who prattled, cavorting before us in cap and bells, doing their pathetic tricks and madly laughing' (11).

In 'Pathologic Forms of Self-Esteem Regulation', her seminal essay on the narcissistic character type, Annie Reich employs a deeply sexualised understanding of the male personality to stress the connection between the inflated ego, contempt for others and underlying insecurity. 'The very process of self-admiration,' she writes, 'involves contempt for others. Undisguised phallic-exhibitionistic impulses [...] generally are combined with unmitigated, primate aggression: the patient 'blinds' others with his magnificence; he 'rubs in' his successes, as though he were forcing his enormous penis on his audience' (Reich, 1986: 53). Reich's language and imagery is no doubt extreme, and her (not untypical) overemphasis on the penis as the overbearing force in the psychology of the male may be somewhat jarring, but she nonetheless gives us a powerful impression of the essential ugliness of the pathological narcissistic worldview. It is a worldview remarkably close to that of Freddie Montgomery.

In describing his relationship with his 'motley court', Freddie's tone is one of high irony and his language is deliberately acerbic, but this sardonic voice only partially masks an essential extremity of vision, an underlying imbalance in his view of himself and the world that can be likened to Reich's analysis. This is not to say that Freddie is insane – he is clearly not; unquestionably he is in full possession of his faculties – but that he is driven by a kind of desperate need to elevate himself above others, and that this need is really a type of anguish, the translation of a certain kind of despair. There is a powerful impulse to see himself reflected in the (supposedly) admiring gaze of these 'poor fools', a need to counterbalance – or overcompensate for – a psychological force which is at once the precise opposite of and the impetus behind his rather extreme sense of personal grandiosity. Freddie's narcissistic visions of himself as a king amongst fools, or as 'a sort of celebrity' are, in other words, a form of psychological indemnity against an underlying sense of feebleness and insubstantiality. 'I looked in their eyes and saw myself ennobled there,' he says, 'and so could forget for a moment what I was, a paltry, shivering thing, just like them, full of longing and loathing, solitary, afraid, racked by doubts, and dying' (1989a: 11).

This underlying anguish, this shame and sense of fragility, is very close to Reich's conception of the inseparability of exhibitionistic grandiosity and self-doubt. For Reich, narcissism is a matter of drastic extremes and rapid reversals: 'Unsublimated, erotized, manic self-inflation easily shifts to a feeling of utter dejection, of worthlessness, and to hypochondriacal anxieties. *"Narcissists" of this type thus suffer regularly from repetitive, violent oscillations of self-esteem*' (Reich, 1986: 52 [emphasis in original]). There is a moment which perfectly illustrates this abrupt swing from self-admiration to self-disdain; a moment where, in Reich's expression, the 'brief rapture of elated self-infatuation is followed by a rude awakening' (52). It occurs at the point of Freddie's introduction, upon arrival at Coolgrange, to his mother's live-in stable-girl, whose name is offhandedly reported as 'Joan, or Jean, something like that'. He makes much of how intimidated she appears to be by him, and he seems deeply impressed by his own charismatic presence. 'I gave her,' he informs us, 'one of my special, slow smiles, and saw myself through her eyes, a tall, tanned hunk in a linen suit, leaning over her on a summer lawn and murmuring dark words' (Banville, 1989a: 46). When he places his hand on the flank of a horse, however, he is started by 'the solidity, the actuality of the animal' and is instantly overcome with a visceral disgust of his own flesh, as though he were somehow unbearably compromised by his very corporeality. He suddenly has what he calls 'a vivid, queasy sense of myself, not the tanned pin-up now, but something else, something pallid and slack and soft. I was aware of my toenails, my anus, my damp, constricted crotch. And I was ashamed. I can't explain it. That is, I could, but won't' (46). It is an important moment in the novel because it illustrates the tenuousness of Freddie's grandiosity, the almost insupportable volatility of his conception of himself. From one moment to the next, he goes from suave leading man to a disconnected assortment of squalid body parts. He comes apart in his own mind; from urbane coherence to obscene fragmentation, a dissolution complete in seconds.

Freddie only fully pays heed to the outside world to the extent that it either reflects him favourably or threatens his image of himself. He is, as such, living a life peculiarly devoid of context. There is very little in the way of background in *The Book of Evidence*: Freddie sketches just enough of an outline of the world that he may appear to stand out against it. One of the more immediately noticeable aspects of his utter self-absorption is his almost total lack of interest – even awareness – of politics or current events. Wars, socio-political struggles, entire cultural movements seem to pass him by more or less unheeded. In his opening description of prison life, for instance, he mentions in passing that things were different when 'the politicals' were kept in the prison, in that they would provide a mildly entertaining spectacle by their marching up and down the corridors and 'barking at each other in bad Irish'. But then, with impressive vagueness, he informs us that 'they all went on hunger strike or something, and were moved away to a place of their own' (5–6). It is the haziness, the wilful detachment of that 'or something' which really marks out Freddie's self-centred lack of engagement with the world of which he is only notionally a part. It is one of only a few moments in the novel where the reader really witnesses the opening of a gap between the author and his narrator. Banville is carefully weighting those two words with ironic significance; Freddie, presumably, is merely dashing them off with supreme indifference.

A similarly impassive reaction to actual political violence is evidenced later on in Freddie's narrative, when he encounters Anna Behrens for the first time in years upon his visit to Whitewater. He takes note of the fact that there is blood spattered on her shoes. It transpires that she has just come from a hospital (her father having suffered 'some sort of mild attack') which had been overrun with victims of a terrorist attack in Dublin: 'A bomb had gone off in a car in a crowded shopping street, quite a small device, apparently, but remarkably effective' (82). Freddie gives the bomb scant further consideration. It is alluded to only as the distant cause of the blood on Anna's shoes, and thus of her mild irritation: '"Look at that", she said. She was peering in annoyance at her bloodstained shoes. She clicked her tongue, and putting down her glass she quickly left the room' (83).

The impression is one of a near-hermetic psychological universe – for the Behrenses as well as for Freddie – where the suffering and death of others and the political turmoil of their own country is of so little concern as to be scarcely worth speaking of. Anna's father mentions the bombing in passing at dinner, but his manner is chillingly detached: 'Five dead – or was it six by now? – from a mere two pounds of explosive! He sighed and shook his head. He seemed more impressed than shocked' (85). The blood on the shoes is both a sinister portent of the blood that will soon be spilled by Freddie's hands and a disconcerting illumination of the callousness and disregard that enables him to spill it.

Similarly, throughout Freddie's recollections of his time spent teaching mathematics in Berkeley during the days of the Vietnam War and the student movement, there is scarcely a hint of political awareness. His primary concern, as always, is himself and the impression he makes on others. He is happy to go to bed with the 'flower children', but he is utterly uninterested in their quaint political engagements:

> One of their little foreign wars was in full swing just then, everyone was a protester, it seemed, except me – I would have no truck with their marches, their sit-downs, the ear-splitting echolalia that passed with them for argument – but even my politics, or lack of them, were no deterrent, and flower children of all shapes and colours fell into my bed, their petals trembling. I remember few of them with any precision, when I think of them I see a sort of hybrid, with this one's hands, and that one's eyes, and yet another's sobs. (Banville, 1989a: 19)

Though it is never stated explicitly, one can well imagine Freddie finding the US government's involvement in 'one of their little foreign wars' and the protests against it equally uninteresting. Politics, as he openly admits, simply does not concern him. Politics is what goes on between states, and between the citizens of those states and their governments – is about the relationships, in other words, between people – and is thus an area which has little relevance for Freddie. As Rüdiger Imhof has put it, Freddie remains an outsider 'because his imagination is tainted by a monstrous deficiency which makes it impossible for him to relate to living things' (Imhof, 1997: 190).

Later, he recollects stepping out into the street having bumped into Anna in a gallery in Berkeley. He notes, in a powerfully evocative series of sensual details, that 'a jet plane was passing low overhead, its engines making the air rattle, and there was a smell of cypresses and car exhaust, and a faint whiff of tear-gas from the direction of the campus' (Banville, 1989a: 63). The significance of the tear-gas from the campus is dampened down, so that it is just one sensory particular among a range of others; it is given importance equal to, but not greater than, that of the passing jet plane and the smells of cypress trees and car exhausts.[8]

Freddie's murder of Josie Bell is at least in part a result of this deeply flawed and incomplete perception of the world. He murders her in a fit of rage for the simple reason that she gets in his way – she is, as Freddie so tellingly puts it, 'the last straw', the last in a long spate of insults and inconveniences dealt to him by the world (110). As he himself admits, other people are primarily experienced as obstacles in his path: 'People got in the way and blocked my view, I had to crane to see past them' (56). In *Ghosts*, looking back upon his crime at the remove of a third-person singular voice, Freddie tells us that he is 'not used to seeing people whole, the rest of humanity being for him for the most part a kind of annoying fog obscuring his view of the darkened shop-window of the world and himself reflected in it' (1993a: 88).

Other people, when they are not providing favourable reflections, are rarely more than a source of frustration and obstruction. As Derek Hand argues, Freddie is roused into violence by Josie's 'actuality, her unassailable presence' and that, 'provoked by the presence of another, he is brought face-to-face with the reality of the world [...] and strikes out at the affront to all those fictions he has created, which have, until now, kept the world at bay' (Hand, 2002: 139). The emotional trajectory in the moments that lead up to the murder is one of extreme irritation building towards blind rage. When he sees her seeing him, his reaction is one of indignation at the world's effrontery: 'This, I remember thinking bitterly, this is the last straw. I was outraged. How dare the world strew these obstacles in my path.

It was not fair, it was just not fair!' (Banville, 1989a: 110). This sense of having been too frequently and too grievously wronged is present even at the moment when he is committing the murder. Between the first and second blows of the hammer, when she launches herself at him 'flailing and screaming', his reaction is almost unbelievably callous and, at the most serious point in the story, provides a moment of grossly inappropriate comedy: 'I was dismayed. How could this be happening to me – it was all so *unfair*. Bitter tears of self-pity squeezed into my eyes' (114 [emphasis in original]).

This strangely unseemly self-pity in the midst of committing a terrible moral transgression is, in fact, something of a Banville hallmark. In *The Untouchable*, for instance, Victor Maskell undergoes a similar bout of excessive, self-absorbed unhappiness whilst putting his mentally handicapped younger brother (also called Freddie) in a home after their father's death. The more upset the brother becomes, the more Maskell feels, not guilty, but outraged by having been put in this position, as though this turn of events were somehow not of his own creation. 'He clutched at me,' Maskell tells us, 'sinking his shockingly strong fingers into my arm [...] That blustering anger boiled up inside me all the stronger, and I felt violently sorry for myself, and cruelly wronged' (1997b: 246).

At both of these moments the reader inevitably feels that there is something extraordinarily childish, and starkly comic, about such self-pity. Freddie Montgomery's reaction in particular is strikingly so, and the language he uses – 'it was all so *unfair*' – reinforces this impression (as does the italicisation, which seems a typographical rendering of the force of a childish tantrum). What he is undergoing here is a specifically narcissistic form of rage. Heinz Kohut, in his 1972 essay 'Thoughts on Narcissism and Narcissistic Rage', explicitly links the concept of narcissistic rage to the emotional reaction of children to slight injuries. When a child is physically hurt in some way, reasons Kohut, 'he gives voice not only to his physical pain and fear, but also to his wounded narcissism. "How can it be? How can it happen?" his outraged cries seem to ask' (Kohut, 1972: 384). The question Freddie asks between the first and second blows of the hammer, it will be remembered, is 'How could this be happening to me?' Two aspects of this question suggest themselves as particularly significant: the bewilderment that this should be happening, and the outrage that it should be happening *to him*. It scarcely needs pointing out that nothing is happening *to* Freddie, as such; what is happening is happening to Josie Bell and is being done by him.

Kohut stresses the similarity between the self-centred incredulity of the injured child and the blind rage of the narcissistically injured individual. He also sees narcissistic rage as related to the frustration a person with a brain defect feels when unable to name a familiar object. That person will often feel outraged, in some sense betrayed by a part of him- or herself. This rage, writes Kohut, is 'due to the fact that he is suddenly not in control of his own thought processes, of a function which people consider to be most intimately their own – i.e., as a part of the self'. When a person suffering from aphasia is unable to name a familiar object such as a pencil, his fury is one of aggrieved denial, explains Kohut: '"It must not be! It cannot be!"' (Kohut, 1972: 382). Narcissistic rage, he maintains, is analogous to this: it is the rage that arises from the uncomfortable discovery, and subsequent denial, of the fact that one is not omnipotent and that the world is not simply an extension of oneself. It is this '"It must not be!"' which Freddie feels so powerfully in the presence of Josie Bell, in the face of the intransigence of the world beyond himself.

What enables Freddie to kill Josie is an integral part of his narcissism – his unwillingness to see her as a person in her own right, to see beyond the obstruction she presents to him. When he looks at her, while he sees her seeing him, he sees right through her. At the moment before he flings her into the back seat of the car, just after he has put the stolen painting into the boot, he takes note of her eyes, and what he sees – or does not see – and the way in which he describes it, is remarkable: he says that her eyes 'seemed transparent', that 'when I looked into them I felt I was seeing clear through her head' (Banville, 1989a: 111). He looks at her, and he sees nothing; it is as though there were nothing there – no person – for him to see. This, Freddie admits in the closing pages of his confession, is what makes it possible for him to kill her and is what constitutes his true crime. When he reads in the paper that she worked for a time as a chambermaid in a hotel he frequented, he marvels at the fact that they might have crossed paths, that he might have noticed her. Immediately, though, he realises that she would have been no more real for him as a chambermaid in a hotel than as a domestic in a manor house or a target for his rage in the back of a car. With respect to Freddie's steadfast solipsism and his realisation that it is what lies behind his crime, the passage is perhaps one of the most enlightening in the novel:

> There would have been no more of her there, for me, than there was in the newspaper stories, than there had been that day when I turned and saw her for the first time, standing in the open french [*sic*] window with the blue and gold of summer at her back, than there was when she crouched in the car and I hit her again and again and her blood spattered the window. This is the worst, the essential sin, I think, the one for which there will be no forgiveness: that I never imagined her vividly enough, that I never made her be there sufficiently, that I did not make her live. Yes, that failure of imagination is my real crime, the one that made the others possible. What I told that policeman is true – I killed her because I could kill her, and I could kill her because for me she was not alive. (Banville, 1989a: 215)

This is the precise experience – or non-experience – of the other person which characterises, for Kohut, the 'insatiable rage' of the narcissistically injured individual. Such a person, he maintains, 'cannot rest until he has blotted out a vaguely experienced offender who dares to oppose him'. Kohut outlines the distinction between the aggression of the normal, or mature person, with that of the narcissist:

> The opponent who is the target of our mature aggressions is experienced as separate from ourselves, whether we attack him because he blocks us in reaching our object-libidinal goals or hate him because he interferes with the fulfilment of our reality-integrated narcissistic wishes. The enemy, however, who calls forth the archaic rage of the narcissistically vulnerable is seen by him not as an autonomous source of impulsions, but as *a flaw in a narcissistically perceived reality*. He is a recalcitrant part of an expanded self over which he expects to exercise full control and whose mere independence or other-ness is an offense. (Kohut, 1972: 386 [emphasis in original])

This seems a strikingly accurate description of the way in which Freddie perceives his victim; her mere other-ness, her recalcitrance in the face of his will, is an intolerable affront to his narcissism. There is only one moment when Josie is actually present to him, in the sense of his experiencing her as separate and distinct from himself, and it is a moment at which, he says, he 'had never felt another's presence so immediately and with such raw force'. It is also, significantly, the moment directly before he lands the first blow of the hammer. She is shielding her face from the oncoming blow, pressing her back into the corner of the backseat of the car and, in looking at her, he is 'filled with a kind of wonder'. 'I saw her now,' he says, 'really saw her, for the first time, her mousy hair and bad skin, that bruised look around her eyes. She was quite ordinary, and yet, somehow, I don't know – somehow radiant' (Banville, 1989a: 113).

It is difficult to know what to make of such an admission. It is as though he were experiencing her aesthetically, in a way not unlike that in which he has experienced the stolen painting. Her strange, inscrutable combination of plainness and radiance certainly links her to the anonymous woman in the portrait. But the 'raw force' of her presence is not, for Freddie, something that can be borne; it provokes him to murderous violence. Where he invents a life for the woman in the portrait, creating a narrative through which he imagines himself into her existence, he does what might be considered the opposite with Josie. Instead of 'creating' her in his mind, he destroys her in reality. The killing is a kind of furious, blind denial of her presence. To him she is a 'flaw in a narcissistically perceived reality' and his reaction to her is a kind of translation of Kohut's drastic imperative of the enraged narcissist ('it must not be!') into violent, devastating action. When Freddie admits to being able to kill her 'because for me she was not alive', he is admitting to his narcissistic *inability* to see her for what she is, as an independent individual who is not simply an obstacle thrown in his path by a recalcitrant world. He kills her because she is a part of that world which will not cooperate with his will.

Freddie never tires of reminding us that he is writing a book and that, in so doing, he is creating the world around him anew, sketching characters and situations; that he is, in this sense, his own literary creation. And for all the moral and existential weight of the events he narrates, there is a peculiar sense that he himself is an oddly indistinct, insubstantial figure. Just as he sees his true 'crime' as 'failure of imagination' – his inability to *realise* Josie Bell – he is beset by the notion of himself as not solidly there, as a kind of sketchy, provisional presence in the world. Recalling an incident from his childhood in which a large branch fell from a tree during a storm and narrowly missed hitting him, he muses upon the frailty of his existence and nature's blind indifference to it:

> It was not fright I felt but a profound sense of shock at how little my presence had mattered. I might have been no more than a flaw in the air. Ground, branch, wind, sky, world, all these were the precise and necessary coordinates of the event. Only I was misplaced, only I had no part to play. And nothing cared. (Banville, 1989a: 185)

This perceived lack of substance has much to do with mortality – with the fact that one's presence is in fact only ever provisional – but it is also a recognition of the truth that he is no more significant to the world than Josie Bell was to him when he ended her life. His idea of himself – the one he presents to us in his book of evidence – is, too, only a flimsy structure, a contingent arrangement of details, half-truths and at least the occasional outright lie. This uncomfortable reality is one which Freddie comes to appreciate when he is presented with a confession written on his behalf by Inspector Cunningham, the investigator in charge of his case. He recognises the author as 'the kind of artist I could never be [...] a master of the spare style, of the art that conceals art'. Worse, Cunningham's narrative presents a version of Freddie – an 'official' fiction – the harsh, empirical light of which is completely at variance with the chiaroscuro of his own narrative. Cunningham's version, affirms Freddie, 'was an account of my crime I hardly recognised, and yet I believed it. He had made a murderer of me' (202–3).

This seems to amount to an admission of failure on Freddie's part, an acknowledgement that his confession, his scrupulously tinted self-portrait, is no more an authoritative account of his self than Cunningham's purely factual rendering. This sense of the contingency of his own presence – the recognition that a contradicting view can undermine his entire self-conception – is at once an affront to, and a constituent element of, his narcissism. Reading and assenting to the confession is a kind of capitulation for Freddie. Finished with it, he 'undressed and lay down naked in the shadows and folded my hands on my breast, like a marble knight on a tomb, and closed my eyes'. Something fundamental is happening here, something as primary as a birth or a death. 'I was no longer myself,' he tells us. 'I can't explain it but it's true. I was no longer myself' (203).

Like Narcissus, who cannot bring himself to look away from his reflection for fear that the object of his love may disappear, Freddie's sense of himself is perilously fragile. Just as a falling branch in a storm might utterly erase his presence, an alternative account of his deeds can make him something other than what he thinks of as himself. Such vulnerability is what lies at the root of Freddie's narcissism. He cannot look beyond himself – cannot make real the presence of another – because to do so would be to risk fracturing the fragile illusion of his own solidity.

3
Missing Twins

In Plato's *Symposium*, Aristophanes offers an explanation as to why people refer to feeling 'whole' when they fall in love. This is due, he announces, to the fact that humans were originally twofold beings with four arms, four legs, two sets of sexual organs and 'two faces, exactly alike, on a rounded neck' (Plato, 1997: 473). These creatures, completely spherical in form, were so strong and arrogant that they saw fit to launch an offensive upon the gods of Mount Olympus. Zeus, enraged but unwilling to destroy them and thereby deprive himself of their offerings and devotions, contented himself with crippling them by splitting them in half. In this way, with a single stroke, he would make them both more numerous and less powerful, doubling their value to the gods. 'Each of us then,' explains Aristophanes, 'is a 'matching half' of a human whole, because each was sliced like a flatfish, two out of one, and each of us is always seeking the half that matches him' (474).

In the Judeo-Christian myth of Genesis, God creates Adam from the dust of the earth and then Eve from one of Adam's ribs. God then brings the first woman before the first man: 'And the man said, "This form is bone of my own bone, and flesh of my own flesh. This shall be named 'woman,' because she was taken from man"' (Genesis 2:23–4). The Bible goes on to state that, as a result of this original consubstantiality of male and female, man shall 'leave his father and his mother and shall unite with his wife; and they shall be one body' (Genesis 2:24–5).

When we consider side by side these Greek and Judeo-Christian myths of origin, what is initially striking is the way in which they both account for the human condition generally, and sexuality specifically, using notions of partition and integration. Both point toward an imagined origin in wholeness and toward a fragmented present, and both explain sexual desire as a manifestation of the deeper longing to return to that state of wholeness. Unity is an important concept in each myth. When men and women seek each other, it is their own selves – an earlier and *intact* version of themselves – for which they are truly searching. In this way, both of these visions of humanity resemble the myth of Narcissus, whose predicament is characterised by a profound yearning for unity with himself, a yearning which is also the result of a divine punishment for his conceit and cruelty. The obvious distinction is that Narcissus desires a reflection of himself, whilst Adam and Eve and Aristophanes' original humans desire a reintegration with split-off parts of themselves. Man and woman are, in these myths, like twins who have been separated and long for reunification. They are of the same flesh: 'two out of one', in Aristophanes' words, 'bone of my own bone' in Adam's.

Yet there is another version of the Narcissus myth, favoured by the second-century Lydian geographer Pausanias in his *Description of Greece*. Pausanias (who is perhaps guilty of being a little too literal-minded) objects that it is 'utter stupidity to imagine that a man old enough to fall in love was incapable of distinguishing a man from a man's reflection' (Pausanias, 1918: 311). Instead, he recounts a second rendering of the myth – 'less popular indeed than the other, but not without some support' – in which Narcissus has a twin sister who is 'exactly alike in appearance', who dresses similarly, and with whom Narcissus falls in love. The twin sister dies and the grieving Narcissus goes to a spring on the summit of Helicon to gaze into its depths. He does so 'knowing that it was his reflection that he saw, but in spite of this knowledge finding some relief for his love in imagining that he saw, not his own reflection, but the likeness of his sister' (311). Ovid's better-known version links Narcissus's predicament with the notion of self-knowledge (Tiresias's cryptic disclosure, it will be remembered, is that Narcissus shall only live a long life 'if he shall himself not know') and, as such, places it in line with the Promethean defiance of Aristophanes' spherical proto-humans and the Bible's Adam and Eve (Ovid, 1986: 61). What is intriguing about the second version, from a psychoanalytical perspective, is the way in which it reconfigures Narcissus' predicament as having to do not with a total absence of object relations but with a specific *kind* of object-relatedness. His love for his twin is his love for himself (despite the difference in their genders, Pausanias asks us to believe that they are still 'identical'), and, following her death, his love for himself is his love for her.

Together, these three myths present a powerful case for understanding interpersonal relationships as rooted in a narcissistic pursuit of unity with a 'missing' part of the self. Each of the myths attempts to make sexual desire intelligible, and each of them does so by explaining it as a form of desire for the self's completion. Myths always express something elemental about human psychology, even – and perhaps especially – when what they express cannot easily be interpreted. What this chapter sets out to do is to take this notion of twinning as somehow fundamental to our experience of ourselves and other people, and use it to obtain access to an understanding of the two of Banville's novels which are most explicitly concerned with the motif of twins: *Birchwood* and *Mefisto*.

There are, on the face of it, many similarities between the two novels. Both narrators are named Gabriel: Gabriel Godkin in *Birchwood* and Gabriel Swan in *Mefisto*. These family names, too, are connected, in that they both hint towards a notional divine provenance: Godkin suggests a kinship with God, whilst the name Swan points the reader in the direction of Castor and Pollux, the twins borne by Leda after her rape by Zeus in the form of a swan.[1] Both Gabriels are twins, but, what is more, both are twins who have, so to speak, lost their other halves. Gabriel Godkin, in the second section of *Birchwood*, sets off on a journey to find his 'lost' twin sister, while Gabriel Swan is haunted by the stillbirth of his identical twin brother. The two novels, in fact, exist in a kind of twinned relationship, each reflecting the other in myriad ways. In an interview not long after the publication of *Mefisto*, Banville himself acknowledged the 'many overt and covert allusions to *Birchwood* made in the novel' (Banville, 1987: 13). Both Gabriels are fundamentally preoccupied with the notion of harmony, of finding some kind of unity of self and experience. They take different approaches toward locating this unity – Godkin joins the circus, hoping to find a sort of improvised symmetry in the artistic life of itinerant performance, while Swan struggles to find it through scientific enquiry – but they are both motivated to search for it by a shared sense of desolation and incompletion apparently arising from the loss of a twin. At the deepest of levels, each of these novels is about the search for unity, for individual wholeness. And this, overwhelmingly, is what psychoanalysis views narcissism as being about. Kohut, it will be remembered, sees the narcissist as suffering from a sense of only partial reality. The 'preconscious centre' from which narcissistic disturbances emanate, he writes, 'is the sense of an incomplete reality of the self' and, in the analytical situation, the client will likely let the analyst know of his 'impression that he is not fully real' (Kohut, 1971: 210).

Though *Mefisto*'s obvious major source is the Faust legend, Gabriel Swan's journey from his home to the outside world in search of a means of ordering the chaos of experience is repeatedly linked to the Pinocchio story.[2] Apart from the fact that the first part of the novel is entitled 'Marionettes', the Mephistophelean figure of Felix makes teasing reference at one point to Gabriel's wish 'to be a real boy' (Banville, 1986a: 142).[3] Elsewhere, Gabriel describes himself as 'a riven thing, incomplete' (130). Similarly, Gabriel Godkin in *Birchwood* is impelled by a feeling of fragmentation and unreality to set out in search of what he imagines is his lost twin sister. 'I was incomplete,' he tells us, 'and would remain so until I found her' (1973: 83).

Birchwood begins as an apparent pastiche of the Irish Big House novel, liberally incorporating elements of the gothic and the farcical, before tacking sharply towards a picaresque quest narrative at roughly the halfway point. The early part of the novel, entitled 'The Book of the Dead', is concerned with the history and downfall of the house of Birchwood, and with the ensnarled family trees of the Godkins and the Lawlesses, in whose possession it has variously lain. Young Gabriel's life is thrown into turmoil upon the arrival of his Aunt Martha and her illegitimate son Michael at Birchwood. The relationship between Martha and her brother Joseph, Gabriel's father, is highly fraught, and hints are repeatedly made toward the possibility of its possessing a sexual element. It later becomes apparent that Gabriel and Michael are in fact twins, born of an incestuous union between Martha and Joseph, a ploy to keep the estate out of the hands of the Lawless family, to which Gabriel's supposed mother Beatrice (who is barren) belongs. Beatrice's mental dissolution is precipitated by the relationship between Martha and Joseph, and by the political turmoil which surrounds them. Martha, determined to secure Birchwood as Michael's inheritance, manipulates Gabriel into believing that he has a twin sister who has run away, so that he will be compelled to set out in search of her. The first section ends with Gabriel setting out on this journey.

Out in the wider world, Gabriel encounters a travelling troupe of performers calling themselves Prospero's Circus. The group, which includes two pairs of twins (Justin and Juliette and Ida and Ada) presents an even more grotesque parody of family life than we find in the first section. Derek Hand, for instance, argues that the novel's second part can be seen 'as a retelling of the first' – an interpretation which would place it firmly in line with *Mefisto*, the two halves of which are in many ways distorted mirror images of one another (Hand, 2002: 29). Gabriel travels throughout Ireland with the circus, and the dissolution of the country, ravaged by famine and devastated by violent political unrest, mirrors the dissolution of the Big House in the first half of the book. Finally, Gabriel comes to understand his twin sister as a fantasy borne of his unwillingness to recognise the true nature of his family. His journey comes full circle and he returns to Birchwood where his climactic confrontation with Michael takes place and where he begins the writing of his narrative.

Gabriel's journey – his search for the 'missing' part of himself – can be understood as a narcissistic quest for self-synthesis. This yearning for wholeness is markedly similar to that experienced by Alexander Cleave in *Eclipse* who leaves his wife and sets out, 'weary of division, of always being torn', for his childhood home in search of what he calls 'the pure conjunction, the union of self with sundered self' (2000a: 70). Gabriel's Aunt Martha reads to him from a book (the title of which he can only recall as *The Something Twins*) which relates the story of two twins, Gabriel and Rose. We are given the following recollected extract: '*Gabriel and Rose lived in a big house by the sea. One day, when she was very young, little Rose disappeared, and Gabriel went away in search of her …*' (1973: 47–8 [emphasis in original]). There is also, in the house, a photograph of an unidentified young girl, 'dressed in white, standing in a garden', by which Gabriel finds himself transfixed. His description of the photograph conveys its enigmatic appeal and the way in which it strikes a chord with a deep-set division or lack in Gabriel's psyche. The picture itself is marked by a 'white crease aslant it like a bloodless vein', and the scene it depicts is half in sunlight, half in shade. Though his mother claims that the photograph is of herself as a child, he is convinced that this is untrue: 'No, I knew this girl was someone else,' he insists, 'a lost child, misplaced in time' (13). Between them, the photograph and the story have a profound impact on Gabriel, convincing him by means of subliminal suggestion that he has a twin sister named Rose.

It is the profound loneliness for this imaginary twin that compels Gabriel to set out on his quest to find her. In many respects, Gabriel's sense of the inner absence of some integral part of himself is consistent with Melanie Klein's notion of 'internal loneliness'. This loneliness, Klein explains, is not caused by the absence or loss of any particular person, but is rather the result of 'a ubiquitous yearning for an unattainable perfect internal state' (Klein, 1988: 300). In Kleinian psychoanalysis, focused as it is upon the central mother–child relationship, the feeling which arises during the breast-feeding process of being completely and pre-verbally understood is what leads in later life to the longing for a return to this condition. For Klein, the need for self-comprehension is inseparable from the desire to be understood by what she refers to as the 'internalised good object'.[4] A common expression of this yearning for an 'unattainable perfect internal state', she maintains, is what she calls 'the universal phantasy of having a twin'. The figure of the twin represents 'those un-understood and split off parts which the individual is longing to regain, in the hope of achieving wholeness and complete understanding'. (Lacan's conception of the *objet petit a* as the unattainable object-cause of desire bears considerable resemblance, in this regard, to Klein's notion of internal loneliness.)[5] These 'split off parts', writes Klein, 'are sometimes felt to be the ideal parts' whilst at other times they also represent 'an entirely reliable, in fact, idealized internal object' (301).

There is a sense in which Gabriel, in inventing an idealised twin sister and rejecting the reality of the malicious actual twin Michael, 'splits' his troubled psyche into 'good' and 'bad' components.[6] The correspondence between his hunt for his 'lost' twin sister and Pausanias's version of the Narcissus myth points us toward a reading of *Birchwood* in which Gabriel is engaged in a narcissistic search for self-unity. The Kleinian analyst Vivienne Lewin, in her book *The Twin in the Transference*, repeatedly stresses the narcissistic elements in both the creation of imagined twins and the relationship between actual twins:

> A characteristic of an imaginary twin is that it provides an illusion of great strength and invincibility, the two combining to pro-vide double strength. The phantasy twin is a narcissistic object, someone like self, created in the child's own image. The phantasy twin might therefore complement the child in what s/he feels s/he lacks, as if the twins were two halves of one person (which indeed they are!). The love of the phantasied twin is a cover for narcis-sistic love, in the guise of object love. (Lewin, 1977: 24)

This narcissistic aspect is further substantiated by Gabriel's narration of his first sexual experience. The local peasant girl with whom he engages in his first erotic fumblings happens to be named Rosie. To recognise that the name 'Rosie' is 'Rose' with an 'I' inserted into it, though it may seem an excessively scrupulous analysis, is no more than Banville demands of his readers: his attention to nomenclatu-ral nuance and overtone has always, from his earliest writing, been a significant characteristic of his work. Though the issue is never addressed by Gabriel, it seems reasonable to assume, then, that Rosie functions as a kind of psycho-sexual placeholder for the ideal of his twin sister. She herself, the quotidian reality of her body, he regards with a fascinated contempt that approaches the misogynistic (their affair, he claims, was 'founded on mutual astonishment at the intri-cacy of things, my brain, her cunt, things like that'), but it is the idea of her which accounts for her appeal. '[T]he actuality,' he writes, 'of my peasant girlchild with her grubby nails and sausage curls seems a tawdry thing, and I suppose it is not her but an iridescent ideal that I remember' (Banville, 1973: 68). It is not Rosie herself so much as the 'I' he has inserted into the 'Rose' that interests him.

One of the most intriguing aspects of this narcissistically motivated dalliance is the way in which Banville uses it to establish an imagina-tive link between the notions of sex and mathematics, between the intricacies of Gabriel's brain and Rosie's 'cunt'. He sweet-talks her, improbable though it may seem to the reader, with numbers:

> I told her about algebra. She stared at me with open mouth and huge eyes as I revealed to her the secrets of this amazing new

world, mine [...] Ah yes, I won her heart with mathematics. She was still pondering those mysterious symbols, her lips moving incredulously, when I delved between her chill pale thighs and discovered there her own, frail secret. (Banville, 1973: 68)

What links the secrets of the body and of mathematics is their potential to reveal something of the harmony Gabriel seeks. Earlier in the novel Gabriel glimpses his mother and father having sex in a clearing in the woods, and feels that he has 'discovered something awful and exquisite, of immense, unshakable calm' (32). Banville assigns the word 'awful' a dual implication here: firstly, there is the perennial sense in which it is awful to catch sight of one's parents having sex, but there is also the more archaic definitions of the word as 'worthy of, or commanding, profound respect or reverential fear' or 'solemnly impressive; sublimely majestic' (*OED*). Thus, from the first, sex is invested with a numinous significance. Gabriel refers to what he has seen as a 'secret', and stresses the idea that he has been granted a brief glimpse of some hidden order behind the apparent chaos of experience: 'O I am not saying that I had discovered love, or what they call the facts of life [...] no, all I had found was the notion of – I shall call it harmony' (33).

The bringing together of disparate things into a new harmony – the unification of fragmented parts – is one of the shared goals of art and of mathematics, and it is one of the overriding motivations of the narcissistic character. The vision of the world that Gabriel tentatively sets down in *Birchwood* is a vision that characterises much of Banville's work. It is one in which humans are essentially isolated from one another and in which experience is almost never intelligible, but where there always exists the tantalising promise of connection and coherence. The following passage is as close to a statement of a philosophical position as we get anywhere in Banville:

Listen, listen, if I know my world, which is doubtful, but if I do, I know it is chaotic, mean and vicious, with laws cast in the wrong moulds, a fair conception gone awry, in short an awful place, and yet, and yet a place capable of glory in those rare moments when a little light breaks forth, and something is not explained, not forgiven, but merely illuminated. (Banville, 1973: 33)

The extraordinary lissomness of Banville's early prose here, the way in which it furtively acknowledges its own irresolution with no less than 13 commas in one long and sinuous sentence, corresponds to the meandering but simultaneously deft movement of the thought it expresses. There is both hesitancy and conviction here in equal measures, both disdain and reverence for that with which it is concerned. These 'rare moments', as Joseph McMinn has identified, are 'usually unexpected intervals of imaginative and sensuous pleasure in which some small, redemptive sense of order and harmony is discovered' (McMinn, 1999: 40).

Significantly, it is Michael who first suggests (again more or less subliminally) the possibility of harmony as offered by art – in this case the performing art of the circus. Having accidentally broken a jigsaw puzzle which Gabriel had spent weeks labouring to assemble, Michael attempts to win his favour again by performing a juggling routine for him. Gabriel becomes utterly transfixed by the act, believing he sees in it the promise of order and symmetry: 'I found myself thinking of air and angels, of silence, of translucent planes of pale blue glass in space gliding through illusory, gleaming and perfect combinations. My puzzle seemed a paltry thing compared to this beauty, this, this *harmony*' (Banville, 1973: 43 [emphasis in original]).

Michael's presence in Gabriel's psychological sphere is, as it is in Birchwood itself, a troubling and contradictory one. They are simultaneously repelled by and attracted toward one another. Even before Gabriel admits to himself (or the reader) that Michael is his twin, he acknowledges this uneasy connection that exists between them:

> I cannot say that I ever liked him, but there was between us a bond which would not be ignored however we tried, and we did try. Here the silences, the disclosures, the sudden charges we made at each other across the distance that separated us, only to be jerked back by our congenital coldness from the final contact, that squelchy slap a human creature experiences when it surrenders to another. (Banville, 1973: 53)

Quite what form this final contact might take is never overtly addressed, but there are hints throughout the novel at an incestuous subtext to their relationship.[7] This attraction/repulsion dichotomy is again present in the relationship between the twin children

Chloe and Myles in *The Sea*. When Max asks Chloe what the 'state of unavoidable intimacy' with her brother feels like, she replies by saying that it is 'like two magnets [...] but turned the wrong way, pulling and pushing'. Max is taken aback by her admission, as though she were 'admitting to something intimate and shameful,' and is fascinated by the 'notion of an impropriety in such closeness' (2005c: 81). Once Gabriel flees Birchwood, all of Michael's subsequent appearances in the novel are in 'female' form, having joined a band of cross-dressing revolutionaries known as the Molly McGuires. Thus an association is established between Michael and the imaginary Rose (as well as, by extension, the actual Rosie). That the 'girl' in the photograph is in fact Michael is never actually confirmed by Gabriel, but it is hinted at. When Gabriel shows Rainbird, one of the members of Prospero's circus, the photograph of his 'sister' for whom he is searching, his response suggests that he knows the 'girl' in the photograph is really Michael: ' "She's a dandy," he said, and sniggered' (1973: 111). Banville's characteristic attentiveness to the various senses in which particular words may be understood is once more noteworthy here. Rainbird appears to be using the word 'dandy' in its archaic sense of 'an excellent thing of its kind', but the word's more familiar definition as 'a man unduly devoted to style, neatness, and fashion in dress and appearance' seems to mock and undermine this more innocent surface meaning (*OED*). The snigger bolsters the sense of double entendre, and the sense, present throughout the novel, that Gabriel is unacquainted with some unpleasant truth to which everyone else appears to be privy.

This cryptic eroticisation of the twins' relationship is intensified in the novel's final pages, when Gabriel returns to Birchwood to find a transvestite Michael whom he resolves to kill, but ultimately finds himself incapable of doing so. When he sees him in drag, he finally recognises him as his twin, as a twisted, parodic form of the sister he has been yearning to find: 'Yes, he was my brother, my twin, I had always known it, but would not admit it, until now, when the admitting made me want to murder him'. Coming to this recognition, he notes that he 'might have been looking at my own reflection' (Banville, 1973: 169). Gabriel's failed attempt to murder his twin brother can be read as a frustrated effort at consummation, or harmony. That the instrument used is that most phallically penetrative of weapons, a dagger, reinforces this: 'From its sheath I slipped the gleaming panther and clasped it in both hands above my head so tightly that the blade shivered and sang under the strain. He stared intently at the wicked weapon and glided backward slowly' (169).

Gabriel's failure to locate the sense of harmony – the ideal of self-synthesis – that he sets out to find is made explicit at the novel's close. The act of writing his narrative seems to present the possibility of attaining a kind of harmony, but that too proves illusory. 'I began to write,' he tells us, 'and thought that at last I had discovered a form which would contain and order all my losses. I was wrong. There is no form, no order, only echoes and coincidences, sleight of hand, dark laughter. I accept it' (174). His search for reconciliation with all his 'losses' is doomed to failure, as is his search for reunion with his 'lost' sister. Order cannot be imposed, cannot be found, because it is never more than a concept and always less than a real possibility.

This search for order and harmony is once again the overriding theme of *Mefisto*, and again the recognition of its inevitable failure is implicit from the very start of the novel. The novel begins with an acknowledgement of chaos as the original and ultimate condition of things, parodying the opening words of the King James Bible: 'Chance was in the beginning' (1986a: 3). As the surviving half of a pair of identical twins, Gabriel Swan is, like Gabriel Godkin, haunted by a feeling of incompletion. 'I seemed to myself not whole,' he writes, 'nor wholly real' (9–10). In his class in school there are two identical twins, and he finds himself utterly captivated by them. What fascinates him, he says, is 'the thought of being able to escape effortlessly, as if by magic, into another name, another self'. What he himself lacks is this mirror image into which he can disappear at will, and it is because of this lack that he feels so incomplete and internally divided. As a child, he imagined himself to be perpetually burdened by 'a momentous absence' from which 'there was no escape' (17):

> A connecting cord remained, which parturition and even death had not broken, along which by subtle tugs and thrums I sensed what was not there. No living double could have been so tenacious as this dead one. Emptiness weighed on me. (Banville, 1986a: 17–18)

The 'vague and seemingly objectless yearning' Gabriel Swan feels – the weight of emptiness under which he strains – recalls the obscure desire experienced by his counterpart in *Birchwood*, as well as the 'ubiquitous yearning for an unattainable perfect internal state' identified by Klein. The narcissistic nature of this desire is hinted at by Gabriel's relation of a childhood incident in which he came across an obstetrical manual in the house of a midwife friend of his mother's, which he 'pored over hotly for five tingling minutes'. It was not, he states, the 'gynaecological surprises' found in the manual that held him 'slack-jawed and softly panting, as if I had stumbled on the most entrancing erotica' but rather a selection of images of 'nature's more lavish mistakes' – 'the scrambled blastomeres, the androgynes welded at hip or breast, the bicipitous monsters with tiny webbed hands and cloven spines, all those queer, inseverable things among which I and my phantom brother might have been one more' (1986a: 18).

What is so intriguing, and so disquieting, about this passage is the way in which it conflates biological aberration – the fusion of things which should by nature be separate (scrambled blastomeres, webbed hands, cloven spines) – with sexual desire. Sexuality and mathematics are for Gabriel Swan, as they are for Gabriel Godkin, bound together from the very beginning. He speculates that it is out of this crypto-erotic fascination with 'queer, inseverable things'– with what he calls the 'mystery of the unit' – from which his mathematical gift has grown (18). Like Pausanias's version of Narcissus or Aristophanes' proto-humans, sexual desire is, for Gabriel, bound up with the notion of a return to an original unity. In a more holistic sense, his entire psychology is – again like Gabriel Godkin and, indeed, like Copernicus and Kepler, his antecedents in the novels of the Science Tetralogy – oriented around a powerful attraction to the idea of harmony. His fascination with mathematics has to do not with the pleasures of play, but with a deeper and more urgent attraction to a sense 'of harmony, of symmetry and completeness' (19). This conception of mathematics as possessed of a numinous beauty comparable to that of great art, as presenting the possibility of bringing the seemingly irreconcilable fragments of experience into harmony, is a central one in *Mefisto*. In this respect, Gabriel's beliefs are consonant with Bertrand Russell's views on mathematics and the sublime:

> Mathematics, rightly viewed, possesses not only truth, but supreme beauty – a beauty cold and austere, like that of sculpture,

without appeal to any part of our weaker nature, without the gorgeous trappings of painting or music, yet sublimely pure, and capable of a stern perfection such as only the greatest art can show. (Russell, 1966: 73)

For Gabriel, mathematics is a quasi-artistic endeavour, a way of sculpting the original and absolute incoherence of the world into a kind of order.

The concept of harmony is deeply informed by notions of balance and wholeness; it is defined as a 'combination or adaptation of parts, elements, or related things, so as to form a consistent and orderly whole' (*OED*). What Gabriel lacks is his 'other half', the 'Castor' to his 'Polydeuces', and it is this lack which ensures that he never feels that he adds up to a consistent and orderly whole (Banville, 1986a: 3). He has lost at birth a mirror image of himself, a reflection into which he might disappear and become whole. As a young child, he remembers wandering off alone and speaking in 'a private language' which 'sounded as if I were conversing with someone' (9). Gabriel, it seems clear, has had to create this fantasy co-conspirator to compensate for the loss of his actual twin, to redress the internal rupture of his self-conception. This creation of an imaginary twin corresponds closely with Lewin's conception of the phantasy twin as a 'narcissistic object, someone like self, created in the child's own image' (24).

In both *Birchwood* and *Mefisto*, the figure of an idealised imaginary twin serves as an emblem for the protagonists' quests for self-cohesion. Both narratives can be read in terms of Klein's idea of the universal twin fantasy, in which, as we have seen, the need to understand oneself is fundamentally bound up with the desire to be understood by 'an internalised good object'. In his desperate search for understanding, Gabriel develops a relationship with Felix, a procurer and a drug-dealer, who introduces him to Mr Kasperl and later to Professor Kosok, thereby granting him access into the realm of knowledge. Again, the concepts of desire and mathematics – of sexual and scholarly initiation – are linked and, in turn, both are connected to the larger ideal of self-cohesion or wholeness. In the first half of the novel, Gabriel spends most of his time at Ashburn, the manor house Felix shares with Kasperl and a young girl named Sophie. Sophie is mute, and her presence in the narrative seems awkwardly figurative, even in a work where the metafictional status of each character as a 'marionette' is continually hinted at. Sophie, with whom Gabriel has his first sexual experience and who introduces him to Kasperl's sheaves of calculations, embodies the link between sex and mathematics in *Mefisto*. (This association is strengthened by the fact that the name Sophie originates from the Greek word 'sophia', meaning 'wisdom'.)

Significantly, Gabriel recalls her bed, where they share their first kiss, as the place where he always felt 'real' and where he had all of a sudden 'a vivid sense of myself'. It is, however, not so much the kiss itself that is significant, Gabriel claims, as the tantalising proximity of knowledge it seems to designate: 'A world had opened up before me, disordered, perilous and strange, and for the first time in my life I felt almost at home' (68). When she takes him to Kasperl's room, he feels 'a vague, almost pleasurable qualm, as if I were being seduced, gently, with sly blandishments, into hazard' (69). Sophie seems therefore to embody the tension in the novel not merely between sexuality and knowledge but also between order and chaos.[8]

One of *Mefisto's* more troubling and ambiguous moments comes when Felix performs a parodic wedding ceremony for the young couple, in which Gabriel wears a bridal gown and Sophie wears a top hat and morning coat. Felix's camp burlesque of the Christian wedding recalls Buck Mulligan's liturgical travesty in the opening chapter of *Ulysses*, but also the Satanic Black Mass, which is marked by its inversions and distortions of Catholic rites:

> Felix bowed before us, blessing the air and mumbling.
>
> In the name of the wanker, the sod and the holy shoat, I pronounce you bubble and squeak. Alleluia. What dog hath joined together, let no man throw a bucket of water over. (Banville, 1986a: 83)

The outward levity of the moment – its surface form of hammy performance and blasphemous but harmless mischief – belies its obscurely sinister content. The aesthetic trappings of inversion and the overturning of sexual signifiers point towards a more significant through-the-looking-glass position. The sham wedding as officiated by Felix seems to bring to the surface Gabriel's underlying anxiety about his own otherness to himself. Again, there is the uneasy conflation of sexuality, knowledge (in the largely symbolic person of

Sophie) and self-dissociation. Dressed, in a sense, as his own bride, Gabriel totters down the aisle feeling 'a hot spasm of excitement' at the sensation that inside his gown there is another presence, 'some other flesh,' He catches his reflection in a 'cracked mirror' and in that instant 'someone else looked out at me, dazed and crazily grinning, from behind my own face' (83).

The banal psycho-symbolism of the cracked mirror recalls the photograph in *Birchwood* with its 'white crease aslant it like a bloodless vein'.[9] The image is echoed in Part Two, when the now disfigured Gabriel describes the mirror of his hospital room: 'A rich, deep, silver crack ran athwart the glass, slicing my face diagonally in two from temple to jaw' (1986a: 133). The moment seems to mark, at least symbolically, the momentary union of Gabriel with his lost half, the absent twin who is also a ghostly reflection of himself. Knowledge here is self-knowledge, the recognition and integration of one's image of oneself, the thwarted process dramatised in the myth of Narcissus. Like Pausanias's version of Narcissus, Gabriel knows that it is his own reflection he sees, but is granted a fleeting sense of integration by imagining he sees the image of his lost twin. In 'Narcissism and the Death Instinct', Ahmed Fayek speculates that 'the core of the narcissistic drama, as it is presented in the myth, is the dilemma of identity, i.e. of becoming and emerging from oblivion to recognition' (Fayek, 1981: 310). Again like Pausanias's Narcissus, Gabriel is bound to his dead twin, unable either to relinquish or properly mourn that loss. The mock wedding offers no resolution, either within the narrative itself or within the psychological issues at which it hints: on both the symbolic and literal levels it remains enigmatic. It is difficult, therefore, to read it with confidence as anything other than a kind of Dadaist gesture – by Banville as by Felix – that resists not just meaningful interpretation but also the very idea of meaning. In this regard, the scene resonates with and in a sense encapsulates the book's thematic concern with the ascendancy of chaos over order. What does, however, come across strongly amid the theatrical absurdity of the episode, is the permeability of Gabriel's identity. Throughout, he is addressed by Felix – who, tellingly, never calls Gabriel by his real name in the course of the novel – variously as 'Hansel', 'bird-boy', 'sweetie' and 'Cinders' (Banville, 1986a: 81–4). He feels himself, in his wedding gown, to be 'not myself but someone else', and it is that someone else who he sees staring at him in the mirror 'from behind my own face' (84).

In this disturbing image we are given a brief premonitory glimpse of Gabriel's immediate future, in which he is horribly disfigured in an explosion at Ashburn. The second of *Mefisto*'s two parts begins with Gabriel lying in hospital after the accident. Just as the first part begins with a swirl of images and associations around the concept of birth, the opening of this second half is pervaded with the language of rebirth. Like a toddler, he must learn to walk again with 'first, faltering little steps'; in his scorched condition, he is 'bent and hobbling, hairless as a babe' (132). It is rebirth of a hellish sort, however, a return from death that does not erase the memory and trauma of dying. Gabriel, in this sense, is even closer now to the ghostly other of his dead brother: 'A riven thing, incomplete. Something had sheared away, when I pulled through. I was neither this nor that, half here, half somewhere else. Miscarried' (130). When his doctor tells him he is lucky that his burns went deep enough to destroy the nerves in his face, Gabriel replies that he can feel, that he is in pain. The doctor informs him that this is impossible, that what he is feeling is 'phantom pain' (130). The idea of 'phantom pain' – of something which is, like a lost limb, both absent and distressingly present in its absence – can be read as representative of Gabriel's psychological condition. Alexander Cleave in *Eclipse* is told by his wife that 'you are your own ghost'; Max Morden in *The Sea* worries that 'I am becoming my own ghost' (2000a: 42; 2005c: 194). Gabriel, similarly, is becoming the thing by which he has always been haunted. In his disfigurement, he has taken on an avian appearance that recalls Felix's favourite nickname for him, 'bird-boy': 'My face now was a glazed carnival mask, with china brow and bulging cheeks, hawk nose, dead eye sockets'.[10] The implication is that he has somehow become his dead twin, or that he has in some sense merged with him: 'But I was different. I was someone else, someone I knew, and didn't know'. He has, he claimed, 'stepped into the mirror' (1986a: 132).

This awareness of being haunted by a phantom version of oneself, of being possessed by an implacable sense of loss, is repeatedly registered in the language of authenticity. The vague scientific venture at the centre of *Mefisto* (neither the nature of the knowledge Gabriel and his successive mentors are seeking nor the use to which they intend to put it are ever defined) seems wholly commensurate with the obscurely conceived project of self-cohesion, of 'becoming real', which is pursued alongside it. Both projects, it seems clear, are concerned with the uncovering of an ultimate, ineffable truth. Gabriel describes what he is searching for – in both the scientific and the existential senses – in a language that seems to reach toward a spiritual register. 'It was here,' he asserts, 'in the big world, that I would meet what I was waiting for, that perfectly simple, ravishing, unchallengeable formula in the light of which the mask of mere contingency would melt' (186). The melting mask imagery establishes a plain link between the revelation of cosmic truth and the revelation of some kind of authentic self. He goes on to explicitly conflate the truth-seeking project with the narcissistic search for his missing twin:

> At times it felt as if the thing would burst out into being by its own force. And with it surely would come something else, that dead half of me I had hauled around always at my side would somehow tremble into life, and I would be made whole. (Banville, 1986a: 186)

Gabriel's monomaniacal search for wholeness, like his search for a universal order, is ultimately and necessarily a failure. Klein, as we have seen, insists that the desire for what she calls 'full integration' is never realisable, and that it is this perpetually thwarted impulse towards cohesion that leads to the 'universal phantasy of having a twin' (Klein, 1988: 300). The last piece of direct speech in the novel is a question, put to Gabriel by Professor Kosok after the death of his drug-addicted daughter Adel: 'Where is your order now?' (Banville, 1986a: 233). This corrosive interrogation admits of no reply, and the book ends with Gabriel's hesitant renunciation of faith in the narcissistic ideal of harmony. He has lost his mathematician's ability (or propensity) to see the world in terms of orderly categories, having woken up one morning to find he 'could no longer add together two and two' (233). He determines, in the future, 'to leave things, to try to leave things, to chance' (234). The novel ends on a note of resignation toward the entropic nature of reality. This conclusion is strongly reminiscent of *Birchwood*, which closes with Gabriel Godkin's announcement that whereof he cannot speak, thereof he must be silent. Rüdiger Imhof's claim that 'both characters move from Cartesian certainty to Wittgensteinian despair' is one which comes close to the truth but ultimately falls short of it (Imhof, 1987: 116).[11]

Imhof is mistaken in seeing the progress of both characters as being from certainty to uncertainty. There is a desire for certainty, but the thing itself is perpetually absent in a manner reflective of the over-bearing absence of the idealised identical twin figure. The intellectual trajectory tracked by both novels is thus from a fixation on the *idea* of cohesion – in both the epistemological and ontological senses – to a renunciation of that fixation; to a realisation that neither the self nor the world in which it exists can be forced into an artificial framework of meaning. What Imhof disregards is the crucial distinction between certainty itself, which is never more than a phantom presence in Banville's work, and the compulsion to seek it as an ideal. *Mefisto*, from its very first words, makes this absence known, even as it links it to the absence of the whole, immutable self: 'Chance was in the beginning' (Banville, 1986a: 3).

The key device through which this cognitive narrative is dramatised is that of the missing twin. The notion of the incomplete self – the sense of there being an absent part, the lack of which presents an insurmountable obstacle to a kind of prelapsarian personal wholeness – can be understood, moreover, in the light of Pausanias's alternative version of the Narcissus myth. The narcissism of Gabriel Godkin and Gabriel Swan is of a form distinct from that of Alexander Cleave, Axel Vander and Freddie Montgomery in that it is less aggressively misanthropic, but they are equally as inward-directed in terms of their psychological orientation. The missing twin device serves the figurative portrayal of this narcissistic search for self-cohesion. As a fictional stratagem, it can be viewed in terms broadly similar to those in which Slavoj Žižek conceives of the Hitchcockian device of the McGuffin: as 'pure absence' after the manner of Lacan's *objet petit a*. 'The McGuffin is clearly the *objet petit a*,' writes Žižek, 'a gap in the centre of the symbolic order – the lack, the void of the Real setting in motion the symbolic movement of interpretation, a pure semblance of the Mystery to be explained' (Žižek, 1992: 8). In both novels, Banville uses the missing twin as a psychological McGuffin, as a catalyst for the more fundamental 'plot' of the narcissistic pursuit of self-unity.

The enduring presence of the ideal of wholeness in Western culture – from Plato to the Bible, from the various renderings of Narcissus to Kleinian internal loneliness and the *objet petit a* – confirms its centrality to the way in which we think about ourselves and our relationships to others. From each of these perspectives, the ideal always remains an unattainable one: the problem of desire is one for which no solution can be offered. To be human is to be always incomplete, forever aware of the missing pieces in the puzzle of one's self. The abortive pursuits of lost twins that impel, in different ways, the narratives of *Birchwood* and *Mefisto*, are fundamentally narcissistic pursuits. They are narcissistic in the way that all human desire – as Plato's *Symposium*, the story of Narcissus, the Judeo-Christian myth of Genesis and much of psychoanalysis confirm – is the self's desire for its own completion.

4
The False Self

When asked in an interview with *The Observer* in 2000 why he chose to make the protagonist of the recently published *Eclipse* an actor, Banville revealed that the decision came at a late stage in the novel's composition. He acknowledged that, at some point, he was 'really going to have to stop dealing with these inauthentic men who have made themselves', and went on to speak about the pervasiveness of inauthenticity among artists:

> If you look at practically anyone – I mean, I find this more and more – the more you look at people the more you find that they've actually manufactured themselves. People whose names that you know. I meet lots of people in my ordinary life, away from writing, who seem to be authentic, who seem to know where they've come from and who they are, but anyone that I deal with in, if you like, my profession, we all seem to have made ourselves. I think artists are all self-made. (Banville, 2000d: 15)

The exchange sheds light on two particular aspects of Banville's approach to the question of selfhood: his recognition, on the one hand, that there does seem to be such a thing as an authentic self, and his prevailing concern, on the other, with those people for whom such authenticity is not an option. His protagonist is indeed an actor, but the implication is that his inauthenticity – his inability to do anything other than perform – is, as it were, ontologically prior to his profession. Banville seems to be saying that what his character does for a living is, if not actually beside the point, not quite central to it either: it is reflective rather than constitutive of his inauthenticity. Almost all his protagonists, after all, are performers of roles in one way or another. There is, in his view, clearly something about the artistic personality (or persona) that forever rings false.

Looked at as a whole, Banville's output reveals his unflagging fascination with postures and impostures. His fiction might be viewed as a sustained exploration of the various ways people find of deceiving themselves and others, as a fiction about the fictions people make of themselves. The present chapter is concerned with examining this fraudulent aspect of Banville's characters in relation to the British psychoanalyst Donald Winnicott's notion of the 'False Self', and demonstrating the ways in which it contributes to an understanding of the narcissistic mechanisms at work in the fiction.

As a theorist working within the object relations school of psychoanalysis, Winnicott has had much to say about the formative relationships between infants and their mothers. In the late paper 'Mirror Role of Mother and Family in Child Development' (1967), he stresses the critical importance to the child's healthy maturation of the mother's face as a mirroring phenomenon. For Winnicott, when the infant looks at the mother – provided, that is, that she is a 'good-enough mother', a mother capable of providing her infant with a reliable 'holding environment' – 'what the baby sees is himself or herself' (Winnicott, 1967: 151). It is through the mother's ample recognition of what he calls the infant's 'spontaneous gestures' that the child begins to develop what was to begin with only a potentiality: a self that feels real and integrated.[1] If the mother is for some reason emotionally withdrawn – if she is not a 'good-enough mother' – and insufficiently capable of responding to the infant's spontaneous gestures, the infant will be unable to see itself in her face, unable to get a sense of itself as 'real'. In a curiously poetic formulation that is fairly typical of Winnicott's style, he writes:

When I look I am seen, so I exist.
I can now afford to look and see.
I now look creatively and what I apperceive I also perceive.
In fact I take care not to see what is not there to be seen
(unless I am tired). (Winnicott, 1967: 154)

It is crucial, then, for that earliest and most important of relationships, that something is returned to the child when it looks at its mother. If there is no such return, the risk is that the child will fail to believe fully in its own reality. This is a kind of psychoanalytical version of Berkeley's *esse est percipii*: in order to feel oneself to be real, one has to see oneself being seen. The condition of the 'True Self' – the self which is communicated through the infant's spontaneous gestures – is contingent upon the mother's responsive engagement with those spontaneous gestures. Met with maternal rejection or unresponsiveness, with a face that does not function as an approving mirror, something in the infant retreats within itself and the strategy of compliance and defence known as the 'False Self' is set in motion.

One of the few mother–son relationships to be explored in any real depth in Banville's *oeuvre* is that between Freddie and his mother in *The Book of Evidence*. Their interactions are overwhelmingly characterised by emotional frigidity and passive aggression. As the creator of his own narrative of self, Freddie finds himself on 'perilous ground' when he comes to the topic of his mother. 'I find myself staggering backwards slowly,' he writes, 'clutching in my outstretched arms a huge, unwieldy and yet weightless burden. She is so much, and, at the same time, nothing' (Banville, 1989a: 41). From a Winnicottian perspective, his brief description of her gives the distinct impression of a mother who would fall short of the 'good-enough' standard. I recall her from my childhood,' Freddie writes, 'as a constant but remote presence, statuesque, blank-eyed, impossibly handsome in an Ancient Roman sort of way, like a marble figure at the far side of a lawn' (41–2). There is a strong sense that the blank eyes of this cold and aloof woman would have failed to function as an approving mirror for the young Freddie. In this sense, it is worth noting that in *Ghosts*, in which Freddie's False Self takes centre stage, the figure of the mother is completely absent.

In 'Ego Distortion in Terms of the True and False Self' (1960), Winnicott writes that 'the False Self has one positive and very important function: to hide the True Self, which it does by compliance with environmental demands' (Winnicott, 1960: 15). He classifies False Self organisations along a continuum, ranging from the most extreme to the normally functioning. At one end of this continuum, the True Self is completely hidden and it is the False Self 'that observers tend to think is the real person'; at the other, the False Self is represented by 'the whole organization of the polite and mannered social attitude, a "not wearing the heart on the sleeve", as it might be said' (10–11). Interestingly – and, with respect to Banville's characters, significantly – when Winnicott addresses the ways in which the infant False Self can form the basis for specific kinds of sublimation the example he chooses is that of when a child grows up to become an actor. 'In regard to actors,' he writes, 'there are those who can be themselves and who can also act, whereas there are others who can only act, and who are completely at a loss when not in a role, and when not being appreciated or applauded (acknowledged as existing)' (19).

For Winnicott, then, there is an intrinsic authenticity which can, depending on the nature of the mother–child relationship, either be nurtured into a condition of strength and creative dominance or caused to retreat behind the protective facade of the False Self. The narcissistic aspect of the False Self – its correspondences to Freud's theory of secondary narcissism, for instance, and to Kohut's notion of the grandiose self – is made explicit in this remark about actors. It emerges and becomes psychically dominant as a form of compensation for the mother's inability to reflect the child back upon itself. Like most of the British school, Winnicott tended to avoid using the word narcissism, but his False Self can be seen as a contribution to the psychoanalytic understanding of the concept. Perhaps his most vivid analogy for the False Self is one which captures both its narcissistic content and its peculiar vacancy: the child, he writes, 'presents a shop-window or out-turned half' to the world (Winnicott, 1965: 135).

Banville's work is endlessly concerned with the divisions and confusions between components of experience: self and world, truth and falsehood, memory and imagination. One such endlessly scrutinised dichotomy is that between the out-turned and the in-turned halves of the self. It is in *Ghosts* that this dichotomy is most thoroughly explored. Appropriately for a novel so concerned with the techniques and strategies of visual art, it is almost completely without narrative impetus; to a greater extent than even *Eclipse* or *The Sea*, it is all setting and no plot. In terms of characterisation, too, it marks a notable break with his usual methods. Freddie Montgomery is the novel's narrator, but he does not reveal himself as such until the novel's 'action' is well underway. In fact, we are never told the narrator's name in *Ghosts*: we merely infer, from an increasingly unsubtle series of hints, that it is Freddie. Whereas *The Book of Evidence* opens with a narcissistic affirmation of Freddie's menacing, preening presence, *Ghosts* begins with uncharacteristic ambivalence, on a hesitantly sounded note of self-effacement: 'Here they are. There are seven of them. Or better say, half a dozen or so, that gives more leeway' (Banville, 1993a: 3). It is not immediately apparent what we are being offered here in the way of narration, whether it is a first-person or third-person voice which speaks to us. In this sense, the novel begins as it means to go on: Freddie's wandering 'authorial' perspective is a feature throughout – a kind of free indirect first-person narrative. He leaps from one 'character' to the next, as he attempts to possess the consciousness of each of the people who are shipwrecked on his island. There is a distinct sense of experimentation to this, as though he were testing his ability to empathise, to make others 'real' by imagining what their inner worlds might be like.

The novel's first short introductory fragment ends with a question, the response to which is more a reformulation of that question than an answer: 'Who speaks? I do. Little god' (3). The question of who speaks, of course, is one that resounds throughout all of Banville's work (it is also the question, it will be remembered, with which *Shroud* begins). We are not sure who this 'I', this 'little god' is – we have no reason at this point to suspect that it might be the murderer from *The Book of Evidence* – but it seems to gesture toward an external, quasi-divine authorial presence, of which the speaking 'I' is perhaps an avatar within the fictional world of the novel. But this initial uncertainty about who is addressing us is no mere sleight-of-hand; it augurs a more profound and prolonged ambivalence about identity in the novel. Freddie is attempting to flee and conceal his shameful past, and the narrative's reticence reflects this. As he himself says of the work of the painter Jean Vaublin (an almost-anagram of John Banville), whose work he is on the island in order to research for the art historian Professor Kreutznaer, 'something is missing, something is deliberately not being said' (1993a: 35). Freddie's 'inexpungible guilt' is like a True Self that will not bear disclosure, that must be protected from the world's gaze, and vice versa. 'My crime,' as he puts it, 'had ramified it; it sat inside me now like a second, parasitic self, its tentacles coiled around my cells' (22). This inexpungible guilt, in other words, is not the *result* of his crime: it precedes it, and is merely intensified by it. Freddie makes reference to the hermitic life of solitude and repentance which he has left his past behind in order to live: 'And so I had come to this penitential isle (there are beehive huts in the hills), seeking not redemption, for that would have been too much to ask, but an accommodation with myself, maybe, and with my poor, swollen conscience' (22).

Self-communion, here as in almost all of Banville's fiction, is, in the fullest sense of the term, the object of the narrative; both the means of representation and that which it represents are oriented towards finding an essential unity. As such, although Freddie's 'project' is about atonement, about attempting to assuage his ineradicable guilt, it is nonetheless narcissistic. In *Eclipse*, Alexander Cleave's desire is to 'give it all up, home, wife, possessions, renounce it all for good, rid myself of every last thing and come and live in some such unconsidered spot as this' (2000a: 70). Freddie here is doing something remarkably similar. He is in a state of retreat, in a kind of early retirement from the world. There is a significant measure of fear, of watchful self-defence, to this retreat. Freddie formulates this as follows: 'How to be alone even in the midst of the elbowing crowd, that is another of those knacks that the years in captivity had taught me. It is a matter of inward stillness, of hiding inside oneself, like an animal, in cover, while the hounds go pounding past'. He denies the implication that he is retreating from the confusion and pain of the real world, the world of others, into the anaesthetising refuge of scholarship, claiming, rather, that it is himself he wishes to escape: 'I was trying to get as far away as possible from everything. I had tried to get away from myself, too, but in vain' (1993a: 26).

All this is strangely contradictory: Freddie denies that he has 'retreated into solitude', but then affirms that he has attempted to escape from everything. He claims that he wanted to get away from himself, but then, less than a page later, informs us that 'I wanted to be simple, candid, natural – I wanted to be, yes, I shall risk it: I wanted to be *honest*' (27 [emphasis in original]). There is something paradoxically enlightening about this confusion and logical inconsistency, something instructive in the way that Freddie is so obviously at variance with himself. 'There is', he admits, 'no getting away from the passionate attachment to self, that I-beam set down in the dead centre of the world and holding the whole rickety edifice in place. All the same, I was determined at least to try to make myself into a – what do you call it – a monomorph: a monad' (26).

Freddie, then, wishes to be something that exists in only one form (a monomorph). He wants to be no longer internally divided, to be 'honest' and authentic. The word 'monad' seems, at first glance, to reinforce this: in Leibniz's *Monadology*, the word denotes a simple and indivisible entity, such as an atom or a human self, which has the property of being ultimately and fully *real* (as distinct from what he calls *phenomena*).[2] Initially, then, the words 'monomorph' and 'monad' would appear to be interchangeable. Typically for Banville, however, there is another sense of the latter word which casts a shadow over this ostensibly humble expression of desire for a simple existence. In various Gnostic heresiologies, the true God was known as the Monad, meaning the One or the Absolute. In *The Lives and Opinions of Eminent Philosophers*, Diogenes Laertius attributes to Pythagoras the belief '[t]hat the monad was the beginning of everything' (Laertius, 2006: 348). So a statement apparently expressing Freddie's desire to be uncomplicated and undivided can equally be read as a cryptic (and perhaps not wholly serious) allusion to his god complex. In a novel scattered with references to *The Tempest*, Freddie is slyly positioning himself as the Prospero of his own island, the 'little god' of his bounded and isolated world.[3] His essential position appears to be one of isolation and internal division. He seems to want to atone for the actions to which his narcissism have led him in the past, but his method of atonement seems uniquely narcissistic. 'My case, in short,' he says, 'was what it always had been, namely, that I did one thing while thinking another and in this welter of difference I did not know what I was' (1993a: 27). Narcissism is, amongst other things, the condition whereby a person's desire for self-unity is perpetually thwarted by the awkward conundrum of self-knowledge. This paradox is elegantly articulated by Marina Warner:

> Mirrors are associated with enlightenment through their association with integration – the self as a bounded object in space – and, less obviously but by extension, with estrangement – the self as separate and elsewhere. It is a profound paradox that when I recognize myself in a mirror, I am seeing myself as an Other, as if seen by someone else (though I may not share or ever know others' response to what they see) [...] For while the self appears

detached and bounded in the mirror, any move or gesture changes the image accordingly, through that indissoluble twinship that makes Ovid's Narcissus cry out in agony when he cannot reach his beloved *alter*. (Warner, 2006: 173)

In this respect, Freddie is incapable of transcending his narcissism because he is incapable of negotiating a reconciliation between the disparate components – the in-turned and out-turned halves – of his self. 'How then,' he asks, 'was I to be expected to know what others are, to imagine them so vividly as to make them quicken into a sort of life?' (Banville, 1993a: 27). Winnicott sees human experience as defined by this kind of profound contradiction, by our simultaneous desires to connect with others and to insulate ourselves. In his most important paper, 'Communicating and Not Communicating Leading to a Study of Certain Opposites' (1990), he describes this formative dialectic as, in its healthy form, a creative and profoundly instinctual playing of hide and seek. Winnicott saw the figure of the artist as representative of the True Self at its most authentic and thriving, and yet most guarded. 'In the artist of all kinds one can detect an inherent dilemma which belongs to the co-existence of two trends, the urgent need to communicate and the still more urgent need not to be found' (Winnicott, 1963: 185). In the same paper, Winnicott – who is never afraid of embracing paradox – represents the creative process as definitive of sanity and madness, describing it as 'a sophisticated game of hide and seek in which it is joy to be hidden but disaster not to be found' (186). There is in each of us, he maintains, a core that remains utterly hermitic, incommunicative and incommunicable, and which is a less extreme version of the hidden self of the pathologically split personality:

I suggest that this core never communicates with the world of perceived objects, and that the individual person knows that it must never be communicated with or be influenced by external reality. This is my main point, the point of thought which is at the centre of an intellectual world and of my paper. Although healthy persons communicate and enjoy communicating, the other fact is equally true, that *each individual is an isolate, permanently non-communicating, permanently unknown, in fact unfound*. (Winnicott, 1963: 187 [emphasis in original])

There is a conspicuous contradiction here. Namely, how can it be true that it is a disaster for the inner self not to be found, and yet also true that each of us is permanently unfound? Is it that human experience is unavoidably a kind of disaster? Winnicott stresses the necessary isolation of the inner core of the person in the most extreme of terms, his language striking a Kleinian note of violent intensity. 'Rape, and being eaten alive by cannibals,' he writes, 'these are mere bagatelles, as compared with the violation of the self's core, the alteration of the self's central elements by communication seeping through the defenses. For me this would be the sin against the self [...] The question is: how to be isolated without having to be insulated?' (187). What seems clear, despite the evident contradictions in Winnicott's ideas and the provocative ways in which they are expressed, is that there is something about communication which represents an intolerable compromise to that part of the person which he considers to be the 'True Self'. For Winnicott, normal human maturation entails a lesser level of the kind of psychic splitting found in the most extreme forms of psychopathology. As he puts it: 'The traumatic experiences that lead to the organization of primitive defenses belong to the threat to the isolated core, the threat of its being found, altered, communicated with. The defense consists in the further hiding of the secret self' (183).

In his book on Winnicott, Adam Phillips addresses this contradiction without attempting to resolve it:

> He proposes an absolute insulation at the core of the self and then also says that the problem for the individual is how to stay isolated without being insulated. It is as though at the end of his life the issue he had always struggled with, of separation and connectedness, had changed from being an inter-psychic problem between mother and child, to being an intra-psychic problem about a person's relationship with the core of himself. And it is worth noting that Winnicott takes his language for an 'essential' self from a simpler form of organic life: the core is the central casing of a fruit that contains the seeds. (Phillips, 1998: 148–9)

These notions of insulation and isolation – of the need to be at once exposed to and inoculated against the presence of others – are central to *Ghosts*, as indeed they are to Banville's work as a whole. Freddie, as we have seen, is concerned with being 'alone in the midst of the elbowing crowd', and he finds that doing so is a matter of 'hiding inside oneself, like an animal, in cover, while the hounds go pounding past' (Banville, 1993a: 26). This kind of anxiety about protecting the inner core against the feral threat of alterity resonates with Winnicott's remark about rape and being eaten alive by cannibals. What is most fascinating about Freddie's formulation – and if there were such a thing as a Winnicottian locution, it might look very much like this – is the way it positions him as the cowering animal, as not the predator but the prey. *The Book of Evidence* begins with Freddie's projection of himself as 'locked up here like some exotic animal', as 'the girl-eater, svelte and dangerous, padding to and fro in my cage, my terrible green glance flickering past the bars' (1989a: 3). What is dangerous now and what is at risk would appear to have switched positions.

Much is made throughout the novel of the allegorical aspect of Freddie's island location (Banville has a great deal of intertextual fun with a lavish miscellany of references, covert and overt, to *Gilligan's Island, Treasure Island, The Island of Doctor Moreau, The Swiss Family Robinson, The Tempest* and *Gulliver's Travels*). Not only is he isolated from the world, but it is a new territory in which he can attempt to reinvent himself as the introverted but harmless man of letters. Islands are, he admits, places which appeal to him because of 'the sense of boundedness' and of 'being protected from the world – and of the world being protected from me' (1993a: 207). And he describes his 'impression of a scholar' as 'a splendid part, the best it has ever been my privilege to play, and I have played many' (34). So Freddie is well aware of the reasons for his self-isolation, of the fraudulence of the face he presents to the world. In its most extreme manifestation – in the kind of drastically inauthentic and split existence Freddie represents – the False Self, Winnicott tells us, 'results in a feeling unreal or a sense of futility' (Winnicott, 1996: 10). Freddie is unable to conceive of himself as having any kind of existential weight: he is 'there and not there' (Banville, 1993a: 40). The title of the novel refers as much to himself as to the various shipwrecked 'characters' with whom he populates his story. Just as, for much of the novel, he is a kind of spectral, omniscient 'little god' presence hovering above and around the narrative – possessing at any given moment the mind of any given character – Freddie is by his own admission a curiously insubstantial presence:

> I felt like something suspended in empty air, weightless, transparent, turning this way or that in every buffet of wind that blew. At least when I was locked away I had felt I was definitively there, but now that I was free (or at large, at any rate) I seemed hardly to be here at all. This is how I imagine ghosts existing, poor, pale wraiths pegged out to shiver in the wind of the world like so much insubstantial laundry, yearning towards us, the heedless ones, as we walk blithely through them. (Banville, 1993a: 37)

Freddie's experience of himself here anticipates Alexander Cleave and Max Morden: he feels that he is becoming his 'own ghost' (2000a: 42; 2005c: 194). And this is something which reflects his strange insubstantiality as a narrator, as the speaking 'I' of the narrative. This absence of any fixed presence behind the text, the ghostliness of the narrating subject, is something which Derrida addresses when he directly asks his reader (whose existence he also throws into question):

> who is it that is addressing you? Since it is not an 'author', a 'narrator', or a 'deus ex machina', it is an 'I' that is both part of the spectacle and part of the audience; an 'I' that, a bit like 'you' [...] [functions] as pure passageway for operations or substitutions, is not some singular and irreplaceable existence, some subject of 'life', but only, moving between life and death, reality and fiction, etc., a mere function or phantom. (Derrida, 2004: 357).

Freddie – who never once names himself in the novel, never truly positions himself as the solid subject of his text – is haunted by this sense of himself as a 'mere function or phantom'. Though Winnicott firmly believes in the existence of a 'True Self', he knows the power such ideas can have; he knows how keenly people can feel themselves as absences. It is the False Self existence, he tells us, which leads to this 'feeling unreal'. Freddie's seeming inability to confront head-on the sins he has committed might be seen, in this sense, as the reason behind his sense of absence from himself. He seems able to countenance himself only at an angle. He does eventually relate the story of the theft of the portrait from Whitewater and his murder of Josie Bell – providing, in so doing, a usefully condensed version of *The Book of Evidence* – but he does so in a curiously furtive and oblique manner. Tellingly, he approaches this painful task of narration by means of the third person, and as though he were merely adumbrating a hypothetical set of circumstances. In this way, he places himself at a double remove from his actions, from the intractable reality of himself: not only were these crimes not really committed, it was not him who committed them. 'Let us take the hypothetical case', he begins, 'of a man surprised by love, not for a living woman – he has never been able to care much for the living – but for the figure of a woman in, oh, a painting, let's say' (Banville, 1993a: 83). Intriguingly, he uses this affected detachment to do a little amateur psychoanalysis on the motives behind the theft of the painting: 'Freud himself remarked that in the passionate encounter of every couple there are four people involved. Or should it be six? – The two so-called real lovers, plus the images they have of themselves, plus the images that they have of each other' (84). Again, he cagily acknowledges his own narcissism and its place in his actions. The woman in the portrait, he relates, is more 'real' to this hypothetical character than the majority of actual people. 'And our Monsieur Hypothesis is not used to seeing people whole, the rest of humanity being for him for the most part a kind of annoying fog obscuring his view of the darkened shop-window of the world and of himself reflected in it' (84). More explicitly, in describing his relationship with Mrs Vanden (a taciturn widow with whom he has a brief tryst) he alludes to the myth of Narcissus. What he lusts after, he tells us, 'is not some sly-eyed wanton but a being made up of stillnesses [...] a pale pool in a shaded glade in which I might bathe my poor throbbing brow and cool its shamefaced fires (I know, I know: the pool and the lover leaning over it, I too caught that echo)' (80).

The primary threat to Freddie's insulation of his True Self is represented by the figure of Felix, who reprises his role from *Mefisto* as a vaguely demonic presence possessed of incriminating knowledge about everyone with whom he comes in contact. His relationship to Freddie is never wholly defined. He often appears to be a kind of personification of Freddie's own bad conscience, a representative of the True Self out in the world, and thus a projection of his own split psyche. Perpetually smirking and snickering, he seems always to be on the brink of disclosing some unspeakable truth about not just Freddie, but everyone else. Professor Kreutznaer, for instance, fears him for the knowledge he possesses about his sometime penchant for picking up rough trade on the city quays of Dublin. He recalls, of such occasions, Felix's omnipresence and omniscience in this milieu: 'And Felix there always, lord of the streets, popping up out of nowhere, horribly knowing, making little jokes and smiling his malign, insinuating smile [...] And that laugh' (113). Similarly, when Freddie is released from prison and attempting to put his past behind him, Felix is a nebulous presence, lurking on the margins and seeming to deny the possibility of self-reinvention. When Freddie telephones his wife immediately upon his release from prison, she informs him that 'someone' has already been looking for him. When she mentions that this person was foreign, or 'pretending to be' and that he 'seemed to think something was very funny', the reader is left in little doubt as to the identity of this 'someone' (161). And when, on his way to catch the ferry to the island, Freddie makes a detour to his former home, he catches sight of a figure we can only assume to be Felix hanging around the fringes of the estate.

The reader is repeatedly given reason to suppose that the connection between Felix and Freddie is of a preternatural sort, that there is some unspoken kinship or parallel between them. Like the Pierrot in Vaublin's *Le monde d'or* – a figure with whom Freddie persistently identifies himself – who 'stands before us like our own reflection distorted in a mirror, known yet strange', there is something equally familiar and foreign about Felix (225). He is referred to by Freddie as 'the dark one, my dark brother, waiting for me [...] to throw down my challenge to him' (240). When he does confront him at the novel's end – and it is, unsurprisingly, a rather anticlimactic confrontation – Freddie confesses that it was 'as if all along we had been walking side by side, with something between us, some barrier, thin and smooth and deceptive as a mirror, that now was broken, and I had stepped into his world, or he into mine, or we had both entered some third place that belonged to neither of us'. It is as though the level of reality in which Felix exists were somehow undetermined, neither wholly external nor internal, and Freddie finds it 'hard to keep a hold of him, somehow'. 'He kept going in and out of focus,' he claims, 'one minute flat and transparent, a two-dimensional figure cut out of grimed glass, the next an overpowering presence pressing itself against me in awful intimacy, insistently physical, all flesh and breath and that stale whiff of something gone rank' (241).

Whether Felix is wholly real is perhaps finally immaterial, in that it is what he represents in Freddie's psyche which is truly important. He knows the truth about him, and in many respects he is the embodiment of that truth. If Felix is sinister and insinuating, if his entire persona seems charged with a treacherous and insistent suggestiveness, it is because he is a kind of manifestation of Freddie's hidden self. *Ghosts* ends on a fatalistic note, with Freddie acknowledging the impossibility of escaping Felix and the ignoble True Self of which he seems to be the avatar or emissary: 'No riddance of him' (244). When the sentiment is repeated in the novel's final words, this time without the third-person singular pronoun – 'No: no riddance' – this can be read as suggesting that what Freddie will never be able to rid himself of is his own self (245). The project of suppression, of what Winnicott would call 'insulation', is one that would appear to be doomed to failure.

The narrative strategy of *Athena*, the final novel of the Art Trilogy which Freddie narrates, is even more radically suppressive than that of *Ghosts*. As Freddie says of the work of the painter Vaublin, 'something is deliberately not being said' (1993a: 35). There is, in *Athena*, a palpable sense of the determined containment of a painful truth. No one in this story goes by their true name. The narrator – whose identity we must once again infer to be that of Freddie Montgomery – has changed his name by deed poll to Morrow. The object of his love is only ever referred to as 'A.', and he speaks of her as revealing to him only 'successive approximations of an ultimate self that would, that must, remain forever hidden' (1995: 48). The villain of the piece, as it were, is a 'master of disguises' known only as 'The Da' (evidently based on the real-life figure of Martin Cahill, the Dublin crime boss known as 'The General'). The real name of Aunt Corky, the distant elderly relative who Freddie is forced to take in is, we are told, unpronounceable, and he confesses that he is 'not sure which of [her] many versions of her gaudy life was true, if any of them was' (22). Likewise, though the city in which the novel is set is presumably Dublin, it is never referred to as such, and all the street names mentioned are fictional. Whenever we come across a proper noun in *Athena*, we are reminded of the novel's strategy of concealment and suppression. Freddie/Morrow occasionally hints at his true identity, but more often than not such slips are quickly glossed over or abruptly cut off before they lead anywhere. The mention of a hammer, for instance, evidently brings to mind the murder of Josie Bell, and so the narrative is suddenly discontinued like a line of thought that is too much to bear:

> Francie ambled forward and picked up a miniature hammer from the workbench and turned toward me and –
> Enough of this. I do not like it down here! I do not like it at all. A wave of my wand and *pop*! here we are magically at street level again. (Banville, 1995: 55)

Shortly afterwards, Freddie permits himself a short polemic against his own perversity. 'I am not good, I never was and never will be,' he begins, appearing at first to relish this admission of his wickedness. 'I am the bogey-man you dream of as you toss in your steamy beds of a night' (59). When he gets too close to the reality of the murder he has committed, however, and to his capability of committing such an act again, he stops himself, denying the actual facts (as opposed to the poetic truths) entry into his narrative:

> I have done terrible things, I could do them again, I have it in me, I –
> Stop. (Banville, 1995: 60)

These aposiopetic ruptures are suggestive of what is going on beneath the narrative surface of *Athena*. Each of the novel's characters is engaged in an improvised performance, and no one sees anyone else for what they are. Freddie's relationship with A., for instance, seems to be no different to any other love affair in Banville's fiction, in that it is defined by a fundamentally narcissistic form of attachment. In the aftermath of his first encounter with her, he admits to being 'full of self-regard ... for as usual it was I who was the real object of all this attentiveness, the new-made, sticky-winged I who had stepped forth from the cocoon that A.'s kiss had cracked' (94). Despite his obsession with her, he admits on more than one occasion to an inability to 'summon up her face in my memory except in a general way'. She herself is 'almost incidental' to the 'swoony ruminations which at their most concentrated became entirely self-sustaining' and which characterise his infatuation (88). Even when he can think of nothing but her, in other words, it is not really her of whom he is thinking. This is the nature of love in Banville's fiction: it is always some or other form of narcissism. Freddie expresses it as follows:

> I know what I am saying here, I know how thoroughly I am betraying myself in all my horrible self-obsession. But that is how it was, at the start, as if in an empty house, at darkest midnight, I had stopped shocked before a gleaming apparition only to discover it was my own reflection springing up out of a shadowy, life-sized mirror. It was to be a long time before the silvering on the back of that looking-glass began to wear away and I could look through it and see her, or that version of her that was all she permitted me to see. (Banville, 1995: 88)

Narcissism and the idea of the false self are linked in the version of erotic obsession with which *Athena* presents us. When one of the two lovers is not consumed by self-regard, he or she only ever has access to a false front presented by the other. It is, in many respects, a rigorously bleak view of human relationships – or rather, of the impossibility of human relationships so conceived. For Winnicott as for Lacan, one is revealed to oneself in the other. As the British psychoanalyst Katherine Cameron puts it, 'to be seen not only *in* but *by* the Other means to discover both yourself and that there is another, though the Winnicottian pendulum has a way of swinging always back to the Self' (Cameron, 1996: 40). Though there is a good deal of tenderness in Freddie's desire for A., it seems to be largely physical in nature, confined to the surface of things (she is, he notes, 'five foot two in her bare, her heartbreakingly bare, red little feet' (Banville, 1995: 118)).[4] But ultimately, A. is less a person than a cipher, a receptacle for Freddie's amorphous desires. Before embarking on the narrator's task of quotidian description, he playfully asks, for instance, 'what shall I dress my dolly in today?' (98). Their entire relationship is a kind of sinister game of make-believe or dress-up, a sustained flirtation with the boundary between fantasy and painful reality (sex, for Freddie, is 'the act, as it is interestingly called', and she plays 'her part' with enthusiasm, though she seems to him 'more interested in the stage directions than the text' (121–2)). She asks him to tell her about his life, and he is 'evasive'; she lies to him about hers but he thinks of them 'not as lies but inventions, rather, improvisations, true fictions' (122). Though it emerges by the end of the novel that she is in fact the daughter, rather aptly, of 'The Da' (and that she was all along positioned as a bait to lure him into a plot to authenticate a collection of forged paintings) she tells him of her invented family, her Swiss diplomat father and her American mother who hails, variously, from Mississippi, Missouri and Missoula.[5] Freddie willingly plays along and, prompted by the 'ominous hints' she drops about her father, imagines a Lolita/Humbert-style relationship with 'a dark, sleek-haired *gentilhomme*, sinisterly handsome – see his skier's tan, his chocolate-dark eyes, his multi-jewelled watch – idly fondling a pale little girl perched in his lap' (123). Each of them knows that the other is lying about who he or she is, but these lies are an integral part of the 'act' that is their relationship. The more or less explicit fictionality of such biographical particulars emphasises the importance of the role played in this relationship by pure invention.

Freddie's insulation of the 'bogey-man' he knows to be contained within him – his concealment, that is to say, of his murderous past, of his True Self – gradually develops into a kind of experimentation with intransigent biographical fact. He toys with the possibility of revelation. 'I know a man,' he tells her, 'who killed a woman once' (127). Evidently more aroused than appalled, she asks him who this man killed, and his reply speaks to the vexed relationship between truth and falsehood that is at the heart of the novel:

> 'A maid in a rich man's house.' How quaint it sounded, like some-thing out of the Brothers Grimm. The bad thief went to the rich man's mansion to steal a picture and when the maid got in his way he hit her on the head and killed her dead. 'Then they took him away,' I said, 'and locked him up and made him swallow the key'. (Banville, 1995: 128)

Rather than presenting fiction as fact, the strategy here is precisely the opposite. The prospect of real connection – of confession leading to redemptive communication – is thus undermined by this treatment of the truth about oneself as a danger to be flirted with, as a psycho-sexual gambit.

Again and again in *Athena*, the tense equipoise between what Winnicott calls the 'urgent need to communicate and the still more urgent need not to be found' is dramatised. The sexual *divertissements* which account for much of the intellectual substance of the novel are all, in one way or another, about revelation and concealment; they are all concerned, as it were, with being watched but not seen. A. devises an elaborate game whereby she and Freddie arrange to meet in the house where he is supposed to be working on the paintings, and he will sometimes (but, crucially, not always) observe her through a specially installed spyhole in the wall for half an hour before the arranged time. She performs a series of strange charades, pretending to entertain an unseen guest, sometimes even moving 'her lips in soundless speech, with exaggerated effect, like the heroine in a silent film' (156). The tableaux, Freddie tells us, inevitably moved from a mood of 'elaborate politenesses' to 'an atmosphere of menace', with sexual violence invariably creeping into the performance. Thus A. seems to hint, in her narcissistic display of sadomasochistic fantasy, at a knowledge of Freddie's inner 'bogey-man'. Her False Self expression is aimed, in a sense, both at concealing her own True Self and insinuating a knowledge of his. Another of her games involves Freddie blindfolding her, binding her hands and positioning her naked in front of a street-facing window, whilst narrating for her the precise reactions of the people watching her (again, though, he only pretends to place her in front of the window, until she requests that he do it for real).What is most curious, and most disturbing, about all of this is that her exhibitionism seems to be more about concealment than revelation: in displaying herself, she is paradoxically obscuring what she appears to be revealing. It all seems a kind of front, or a convoluted tease: 'She desired to be seen, she said, to be a spectacle, to have her most intimate secrets purloined and betrayed. Yet I ask myself now if they really were her secrets that she offered up on the altar of our passion or just variations invented for this or that occasion' (158–9). Winnicott conceived of human relationships, as we have seen, in terms of a highly sophisticated, and highly fraught, game of hide-and-seek. The relationship at the centre of *Athena* consistently illustrates this paradigm, and frequently pushes the notion of such game-play out of the realm of metaphor and into the literal space of real actions, of symbolically weighted performances.

For both of them, lying becomes a kind of end in itself. This pretence – which Freddie refers to as 'the fragile theatre of illusions we had erected to house our increasingly exotic performances' – is a source of intense pleasure. 'How keen the dark and tender thrill that shot through me when in the throes of passion she cried out my assumed – my false – name and for a second a phantom other, my jettisoned self, joined us and made a ghostly troilism of our panting labours' (160). When A. takes him to a brothel in order to make love to her in front of a prostitute, he feels, as he puts it, 'perused' and is unable to maintain an erection, but she insists that he 'pretend' and so they perform a charade for the prostitute. She invests herself thoroughly in the performance, biting and thrashing and 'crying out foul words, things that she never did when we were alone and not pretending, or not pretending as much as we were now' (164–5). Freddie's admission of feeling 'perused' is worth examining here: the term suggests a good deal more intensity than merely being observed. Freddie cannot perform, as it were, precisely because he feels vulnerable, exposed. The threat of being 'found', in Winnicott's sense of the term – and perhaps, in another sense, of being 'found out' – appears to be what is overwhelming him here, and forcing him to substitute one kind of performance, or 'act', for another. The core of his True Self, which for Freddie is both threatening and threatened, is what, in Winnicott's words 'must never be communicated with or be influenced by external reality' (Winnicott, 1965: 187).

This treacherous dalliance between performance and reality finally reaches a fatal convergence when A. requests that Freddie beat her during sex, urging him to '"*Hit me, hit me like you hit her*"' (Banville, 1995: 171 [emphasis in original]). Crucially, the self-image Freddie employs at this instant is that of an 'animal caught on open ground' – one which recalls Winnicott's notion of the threat to the True Self as being more intense than that of 'being eaten alive by cannibals'. He is finally left without any doubt, at this point, that he has been found. He consents to inflicting a series of 'tender beatings', and derives a 'frightful exultation at being allowed such licence' (174). Much like Felix in *Ghosts*, A. possesses the strange power to lay bare the part of himself Freddie desperately wishes to conceal. She wields it, however, more subtly and finally more damagingly, because she makes him complicit. The harder he hits her the more free he begins to feel; the more violent he becomes, the less clear it is who is the victim and who the aggressor. This violent performance is, as a ritual re-enactment of past violence, a *release* in both a sexual and an existential sense. The image of the monster, the primitive and instinctual predator, as representative of the authentic inner self is a significant one here, not least in the way in which it contrasts to the previous image of the inner self as a hunted animal:

> I saw myself towering over her like a maddened monster out of Goya, hirsute and bloody and irresistible. Morrow the Merciless. It was ridiculous, of course, and yet not ridiculous at all. I was monster and at the same time man. She would thrash under my blows [...] and I would not stop, no, I would not stop. And all the time something was falling away from me, the accretion of years, flakes of it shaking free and falling with each stylised blow that I struck. (Banville, 1995: 174–5)

This image of Freddie is in many ways a classic Banvillean representation of authenticity as a form of quasi-artistic self-creation. He is a monster here, but he is a monster out of a Goya etching and his blows are 'stylised'. The more he indulges his violent inner self, the more he shakes off the 'accretion of years' – the protective layers of the False Self which have grown around his animalistic core – and the more he becomes like a work of art. There is, disturbingly, something of the creative act about this oddly formalised sexual violence. Winnicott asserts that 'the spontaneous gesture is the True Self in action' and that 'only the True Self can be creative and only the True Self can feel real' (Winnicott, 1996: 17). What this represents, then, is the emergence of Freddie's True Self in its most feral form. The paradoxical crux is that Freddie has released, or exposed, what appears to be his truly authentic inner core through a kind of performance. Through the re-enactment of his most terrible deeds, he has liberated some essential part of himself in a way that recalls *The Book of Evidence*: 'To do the worst thing, the very worst thing, that's the way to be free' (Banville, 1995: 124). From the very beginning of the Art Trilogy, Freddie has always identified his inner self – the self he refers to in *The Book of Evidence* as 'Bunter' – with the monstrous and the unappeasably bloodthirsty. One of the things that sustains Freddie's story through the three books is the pivotal tension between what he appears to be and what he believes himself to be at his core – the tension, in other words, between the performance and the reality it attempts to mask. In *Ghosts*, Freddie says he agrees with Diderot – and one suspects Banville does too – about 'how much of life is a part that we play', about how living is 'a form of necessary hypocrisy, each man acting out his part, posing as himself'. Freddie's problem would appear to be that he is both overly invested in his role and insufficiently persuaded by it – a condition that could be identified as uniquely narcissistic. 'I am not convincing, somehow,' as he puts it, 'even to myself' (1993a: 198).

Shroud evinces a similar concern with the idea of personality as a carefully staged performance, as character rather than self. As with Freddie in *Ghosts* and *Athena*, the elements that constitute Axel Vander's social identity – his name, the details of his past, the epiphenomena of his personality – are all consciously assumed. Like Freddie, too, he takes a kind of perverse delight in his own inauthenticity. 'What a fabulist I was; what an artist!' as he declares (2002: 43). Elsewhere, he speaks of the work he has invested into making his performance credible: 'So difficult it was, to judge just so, to forge the fine discriminations, to maintain a balance – no one could know how difficult. If it had been a work of art I was fashioning they would have applauded my mastery' (7).

In *Shroud*, Banville once more scrutinises the dialectic of the True and the False Self. When Cass Cleave appears in Vander's life, she brings his suppressed past with her. Cass has been tipped off about Vander's shameful wartime past by a character named Max Schaudeine, whom Banville endows with just enough detail for us to suspect that he is yet another incarnation of the protean Felix. Vander's physical description of him tallies with the descriptions of Felix in *Mefisto* and *Ghosts* – a vulpine figure with striking red hair, a mocking smile and comically ill-fitting clothes. Schaudeine is introduced as having hair of 'an almost orange shade, wearing 'a grin of happy malice' and 'shapeless trousers too long in the leg' with a too-tight overcoat (92–3). The name 'Schaudeine' hints at the unmasking role the character plays in the story: 'Schau', in German, means 'to show', 'to display', or 'to exhibit'; 'deine' means 'yours'. It was Schaudeine who, as an operative of the occupying Nazi forces, facilitated Vander's adoption of his false identity and aided his escape from Belgium to England. He does this, apparently, for no cause more noble than his own amoral entertainment. As Vander puts it, 'I suspect he saved me […] for no other reason than that it amused him that I had escaped seizure and deportation simply by not being at home' (163). So it is Schaudeine who enables Vander's self-reinvention, just as it is he who finally blows the whistle on

Vander's False Self, using Cass Cleave as a proxy. In this respect, he occupies a similar role to Felix in *Ghosts*: he is the possessor of dangerous knowledge, the insinuating and nebulous figure who embodies the shameful truth about the protagonist's real self.

The philosophical question at the centre of *Shroud* is that of the existence or non-existence of the self, an issue which has defined Vander's academic career. His professional insistence on the insubstantiality of the self – indeed, on the speciousness of the very notion – is one which, as discussed in Chapter 1, serves Vander remarkably well. Living in the American West Coast academic enclave of Arcady (a gentle caricaturing, presumably, of Berkeley) he remarks that there are 'times when that entire coastal strip seems a film set and everyone on it a character actor' (15). The relationship he falls into with the aristocratic Laura in England is repeatedly registered, on both sides, as a performance. All he sees of her, he recalls, is 'the brittle, bright facade she chose to present to the world at large' (172). So, although his conviction that inauthenticity is the natural order of things is largely self-serving, Vander's philosophical positions do appear to be genuinely, if tentatively, held. At times, however, he finds himself unable to shake the suspicion that there is indeed such a thing as a self:

> I spent the best part of what I suppose I must call my career trying to drum into those who would listen among the general mob of resistant sentimentalists surrounding me the simple lesson that there is no self: no ego, no precious individual spark breathed into each one of us by a bearded patriarch in the sky, who does not exist either. And yet ... For all my insistence, and to my secret shame, I admit that even I cannot entirely rid myself of the conviction of an enduring core of selfhood amid the welter of the world, a kernel immune to any gale that might pluck the leaves from the almond tree and make the sustaining branches swing and shake. (Banville, 2002: 18)

The substance of this idea can be seen as broadly Winnicottian, in that it posits an inner self which is steadfastly separate from the world as a whole – one which is literally self-contained. Moreover, the language used to express it is remarkably reminiscent of Winnicott's distinctive psychoanalytic idiolect. Winnicott, as we have seen, employs similar images of cores and kernels in his description of a True Self which is insulated from the world of experience. The novel's typically multivalent title reflects this central concern with protection and secretion, referring as it does to any number of 'shrouds': the (fraudulent) winding sheet of Christ; the shroud of obfuscation within which Vander protects his true identity; the narrative itself, shrouded in ambiguity. What is ultimately shrouded, however, is Vander, and the narrative is that which shrouds him. The novel's recurrent use of the motif of masks underlines this preoccupation with self-concealment and self-protection. Vander, for instance, is repeatedly identified with the Harlequin, the masked and mute jester who was a stock character of the Italian *commedia dell'arte*. The Turin Shroud, to which Cass and Vander make a failed pilgrimage, is also continually linked to the latter's inveterate inauthenticity. Widely believed to be a medieval hoax, it provides a spectral image of a false face at the centre of the novel. Like Winnicott's False Self, what it claims to reveal (the face of Christ) it rather serves to obscure and falsify. When Cass tries to tell Vander about its history, he dismisses her by telling her that 'he knew about fakes' and asks her derisively whether she really believes 'it was the image of the crucified Christ?' (196). When she points out that the image of the face on the shroud looks just like him, we are left in little doubt as to the emblematic position the relic occupies in the novel. For Vander, as for Banville, to be human is to be guilty of fraud. Dishonesty, rather than disobedience, is the original sin that defines mankind in Banville's moral universe. Lies, as Vander puts it, 'are life's almost-anagram' (8).

The fundamental conundrum of the novel is one which is never resolved, perhaps because such a resolution is unattainable. Namely, if there is no such thing as the self, as Vander claims to believe, what precisely is the nature of his crime in pretending to be someone he is not? There can be no doubt as to his profound inauthenticity, which is literally inscribed on every page of his story, but the question this story raises above all others is whether an authentic existence might be possible and, if so, what it might be like. The most that Vander can offer by way of an answer is the cryptic and profoundly paradoxical remark that 'to be someone else is to be one thing, and one thing only' (181). We can view this sentiment as being consistent with Freddie's comment in *Ghosts* about his determination to make of himself a 'monomorph' or 'monad'. What is at issue here, once more, is the narcissistic desire for self-unity which is such a major theme of Banville's work. By investing himself entirely into the False Self component of his personality, Vander is seeking a way to circumvent the 'insupportable medley of affects, desires, fears, tics, twitches' that constitutes 'mere being' – what Philip Roth refers to as 'the terrible ambiguity of the I' (Roth, 1990: 98). Winnicott's observation in 'Ego Distortion in Terms of the True and False Self' about actors who are 'completely at a loss when not in a role' seems to be particularly germane here. Like his counterpart Alexander Cleave in *Eclipse*, Vander is totally confounded by his own subjectivity when not performing a narcissistic version of himself. In an effort to explain the importance of disguise to his conception of himself, Vander imagines a veteran 'actor of the ancient world [...] an old trouper'. This actor, when onstage, always wears a mask which he considers his 'talisman' (Banville, 2002: 181). Gradually, this mask becomes more familiar to him than his own face:

> Increasingly, indeed, he thinks the mask is more like his own face than his face is. At the end of a performance when he takes it off he wonders if the other actors can see him at all, or if he is just a head with a blank front, like the old statue of Silenius in the marketplace the features of which the weather has entirely worn away. He takes to wearing the mask at home, when no one is there. It is a comfort, it sustains him; he finds it wonderfully restful, it is like being asleep and yet conscious. Then one day he comes to the table wearing it. His wife makes no remark, his children stare for a moment, then shrug and go back to their accustomed bickering. He has achieved his apotheosis. Man and mask are one. (Banville, 2002: 181–2)

'Apotheosis', in its associations with the ideas of self-perfection and deification, is a key term in Banville's later work. As we have discussed, the narcissistic content of the word as he tends to use it is connected to the notion of the self as a work of art. Self-synthesis, as always, is an overriding concern. If Vander never reaches his own apotheosis, his own ascension to monadic harmony, it is because he never manages to become one with the mask he wears. There are too many conflicting self-images ricocheting about his text, too many echoes and doppelgängers surrounding him for his fragmented self-image to ever cohere. He never believes fully enough in his own performance; he is, like Freddie Montgomery, unconvincing even to himself. Like so many of the postures and impostures in Banville's novels, Vander's are arranged to conceal something which may not actually be there. The True Self, the self which his entire persona is intended to mask, may finally be a chimera. When Vander remarks that he is 'a thing made up wholly of poses', we might understand him to mean that his entire existence is contingent upon being seen. This, as we have observed, is how Winnicott conceives of the False Self: 'When I look I am seen so I exist' (Winnicott, 2005: 154). Because Vander has lived his entire life under the awareness or illusion of 'being constantly under scrutiny', he is, as he puts it, 'all frontage'. If the question with which *Shroud* begins – 'Who speaks?' – is that which motivates everything that follows, the answer Vander seems to be suggesting here is 'no one'. 'I have manufactured a voice, as once I manufactured a reputation, from material filched from others. The accent you hear is not mine, for I have no accent' (Banville, 2002: 210).

What links *Ghosts*, *Athena* and *Shroud* is their overriding concern with the ways in which identities are performed; the novels are also engaged with the ways in which the masks people wear can, over time, come to usurp the faces they once served to protect and conceal. Amongst the most perplexing problems presented by Banville's fiction is that of the relationship between truth and falsehood. Is authenticity constituted merely in what is believed to be true of a person and what that person believes to be true of themselves? Is there a point, to phrase it in Winnicott's terms, when the False Self to all practical purposes *becomes* the True Self, and the True Self ceases to exist? If we conceive of the self, as Freddie Montgomery and Axel Vander do, as a kind of ongoing work of art, and if we accept the permeability of that self's boundaries as a condition of its existence in the world, must we then accept that there is no such thing as an 'enduring core of selfhood'? Despite the protagonists' exhaustive attempts to answer these questions, there is always a sense of their ultimate insolubility.

Psychoanalysis is premised on the idea that each of us is, to a greater or lesser extent, concealed from ourselves; that we are never – or never just – the people we recognise ourselves to be. For a theoretical system that is aimed, however indirectly, at self-knowledge, it is staunchly sceptical about the viability, as categories, of 'self' and 'knowledge'. Freud was notoriously mistrustful of the idea of biography, of the belief that it was somehow possible to tell the truth about a whole life. Psychoanalysis, in this sense, has always advanced the view that every self is a False Self, that we are never who we would have people, ourselves included, believe we are. As such, Winnicott makes explicit and specific something that was always, in Freud's writing, implicit and general.

The view of relationships in Banville's fiction as elaborate games of revelation and concealment shares a profound affinity with Winnicott's hide-and-seek notion of intersubjectivity. Novels such as *Ghosts*, *Athena* and *Shroud* are motivated by the question of what constitutes a True Self; by the question of whether such a thing exists and, were it to exist, what form its revelation might take. Perhaps the ultimate question these novels present us with is whether, when it comes to the vexed issue of selfhood, such concepts of truth and falsehood are even applicable. If, as Winnicott tells us, secrecy and self-enclosure are primary components of the way in which we relate (or fail to relate) to one another, Banville's fiction confronts an elemental and unsettling aspect of human experience.

5
Shame

The topic of shame is one which previous chapters of this book have touched upon in various ways. What has thus far been implicit in much of the discussion is something that this chapter will aim to make explicit: that shame is a key issue in Banville's work and that it is inseparable from that of narcissism. It is a central affect throughout the *oeuvre*, prominent to varying degrees in the protagonists of each of the novels and, while this chapter will make reference to many of these works in support of its argument, it is *The Untouchable, Shroud* and *The Sea* that will provide the foundation of this discussion.

In order to clarify the sense (or senses) in which I am using the term 'shame' here, and in order to define its fundamental connection to narcissism, it will be useful at this point to provide some context with regard to the ways in which this term is understood within psychoanalytic theory. Like almost all psychoanalytic concepts, shame is defined and positioned in a variety of ways by a variety of theorists. Though there is no strict agreement on its overall importance or on its relationship to narcissism, there is enough broad consensus to satisfy the need for a useful definition. Among those psychoanalysts who have written on the topic, there is agreement that shame is the result of some shortfall between a person's idealised image of him- or herself and the reality.

The notion of what Freud in his early writings called the 'ego ideal' is central to a psychoanalytic conception of shame. In one way or another, it is the ego ideal which lies at the root of almost every major theorist's understanding of the term. The concept was first introduced by Freud in 'On Narcissism' in 1914 and, just as narcissism was subsequently neglected as a metapsychological principle by Freud, the ego ideal was, by the time he wrote *The Ego and the Id* in 1923, radically revised to become the superego. For Freud, while the superego is born of the Oedipus complex, the ego ideal is born of primary narcissism. It is, as he puts it:

> now the target of self-love which was enjoyed in childhood by the actual ego. The subject's narcissism makes its appearance displaced on to this new ideal ego, which, like the infantile ego, finds itself possessed of every perfection that is of value. As always where the libido is concerned, man has here again shown himself incapable of giving up a satisfaction he had once enjoyed. He is not willing to forgo the narcissistic perfection of his childhood: and when, as he grows up, he is disturbed by the admonitions of others and by the awakening of his own critical judgement, so that he can no longer retain that perfection, he seeks to recover it in the new form of an ego ideal. What he projects before him as his ideal is the substitute for the lost narcissism of his childhood in which he was his own ideal. (Freud, 1986: 36)

In formulating their concepts of shame, those post-Freudian theorists who have written on the topic have almost all used this notion of the ego ideal, or some version of it. Annie Reich was one of the first to specifically link shame to Freud's ego ideal and, thereby, to narcissism. 'Pathologic Forms of Self-Esteem Regulation' (1960) explores how narcissistic personalities heighten their self-esteem through vividly grandiose self-images, and how they suffer painful feelings of worthlessness and narcissistic rage when these self-images are not realised. These pathological narcissists, Reich maintains, are subject to violent vacillations in their levels of self-esteem. Reich stresses the suddenness with which such people can be overwhelmed with shame upon incurring narcissistic injuries.

The link between – and the consubstantiality of – shame and narcissism is almost universally recognised in psychoanalysis. Theories vary as to the specifics of this relationship, but that it exists and that it is important are not in doubt. The broad psychoanalytic consensus about shame is that it is proportionate to the distance between a person's narcissistic self-conception and the reality it never wholly succeeds in masking. In *Intimacies*, their collection of collaborative essays about what they term 'impersonal narcissism', Adam Phillips and Leo Bersani connect the concept explicitly to that of shame: 'In shame we are (violently) separated from our preferred image of ourselves – in psychoanalytic language we betray or sacrifice our ego ideal – and so to bear with the experience of shame, to go through it rather than be paralysed by mortification, is to yield to a radical reconfiguration of oneself' (Bersani and Phillips, 2008: 110). It is in shame that we see our illusions about ourselves for what they are, faced with the 'unbridgeable gulf between who one feels oneself to be, and who one should be' (116).

One of the things at which Banville is especially adept is bringing to light the ways in which people's preferred images of themselves are always at variance with reality. His protagonists are endlessly pre-occupied by their own grandiose ideas about themselves, and many of his most vivid and memorable passages are concerned with what happens when the world refuses to reflect these notions. A central symbol in the *oeuvre* is that of the statue. It occurs, in one way or another, in almost every novel from *The Book of Evidence* onwards. In *Ghosts*, Freddie references Diderot's imperative that we 'become sculptors of the self' through 'a kind of artistic striving, cutting and shaping the material of which we are made, the intransigent stone of self-hood, and erecting an idealised effigy of ourselves in our own minds and in the minds of those around us' (Banville, 1993a: 196). The notion is restated in similar terms by Victor Maskell in *The Untouchable*. He tells Vivienne 'Baby' Brevoort, the young woman who will later become his wife, about his fascination with Diderot's statue theory:

> Diderot said that what we do is, we erect a statue in our own image inside ourselves – idealised, you know, but still recognisable – and then spend our lives engaged in the effort to make ourselves into its likeness. This is the moral imperative. I think it's awfully clever, don't you? I know that's how *I* feel. Only there are times when I can't tell which is the statue and which is me. (Banville, 1997b: 86)

This idea of a platonic form of personal identity, of an internal model against which one continually measures oneself, clearly has a great deal in common with the concept of the ego ideal.

The imaginary statue spoken of by Freddie Montgomery and Victor Maskell represents a petrification of their own narcissism, a permanent standard possessed, as Freud puts it, 'of every perfection that is of value'. Though Max Morden in *The Sea* does not use Diderot's metaphor, his narrative is scattered with references to an ideal self-conception that is notably similar in its imagery. He writes at one point of entering a party in London with his wife Anna, and the self-depiction he conjures evokes, in its static majesty, the notion of the statue. 'How grand we must have looked,' he marvels, 'the two of us making our entrance, taller than everyone else, our gaze directed over their heads as if fixed on some fine vista that only we were privileged enough to see' (2005c: 101). The monumentalism of the image resonates with a description just two pages earlier of a much older Max and Anna, in the immediate aftermath of her diagnosis with fatal stomach cancer. They lie in bed together, cowed by the cruel blow reality has dealt them, 'side by side in the darkness, toppled statues of ourselves' (99). One interpretation these paired images appear to invite is that the inevitable intrusion of reality upon our self-deceptions is a kind of deposition of the ego ideal, a violent overthrow of narcissism's symbolic mastery over the imagination.

The similarities between *The Untouchable*, *Shroud* and *The Sea*, and between their protagonists, are striking. Both Victor Maskell and Max Morden are art historians, although the former has reached the apex of his profession while the latter is, by his own admission, little more than a dilettante. Both come from lower-middle-class Irish backgrounds, and both marry upper-class English women whose sophisticated families are repeatedly described in such a way as to vividly contrast with their own. Both men are eventually widowed, and have fraught, but ultimately (and uncharacteristically) loving, relationships with daughters whose guilelessness is a perennial source of bewilderment to them. *Shroud*'s Axel Vander is also an ageing academic, who comes from a lower-middle-class background of which he is deeply ashamed, though he is a Flemish Jew rather than an Irishman. He is also recently widowed, although it eventually becomes apparent that he has had a hand in facilitating the death of his senile wife.

A particularly significant aspect of these three novels is the shame felt by their protagonists about their unsophisticated backgrounds, and how this continually reoccurs in various guises throughout their lives. In *The Untouchable*, Maskell's polished and urbane persona as a successful Cambridge academic and mover within London society circles belies the obscure shame he feels at his bourgeois Irish origins. His Ulster upbringing by his Church of Ireland bishop father, and stepmother Hettie, is a source of acute social discomfort for him in his English life, and he is almost agonisingly attuned to perceived slights about his Irishness. Social class is certainly an issue – the milieu Maskell moves in, as a Soviet double agent at the heart of the British establishment, is overwhelmingly upper class and aristocratic – but it is one which is secondary to, and in certain respects a corollary of, his Irishness. Maskell clearly considers himself to have outgrown and transcended the moral certainties and cultural crudeness of his background. He imagines himself, at one point, as having undergone 'the exquisite agony of the caterpillar turning itself into a butterfly, pushing out eye-stalks, pounding its fat cells into iridescent wing-dust, at last cracking the mother-of-pearl sheath and staggering upright on sticky, hair's-breadth legs, drunken, gasping, dazed by the light' (Banville, 1997b: 63). In these peculiar self-images – of the embryonic and the mature, the gauche and the graceful – can be glimpsed Maskell's internalised iconography of shame and aspiration. His condition is that of the butterfly which cannot quite erase the consciousness of its larval origins.

One of the novel's most painfully funny sections is that in which Maskell is persuaded by Nick Brevoort, with whom he is secretly infatuated, to take him on a trip back to Ireland to visit his family home. It emerges towards the end of the novel that Nick has all along also been a Soviet double agent unbeknownst to his friend, and that it is he who eventually betrays him. Eibhear Walshe highlights the significance of the fact that Nick is the only one of Maskell's English friends to visit Carrickdrum, his family home near Belfast, and that he is 'thus aware of his weak point and armed with knowledge of his source of vulnerability' (Walshe, 2006: 109). Maskell wonders, indeed, whether Nick's intention was 'to get the goods on me, nose out my family secrets [...] place me in my class?' (Banville, 1997b: 63). In a novel where much of the dramatic tension is provided by the persistent threat of exposure, this fear of being placed in one's class is a constant presence. It is there in moments like this, where Maskell is jolted out of his complacency by Corporal Haig, his inferior in both social class and military rank, who casually raises the issue of his Irishness:

> 'Mind my enquiring, sir, but were you called up or did you join?'
> 'Good heavens,' I said, 'what a question. Why do you ask?'
> 'Well, I just wondered, you being Irish and all.'
> I registered the familiar faint shock, like a soot-fall in a chimney.
> 'Do I seem very Irish to you, Haig?'
> He looked at me askance, and chuckled.
> 'Oh, no, sir, no,' he said, and lowered his face over his soup plate.
> 'Not so's you'd notice.' (Banville, 1997b: 210–11)

Here we are given the impression of an Irishman trying his utmost to appear English, putting in what he considers to be a convincing performance, and being made to realise that the pretence is in reality quite obvious. The social comic set-piece, as narrated by Maskell, is made all the more masochistically funny by the fact that it takes place over a dinner in France ('an informal mingling of the ranks') in which Maskell insists that his Cockney companion sample oysters and drink the 'rather good local white' rather than the beer he would prefer. The social awkwardness is, at first, all on Haig's side as he waits to see which pieces of cutlery his cultured fellow diner will pick up first and as he fumbles with the oysters, 'making them clack like false teeth' (210). At the merest mention of Maskell's Irishness, though, the old insecurities come to the fore. Maskell imagines him 'sitting in the canteen at HQ with his fellow drivers, a mug in one hand and a fag in the other, putting on a snooty face and mimicking my accent: *But my dear Haig, I'm hardly Oirish at all, at all*' (211).

So when Maskell travels to Ireland with Nick, he is undertaking considerably more than just a trip home. He is risking laying himself bare, exposing himself to the obscure shame of his nationality, of not being English (of being, to paraphrase Beckett, the *opposite* of English). His experience is in line with the psychoanalysts John O'Leary and Fred White's description of shame as 'a sudden, painful experience of being seen by present and/or internalized others as defective, debased or weak in a manner that seems to capture a selectively unattended truth about oneself'. Such an experience, they claim, is characterised by 'the sense that one's private world has been punctured and that one stands helplessly and glaringly revealed' (O'Leary and White, 1986: 330). As their train approaches Carrickdrum, Maskell is seized by a conviction that he has done something very foolish in bringing the sophisticated, cosmopolitan Nick to his home. He is deeply ashamed of his family and his place of origin, and in travelling there he feels he is exposing himself. There is a ruthless, almost self-lacerating quality to Maskell's description of his own mortification at the backwardness of the world he has come from:

> By now I had realised the full magnitude of the mistake I had made in bringing him here. The home returned to is a concatenation of sadnesses that makes one want to weep and at the same time sets the teeth on edge. How dingy the place looked. And that smell! – tired, brownish, intimate, awful. I was ashamed of everything, and ashamed of myself for being ashamed. I could hardly bear to look at my shabby father and his fat wife. (Banville, 1997b: 68)

Maskell's humiliation is palpable in the sad contempt of those four words: 'tired, brownish, intimate, awful'. If the smell is 'intimate' and 'awful', it is because it somehow hints at something obscurely shameful about Maskell himself, about his past. The 'shabby father and his fat wife', the Ulster fry he fears will be 'slapped' down in front of Nick – each detail adds to the intensity of Maskell's discomfiture. He can barely stand to look at his mentally handicapped brother Freddie; it is as though Freddie's condition somehow implicated Maskell himself. When Freddie makes his first appearance, 'lumbering diagonally across the lawn to meet us with his arms spread, grinning and gibbering', Nick – to whom Maskell has not even mentioned having a brother – asks whether Freddie is the son of the gardener and handyman who has been sent to pick them up at the ferry. Maskell's wordless response speaks volumes: 'In my agitation and shame', he admits, 'all I did was shake my head and look away' (65). As appalled as he is by the general character of his family home, it is Freddie, he admits, who is his 'greatest shame'. As children, he says, he 'had not minded him, deeming it right [...] that anyone born into the family after me should be defective' (68). In the presence of Nick, however, he is forced to see him as he imagines his friend must, as 'a poor, shambling, damaged thing with my high forehead and prominent upper jaw'. His shame is such that he finds himself in a 'hot sweat of embarrassment' and unable to 'meet Nick's amused, quizzical gaze' (69).

That Freddie bears a physical resemblance to his older sibling is a crucial detail here. Maskell is not so much ashamed of Freddie as he is ashamed of himself for having him as a brother. He is ashamed, in a way that he never quite brings himself to articulate, of the part of himself that *is* Freddie. He sees him with Nick's eyes – through the eyes of the Other – and what he sees in that physical resemblance is a kind of primitive, brute version of himself. His inability to meet Nick's gaze, his 'hot sweat of embarrassment': these reactions seem close to what one might expect to experience at a moment of exposure, of nakedness. Shame, as Sartre puts it, 'is in its primary structure shame *before somebody* [...] the Other is the indispensable mediator between myself and me. I am ashamed of myself *as I appear* to the Other' (Sartre, 1943: 221–2 [emphasis in original]). The person who experiences shame is, like Narcissus in Ovid's myth, seeing him- or herself as though through the eyes of another. Maskell, in returning to Ireland, sees himself through Nick's English eyes and is deeply ashamed of what he sees. 'Experiences of shame', as Helen M. Lynd writes, 'appear to embody the root meaning of the word – to uncover, to expose, to wound. They are experiences of exposure, exposure of peculiarly sensitive, intimate, vulnerable aspects of the self' (Lynd, 1958: 27–8).

There are moments of exquisite social comedy here, too, when Maskell's pretensions to social superiority, his image of himself as a 'polished man of the world', are undermined by his family's lack of sophistication (Banville, 1997b: 91). At one point, during a discussion about the ongoing rise of fascism in Europe and the possibility of war, Maskell's mortification at his father's *naïveté* is palpable. That it is compounded by a parallel humiliation at the provincial dreariness of the food being served – a traditional Irish dish called 'fadge' – makes for a bitterly funny scene:

'Say what you like about Chamberlain,' he said, 'but he remembers the Great War, the cost of it.'
I glared at a sausage, thinking what a hopeless booby my father was.
'Peace in our time,' Hettie murmured, sighing.

'Oh, but there *will* be a war,' Nick said equably, 'despite the appeasers. What is this, by the way?'
'Fadge,' Mary blurted, and blushed the harder, making for the door.
'Potato cake,' I said between clenched teeth. 'Local delicacy.'
Two days ago I had been chatting with the King.
'Mm,' Nick said, 'delicious.' (Banville, 1997b: 69)

There is something not just about the constitution of this potato-based 'local delicacy', but also the word 'fadge' itself – its almost comical stodginess as a spoken sound – that bespeaks a terrible lack of sophistication. That Maskell's father should foist his uninformed, provincial opinions about the war on someone like Nick Brevoort is bad enough; that it should be compounded by the serving of such humiliatingly humble fare as mashed potatoes fried in bacon grease is unforgivable.

At this point, Maskell observes his father 'blinking in distress' as the light streaming through the kitchen window 'glinted on his balding pate'. Rather than being struck by the peculiar pathos of this sight, he indulges his tendency to reduce others to caricatures: 'Trollope, I thought; he's a character out of Trollope – one of the minor ones' (70). It is suggestive of just how little regard Maskell has for his father that he cannot conceive of him as anything other than a minor creation of a writer he would presumably consider to be likewise minor. Shortly thereafter, as they stroll through the village, Nick approvingly calls Maskell's father 'a fighter', and his response is ruthlessly dismissive: '"You think so? Just another bourgeois liberal, I would have said"' (72).

The low comedy of Maskell's own family – at one point he frets that the visit will disintegrate into 'ruinous farce' – is vividly contrasted with the sophistication of Nick's home (66). The Brevoorts are wholly consistent with Maskell's idealised notion of the cultured and cosmopolitan family. The novel's first flashback relates his first visit, in 1929, to their North Oxford house to discuss with Nick's father, Max, the possibility of his publishing an essay Maskell has written (10). It is also Maskell's first encounter with Nick, with whom he becomes immediately infatuated. The house is characterised by what he calls 'slovenly opulence', with 'lots of faded silk and *objets* supposedly of great value [...] and a rank smell everywhere of some sort of burnt incense'. Of the cluster of details here, the faded silk is a particularly effective emblem of the combined qualities of wealth and apparent indifference to it that the young Maskell seems especially to revere. He is impressed, too, by the house's atmosphere, which has 'something thrillingly suppressed in it, as if at any moment the most amazing events might suddenly begin to happen' (10). The brief scene ends with an image of explicitly self-conscious theatricality, a *tableau vivant* the composition of which likely owes more to Maskell's memory than to reality: 'I backed out and the three of them held their places, as if waiting for applause, the parents beaming and Nick darkly amused. Baby was still upstairs, playing her jazz and rehearsing for her entrance in act two' (12–13).

The contrast between the two families, and the two social worlds they inhabit, could hardly be more pronounced, the one with which Maskell identifies himself hardly more clear. He immediately recognises in the beau monde of the Brevoorts a vision of himself which he has long held as an ideal. Nick can be seen as what Kohut would refer to as a 'selfobject' or an 'idealised object' – as a partially internalised other forming a crucial aspect of Maskell's own preferred self-image. It is possible, therefore, to see Nick as the object upon which Maskell has projected his own idealised self-image, to view his idolisation of Nick as a kind of narcissistic object-love. He seems to come close to acknowledging this as the novel reaches its tragic ending (and *The Untouchable*, beneath its gleaming comic veneer, is essentially tragic in its form): 'That was what I was for,' he writes immediately before his suicide, 'that was always my task, to keep his image in place, to kneel before him humbly with head bowed and hold the mirror up to him, and in turn to hold his image up to the world's inspection' (390).[1] It is presumably no mere coincidence that, as the novel ends, Maskell has just finished what he refers to as a 'posthumous article' on 'erotic symbolism in Poussin's *Echo and Narcissus*' (397). That Maskell sees his relationship with Nick in the light of this classical myth seems plain. Poussin's painting, for instance, depicts Narcissus sleeping in the shade of a tree as a languishing Echo gazes on, sprawled against a rock, accompanied by an evidently impotent and frustrated Cupid. Maskell's first visit to the Brevoorts is described in similar terms: he waits in the garden, feeling 'foolish, dithering there' while Nick dozes in a hammock 'holding himself in his arms' (Banville's painterly eye is evident in the subtly symbolic significance of this detail, signalling as it does the self-contained impenetrability that will come to light as Nick's predominant characteristic). The final confrontation with a now-elderly Nick also takes place in a garden, and Maskell finds him there in repose against 'a great dense dark-green stand of laurel'. He wonders whether it is 'for me he had got himself up in this nice silk shirt, these slim-fitting slacks and slip-on shoes (with a decorative gold buckle on the instep, of course) and posed himself here against all this green?' (398–9). At the conclusion of this climactic scene – to which Maskell, with characteristically self-mocking portentousness, gives the title *The Agony in the Garden* – he notes that Nick has a bit of laurel stuck to his brow and is prompted to marvel at how he 'once thought him a god' (398, 404).

Maskell never feels wholly secure in, or deserving of, Nick's company. At one point, he describes their eating breakfast at Carrickdrum, imagining how they both must look to his father and his stepmother: 'Hettie and my father sat and watched us in a sort of hazy wonderment, as if we were a pair of immortals who had stopped off at their humble table on the way to some important piece of Olympian business elsewhere' (69). It is a moment that should perhaps be comical, but is in fact poignant. It isn't immediately clear what makes it so – whether it is the thought of the older couple actually conceiving of their son and his friend in this way, or the thought of their son imagining them doing so. Banville gives no indication that things might be otherwise than how Maskell sees them, so the reader can only guess at what the bishop and his wife might really be thinking. That Maskell is unable to conceive of his family as anything other than simple, goodhearted country folk is a consequence of his shame-ridden narcissism. Thus he assumes that they must be as in awe of him and his friend as he himself is, that they must see themselves as mortals in the presence of gods.

The relationship between Axel Vander and the original Vander family in *Shroud*, in many respects, is similar to that between the Maskells and the Brevoorts in *The Untouchable*, and between the Mordens and the Graces in *The Sea*. The difference here, however, is that Vander's shame is religious and racial in its origins, where Maskell's is national and class-based, and Morden's merely class-based. Mr Vander (the father of the original Axel Vander, that is, as distinct from the one who narrates the novel) is an extremely wealthy diamond merchant, and the family home is described as 'the very epitome of taste and discreet luxury' (Banville, 2002: 130). The narrator's father, by contrast, is a seller of second-hand clothes, and their home is a small flat, described as a 'dim warren'. The sensuous evocation of this Antwerp flat is remarkably similar to Maskell's description of his 'dingy' Carrickdrum family home, with its 'tired, brownish, intimate, awful' smell: *Shroud*'s narrator remembers his family's 'underground life', and has a sense of something 'torpid, brownish, exhausted'; the smell, as he puts it, 'is the smell of re-breathed air' (131).[2]

Like the Brevoorts and the Graces, the Vanders represent a far more desirable form of life against which the narrator projects his ego ideal: 'In those days [...] the Vanders were for me the very ideal of what a family should be: civilised, handsome, amused and amusing, at ease with themselves, knowing precisely their position in the world'. He sees himself 'moving amongst them, my face on fire with their reflected light, like a rough youth who has been invited up from the stew of groundlings to take part, in however small and passive a role, in the performance of a marvellous, sophisticated, glittering comedy of manners' (131). Once again, Banville employs a theatrical analogy to highlight the generic difference between the two families. But there is also a slyly anti-Semitic tone to these comparisons. The narrator, for instance, acknowledges that although his family are of a lower class than the Vanders, he 'had not exactly been spawned in an estaminet, as the poet so prettily puts it' (131). The poet referred to here is Eliot, and the poem is that which is most often submitted as evidence of his anti-Semitism, 'Gerontion', in which 'jew squats on the window sill' and is 'Spawned in some estaminet of Antwerp' (T. S. Eliot, 1974: 29). Eliot's spawned and squatting Jew – alien and external, yet proprietorial – is more a stylised hieroglyph for cultural degeneration than a character. Banville references this poisonous poetic image partly in order to connect *Shroud*'s narrator to a larger current of anti-Semitism in pre-war European culture, but primarily to identify the way in which he has internalised that loathing, channelling it into the larger reservoir of his own shame and self-hatred. The invocation of Eliot's Jew-as-rodent reverberates with the narrator's own descriptions of his family's 'underground life' and the 'low, dim warren' in which they live it.

Significantly, there is a parallel allusion in *The Untouchable*. In this case the poem is Yeats's 'Under Ben Bulben', the class contempt of which is as pronounced as the anti-Semitism of 'Gerontion'. After the section in which Maskell details the visit with Nick to Carrickdrum, he reveals that his father's family were in fact natives of Co. Mayo – 'the mighty O Measceoils, warriors, pirates, fierce clansmen all' – and that they were Catholics who, in order to avoid starving to death in the Famine, had 'changed their religion and Anglicised the family name and turned themselves into Yeats's hard-riding country gentlemen'. Despite telling his father he will take a trip to Mayo with Nick, he decides against it. He had no wish, as he puts it, to walk with Nick 'through the sites where had stood the stone cottages of my forebears and the base beds from which they had sprung' (Banville, 1997b: 77). What is intriguing here is the fusion, in the person of Maskell, of the twin poles of racial pride and class contempt that characterise Yeats's poem. In him, the 'hard-riding country gentlemen' exist in uneasy ascendancy over the 'base-born products of base beds' to whom he alludes (Yeats, 2001: 168).

Banville employs the imperious racial disdain of 'Gerontion' and 'Under Ben Bulben' as a way of dramatising the psychological chasm that exists between the narrators' idealised and actual selves, and the shame that arises out of that disparity. Axel Vander is both Jew and anti-Semite. The original Vander, whose name and identity he opportunistically appropriates, has made a name for himself writing a series of pro-Nazi articles arguing that 'nothing of consequence would be lost to the cultural and intellectual life of Europe' were the Jews to be 'removed' (Banville, 2002: 137). This is a sentiment with which the narrator largely agrees, taking issue only with its lack of vehemence. 'I would,' he claims, 'have been far fiercer on the threat to our – their! – Culture that my people were supposed to represent, if it had been asked of me [...] I would have sold my soul, I would have sold *my people*, for one sustained moment of the public's attention' (136 [emphasis in original]). He is perfectly willing to laugh gamely at Mr Vander's dinner table performance involving two grotesque Jewish stereotypes:

> Axel's father liked to divert the table with a routine he had developed, involving an archetypal couple, Moses and Rahel, both of which parts he would play in turn, screwing up his eyes and bowing from the shoulders and crooning and rubbing his hands, until his wife, laughing tearfully, would flap her napkin at him and cry, 'For shame, Leon, for shame, you will bring a judgment on us!' It did not occur to anyone around that table,

not even to me, on the few, treasured occasions when I was invited to dine there, that I should feel insulted or humiliated by what was, after all, only a piece of good-humoured mimicry. (Banville, 2002: 132)

Mr Vander's hand-rubbing, screw-eyed caricatures may not be quite as noxious as Eliot's verminous Jew, but the description of them as 'good-humoured mimicry' is tellingly disingenuous. Vander's willingness to accept this routine, and even to enjoy it, points toward his own shame about belonging to a race he imagines to be less than fully human. He is their pet Jew, the one they have allowed into their home, and for this he is pathetically grateful: 'they had assimilated me; I was Axel's friend, and therefore a special case, exempt from the general distaste – I would not put it more strongly than that – with which the Vanders regarded what in my presence were referred to delicately as *your people*' (132 [emphasis in original]).

That this is a pattern that repeatedly manifests itself in Banville's work is highly significant. Again and again, we are presented with the figure of a protagonist who is ashamed of his own origins and who disclaims those origins in order to occupy a tentative place in a kind of surrogate family. Banville's characters are never comfortable in their own identities – are often uncomfortable, moreover, with the very concept of identity – and their stories are frequently complicated accounts of the ways in which they have tried to become something other than what they are. The families who are defined in opposition to their own (the Brevoorts, the Vanders, the Graces) are objects of their narcissistic yearnings to realise the fantasy of their ego ideals. As real as they are, these idealised families are, on a distinct but equally important level, also figments of their narcissistically preoccupied imaginations. They are enchanted not by their sophistication and refinement per se, but by what these qualities represent in terms of their own ideal notions of themselves.

There is an important paradox here: the more preoccupied these narrators are by these idealised others, the more solipsistic those preoccupations tend to be. There is, finally, very little about their engagements with the world that cannot be seen as a secondary corollary of their engagements with themselves. Likewise, these characters' shame of their own families is ultimately a projected form of their shame about themselves. That this shame is often expressed in terms of narcissistic self-images – in images of the ego ideal – is evidence of the intimate link between shame and narcissism. With a typical combination of ambivalence and ostentation, Vander explains how he looks back upon his family. As is customary with Banville, it is as much an obfuscation as an illumination:

> I do not intend to oppress you with reminiscences of my family. It is not that they are any longer an embarrassment to me – I have so many, more recent, things to be ashamed of – but because, because, well, I do not know. Father, mother, my older brothers and sisters, those botched prototypes along the way to producing me, and the many younger ones who were always under my feet, they have in my memory a quaint, outmoded, in some cases badly blurred, aspect, like that of the incidental figures standing about self-consciously in very old photographs, smiling worriedly and not knowing what to do with their hands. Among them I was too big, in all ways; I was the giant whose head threatened to knock a hole in their ceiling, whom they must feed and tend and humour, and encourage away from the windows lest the neighbours look in and be frightened. (Banville, 2002: 131–2)

Like Victor Maskell, who sees his younger brother Freddie's mental disability as an appropriate counterpoint to his own narcissistic grandiosity ('deeming it right, I suppose, that anyone born after me should be defective'), the narrator sees his older siblings as 'botched prototypes' (Banville, 2002: 67).[3] There is a suggestion here of the familiar statue image, of the ego ideal as monumental artifice. But this narcissistic self-conception gives way, with remarkable fluency, to something very like shame. His sense of his own superiority to his family is transfigured into an image of himself as outlandishly large and grotesque, and liable to frighten the neighbours. In this way, it becomes impossible to separate the narrator's narcissism from his shame; it becomes impossible, in turn, to separate his shame about his family from his shame about himself.

In *The Sea*, Banville returns once again to this motif of opposition between two families. The Graces occupy a similar position in the mind of the young Max Morden as the Brevoorts in *The Untouchable* and the Vanders in *Shroud*. Again and again in the novel, Max's own lower-middle-class parents are depicted in pitiful contrast with the sophisticated and worldly Graces. From the novel's first line onwards – 'They departed, the gods, on the day of the strange tide' – they are referred to in an imaginative language of divinity (Banville, 2005c: 3). (The name Grace is, of course, itself suggestive of this notional godliness.) The first thing Max sees of them upon their arrival in Ballyless, the seaside town in which he and his parents spend their summers, is their 'motor car' (one of Banville's cherished archaisms) (6).[4] The fact that they possess such a thing in the first place, like the fact that they stay in a rented house while the Mordens stay in a chalet, sets them immediately apart. The reader is aware of the social and cultural chasm separating the Mordens from the Graces before the latters' first appearance in the novel. Its unbridgeable span is revealed by a few objects, strewn heedlessly by the Graces beneath the back windscreen of their car: 'Books with bleached and dog-eared covers were thrown carelessly on the shelf under the sportily raked back window, and there was a touring map of France, much used' (6). The Graces do not fail to live up to the expectations of sophistication aroused by those initial details. They appear to Max to be from another world. The webbed feet of Myles (the mute twin of Chloe, with whom he falls in love) are an eerie emblem of their otherness, and of the aura of divinity which they seem to diffuse.

Even before Max gets to know the Graces, he is ashamed of what they might make of the ignoble spectacle of his own parents. His recollections of his parents' awkward capering on the shore throb with the heat of humiliation. He notes of his mother – who cannot swim and who instead 'wallows with small, mistrustful pleasure' on in the 'soupy' shallows, 'straining to keep her mouth above the lapping wavelets' – that she:

> wore a crimplene swimsuit, mouse-pink, with a coy little hem stretched across tight just below the crotch. Her face looked bare and defenseless, pinched in the tight rubber seal of her bathing cap. My father was a fair swimmer, going at a sort of hindered, horizontal scramble with mechanical strokes and a gasping sideways grimace and one starting eye. At the end of a length he would rise up, panting and spitting, his hair plastered down and ears sticking out and black trunks abulge, and stand with

hands on hips and watch my mother's clumsy efforts with a faint, sardonic grin, a muscle in his jaw twitching. He splashed water in her face and seized her wrists and wading backwards hauled her through the water. She shut her eyes tight and shrieked at him furiously to stop. I watched these edgy larks in a paroxysm of disgust. (Banville, 2005c: 36)

Coming at the end of this long descriptive passage, the line about Max's disgust seems an unnecessary disclosure. The details themselves reveal more than enough. And there is, in these details, a faint but unmistakable trace of sexual revulsion: the 'coy little hem' of the mother's 'mouse-pink' swimsuit 'stretched across tight just below the crotch'; the father's 'trunks abulge'; the twitching muscle in his jaw as he watches the mother's 'clumsy efforts' before he hauls her against her will through the water. All of this seems to tiptoe in distaste around the intractable fact that his parents' relationship is, whether he likes it or not, at least in part a sexual one. When Mr Morden then laughingly turns on Max and pushes him 'wheelbarrow fashion off the edge of the sandbank', the extent to which the boy does not enjoy it is clear: 'I swallowed water, and twisted out of his grasp in a panic and jumped to my feet and stood in the surf, retching' (36–7).

The ignominy of this familial farce is all the more acute for the fact that the Graces are looking on as it happens. Again, as in *The Untouchable*, the favoured analogy of theatrical genre is employed to indicate the cultural gap between the high-brow Graces and the low-brow Mordens:

They stood regarding us without expression, as if we were a show, a comic turn that had been laid on for them but which they found not very interesting, or funny, but peculiar only. I am sure I blushed, grey and goosepimpled though I was, and I had an acute awareness of the thin stream of seawater pouring in an unstoppable arc out of the sagging front of my swimming-trunks. Had it been in my power I would have cancelled my shaming parents on the spot, would have popped them like bubbles of sea spray, my fat little bare-faced mother and my father whose body might have been made out of lard. (Banville, 2005c: 37)

Banville manages to extract a great deal of comic pathos from the precise quality of indignity that is specific to the wearing of swimwear: the mouse-pink crotch of the mother; the bulging of the father; the sagging and trickling of the son. Again, too, the sense of bodily repugnance is unmissable: it is their fatness, their physical inelegance, that shames him more than anything else. The concern with fleshiness here is bound up with the central dichotomy of divinity and mortality in young Max's imagination. The Graces seem somehow to be almost incorporeal, or at least unencumbered by the indignity of excess flesh, whereas Max's mortal parents are by contrast deplorably human.[5] If the Graces are gods and Max is a mortal, it is his parents who are to blame for his inferior ontological status.

There is a faint echo, in this beach scene, of the moment in *The Untouchable* where Maskell recalls his stepmother taking the sun on the seafront: 'Hettie sat placidly in the middle of a vast checked blanket doing her knitting,' he writes, 'sighing contentedly and talking to herself in a murmur, her big, mottled legs stuck out before her like a pair of windlasses and her yellow toes twitching'. Maskell then notes parenthetically that 'a parishioner once complained to my father that his wife was down on the strand "with her pegs on show for all the town to see"' (72). Neither Victor Maskell nor Max Morden are especially prudish characters – the former, in fact, is positively a libertine – but both seem gripped by an oddly puritan distaste when confronted with their parents' flesh. Parents, for Banville's protagonists, are almost always a rich and complex source of shame, and it is almost always entangled with the protagonists' shame about themselves. Lynd stresses the severe nature of the shame that is aroused by parents in their children:

Because of the pervasive and specifically unalterable character of experiences of shame, shame for one's parents can pierce deeper than shame for oneself, and sense of continuity with one's parents is correspondingly important. No matter how disgusted I am with myself, in some respects I can perhaps change. But the fact that these are my parents, that I am the fruit of their loins, is unchangeable [...] The overall quality of shame involves the whole life of a person, all that he is, including the parents who have created and nurtured that life. (Lynd, 1958: 53–6)

Like Maskell and Vander, though in a less drastic fashion than either, Max does attempt to distance himself from the obscure shame of his background. He pursues his ego ideal through a series of changes to his identity. His manner of speaking is different from that of his parents. He uses 'holiday' as a verb, something which he acknowledges would not have been done in his family: '*We came here for our holidays*, that is what we would have said. How difficult now it is to speak as I spoke then' (Banville, 2005c: 34 [emphasis in original]). The reader is made to picture Max, at this point, sitting at his desk in his book-lined study, shuddering at the recollection of the lexical improprieties of his youth.

'I did not hate them. I loved them, probably. Only they were in my way, obscuring my view of the future. In time I would be able to see right through them, my transparent parents (35)'. This is Max Morden speaking, but it could just as well be Victor Maskell, Alexander Cleave or Axel Vander. Though it is the Graces who first give the young Max an inkling that it might be possible to extricate himself from his parents' social position, and that such an extrication might be desirable, it is his eventual marriage to Anna that ultimately allows for the self-transformation at which he has all along been aiming. Not long after the wedding in London, to which Mrs Morden was not invited, Max brings his new bride home to visit her ('home: the word gives me a shove, and I stumble' (209)). She is at this point living (and dying) in a dingy canal-side flat in Dublin, and her resentment of her son's upward mobility, and of his concomitant neglect of her, is palpable. At one point, she asks confusedly why her son is addressed by his wife as 'Max'. It is the first and only intimation in the novel that Max is presumably not the name his parents gave him, and it places him in the company of Axel Vander and the narrator of *The Newton Letter*, as Banville narrators whose real names we are never actually told:

> 'Why does she keep calling you Max?' she hissed at me when Anna had gone to the counter to fetch a scone for her. 'Your name is not Max.'
> 'It is now,' I said. 'Did you not read the things I sent you, the things that I wrote, with my name printed on them?'
> She gave one of her mountainous shrugs.
> 'I thought they were by someone else.' (Banville, 2005c: 210)

Max is not the person, or does not see himself as the person, his mother brought into the world. He never examines his own guilt about the way he has treated her – his guilt about his shame – but his reticence seems to signal its problematic presence.

Having just witnessed the spectacle of a masturbating baboon at the zoo to which they have patronisingly brought her to visit, Mrs Morden turns on her son: '"Huh," she said, "this place. I suppose you'd like to leave me here, put me in with the monkeys and let them feed me bananas" (210–11). Attempting to mollify her, Max says the word 'Ma', to which she replies '"Don't *Ma* me"' (211). This is presumably not a name by which Max would choose to call her if he were to have his way. It is too unsophisticated, too working class, too cloyingly familiar and childish. And yet he does call her 'Ma', and there is a small capitulation in this (Max is presumably the type of person who would rather call his mother 'Mother'). Her rejection of the word – 'Don't *Ma* me' – is a rejection of half measures, a rejection of partial reparations. She knows that he is ashamed of her, and, perhaps for the first time now, he knows that she knows. The passage that follows, in which Max never acknowledges the guilt with which his words are laden, is one of the most moving Banville has written:

> But when we were leaving she wept, backing for cover behind the open door of the flat, lifting a forearm to hide her eyes, like a child, furious at herself. She died that winter, sitting on a bench by the canal one unseasonably mild mid-week afternoon. Angina pectoris, no one had known. The pigeons were still worrying at the crusts she had strewn for them on the path when a tramp sat down beside her and offered her a swig from his bottle in its brown-paper bag, not noticing she was dead. (Banville, 2005c: 211)

There is hardly a need for Max to explicitly concede his own culpability here; it is structural to the facts he is relating. That no one had known of her illness; that a tramp had assumed sufficient fellowship to offer her a swig from his bottle; that she died alone on a canal-side bench surrounded by pigeons: all these sad specifics are contingent upon the general fact of Max's failure as a son. His mother's misfortune is that she does not conform to – is in fact a kind of long-standing outrage against – his preferred image of himself. She is a victim, not of his indifference to her, but of his shame.

Max's relationship with Anna is, at least in part, conceived as a means of escaping the shabbiness of his upbringing. She is, in this sense, a kind of reincarnation of Chloe Grace, in that she represents everything he was not born into; the world she inhabits is everything his world is not. ('What was it,' he asks, 'that I wanted from Chloe Grace but to be on the level of her family's superior social position, however briefly, at whatever remove?' (207).) The course of marriage as social migration has already been charted in *Eclipse*, in which Alexander Cleave's relationship with his wife Lydia is represented as a fulfilment of his narcissistic self-image. 'I had come from nowhere,' as he puts it, 'and now at last, through Lydia, I had arrived at the centre of what seemed to me to be somewhere' (Banville, 2000a: 36). This is a familiar component of Banville's fiction: his protagonists have a genius for marrying well. Max readily admits that it is not Anna herself to whom he is primarily attracted so much as the idea of her, the sophisticated daughter of an apparently obscenely wealthy – and alluringly shady – London entrepreneur. So Anna's wealth, and the air of dissolute sophistication that surrounds her family life, allow Max to create a version of himself his own upbringing would not have permitted. What he wants to be is a gentleman scholar – a man, as he puts it, of 'leisurely interests and scant ambition' – and Anna provides him with the necessary resources to pursue this version of himself (2005c: 94). He is unconcerned, indeed delighted, about being a 'kept man': 'I was born to be a dilettante, all that was lacking was the means, until I met Anna'. In a more negative sense, however, his marriage to Anna allows him to escape a past with which he was never comfortable ('I will not deny it, I was always ashamed of my origins [...] From the start I was bent on bettering myself' (207)). What he found in Anna from the very beginning of their acquaintance, he admits, was 'a way of fulfilling the fantasy of myself' (215). As with Lydia in *Eclipse*, and as with Nick Brevoort in *The Untouchable*, Anna can be viewed as what Kohut terms a 'selfobject', the internalised object of a narcissistic fixation:

> From earliest days I wanted to be someone else. The injunction *nosce te ipsum* had an ashen taste on my tongue from the first

time a teacher enjoined me to repeat it after him. I knew myself, all too well, and did not like what I knew [...] Anna, I saw at once, would be the medium of my transmutation. She was the fairground mirror in which all my distortions would be made straight. (Banville, 2005c: 216)

The extent to which Max's attraction to Anna is a narcissistic one is openly acknowledged here. As a 'fairground mirror', she offers self-cohesion – consistency between ego and ego ideal – where otherwise there would be conflict. She offers him, in other words, the possibility of turning his cherished illusions about himself into something resembling reality. This, again, is one of the stock female roles in Banville's fiction. The women in the narrators' lives are frequently conceived of (sometimes in moments of self-recrimination, sometimes almost complacently) in terms of their specular functions; as facilitators and repositories of narcissistic self-images – as de Beauvoir's 'mirror in which the male, Narcissus-like, contemplates himself' (de Beauvoir, 1997: 173).

Viewed in a certain way, *The Sea* is a novel, like so many of Banville's other novels (*The Newton Letter*, *Eclipse* and large parts of the Trilogy), about what happens to a man when he is left entirely to his own devices; when he is left without a mediating presence between himself and his own image. Primarily, Max is mourning Anna's death and the more distant deaths of Chloe and Myles, but on another level he is mourning a way of seeing himself with which these people provided him. The Max who is writing this narrative, as opposed to the various Maxes he narrates, is almost completely bereft of illusions about himself, and this specific loss is a significant component of the more general sense of bereavement with which he is attempting to cope. Death, in this sense, is the ultimate destroyer of happy misconceptions. This is why he and Anna become 'toppled statues' of themselves in the aftermath of her diagnosis, and it is why their shared reaction to that diagnosis is so strangely close to shame. It is a reaction of profound embarrassment and humiliation more than grief or actual shock. Anna's word to describe the disclosure of her illness – 'inappropriate' – is especially telling (Banville, 2005c: 19). The diagnosis has made it impossible to continue with these happy misconceptions: 'Henceforth,' as he puts it, 'I would have to address things as they are, not as I might imagine them, for this was a new version of reality' (20). Impossible and yet absolutely imperative: two pages later, Max asserts that the only way for them to live with the horrific fact of Anna's dying is to ignore it. Again, the sense of mortality as somehow shameful and painfully compromising is evident here: 'It was as if a secret had been imparted to us so dirty, so nasty, that we could hardly bear to remain in one another's company yet were unable to break free, each knowing the foul thing that the other knew and bound together by that very knowledge. From this day forward all would be dissembling. There would be no other way to live with death' (22–3).

What seems to be at stake here, as much as life itself, is the set of illusions that are necessary to make it liveable. One of the most notable aspects of *The Sea* is its ruthless dismantling of the structures of self-deception. Just as the young Max realises that Mrs Grace is not a god but 'herself only, a mortal woman' when he sees her open her legs (when her mortality is revealed, that is, in her sexuality), the adult Max is similarly disabused of his own illusions about himself by his wife's death (118). The body itself – the brute fact, as it were, of corporeality – is the agent of these shameful truths of mortality. Like King Lear looking upon the wasted spectacle of Edgar, Max is horrified by the truth of the 'poor bare, forked animal' that is 'unaccommodated man' (see *King Lear* Act 3, Scene 4, 90–3). He has become painfully aware of his own frailty and perishability. When he takes a 'long, grim gander' in the mirror, any remaining narcissistic self-conceptions are undercut:

> Usually these days I do not dally before my reflection any longer than is necessary. There was a time when I quite liked what I saw in the looking glass, but not any more. Now I am startled, and more than startled, by the visage that so abruptly appears there, never and not at all the one that I expect. I have been elbowed aside by a parody of myself, a sadly disheveled figure in a Hallowe'en mask made of sagging, pinkish-grey rubber that bears no more than a passing resemblance to the image of what I look like that I stubbornly retain in my head. (Banville, 2005c: 127–8)

Max is attempting to see himself whole and entire, without illusions, and to represent accurately what he sees. Looking in the mirror he is reminded of the self-portraits of Bonnard and Van Gogh, both of which are remorseless in their depictions of their creators' frailties. But as so often with Banville, there is an undercurrent of bodily disgust, of what seems an almost religious sense of shame about bodily contingency, of flesh as inherently corrupt. Before Anna's illness, he tells us, he had held his 'physical self in no more than fond disgust, as most people do [...] tolerant, necessarily, of the products of my sadly inescapable humanity, the various effluvia, the eructations fore and aft, the gleet, the scurf, the sweat and other common leakages'. After her diagnosis, however, he developed what he calls a 'crawling repugnance of my own flesh' (70). This self-disgust seems, deliberately or otherwise, to evoke the vivid depictions of his boyhood shame at his parents' flesh discussed above. It recalls, too, the moment in *The Book of Evidence* when Freddie, desperately hung-over, places a hand on the hindquarters of one of his mother's horses and is overcome with a 'vivid, queasy sense' of himself as 'something pallid and slack and soft', and is inexplicably 'ashamed' (Banville, 1989a: 46).

One of the crucial components at work in the complex mechanism of shame is that of exposure. As we have seen, Helen M. Lynd asserts that in shame, 'the thing that has been exposed is what I am'. Banville's protagonists tend to spend large portions of their time and energy concealing themselves from others and from themselves, but there are always crucial moments at which their covers are blown, where, in Winnicott's phraseology, the mask of the False Self slips and the True Self is fleetingly revealed. Max relates one such instance, where Anna, an accomplished amateur photographer, took a series of photographs of him. The results, as he puts it, were 'shockingly raw, shockingly revealing'. In these black-and-white portraits he seems to himself 'more starkly on show than I would have been in a full-length study wearing not a stitch'. He was at the time 'young and smooth and not unhandsome' but in these images he appears 'an overgrown homunculus' (2005c: 173). Worse than the visual image the portraits present, though, is the moral weakness they seem to reveal:

> My expression was uniformly winsome and ingratiating, the expression of a miscreant who fears he is about to be accused of a crime he knows he has committed yet cannot recall, but is

preparing his extenuations and justifications anyway. What a desperate, beseeching smile I wore, a leer, a very leer. She trained her camera on a fresh-faced hopeful but the pictures she produced were the mug-shots of a raddled old confidence trickster. Exposed, yes, that is the word, too. (Banville, 2005c: 173–4)

What is so shocking for Max in these photographs is, it seems, their representation, and thereby their violation, of his insular quiddity. There is, in this notion, something of the common primitive belief in the camera as a snatcher of spirits. 'Exposed' is the word because he feels compromised and laid bare by these likenesses. He is disturbed by how the camera seems to know him in a way that he himself, with his idealised visions of who and what he is, does not.

The passage about the photographs is subtly paralleled by an incident Max relates from his own childhood. He is playing on the beach with the twins when Chloe decides, out of a child's deadly combination of boredom and sadism, to torment a boy Max knows from home – a 'townie', as he calls him. Keen to impress his new girlfriend, Max leads the offensive, giving him a shove and knocking him against a wall before Chloe begins an improvised interrogation. At one point, Myles strikes him on the side of the head and the townie, 'poor slow sheep that he was, only looked startled, and put up a hand and felt his face as it to verify the amazing fact of having been hit' before giving a 'sad shrug' and shambling away (171). What haunts Max about the incident, though, is not the victimisation or the violence, but the look which the boy gives him before walking away. 'He knew me,' Max tells us, 'knew I was a townie too, like him, whatever I might try to seem'. What unsettles him particularly is not an unspoken accusation of betrayal – betrayal of their sort of people – but the 'expression of acceptance in his glance, the ovine unsurprisedness at my perfidy'. It is shame that motivates Max's taking sides against the townie, shame of their shared class, and the townie's stoical recognition of this fact leads, in turn, to more shame: to shame about the shame. The young Max clearly sees himself as having broken deliberately and decisively away from the herd from which this young boy has merely strayed. He is still a 'poor, slow' sheep with his 'ovine' expression, whereas Max is now something else: a wolf, or a sheep in wolf's clothing. His recognition of him ('he knew me') is a kind of penetration of the false barriers that Max has erected between himself and his social class, and between his ideal image of himself and the reality. Both penetrating gazes – that of the camera and of the townie – represent a threat to Max's delicate sense of himself: they are intimate, close to the bone, in a way that he finds deeply unsettling, compromising and ultimately shaming.

There is a sense, in these moments, not just of being seen, but of being seen through. Victor Maskell, whose duplicities are of a far higher order than those of Max Morden, is acutely sensitive to this kind of shaming gaze. He knows that his entire identity (English, upper class, heterosexual, loyal servant of the Crown) is a kind of grandiose sham, that the statue he has erected of himself bears precious little resemblance to the reality, and it is the moments at which he is closest to his bourgeois Ulster background that his fraudulence seems most in danger of being revealed. When he returns to Carrickdrum after his father's death (the second such return), a Mrs Bleckinsop (who, like the townie in *The Sea*, appears nowhere else in the novel) poses just this kind of threat as they sit in the kitchen drinking tea before the funeral. 'The Bleckinsop woman,' Maskell recalls, 'was looking hard at me, and seeming not to approve of what she saw. It is always the most unexpected people who see through one' (Banville 1997b: 238–9).

The sources of Maskell's shame here are numerous, though perhaps it would be more accurate to speak of his guilt about his shame. There is the perennial unease about his Ulster provenance, and his abandonment of it for a carefully sculpted English identity; there is the guilt about his neglect of his stepmother and deceased father; there is, also, and perhaps most piercingly, the guilt about what he is preparing to do before he returns to London: to commit his brother Freddie to a home. Read symbolically, it is a kind of renunciation of the self which he had no hand in creating. As the culmination of a lifetime of smaller betrayals, it has an emotional finality to it. The scene in which he leaves Freddie at the home is an upsetting one, and its emotional weight is of a similar order – and a similar origin – to those passages in *The Sea* in which Max relates his final contacts with his dying (and all but abandoned) mother. Freddie is a standing affront to Maskell's narcissistic image of himself. There is no place for him in the life his only living relative has (in the fullest sense of the

term) forged for himself. Even as children, Maskell's relationship to
Freddie was a disturbingly cold and narcissistic one:

> When we were children I had not minded him, deeming it
> right, I suppose, that anyone born after me should be defective.
> He had been someone for me to order about, a makeweight in
> the intricate games that I devised, an uncritical witness to my
> cautiously daring escapades. I used to perform experiments on
> him just to see how he would react. I gave him methylated spirits
> to drink – he gagged and retched – and put a dead lizard in his
> porridge. (Banville, 1997b: 67)

Maskell is putting his brother in a home primarily because it is the
convenient thing to do, but he also recognises that, in putting him
away, he is putting away a part of himself which cannot be reconciled
with the narcissistic ideal he has for so long laboured to make real.
The chaos of the home's common room seems strangely familiar to
him, and he is gripped by the notion that he has been there before,
as though 'some essential part' of himself had always been there.
'The room,' he tells us, 'looked like nothing so much as the inside
of my own head: bone white, lit by a mad radiance, and thronged
with lost and aimlessly wandering figures who might be the myriad
rejected versions of my self, of my soul' (245–6).

What this remark reveals above all is Maskell's profound solipsism.
Faced with a room full of suffering and fragile strangers, psychiatric
inmates amongst whom his own younger brother will be spending
the rest of his life, he immediately refashions the scene into a symbol-
ist representation of his own interior life. What it represents to him is
a vision of his own narcissistic self-reinvention, but this recognition
increases, rather than mitigates, the severity of Maskell's narcissism.
It is largely Maskell's sense of shame about himself – about that part
of him which Freddie represents – that has led to this cruel betrayal
in the first place, but his guilt about that shame is something he
acknowledges only obliquely. There is a point at which it seems to
threaten to overwhelm him, before it is converted into an outward-
directed anger. Maskell's reaction at this moment is very close to the
narcissistic rage experienced by Freddie Montgomery in the midst of
his brutal murder of Josie Bell in *The Book of Evidence*, as discussed in
Chapter 1. Between the first and second fatal hammer blows, it will be

remembered, Freddie is gripped by an oddly comic fit of narcissistic pique: 'I was dismayed. How could this be happening to me – it was all so *unfair*. Bitter tears of self-pity squeezed into my eyes' (Banville, 1989a: 114 [emphasis in original]). Similarly, at the point when Freddie Maskell realises what is happening – 'that this was no treat laid on for him, a sort of pantomime, or an anarchic version of the circus, but that here was where he was to be abandoned [...] for the rest of his life' – his older brother nimbly sidesteps his own culpability by shifting into a mode of defensive self-righteousness: 'That blustering anger boiled up inside me all the stronger, and I felt violently sorry for myself, and cruelly wronged' (Banville, 1997b: 246). Just as Freddie Montgomery's self-pity provokes the reader's scandalised laughter at *The Book of Evidence*'s most serious point, Maskell's preposterous sense of his own victimhood strikes a note of wholly inappropriate comedy here. His narcissism has momentarily brought the scene perilously close to the line separating the tragic from the farcical.

So Freddie Maskell, in his childlike innocence and stoic forbearance, is like a kind of sacrificial lamb – sacrificed, that is, to the larger cause of his brother's ego ideal. What drives the institution scene, like the incident with the townie in *The Sea*, is guilt, and what drives the guilt is shame. One of the more instructive similarities between Maskell, Vander and Morden is the way in which so many of the people in their lives tend to be grouped on either side of a notional dividing line. These people are psychologically linked either with their ego ideals or with their senses of shame about themselves – with who they wish to be or with who they 'really' are. In *The Untouchable*, there are those characters (chiefly the Brevoorts) who serve as models for the 'idealised effigy' Maskell is attempting to erect within himself, and there are those (his own family and anyone connected with his Ulster upbringing) who are associated with the frustration of that attempt. In *The Sea*, the same distinction can be made between the Graces and Max's own family, as it can, in *Shroud*, between Vander's own family (who are never named) and that of his friend.

This can be seen as a kind of narcissistic polarisation of identification, which in certain respects is similar to Klein's conception of the way in which we 'split off' aspects of experience into 'good' and 'bad'. Banville's narrators are almost – though not, as we shall see, completely – incapable of relating to other people per se, of seeing them as anything other than ways of seeing themselves. By a kind of process of projective identification, others are viewed in terms of the versions of the self with which they are associated. There are those who are aligned with (who contribute to the strength of) the ego ideal, and those who are aligned with the sense of shame. And so just as narcissism can be seen as the obverse of self-consciousness, these others, both idealised and rejected, can be seen as contrasting projections of the narrators' own narcissistically divided selves.

6
Narrative Narcissism

As an exploration of narcissism in Banville's novels, the focus of this book has so far lain primarily upon the characters, upon the representations of their inner lives and their interactions with one another. The understanding of the concept previously employed has, in other words, been a more or less exclusively psychological one. The present chapter is intended to broaden the scope of the discussion to encompass a consideration of formal and stylistic elements of the novels. This involves a somewhat altered stance with respect to the concept of narcissism, so that it denotes not a specifically psychoanalytic view of a particular personality type, but rather a more general description of various self-reflexive approaches to fiction. More simply put, what this chapter explores is not narcissism in the novels, but the narcissism *of* the novels (though with an understanding of the implicit links between the two).

Throughout, what is intended by the term narcissism will be broadly in line with the kinds of self-conscious narrative strategies and devices that are commonly discussed under the general rubric of metafiction. As such, the reading of the novels in this chapter will not, per se, represent any significant departure from the mainstream of Banville scholarship. Critics have, after all, been discussing the work in this way since *Nightspawn*. The background against which this chapter discusses such self-reflexivity, however, offers a new perspective on the novels. The aim is to present this tendency towards conspicuous self-consciousness – what Linda Hutcheon calls 'narrative narcissism' – as something which is of a piece with the novels' overarching concern with the psychology of self-absorption.

In this sense it presents, within the context of this study as a whole, a straightforward argument about the relationship between form and content. Although self-reflexivity is one of the more notable characteristics of Banville's work, the focus here is only on those novels in which it manifests itself as a structural rather than a merely stylistic quality.

This chapter examines the first three works in the so-called Scientific Tetralogy (*Doctor Copernicus*, *Kepler* and *The Newton Letter*) and the later novels *Ghosts* and *Athena*, which form two thirds of the Art Trilogy. There is an obvious case to be made for considering all four volumes in the Tetralogy together – Banville originally intended them, after all, as a group of interrelated works on the theme of science. But in most significant respects, *Mefisto* has no more in common with the other three novels (especially *Doctor Copernicus* and *Kepler*) than it has with anything else in Banville's *oeuvre*, and is best viewed in relation to the work which follows it. *Doctor Copernicus*, *Kepler* and *The Newton Letter*, (republished by Picador in an omnibus edition as *The Revolutions Trilogy*) are looked at in terms of how they identify the figure of the scientist with that of the artist, and how they appear to offer straightforward biographical fictions while in reality presenting explorations of the motives and difficulties of artistic creation.

Ghosts and *Athena* are also considered as examples of a particular form of self-reflexive writing which has hitherto been largely unexplored with respect to Banville's work. His use of *mise en abyme* – the device whereby the themes and preoccupations of a work are mirrored by a fictional work of art placed within it – is examined as a means of narcissistic self-reflection. *Mise en abyme* is discussed in terms of André Gide's definition and theorisation of the concept, and Banville's employment of it as a narratological device is examined alongside two paradigmatic applications – Gide's in *The Counterfeiters*, and Nabokov's in *The Real Life of Sebastian Knight*.

The concept of harmony is one of the major unifying factors of Banville's fiction. Each of the novels is in some way concerned with a search for a means of imposing order on experience. From the quests for missing twins which motivate the action of *Birchwood* and *Mefisto* to Alexander Cleave's and Max Morden's withdrawal into themselves from the painful incomprehensibility of the world in *Eclipse* and *The Sea*, there is always an anxiety about making sense of the things that seem to resist meaning. With these first-person narratives, the act of writing is itself an attempt at ordering experience. Banville's narrators are always motivated by a kind of elemental confusion – about the world, about their own selves, and about the endlessly enigmatic relationship between the two. As he put it in a 2005 interview with Derek Hand: 'Puzzlement, bafflement, this is my strongest sensation, my strongest artistic sensation' (Banville, 2006b). In another interview from around the same time with the American novelist Mark Sarvas, he joked about how he had recently realised 'that I've been through the astonished/baffled/amazed/puzzled parts of the thesaurus so many times [...] they're getting worn away' (Banville, 2005b).

Confusion, then, is a key concept in the work. It is what motivates the protagonists to create their narratives, just as, by his own admission, it is a large part of what motivates the author himself. Fiction, in common with art generally, has long been thought of as a product of humanity's impulse to make meaning from the apparent meaninglessness of experience. In *The Sense of an Ending* (1967), for instance, Frank Kermode advances a concept of fiction-making as arising from the desire for an ultimate conclusion that will retrospectively invest with meaning everything which preceded it. Similarly, the philosopher Paul Ricoeur's notion of 'narrative identity' attempts to explain our conception of ourselves as having 'selves' – as being internally coherent and consistent unitary beings – through an act of inner narration of our own experiences. The self, in Ricoeur's analysis, is in this sense a product of imaginative, creative work: 'life,' as he puts it, 'is a cloth woven of stories told' (Ricoeur, 1998: 246).

This idea of narrative as the process by which we make sense of the world – by which, to use Banville's preferred term, we attempt to resolve our bafflement about things – is at the heart of Linda Hutcheon's concept of 'narrative narcissism'. In *Narcissistic Narrative: the Metafictional Paradox* (1984), Hutcheon uses the notion of narcissism to define and explore metafiction. She defines narcissistic fiction as that which includes within itself some form of commentary on its own linguistic and narrative origins. At pains to liberate this narrative self-consciousness from the historically specific classification of postmodernism, Hutcheon points to the playful self-referentiality of many early novels (such as *Don Quixote* and *Tristram Shandy*) to justify her claim that narcissism is a tendency inherent in the form itself. Echoing Freud's assertion, in 'On Narcissism', that narcissism was the universal original condition of mankind, Hutcheon argues that it is also 'the "original condition" of the novel as a genre' (1984: 8). On this matter, she is in agreement with Patricia Waugh, who points out that 'although the term "metafiction" might be new, the *practice* is as old (if not older) than the novel itself' (Waugh, 1984: 5 [emphases in original]). Where self-referentiality has always been a vital element of fiction, what Hutcheon calls the 'more modern textual self-preoccupation' is distinguished by 'its explicitness, its intensity, and its own critical self-awareness' (Hutcheon, 1984: 18). Such quantitative rather than qualitative progression is, as well as being identifiable with a change in the way we think about language, 'perhaps also a matter of finding an aesthetic mode of dealing with modern man's experience of life as being unordered by any communal or transcendent power – God or myth – and his new scepticism that art can unproblematically provide a consolatory order' (19).

Where realist novels of the nineteenth century, with their well-turned plots and convincing characters, reinforced either a sense of the ultimate meaningfulness of human action or a sense of art as capable of conferring meaning upon experience, the modern 'ambiguous' and 'open-ended' novel suggests something very different. Such modern fiction, she claims, indicates 'less an obvious new insecurity or lack of coincidence between man's need for order and his actual experience of the chaos of the contingent world, than a certain curiosity about art's ability to produce "real" order, even by analogy, through the process of fictional construction'. Hutcheon recognises a causal link between this uncertainty or curiosity about art's ability to generate meaning and what she calls 'the new need, first to create fictions, then to admit their fictiveness, and then to examine critically such impulses' – a general trend in all forms of fiction which she identifies as 'narcissistic' (18–19). Waugh (1984) makes a similar point, contending that:

> Metafictional novels tend to be constructed on the principle of a fundamental and sustained opposition: the construction of a fictional illusion (as in traditional realism) and the laying bare of that illusion. In other words, the lowest common denominator of metafiction is simultaneously to create a fiction and to make a statement about the creation of that fiction. The two processes are held together in a formal tension which breaks down the distinctions

between 'creation' and 'criticism' and merges them into the concepts of 'interpretation' and 'deconstruction'. (Waugh, 1984: 6)

Banville's fiction is continually distinguished by this kind of sustained opposition. One of the most significant aspects of the Science Tetralogy (in particular *Doctor Copernicus* and *Kepler*) is the way in which it synthesises the universal human need for a sense of order and harmony with this kind of postmodern questioning of the roles of art and fiction. What makes these novels so much more interesting than the genre they appear to be operating within – that of the straightforward biographical novel – is this concern with fiction which at all times shadows the manifest subject matter of the books. In *Doctor Copernicus*, the eponymous astronomer whose heliocentric cosmography displaces earth – and thereby mankind – from its position at the centre of creation is in this sense an ideal model for the dual significance with which Banville invests the novel. Copernicus is, at least according to this rendering of him, a kind of symbol for all that unites art and science. He evokes both *Birchwood*'s Gabriel Godkin and *Mefisto*'s Gabriel Swan in his childhood conviction that numbers have the capacity to reveal an essential harmony apparently belied by the chaos of experience. It is, we are told, 'in the grave cold music of mathematics' and 'in logic's hard bright lucid, faintly frightening certainties' that he finds the harmony which sets off 'within him a coppery chord of perfect bliss' (Banville, 1976: 19). Copernicus's search, like those of Godkin and Swan, is a search for harmony. He aims to map the planets and to chart their movements in order to reveal a logic that is not of mankind's making, but which inheres in the universe itself. And like Godkin and Swan, he is haunted by the notion that the present is characterised by a falling away from this original prelapsarian order. The language in which this is expressed is at once Cartesian, Christian and Platonic, in that it posits the existence of a world of pure forms, and a separation between that world and the world of experience, in which the human form itself is a corrupt and weakened version of some ideal other:

There were for him two selves, separate and irreconcilable, the one a mind among the stars, the other a worthless fork of flesh planted firmly in earthly excrement. In the writings of antiquity he glimpsed the blue and gold of Greece, the blood-boltered majesty of Rome, and was allowed briefly to believe that there had been times when the world had known an almost divine unity of spirit and matter, of purpose and consequence: was it this that men were searching after now, across strange seas, in the infinite silent spaces of pure thought.

Well, if such harmony had ever indeed existed, he feared deep down, deep beyond admitting, that it was not to be regained. (Banville, 1976: 27)

The sense of loss here is figured in terms that are both personal and universal. The vanished order of civilisation's Greco-Roman origins is linked to the lost coherence of Copernicus's own childhood, in which everything seemed to make sense, and everything had its place. 'The sky is blue, the sun is gold, the linden tree is green,' we are informed by the *faux-naïve* voice of the early pages. 'Day is light, it ends, night falls, and then it is dark. You sleep, and in the morning wake again. But a day will come when you will not wake. That is death. Death is sad. Sadness is what happiness is not. And so on. How simple it all was, after all! There was no need even to think about it. He had only to be, and life would do the rest' (4).[1] The repetition of blue and gold imagery in these two passages of harmony and disharmony (the 'blue and gold of Greece' and the blue sky and gold sun of childhood) provides a subtle link between the two worlds of childhood and adulthood, and between the loss of a universal order and the loss of the order – or innocence – of childhood. Everything – even death – makes sense for the child Copernicus in a way that nothing does in adult life. As Elke D'hoker puts it, 'Nicholas's childhood depicts a romanticized version of the premodern faith in a basic unity of self and world, of mind and matter, or of words and things. Although no explicit reference to God is made, one can just imagine a bearded old man on a cloud drifting over the scene, deciding that all is well' (D'hoker, 2004b: 55).

Science is Copernicus's only defence against this breakdown of order. Significantly, this is described in terms which are subtly evocative of narrative and dramatic art: as 'a deeply earnest play-acting' and as 'a form of ritual by which the world and his self and the relation between the two were simplified and made manageable'. Copernicus's scientific endeavours 'transformed into docile order the hideous clamour and chaos of the world outside himself, endistanced it and at the same time brought it palpably near, so that, as he grappled with the terrors of the world, he was terrified and yet miraculously tranquil'. Banville sets up a crucial division between these endeavours and the 'real world', strengthening the scientist-as-artist metaphor. It is as though science, like art, were a way of imposing an artificial order on things rather than an empirical revelation of the *actual* order inherent in them. 'Nothing was stable: politics became war, law became slavery, life itself became death, sooner or later. Always the ritual collapsed in the face of the hideousness. The real world would not be gainsaid, being the true realm of action, but he must gainsay it, or despair. This was his problem' (Banville, 1976: 28). The problem, in this sense, is very much an artistic one: that of trying to generate a sense of harmony in the face of the world's violent incoherence. As Banville himself has claimed in an interview with Rüdiger Imhof, ideas such as causation, along with 'mathematics and [...] theology', are 'invented by men in order to explain and therefore make habitable a chaotic, hostile and impassive world'. He goes on to comment that the Tetralogy's 'hidden theme' is the 'similarity between the workings of the artistic mind and the scientific mind; indeed, I sometimes feel that one could substitute the word "identity" for "similarity"' (Banville, 1987: 13).

The author's metafictional strategy in *Doctor Copernicus* is to surreptitiously write about writing whilst appearing to write about science. There are passages in which it is difficult to avoid the suspicion that Banville is engaging in a kind of covert auto-representation. In a language and sentiment which seems deliberately to recall Beckett's aphorism that 'to be an artist is to fail as no other dare fail, that failure is his world, and to shrink from it desertion', Copernicus describes his own work as 'a process of progressive failing' (Beckett, 1983: 145; Banville, 1976: 92). Like an author whose ideas are violated by attempts to render them into language, he is horrified by the forms into which he must twist his ideas in order for them to 'work out' mathematically. Copernicus at work is described as follows:

> He moved forward doggedly, line by painful line, calculation by defective calculation, watching in mute suspended panic his blundering pen pollute and maim those concepts that, unexpressed, had throbbed with limpid purity and beauty. It was barbarism

on a grand scale. Mathematical edifices of heart-rending frailty and delicacy were shattered at a stroke. He had thought that the working out of his theory would be nothing, mere hackwork: well, that was somewhat true, for there was hacking indeed, bloody butchery. He crouched at his desk by the light of a guttering candle, and suffered: it was a kind of slow internal bleeding [...] He dipped his pen in ink. He bled. (Banville, 1976: 92)

Banville himself has been vocal not just on the difficulty of the process of fiction writing, but on the inevitable disappointments one faces when setting out to convert the pure germ of an idea into the finished product of prose. After Colm Tóibín created a minor media stir by claiming (surely somewhat mischievously) to derive no pleasure from the act of writing and that the best thing about it was 'the money', the *Guardian* asked a number of novelists, including Banville, whether writing for a living was 'a joy or a chore'. His response resonates with Copernicus's notion of his work as a painful drawing of blood performed with a 'blundering pen'. Writing, he claimed, whether it be a novel or a letter to a bank manager, is 'difficult and peculiarly painful':

> The struggle of writing is fraught with a specialised form of anguish, the anguish of knowing one will never get it right, that one will always fail, and that all one can hope to do is 'fail better', as Beckett recommends. The pleasure of writing is in the preparation, not the execution, and certainly not in the thing executed. (Banville, 2009e)

Copernicus, then, is not just presented as an artist, he is presented as precisely the kind of artist John Banville sees himself as being. He is an artist, in other words, with a post-Beckettian awareness of the simultaneous futility and necessity of the struggle to express profound truths using crude representational tools. The novel continually directs its readers' attentions in several directions at once, constantly reflecting upon itself and the difficulties attendant upon its own creation. At one point the astronomer, whose progress is one of continual movement away from all notions of certainty and objective truth, chides his young disciple Rheticus for believing that his master's work can express anything beyond itself, can communicate anything meaningful. 'You imagine that my book is a kind of mirror in which the real world is reflected; but you are mistaken,' he tells him. 'In order to build such a mirror, I should need to be able to perceive the world whole, in its entirety and in its essence. But our lives are lived in such a tiny, confined space, and in such disorder, that this perception is not possible. There is no contact, none worth mentioning, between the universe and the place in which we live' (Banville, 1976: 206). Like so much else in the novel, this statement incorporates multiple meanings. It is, firstly, very much in line with poststructuralist ideas about the subjectivity of truth and the inadequacy of language as a mirror for reflecting the world. Secondly, it seems to express a hopeless resignation about the insularity of human experience, an anxiety (inherent, as I have been arguing, in much of Banville's work) about the impossibility of connecting meaningfully with the world outside of the self. Thirdly, and perhaps most forcefully, it seems to refer to the novel itself, to be a reflection upon its own self-reflection: an admission of a kind of compound narcissism.

In the same way as Banville posits the 'identity' of artists and scientists, Copernicus's book becomes an allegorical representation of Banville's. When Copernicus tells Rheticus that 'my book is not science – it is a dream', we hear the voice of the author in chorus with that of his creation (207). Just as the Tetralogy as a whole can be seen as charting a movement away from certainty – from faith in all its senses – *Doctor Copernicus* can be seen as examining a loss of faith in the power of art somehow to speak poetic truth. We are told that Copernicus 'ceased to believe in his book', that instead of approaching 'the crucial Word, it was careering headlong into a loquacious silence'. Whereas once he had believed it possible to express truth, he now 'saw that all that could be said was the saying. His book was not about the world, but about itself'. When he condemns his work as a 'hideous ingrown thing', we detect a darkly ironic comment by the novelist on his own creation (116). *Doctor Copernicus*, as Hutcheon puts it, is 'a self-conscious meditation on the relationship between names and things, and therefore between theory and the universe: it is both science and history as metafiction' (Hutcheon, 1984: xiv).

Throughout, Banville undermines the effect of historical realism by intermittently alluding to the fictive nature of the novel's world.[2] This metafictional strategy is at its most deliberately jarring in a scene towards the end where an argument between Copernicus and Rheticus is rendered using italicised fragments of dialogue drawn from the writings of some of the most pivotal intellectual figures of the nineteenth and twentieth centuries. Copernicus begins with a quotation from Kierkegaard's *Fear and Trembling*, to which Rheticus replies with a quotation from Einstein. The argument continues with this highly stylised method of dialectic anachronism, via further quotations from Arthur Stanley Eddington, Meister Eckhart, Max Planck and Wallace Stevens (Banville, 1976: 208). The primary effect of this is to draw attention to the constructed nature of the fiction, and to the status of the two interlocutors as marionettes in Banville's puppet theatre. Coming so close to the end of the novel, the moment is positioned to achieve an optimum level of disruption. By putting the words of others – of writers and scientists – into the mouths of his own characters, Banville is making an artfully metafictional comment about the affinity between the artistic and scientific projects. He is also, and perhaps more significantly, revealing his own hand to the reader. In italicising the quotations, he draws attention not just to the fact that they are quotations, but also to his own manipulation of them as text, to his own commanding presence behind the words we read. The strategy of deliberately breaking his or her own meticulously constructed illusion is a risky one for any author to take, and it is perhaps somewhat too heavy-handed to work in the novel's favour here. But it is nonetheless an interesting and instructive moment, for the way in which it indicates Banville's acute self-consciousness and his desire to induce a similar self-consciousness in the reader.

Kepler, with its highly convincing characterisation and its persuasive reconstruction of early modern Europe, maintains a similarly delicate balance between realism and the metafictional strategies of intertextual and self-reflexive interjection. In the novel's opening line, Banville shows us Kepler asleep 'as he dreamed the solution to the cosmic mystery' (1981c: 3). It is no accident that this first glimpse we are given of the astronomer is as a literal dreamer, as someone whose solutions are found in creative reverie: Kepler, like his predecessor Copernicus, is presented from the very beginning as a kind of artist. Banville, in this sense, is setting out his self-reflexive stall at the earliest possible opportunity, flagging in the first words the 'similarity between the workings of the artistic mind and the scientific mind' (1987: 13). One of the general principles which comes across strongest in the Tetralogy is that of the subjectivity of truth and experience. The reader is continually reminded that the 'realities' of *Doctor Copernicus* and *Kepler* are imaginative creations of John Banville, and that these scientists' visions of the world are similarly imaginative in their origins. As he put it to Melvyn Bragg in an interview for a *South Bank Show* special on his work in 1993, it is, for Copernicus and Kepler, 'not the world "out there" that matters, it's the world "in here", it's what I make of it, it's what we make of the world by the power of imagination, the way that we mould the world into our own image. That's what's powerful' (1993b). *Kepler* ends, as it begins, with its hero awakening from a dream, this time right at the moment of his death. His final words (in the book as, presumably, in life) reinforce this sense of him as essentially a creative figure, one whose work is the product of imaginative exploration: 'Such a dream I had, Billig, such a dream. *Es war doch so schön* [...] Ah my friend, such dreams ...' (191). That the novel begins with sleep, and ends with an awakening before death, implies that what passes between is a kind of dream: the dream of fiction and the larger 'dream' that is life.

Like *Doctor Copernicus*, *Kepler* is scattered with strange intertextual anachronisms and deliberate revelations of the authorial hand. At one point, Kepler writes these lines in a letter to his mentor Mästlin: '*I do not speak like I write, I do not write like I think, I do not think like I ought to think, and so everything goes on in deepest darkness*'. Just as, during their argument, Banville feeds Copernicus and Rheticus lines from key figures in modern letters and science, Kepler's italicised words are direct transpositions from a letter written by Kafka to his sister Ottla in July 1914.[3] Kepler, baffled by the words he has just written, asks himself 'where did these voices come from, these strange sayings' and reflects that it is as though 'the future had found utterance in him' (1981c: 86). This is precisely what is happening. The illusion is suddenly broken and we see Kepler not as a fleshed-out historical figure but as a character in a novel, as a puppet designed to do no more or less than his master's bidding. The future has found utterance through him in two separate senses, one metaphorical and the other literal: the historical Kepler hastened the modern era through his discovery of the laws of planetary motion, thus allowing the future to speak, as it were, through him, while Kepler the 'character' is being used by the Banville of 1981 to channel the Kafka of 1914.

The focus of this telescoping, and the real object of this display of metafictional necromancy, is not Kepler but Banville himself.

In the final pages of the novel, Kepler is approached at his lodgings in Linz by two 'kinsmen' of Tycho Brahe, the Danish astronomer under whom he earlier worked. The men are on their way to England, and offer to take him with them. He briefly considers their proposition, as he has previously been invited to travel there by King James's ambassador to Prague, but ultimately decides against it, and the two travellers disappear from the novel. Their names, however, give this fleeting encounter a relevance beyond its minor significance to the narrative: they are 'Holger Rosenkrands the statesman's son and the Norwegian Axel Gyldenstjern' (186). The Scandinavian spellings scarcely conceal the characters' real – which is to say, fictional – provenance: they are *Hamlet's* Rosencrantz and Guildenstern, the treacherous courtiers recruited by Claudius to escort the young prince to England, there to facilitate his execution. Had Kepler travelled with them, he would have stepped into a parallel and contemporaneous fiction. As readers we are reminded that Kepler – or Banville's version of him – is an imagined figure who can be made to inhabit the same fictional realm as *Hamlet's* minor dramatis personae. In referencing Shakespeare in this way, Banville is primarily referencing himself, the ultimate agency behind the action of the novel who can expose at will the fictive nature of the narrative. This kind of self-revelation – of the narrative's origins in imagination and of the author's ultimate power over it – is a form of narcissism, with the fiction reflecting upon its own fictionality and leading the reader to do likewise.

Hutcheon describes narcissistic texts as being 'explicitly aware of their status as literary artefacts, of their narrative and world-creating processes, and of the necessary presence of the reader'. In what she terms 'diegetic narcissism', the text displays itself as narrative, as the gradual building of a fictive universe complete with character and action' (Hutcheon, 1984: 28). *Kepler* is explicit not just about its own status as fiction, but also about the building of that fiction – about the details of its own design. The most formally ambitious of Banville's works, it is fastidiously constructed in order to mirror the historical Kepler's (entirely mistaken) idea that between the orbits of the six known planets could be inserted five distinct geometrical figures. As such, there are five sections in the novel, each of which is named after one of Kepler's works, and each of which is structured after one of these geometrical shapes. Thus Part One, with six chapters (or 'sides') is a cube; Part Two, with four, is a tetrahedron; Part Three, with twelve, is a dodecahedron; Part Four, with twenty chapters (or individual letters, as this section constitutes a detour into the epistolary mode), is an icosahedron, and Part Five, with eight, is an octahedron. Even within this internal construction of its parts, the chapters themselves are all of equal length, and the narrative, as Rüdiger Imhof has identified, is 'elliptical' in the uneven circularity of its progress (Imhof, 1997: 139).

In addition to these overall formal constraints, Banville has also constructed the novel so that the first letters of each of its 50 chapters spell out the names of four central figures in the history of science: Johannes Kepler, Tycho Brahe, Galileo Galileus and Isaac Newton. In this way the entire novel becomes, in terms of its textual arrangement, a kind of giant acrostic. This wordplay is nothing unusual per se in Banville – as early as *Nightspawn*, he utilises puzzles and riddles to emphasise the linguistically fabricated nature of his narratives – but the degree to which it has become central is notable in *Kepler*. Once the reader knows about these authorial restrictions and flourishes, it becomes difficult to read the novel as a work of historical realist fiction. The novel is assembled in such a way that the fact of its being assembled (and the figure of its assembler) become a major feature of our experience of it. As Hutcheon writes of this kind of wordplay (using Nabokov and John Barth as its exemplars), it is a form of 'overt linguistic narcissism' which calls the reader's attention 'to the fact that this text is made up of words, words which are delightfully fertile in creative suggestiveness' (Hutcheon, 1984: 120–1).

By using Kepler as an emissary between himself and the reader to convey the secrets of the novel's construction, Banville goes a step further in his self-reflexive contrivances. When Kepler reflects upon his own work, such reflections invariably contain an embedded reflection on the novel itself. While ostensibly referring to his own work (in a letter to one Hans Georg Herwart von Hohenburg), he effectively discusses the extraordinary architectural arrangements of the novel of which he himself is the protagonist:

> before I have any clear knowledge of what the contents might be, I have already conceived the form of my projected book. It is

ever thus with me: in the beginning is the shape! Hence I foresee a work divided into five parts, to correspond to the five planetary intervals, while the number of chapters in each part will be based upon the signifying quantities of each of the five regular or Platonic solids which, according to my *Mysterium*, may be fitted into these intervals. Also, as a form of decoration, and to pay my due respects, I intend the initials of the chapters shall spell out acrostically the names of certain famous men. (Banville, 1981c: 148)

This is a blatant act of self-revelation on Banville's part. As he does with Copernicus, whose 'book was not about the world, but about itself', the author is overtly using his character as a ventriloquist's dummy in order to speak about his own book. As a passage which reflects upon fictional strategies which are already in themselves highly narcissistic, this is an example of compound narrative narcissism. Because *Kepler's* structure is intended to reflect Kepler's, when Kepler in turn reflects upon *Kepler's*, it creates a dizzying hall-of-mirrors effect, in which form reflects content, which in turn reflects form. (This use of *mise en abyme* is, as we shall see, something of a stylistic trademark of the author's work.) Banville has justified the novel's formal arrangement by explaining it as 'the means by which I attempt to show forth [...] the intuitive shape of the particular work of art that is *Kepler*, and which was there, inviolate, before and after the book was written' (Banville, 1981d: 6). Banville is plainly fixated on the idea that a work of art, like a scientific concept, has a kind of Platonic form which pre-exists that work in its physical manifestation. That he wants to 'show forth' this 'intuitive shape' conveys something foundational about his approach to his work in the Tetralogy: he is as interested in representing the process of representation as he is in representing its subject.

This dual allegiance – to the creation of a convincingly rendered fictional universe and to the disclosure of the methods, the authorial tricks, by which it is rendered – constitutes a structural tension in *Doctor Copernicus* and *Kepler*. We read these novels, by and large, as though they were persuasive works of historical realism (as, much of the time, they are) and yet this reading is frequently, and at crucial junctures, undermined by the author's own self-reflexive intrusions. This is precisely the kind of tension Waugh identifies as a paradigmatic characteristic of metafictional writing when she writes of 'the construction of a fictional illusion (as in traditional realism) and the laying bare of that illusion' (Waugh, 1984: 6). The effect of this is doubly narcissistic: the reader is led to reflect upon his or her role as reader by the novel's reflections upon its own role as fiction. This is close to what Hutcheon refers to as the 'metafictional paradox' posed by such self-reflexive works. 'In narcissistic texts,' she suggests, 'there is a two-way pull of contradictory impulses in regarding the language of fiction – for both writer and reader. There is the impulse to communicate and so to treat language as a means (to order as well as to meaning), and there is also the impulse to make an artifact out of the linguistic materials and so to treat the medium as an end' (Hutcheon, 1984: 117).

The novella which follows *Kepler* in the Tetralogy, *The Newton Letter*, is self-reflexive in a way that goes beyond the metafictional strategies of the previous two volumes. Despite its slightness, it can be seen as a pivotal point in the trajectory of Banville's oeuvre, marking as it does the beginning of an unbroken sequence of first-person confessional narratives which continues right through until *The Sea*. It is also the first of a smaller sub-group of works concerned with narrators who withdraw themselves from the world, establishing themselves in a rural setting in order to write and make sense of their lives – a situation repeated in *Ghosts*, *Eclipse* and *The Sea*. The novella's full title, *The Newton Letter: An Interlude*, alludes to both its position within the Tetralogy as a whole and to its content. In the ancient Greek theatre, a tetralogy was a series of four related dramas consisting of three tragedies and one satyr play. *The Newton Letter* is positioned as a kind of comic interlude in the programme of otherwise broadly 'tragic' works which make up the Science Tetralogy. It centres on an interlude in the life and career of the narrator, a historian failing to write a biography of Isaac Newton.

It is worth noting the fact that, of all Banville's novels, *The Newton Letter* is the one text whose protagonist goes without a name.[4] It might be argued that this indicates a greater proximity to the author himself. Banville has spoken in numerous interviews of how his original intention with the Tetralogy was to write four biographical fictions: the first on Copernicus, the second on Kepler, the third on Newton and the fourth on a twentieth-century physicist such as Einstein or Heisenberg. That this third instalment in the series is the first to deviate from this blueprint, and that the novella itself deals with a writer whose plans for a book about Newton have buckled under the pressure of a kind of crisis of faith, are surely relevant and interrelated facts. *The Newton Letter* marks the point at which Banville's plans for his Tetralogy become derailed, and it fictionalises just such an 'interlude' of derailment.

The opening words reflect this anxiety about creative defeat: 'Words fail me, Clio' (Banville, 1982: 1). 'Clio' is a diminutive of 'Cliona', the otherwise unidentified person to whom the narrative is addressed, but its more significant referent, as numerous critics have pointed out, is the Greek and Roman Muse of history. And so, before the reader knows anything else about the novella, he or she knows one of its major concerns: creative anxiety. The historian, like Banville (and like Alexander Cleave and Max Morden), is a native of County Wexford. It is to Wexford (specifically Ferns, a small town in the middle of the county) that he returns in an effort to rescue his failing academic project. 'I was born down there, in the south,' the narrator tells us. 'The best memories I have of the place are of departures from it' (11). These sentiments, as John Kenny points out, correspond 'with Banville's youthful attitude to his native County Wexford' (Kenny, 2009: 72–3). Banville himself has touched upon these autobiographical aspects of the novella. As the 'satiric' component of the Tetralogy, he has spoken of it as a self-parodic venture, as a means, as he phrases it in one interview, of 'sending myself up' (Banville, 1986b: 18).

The Newton Letter, of course, is about much more than the anxieties and circumstances of its own creation; like all of Banville's metafictions, it offers significantly more than mere involution. Derek Hand, for instance, has convincingly argued for an understanding of the satiric character of the work as proceeding primarily from its ironic engagement with the Big House genre of Irish writing.[5] But when we consider it within the overall context of the Tetralogy, its self-consciousness about this context and about its own position within it seem integral, as the 'Interlude' subtitle would appear to suggest. One of the things the novella dramatises is its own (or its author's) unease with the very agency of its existence: written language. Its narrator has, as he puts it on the opening page, lost 'faith in the primacy of text'. Part of the reason for this is the intrusion of real lives, of other people, into the historian's consciousness. The Newton project has been robbed of its impetus by worldly distractions: 'Real people keep getting in the way now, objects, landscapes even' (Banville, 1982: 1). The historian is completely bewildered by the task of setting down the truth about his subject; there is a sense of despair about the possibility of anything approaching knowledge of any other person, let alone one who has been dead for centuries. Just as *The Newton Letter* satirises its narrator's received ideas about the Lawless family with whom he is lodging in Ferns, he himself has grown contemptuous of all received ideas about Newton. He makes fun of the disclaimer provided in a life of Newton recently published by Popov, one of his academic rivals – a disclaimer which Popov, who reminds him of 'an embalmer', quickly sets about negating: *'Before the phenomenon of Isaac Newton, the historian, like Freud when he came to contemplate Leonardo, can only shake his head and retire with as much good grace as he can muster.* Then out come the syringe and the corpse [...]' (21 [emphasis in original]). Retiring is precisely what the narrator himself is doing. In the same way that he has come to be in awe of what he calls 'the insistent enigma of other people', he is mystified by the historical conundrum of Newton's life, and by the task of representing it (19).

One of the book's many enlightening ironies is that, as mystified as the narrator is by Newton and the apparent breakdown he suffered in 1693, his own situation – his crisis of faith – seems to exist as an uncanny reflection of this. He imagines the scientist's reaction to a fire in his rooms in Cambridge, caused by his dog knocking over a candle, in which much of his work is destroyed. He insists that the story itself is 'rubbish', that 'even the dog is a fiction', and yet he finds himself imagining Newton 'standing aghast in the midst of the smoke and the flying smuts with the singed pug pressed in his arms. The joke is, it's not the loss of the precious papers that will drive him temporarily crazy, but the simple fact that *it doesn't matter*. It might be his life's work gone [...] and still it wouldn't mean a thing' (22 [emphasis in original]). The loss of faith in his work, and in the very concept of meaning, which the narrator attributes to Newton mirrors his own loss of faith. In a further telescoping of the book's self-reflexive planes – in which the author is reflected in a protagonist who, as an author himself, is reflected in his biographical subject – this appears to mirror the diversion of the initial scheme for the Tetralogy which has led to the writing of the novella. When the narrator speaks of his original plan for the Newton biography, there is a sense in which we are being addressed by a heavily ironised version of Banville himself:

> Oh, yes, you can see, can't you, the outline of what my book would have been, a celebration of action, of the scientist as hero, a gleeful acceptance of Pandora's fearful disclosures, wishy-washy medievalism kicked out and the age of reason restored. But would you believe that all this, this Popovian Newton-as-the-greatest-scientist-the-world-has-ever-known, now makes me feel slightly sick? (Banville, 1982: 21).

The novella is full of sly intimations of its own fictionality, of momentary crossings of the border between author and protagonist, and of that between biographer and subject. The 'plot', such as it is, revolves around another interlude, a rather tepid and self-consciously provisional affair between the narrator and Ottilie Lawless, the niece of the couple who own the house at Ferns. The affair begins when Ottilie calls on the narrator in his lodge to thank him for coming to the aid of her young son Michael after a minor accident. If the book can be seen as providing an account of the narrator's renewed engagement with other people, with his 'discovery' of alterity, then this is the incident which provides the catalyst for such a discovery. The fact that it involves Michael's falling out of a tree is no doubt a playful allusion to the famously apocryphal story about Newton's 'discovering' gravity upon being struck on the head by a falling apple. The story has in fact been alluded to twice already. The narrator refers, at one point, to the 'sense of harmony and purpose I had felt in the orchard' and, when he tells Ottilie about the subject of the book he is supposed to be writing, she asks him whether Newton was 'the fellow that the apple fell on his head and he discovered gravity' (9). Beyond the Newtonian allusions, the novella is also crowded with intertextual references to earlier fictions, the most central of which are Goethe's *Elective Affinities* and Hugo von Hofmannstahl's *Ein Brief*. Names of minor characters (the Mittler family, for instance) and certain plot elements are taken directly from the former, and the fictional 'second' letter written by Newton to John Locke is based, Banville reveals in a note at the end of the book, on the latter.[6] In addition to this, there are a number of artful references to Yeats throughout the text which reflect the narrator's (entirely mistaken) belief that the Lawlesses are of Anglo-Irish stock – he sees them as literary 'types', as though he were somehow witnessing the action of a Big House novel from within. A chestnut tree on the estate is described, for instance, as a 'great rooted blossomer', and elsewhere Newton is described as a 'fifty-year old public man' (19; 22). Both are references to Yeats's 'Amongst School Children.' John Kenny has identified a less reverent form of Yeatsian allusion in the moment where the narrator observes Edward beginning 'unceremoniously to piss against the trunk'. We can assume, writes Kenny, that in this incident 'the whole Yeatsian Big House symbolism is being disrespected here along with the tree itself' (2009: 76).

This intertextuality has a function other than giving the text a resonance outside of its immediate concerns: it establishes it as a fiction among fictions, historical as well as literary. Metafiction, as Waugh points out, tends to suggest 'that writing history is a fictional act' (1984: 48). By invoking the Newtonian myths of the Cambridge fire and the falling apple, Banville hints at the ways in which real lives are often fictionalised, in which people are made to become 'characters'. *The Newton Letter* is as reflective, that is to say, about the fictions of 'real' life as it is about its own. One of Banville's more notable achievements in the work, in fact, is his shrewd conflation of the two. Much of the novella's humour, its 'satirical' content, is derived from the narrator's consistent misinterpretations of the Lawless family and the nature of the relationships between its members. He is convinced, not without some misleading evidence, that he knows exactly the type of people they are. In fact, 'type' is a crucial word with respect to the book's metafictional comedy of misapprehensions. His complacent belief that he knows exactly what they are like based on a few hazy cultural signifiers – many of which are rooted in the Anglo-Irish literary tradition of the Big House novel – is a frequent focus of satire in the work. Before he even meets them he is already placing the Lawlesses within a particular kind of cultural (and specifically literary) frame: Ferns House, upon his first glimpse of it, is described as 'the kind of place where you picture a mad stepdaughter locked up in the attic' (Banville, 1982: 3). The narrator becomes obsessed with a romanticised vision of the place as an anachronistic outpost of Anglo-Irish aristocracy, and with the Lawlesses as its highly refined denizens:

> I had them for patricians from the start. The big house, Edward's
> tweeds, Charlotte's fine-boned slender grace that the dowdiest of

clothes could not mask, even Ottilie's awkwardness, all this seemed the unmistakable stamp of their class. Protestants, of course, landed, the land gone now to gombeen men and compulsory purchase, the family fortune wasted by tax, death duties, inflation. But how bravely, how beautifully they bore their losses! [...] Shorn of the dull encumbrances of wealth and power, they were free to be purely what they were. (Banville, 1982: 12)

Banville has a good deal of fun at his narrator's expense (as well as, indirectly, his own) by placing in his path clues of increasing prominence as to the reality of the situation. Edward's sister Bunny is a bloodthirsty supporter of violent republicanism. Even her dismissal of her brother as a 'West Brit, self-made' and her proposal that a street should be named in honour of the IRA's murder of Lord Mountbatten are blithely (and absurdly) converted by the narrator into evidence of her quintessential Anglo-Irishness. Later in the same drawing room scene, when Edward threatens an unruly Michael with a hurley – amongst the more culturally encoded of objects with respect to the religious divide in Irish history – and growls '"Do you see this ...?"', it is passed over by the narrator without reflection (37–8). This is not the hurley's first appearance in the text but it is Banville's most blatantly self-conscious use of it as a device. Edward's '"Do you see this ...?"' seems directed more at the narrator's wilful blindness than at the child's wilful disobedience. It is only much later in the novel, when Ottilie mentions a family excursion to Mass, that he finally realises that they are Catholics, and that he has been interacting all along not with the Lawlesses themselves but with his own misconceived, and in a sense fictive, version of them.

In this way, *The Newton Letter* satirises the fictionalising tendencies of both its protagonist and its author. One of its neater and more self-reflexive ironies is the fact that the family the narrator can't help 'reading' through the lens of fiction are named Lawless. The name is a backward nod in the direction of *Birchwood*, whose warring Lawless and Godkin families are in many respects parodic versions of Gothic and Big House stock characters.[7] The novella's narrator 'misreads' the Lawlesses of Ferns in precisely the kinds of terms in which Banville himself has represented the Lawlesses of *Birchwood*. Unbeknownst to himself, he is forcing everyone at Ferns to conform to some or other literary standard. He casts Edward as the 'fortune hunter' who has married into Charlotte's wealthy family, a 'sot' and a 'waster' (1982: 19). Mr Prunty, the local businessman who is in talks with the Lawlesses to buy the estate is cast as a gombeen man. In an instance of characteristic dramatic irony, the narrator informs us of his familiarity with this kind of person: 'I had seen him before: he was a type' (62). His affair with Ottilie is similarly refracted through the prism of fictional cliché. As they walk toward the house with the injured Michael after his fall from the tree, the narrator observes that the three of them 'must have looked like an illustration from a Victorian novelette', and wonders whether Ottilie had 'her hands clasped to her breast' (24). Neither is she herself immune to this kind of fictionalisation of her own and others' lives. She imagines her parents, who died in a car accident when she was a child, as 'a kind of Scott and Zelda, beautiful and doomed, hair blown back and white silk scarves whipping in the wind as they sailed blithely, laughing, down the slipstream of disaster'. His affair with Ottilie, he claims, is conducted through 'the intermediary of these neutral things, a story, a memory, a dream' (26). *The Newton Letter* is a fiction about the way fiction affects peoples' views of each other, about how real people are forced into the straitening frames of characterisation. It is, in this respect, a comedy of mistaken identities.

There is a sense in which the novel can be taken as an elaborate and extended practical joke played on its protagonist, a self-reflexive conspiracy of misreadings in which author and reader collude at the expense of the narrator. The novels of the Tetralogy are characterised by a common search for understanding, by a quest for knowledge of what is referred to in *Doctor Copernicus* as 'the thing itself, the vivid thing' (Banville, 1976: 85). In each of the novels, the notion of truth becomes increasingly nebulous in the eyes of the respective protagonists. Where Copernicus, Kepler and Gabriel Swan move towards despair in their quests for certainty about the universe, *The Newton Letter*'s historian (the only non-scientist protagonist of any of the novels) seems to proceed toward an analagous kind of despair about accessing the 'truth' of others. By the end, he stands uttterly baffled before the 'insistent enigma of other people' and his own 'wilful blindness' towards them (1982: 19; 80). What is at issue here, finally, is his inability to truly see other people. This is a crucial problem in Banville's work as a whole. It is, as we shall see, a major theme of *Ancient Light*, and one which will be further explored in the final chapter.

In *Doctor Copernicus, Kepler* and *The Newton Letter* – with their allegorical artist protagonists and their problematic *magnum opera* – Banville makes use of the self-reflexive device of the work within the work. In *Ghosts* and *Athena*, his two most cryptic and multivalent fictions, he exploits it to the point that it becomes arguably the dominant feature of both novels. In *Ghosts*, the narrator Freddie Montgomery is living on an unnamed island off the southern coast of Ireland, assisting the art historian Kreutznaer with his research on a painter named Vaublin. A group of day-trippers are run aground off the shore of the island and spend a day killing time about the house. The way in which these characters mirror and are mirrored by a Vaublin painting called *Le monde d'or* – along with the consequent ambivalence as to whether these characters are invented – provide the novel's only real friction. In *Athena*, Freddie is engaged to authenticate a cache of counterfeit old masters, and the narrative is interspersed with faux-academic critical appraisals of the works which coyly reflect upon the novel itself, and upon Banville's own style and preoccupations. Self-reflexivity is a presiding characteristic of Banville's work, but nowhere is it more conspicuously in evidence than in these two interlinked novels.

Banville's use of *mise en abyme* is structurally critical to both works. The artists and paintings at the centre of the novels provide a series of warped mirrors in which the author displays various creative distortions of his own image and of the narratives themselves. There is a tendency to associate this narratological device with postmodern metafiction, but arguably its most successful use in literature – and certainly its most famous – is the play staged by Hamlet in order to 'catch the conscience of the King', and which provides a miniaturised reflection of *Hamlet* as a whole (Act 2, Scene 2). The term was coined by André Gide in 1893 to describe the kinds of nested narrative reduplications his own novels, in particular *The Counterfeiters*, would go on to exemplify. 'In a work of art,' wrote Gide, 'I rather like to find thus transposed, at the level of the characters, the subject of the work itself. Nothing sheds more light on the work or displays the proportions of the whole work more accurately'. The term *mise en abyme* comes from Gide's likening of such transpositions to 'the device from heraldry that involves putting a second representation of the original shield "en abyme" within it' (Gide, 1978: 30–1). The critic Lucien Dallenbach defines a *mise en abyme* as 'any aspect enclosed within a work that shows a similarity with the work that contains it' (Dallenbach, 1989: 7). Hutcheon, meanwhile, categorises it as an 'overt form of narcissism', and sees it as one of the more direct forms of challenge to novelistic realism and as one of the best examples of self-reflexivity in narrative. One of its effects as a device, she argues, is to 'shift the focus from the "fiction" to the "narration" by [...] making the "narration" into the very substance of the novel's content' (Hutcheon, 1984: 28).

Ghosts is the most conspicuously plotless of all Banville's novels. Derek Hand refers to it as 'hardly a novel at all in the traditional sense' (Hand, 2002: 145). Joseph McMinn sees it as 'a kind of interregnum in the progress of Banville's fiction, an opportunity to isolate the idea of representation, and to do so in a fictional landscape which is itself isolated from the demands and expectations of conventional narrative' (McMinn, 1999: 118). In one of the novel's more favourable reviews, Thomas Kilroy described it in *The Irish Times* as a 'fiercely intelligent pursuit of certain ideas about writing and their relationship to what we optimistically call the real world' (Kilroy, 1993: 36). So the novel's lack of plot (conventional or otherwise) and its examinations of the complex interrelations between fiction and reality have tended to be its most critically observed characteristics. Banville's aim in this essentially static fiction is precisely the kind of focal shift onto narrative that Hutcheon identifies as a primary effect of *mise en abyme*. To a degree that exceeds even the novels of the Tetralogy, *Ghosts* and *Athena* are fictions which are focused inward, and with narcissistic intensity, upon themselves. The mode – or, more accurately, modes – in which they are narrated becomes a central issue of the narrative. Freddie's enigmatic self-introduction at the beginning of *Ghosts* ('Who speaks? I do. Little god') establishes him as a kind of omniscient third-person-narrative voice, implicitly associated with the all-seeing eye of a minor deity (Banville, 1993a: 4). He tells us things about the shipwrecked day-trippers that only an author could know of his characters or a god of his creations. He refers to them as his 'foundered creatures' (5). This oblique designation is typical of Banville's capacity for exploiting language's loopholes and ambiguities: among the things the word 'creature' can be understood to mean are 'a fictional or imaginary being, typically a frightening one' and 'a person or organisation considered to be under the complete control of another' (*OED*). The word itself has its origin in the Latin verb *creare*, meaning 'to create'. So these 'creatures' of Freddie's are the novel's titular ghosts, neither wholly present nor wholly absent, and under the apparent control of their quasi-divine creator.

The novel is remarkable for the way in which it relates the problem of third-person narration – of intimate imaginings of other minds – with solipsism (referred to in *Athena* as 'my besetting sin' (Banville, 1995: 34)). Freddie is the author of his world in two distinct but affiliated senses: he 'creates' the shipwrecked day-trippers by conjuring their inner lives through a kind of free indirect style, itself embedded within the wider frame of his first-person narrative, and he 'creates' them, in a non-literary sense, by being conscious of them. In this way the ontological status of his 'creatures' becomes uncertain not just within the fictional world of the novel – whether, that is, Freddie has invented them – but also at the level of his consciousness. Even his own reality, as anything other than the ghostly, watchful presence that enables the existence of these others, is doubtful. He is, as he puts it, both 'there and not there' at the moments he narrates. In a phrase which hints at his awareness of his own author-status within the novel's fictional world, he describes himself as 'the pretext of things'. Two senses could be ascribed to this phrase: that which gives the justification for all else, and that which *precedes* the text. Without him, 'there would be no moment, no separable event, only the brute, blind drift of things'. It is his consciousness of phenomena which make those phenomena real and coherent; he is himself the form which he imposes on external chaos, the eye without which things would be only a 'blind drift'. And yet, he admits, though he is 'one of them', he is 'only a half figure, a figure half-seen [...] and if they try to see me straight, or turn their heads too quickly, I am gone' (Banville, 1993a: 40). Freddie and his 'creatures' seem to exist on separate but enigmatically overlapping ontological planes; they exist in each others' respective worlds as ghosts rather than real presences. As such, *Ghosts'* concerns are as much metaphysical as they are metafictional; what is more, each set of concerns mirrors the other to the extent that they become almost indistinguishable.

Le monde d'or, the painting by Jean Vaublin, is referenced by Freddie so frequently and in such exhaustive detail that it threatens to usurp the main narrative as the novel's focal point. What very quickly becomes apparent about the painting is that the scene it depicts is a sort of pictorial mirroring of the novel itself, with each of the main characters represented within it. What is never clear, however, is whether it is the painting which precedes the narrative or vice versa; we are never sure which is real (or 'real', at least, at the level of the fiction itself) and which imagined. The presence of the painting, along with Freddie's discussions of the somewhat indistinct figure of Vaublin, puts further pressure on the already tense relationship in the novel between the real and the unreal. In the absence of any kind of compelling plot, this is what gives the novel purchase, what provides it with a necessary degree of structural tension. We can never be sure whether Freddie is a creation of the Banville-like persona of Vaublin, or whether Vaublin is a creation of Freddie. There is, too, an unsettling amount of correspondence between these parallel planes of reality, between the levels of the narrative's integral *mise en abyme*. This creates a kind of hall-of-mirrors effect, whereby the reader loses all sense of distinction between which surfaces are being reflected and which are doing the reflecting. In one of the novel's numerous instances of cryptic self-contemplation, Freddie makes the following assessment of the troubling relationship between fiction and reality, and between self and other:

> Worlds within worlds. They bleed into each other. I am at once here and there, then and now, as if by magic. I think of the stillness that lives in the depths of mirrors. It is not our world that is reflected there. It is another place entirely, another universe, cunningly made to mimic ours. Anything is possible there; even the dead may come back to life. Flaws develop in the glass, patches of silvering fall away and reveal the inhabitants of that parallel, inverted world going about their lives all unawares. And sometimes the glass turns to air and they step through it without a sound and walk into *my* world. (Banville, 1993a: 55 [emphasis in original])

What is remarkable about this passage, and the book more generally, is its conflation of the mysteries of artistic creation with those of interpersonal perception. The mirror analogy provides a seamless link between the two fields of signification here, between the two types of narcissism to which Freddie simultaneously refers. Brendan McNamee sees in this passage the opposition between two conceptions of reality, two modes of perception: 'the Cartesian outlook which says the world is simply *there*, and what you see – and label – is what you get; and the pre-Socratic outlook which says in effect that reality is an on-going creation, a bargain between phenomena and imagination' (McNamee, 2005: 73). This is a particularly illuminating reading in that it captures the novel's central ambivalence as to the objectivity or subjectivity of experience. This is a key question in Banville, and represents a meeting point for two perennial concerns, the aesthetic and the interpersonal. It is also one which is of a piece with the psychoanalytic conception of narcissism as a problem, or set of problems, surrounding the interaction of the self with the outside world. As such, *Ghosts* can be read as a kind of dual allegory – albeit a highly evasive one – about the relationships between self and other, artist and art. Freddie's perception of Flora, the beautiful and innocent young woman by whom most of the male characters in the novel are beguiled, is emblematic in this respect. What he sees in her, he claims, is the potential for self-renewal (and, one assumes, for deliverance from his past crimes). He sees her as 'pure clay awaiting a grizzled Pygmalion to inspire it with life', an image which reinforces his central self-conception as author-god. 'Not love or passion,' he insists, 'not even the notion of the radiant self rising up like flame in the mirror of the other, but the hunger only to have her live and to live in her, to conjugate in her the verb of being' (70). Just as the narrator of *Shroud* inhabits his lover Cass Cleave, 'creating' her as a character by means of free indirect narrative and seeing in her 'my last chance to be me', Freddie's sexual desire for Flora and his occupation of her as a linguistic construction become lexically ensnarled. This is something which can be seen most clearly in the densely packed sex/language metaphor of conjugating 'the verb of being' (2002: 210).

The process of fiction-making, of creating characters and plots, can be seen as a kind of cipher for interpersonal relations, for the way in which one's own self and the selves of others are always in some sense imaginative 'creations'. If one looks at solipsism as the only fully rational approach to both epistemology and ontology – and there have always been philosophers who have argued that it is precisely that – then to ascribe inner lives or selves to others requires a kind of imaginative leap of faith. Freddie has to struggle against the lure of solipsism, admitting that 'I could not rid myself of the conviction that somehow I was – how shall I put it? – required' (1993a: 25).

He admits, too, to having no idea how he is 'to be expected to know what others are, to imagine them so vividly as to make them quicken into a sort of life' (27). It was, after all, 'because for me she was not alive' that he could kill Josie Bell (1989a: 215). And so fictional creation, as a means of transcending solipsism, becomes something like an ethical imperative. To make others real, to make them 'live', he must imagine them. Like his creation the photographer Sophie, for whom things 'were not real any longer until they had been filtered through a lens' – and like his creator John Banville – it is, for Freddie, through the medium of art that things seem to become real (1993a: 56).[8]

All this is, of course, richly contradictory, and all but resistant to logical analysis. It is morally necessary that Freddie make others real, that he make them 'live', but in order to do this he must become a maker of fictions. This is the fundamental enigma of the novel. To further add to this perplexity, Freddie's own fictionality – both in the sense of his lack of a coherent and immutable self and his status as the narrator of a novel by John Banville – is repeatedly flaunted. He is in a permanent state of fluctuation between the anxieties of determinism and the anxieties of free will, as though he were fully conscious of being both a character in a fiction and that fiction's author. 'Freedom, formless and ungraspable, yes, that was the true nature of my sentence,' he announces at one point, taking full advantage of the dual implication of the word 'sentence'. Then, quoting directly from Gide's *The Immoralist*, he laments that 'this objectless liberty is a burden to me'. Formless and ungraspable freedom might be viewed as one of the fundamental difficulties of writing fiction, as the quasi-existential crisis every author is faced with: the peculiar paralysis of unlimited choice. And yet he speaks of a suspicion that there is some hidden order of things that remains concealed to him, some immense 'secret everyone is in on, except me'. At such points, we as readers are made to feel like voyeurs at risk of discovery by the object of our perception. Freddie's sense of some invisible conspiracy which covertly governs his every move intimates what seems a partial consciousness of his status as the object of perusal and control: 'When I look back all seems inevitable, as if under everything there really were a secret structure, held immovably in place by an unknown and unknowable force' (195). Waugh identifies this concern with agency and determinism – with what she calls 'the problem of human freedom'– as a common one among metafictional novelists. It is, as she puts it, 'a consequence of the perceived analogy between plot in fiction and the "plot" of God's creation, ideology or fate. It is a concern with the idea of being trapped in someone else's order' (Waugh, 1984: 119).

It is into this uncertain territory that the *mise en abyme* device is inserted as a means of at once reflecting and deepening the novel's anxieties about the permeability of the border between the real and the fictional. As an uncanny pictorial replica of the novel itself, of its characters and its pervasive mood of gravid silence, *Le monde d'or* is exactly the kind of transposition of subject Gide refers to in his formulation of the concept of *mise en abyme*. The figure of Vaublin allows Banville to reflect upon his own techniques and concerns, to assert his own presence in the novel without actually inserting himself into it as he does in *Ancient Light*.[9] Freddie's rather approving assessment of Vaublin's painting style is easily readable as an assessment by the author of his own writing style:

> His pictures hardly need to be glazed, their brilliant surfaces are themselves like a sheet of glass, smooth, chill, and impenetrable. He is the master of darkness, as others are of light; even his brightest sunlight seems shadowed, tinged with umber from these thick trees, this ochred ground, these unfathomable spaces leading into night. There is a mystery here, not only in *Le monde d'or*, that last and most enigmatic of his masterpieces, but throughout his work; something is missing, something is deliberately not being said. Yet I think it is this very reticence that lends his pictures their peculiar power. He is the painter of absences, of endings. His scenes all seem to hover on the point of vanishing. (Banville, 1993a: 35)

As Gide wrote of his ideal representational device, 'nothing sheds more light on the work or displays the proportions of the whole work more accurately'. Banville does indeed shed light on his work here, but it is, in keeping with the terms of this elliptical self-assessment, a shadowed kind of light. It darkens as much as it illuminates. In encountering an encrypted description of the novel we are currently reading, within that novel's fictional world, we are made conscious of the status of the novel as fiction, but also of the nebulous distinction between the author, the narrator and the object of his narrative. It is one of the many moments in the novel at which, through the telescoping effect of fictions within fictions – or 'worlds within worlds' as Freddie puts it – Banville, Freddie and Vaublin become consubstantial, as though they formed a kind of three-personed godhead within the cosmos of the fiction. Used in this way, the *mise en abyme* device inevitably forces the reader to reflect upon the way fiction and reality might be thought of as relative rather than absolute concepts. There is something of the optical illusion to this effect, in the way it seems to unsettle our notions of what is and is not real. In his 1939 essay 'When Fiction Lives in Fiction', Jorge Luis Borges, though he never uses the term *mise en abyme*, writes about the peculiar effects such devices can have on a reader. He takes issue with a remark of De Quincey's about *Hamlet's* play within a play to the effect that its deliberately heavy-handed style 'makes the overall drama that includes it appear, by contrast, more lifelike'. Borges' divergence with De Quincey is in keeping with the effects of his own use of the device in the stories he would go on to publish in the 1940s: its 'essential aim,' he writes, 'is the opposite: to make reality appear unreal to us' (Borges, 2001: 161). Banville's use of *mise en abyme* likewise forces the reader to question the distinctions between the real and the invented.

In both *Ghosts* and *Athena*, the deliberate complication of this distinction is compounded by the fact that the paintings that occupy such central positions in the narratives are revealed to be fakes. The concept of forgery is a significant one in Banville's work. His characters, usually intellectuals or artists *manqués*, are almost always frauds of one sort or another. Paintings in the art novels – in *Ghosts*, in *Athena*, in *The Untouchable* (though not in *The Book of Evidence*) – are likewise commonly forged. As such, both types of fraudulence reflect and intensify the other. The series of seven bogus paintings in *Athena*, faux-academic studies of which intersperse the main narrative, offer a kind of extended ironic inquiry into the concept of fraudulence. As a *mise en abyme* device, they intensify the novel's narcissistic preoccupation with its own fictionality. Each of the paintings is the work of an artist whose name is an anagrammed or otherwise disguised version of the novelist's, and each represents a scene which the reader is made to view as an enigmatic depiction of the novel itself. So the paintings are, as it were, doubly forged: they flaunt their own fictionality to the reader, and are fictions within the larger fiction of the novel itself. Perhaps more importantly, they lead us to question the veracity of the narrative within which they are placed and, consequently, the vexed relationship between fiction and reality in general. Both novels are concerned with the relationship between the true and the false. In *Ghosts*, it is the reader who is kept in the dark as to the reality or otherwise of the events being narrated. In *Athena*, it is the narrator 'Morrow' (Freddie's new – which is to say fake – identity) who is deceived. The entire plot of the novel – his employment as an authenticator and evaluator of paintings, his love affair with the mysterious A. and his eventual abandonment by her – is a result of his being drawn into a web of falsehoods; on a basic level, it is a story about his inability to separate truth from fiction. Even Freddie/Morrow's own Aunt Corky, the elderly spinster who moves in with him and dies in his home, is a kind of living fiction: she is not his aunt, and neither is her name Corky. She is entirely her own invention. He is, as he puts it, 'still not sure which one of Aunt Corky's many versions of her gaudy life was true, if any of them was. Her papers, I have discovered, tell another story, but papers can be falsified, as I know well'. She had, he tells us, the ability to lie 'with such simplicity and sincere conviction that really it was not lying at all but a sort of continuing reinvention of the self' (1995: 22–3). This is equally true of every major character in the novel: nobody, least of all the narrator himself, is who they say they are. The villain behind the forged paintings Freddie is working on authenticating, and who is secretly pulling the strings of his affair with A., is the master criminal 'The Da'. A.'s true identity is never revealed, either to the reader or to the narrator himself. At every turn, at the level of both its plot and its narration, *Athena* discredits any idea that reality and fiction might be mutually exclusive.

In their parallel concerns with the concept of fraudulence and their use of the *mise en abyme* as a narcissistic auto-representative device, *Ghosts* and *Athena* have much in common with Gide's *The Counterfeiters*. The latter is concerned with a group of young Parisian novelists and poets and their upper-middle-class social milieu. As a plot device representing the propagation of artistic and personal fraudulence, Gide has a cabal of corrupt aesthetes entangling a younger generation in a plot to circulate counterfeit coins. The novel also features a highly prominent use of *mise en abyme*, whereby one of the novel's central figures, the aspiring young writer Bernard, secretly reads the journal of the established novelist Edouard (modelled after

Gide himself), in which it is revealed that he is planning to write a novel entitled *The Counterfeiters*, the plot of which is clearly a 'fictionalised' version of the 'real' events in the novel. Like Banville, Gide fully exploits the self-representational opportunities afforded by the device of the work within a work. Edouard claims at one point that his aim in writing his novel is 'to represent reality on the one hand, and on the other that effort to stylize it into art'. Here, the *mise en abyme* contrivance permits Gide to represent – 'at the level of the characters', as he puts it in his diary – the process of representation, and in turn to represent that act of auto-representation. In order to achieve this effect, he says, 'I invent the character of a novelist, whom I make my central figure; and the subject of the book, if you must have one, is just that very struggle between what reality offers him and what he himself desires to make of it' (Gide, 1966: 168–9).

The playful critical examinations in *Ghosts* and *Athena* afford Banville a similar means of auto-representation, and of depicting the struggle to make art from experience. In the latter novel, the first painting anatomised is entitled 'The Pursuit of Daphne', attributed to one Johann Livelb. The name is both an anagram of the author's and a reference to one of his earlier novels (in *Birchwood*, the pseudonym Gabriel Godkin uses while performing with the circus is 'Johann Livelb'). The critical appraisal – which, like the others, takes the form of a catalogue entry, complete with dates, materials used and canvas dimensions – seems to allude obliquely not just to the novel's thematic content, but also to its position as the final part of a trilogy which can be understood (if at all) only within that context:

> The action, proceeding from left to right, strikes the viewer as part of a more extended movement from which the scene has suddenly burst forth, so that the picture seems not quite complete in itself but to be rather the truncated, final section of a running frieze. (Banville, 1995: 17)

A later entry examines a painting by an artist named Giovanni Belli, and notes its 'highly worked, polished textures and uncanny, one might almost say macabre, atmosphere'. Also invoked is the artist's 'concern with the theme of death' which manifests itself in an 'obsessive pursuit of stillness, poise, and a kind of unearthly splendour'. This 'constant effort of transcendence', we are told, 'results in a mannered, overwrought style', in a work that is 'too self-conscious, too deliberate in its striving for pure beauty' (75–6). Similarly, the work of the artist Job van Hellin is adjudged to be marked by a certain 'coolness of approach – a coldness, some critics would say' (103). There is a sense here of an author not merely engaging in a narcissistic contemplation of his own work, but mischievously pre-empting – and thereby further goading – his own critical detractors. It would be wrong to characterise this as an exercise in self-parody, but there is an unmistakably arch quality to Banville's self-reflections here, as though he were deliberately and provocatively positioning himself as his own most perceptive critic. Formally, these *mise en abyme* interludes are an extremely skilful performance, not least for the way they attain two distinct registers at once. We read them, that is to say, as cryptic appraisals by the author of his own work and as slightly skewed ventures in art history by a narrator who can never quite keep his own emotions – his own guilt and pain – from derail-ing his attempts at a critical high style. As the novel progresses, the detached poise with which they are composed becomes more and more unstable, until there is a breakdown of the boundary not just between these interludes and the main narrative in which they are contained, but between the author, his narrator, and their critical subjects. And so by the sixth of the seven entries, on 'Revenge of Diana' by J. van Hollbein, Freddie/Morrow is openly confusing the scenes depicted in the paintings with the dissolution of his own love affair with A. The division between art and real life – or between 'art' and 'real life' – is not only indistinct, but insignificant:

> How well the artist has caught the divine woman in her moment of confusion, at once strong and vulnerable, athletic and shapely, poised and uncertain. She looks a lot like you: those odd-shaped breasts, that slender neck, the downturned mouth. But then, they all look like you: I paint you over them, like a boy scrawling his fantasies on the smirking model in an advertising hoarding. (Banville, 1995: 168)

Banville's most recent book is perhaps his most openly self-referential one. *Ancient Light* (2012) is the third volume in what amounts to a loose trilogy with *Eclipse* and *Shroud*. Here, Alexander Cleave looks back on a brief affair, at the age of 15, with his best friend's mother.

In a parallel plot strand which unfolds in a sort of narrative real-time as he writes his account, Cleave is given the lead role in a film adaptation of a book entitled *The Invention of the Past*. The book, it soon emerges, is a biography of Axel Vander, and so the film in which Cleave is starring is essentially a movie version of *Shroud*. In *Eclipse* and *Shroud* – which were, as we have seen, originally conceived as a single novel – there are numerous hints about the doubled relationship between the two protagonists (not least of which is the anagrammatic relationship between their first names). In *Ancient Light*, the two characters finally come to an ironic convergence; in taking on the role of Vander, Cleave sees himself as becoming 'a sort of him, another insubstantial link in the chain of impersonation and deceit' (2012: 82). It's an audacious move on Banville's part, but it isn't merely a clever way of writing himself a blank cheque for metafictional self-reflexivity; it also allows him to offer the sketched summary of *Shroud* that is necessary to fill the reader in on the events which have led to Cleave's present grief-stricken state (most crucially Cass's suicide after a brief relationship with Vander 10 years previously).

When Cleave reads *The Invention of the Past* in preparation for his role as Vander (he knows nothing about Cass's connection to him at this point) his reaction to the book immediately recalls the passages about paintings in *Ghosts* and *Athena*. What strikes him most forcefully about the biography is the author's prose style ('Rhetorical in the extreme, dramatically elaborated, wholly unnatural, synthetic and clotted' (80)). The author, he informs us, is 'widely but unsystematically read, and uses the rich titbits that he gathered from all those books to cover up for the lack of an education [...] although the effect is quite the opposite, for in every gorgeous image and convoluted metaphor, every instance of cod learning and mock scholarship, he unmistakably shows himself up for the avid autodidact he indubitably is' (80–1). At this point, the reader begins to suspect that not only is the biography a fictionalised – or re-fictionalised – version of *Shroud*, but that its author is recognisably another self-portrait (Banville never attended university, and regularly refers to himself in interviews as an autodidact). The biographer, it turns out, is also the screenwriter for the film adaptation; when he turns up on the set, he is introduced by the initials JB, and the readers' initial suspicions are wholly confirmed. Cleave describes this 'teller of our tale' as 'a somewhat shifty and self-effacing fellow of about my vintage', and remarks that he seems 'ill at ease' on the set, presumably because he 'considers himself many cuts above mere screenwork'.[10] This self-insertion (which is, in an obvious sense, the precise opposite of self-effacement) is reminiscent of the authorial self-representations in J. M. Coetzee's work, but even more strongly of Martin Amis's small but pivotal role in his own novel, *Money*. Where that novel's narrator John Self is decidedly unimpressed by Amis (whom he estimates can't make much money from his work), Cleave, when he finally meets JB for a drink towards the end of *Ancient Light*, is bewildered by the 'distinctly odd' and reticent author. 'He maintains a furtive, anxious air,' Cleave tells us, 'and gives the impression of always being in the process of edging nervously away.' JB is then revealed to be an instigator of the events leading up to this point in the novel, as Cleave informs us that he was in the audience on the night of his disastrous performance of Amphitryon 10 years previously, and was so 'impressed' that he recommended Cleave for the role of Vander. It is also JB who finally reveals to Cleave – perhaps inadvertently, perhaps not – that the character he has been playing in a film had been having an affair with his daughter when she committed suicide. Banville has, in a sense, cast himself in the role of his own *deus ex machina*.

Ancient Light is structured around a central cluster of dramatic ironies. Like the narrator of *The Newton Letter*, Cleave is largely ignorant of the crucial facts about the story he is narrating. On one hand, he is entirely unaware of the fact that Mrs Gray was terminally ill at the time of their affair (he is, as it were, narcissistically focused on his own story at the expense of paying proper attention to the details of hers). But he is also denied access to privileged information about the story he himself is narrating; we as readers (particularly those readers who have already read *Shroud*) understand far more about what he is telling us than he understands himself. Cleave is, in this odd sense, the ironic inverse of an unreliable narrator. That scene late in the novel, where Cleave and JB sit down and talk face-to-face, is deeply ambiguous, but one of the ways in which the author's 'furtive, anxious air' might be explained is as a result of his guilt about his manipulation of Cleave as a character. There's an obvious element of self-satire here, of course – Banville would be unlikely to feel anything toward his characters, least of all guilt – but JB does seem to be suffering some discomfort in the scene, and this might be read as an ironic gesture towards the situation in which he has contrived to place his 'protagonist.' When he informs Cleave that Vander had been in Portovenere, the remote Italian village where Cass committed suicide, and that he suspected it was a research assistant of the Nebraskan academic Fargo DeWinter who had unearthed Vander's past, Cleave finally puts the elements of the story together. JB seems to understand the nature of Cleave's realisation, and his uneasiness is obvious. He looks away from Cleave, 'frowning, and making a faint distressed humming noise at the back of his throat' (235).

It's difficult to avoid reading this moment as, on some level, a kind of dark and veiled joke about the discomfort the author would feel about his treatment of his protagonist were he, in reality, to have to sit down and share a drink with him at a gentleman's club. The relationship between 'reality' and 'fiction' – the relationship, that is, between levels of fiction – has become so incestuously complex in *Ancient Light* as to amount to a kind of bleak sexual-ontological farce. Just as the Oedipal nature of the relationship between the young Alex and Mrs Gray is almost comically overdetermined, the line between Vander (his daughter's much older lover) and himself has been troublingly obscured. He is Vander's avatar in the fictional world of a film about the relationship between him and a young lady he does not know is Cass. Furthermore, his relationship with the actress playing Cass in the film (called 'Cora' in the screenplay) has grown into a distressingly ambiguous hybrid of the romantic and the filial. Cleave has unwittingly been playing a role in a production based on a 'true story' which is much closer to his own life than he has been aware. If the trilogy of *Eclipse*, *Shroud* and *Ancient Light* is taken as one composite work of art, *The Invention of the Past* is an intertextual version of the classic *mise en abyme* as defined by Gide, a transposition 'at the level of the characters [of] the subject of the work itself.'

In Banville's use of *mise en abyme*, however, the influence that is most prominent is not that of Gide, but of Nabokov. It is perceptible not merely in the distinctly Nabokovian use of encrypted versions of the author's name, but more significantly in the tactic of outlining a fictional work as a means toward reflecting the actual work at hand. Banville's *mise en abyme* follows the pattern of the outlined plots of the eponymous author's novels in *The Real Life of Sebastian Knight*. The narrator of Nabokov's novel designates himself only as V, the supposed half-brother of the supposedly deceased novelist Sebastian

Knight. Enough oblique hints are dropped, however, for the reader to suspect that the narrative, which presents itself as a kind of hybrid critical biography/detective fiction, might well be the work of Knight himself. Just as with the paintings in *Ghosts* and *Athena*, the discussions of Knight's fictional novels are all covert discussions of the actual novel we are reading. The narrator's appraisal of Knight's masterpiece, entitled *The Doubtful Asphodel*, reads as a direct reflection of not just the book itself, but of our own experience of it as readers. The mystification which characterises V's reading experience mirrors our own with eerie precision: 'I sometimes feel when I turn the pages of Sebastian's masterpiece that the "absolute solution" is there, somewhere, concealed in some passage I have read too hastily, or that it is intertwined with other words whose familiar guise deceived me. I don't know any other book that gives one this special sensation, and perhaps this was the author's special intention' (Nabokov, 2001: 151). At a point near the end of the novel where we as readers begin to feel ourselves at the cusp of some sudden revelation about the identities – or identity – of Sebastian and V, the narrator says of Knight's novel: 'At this last bend of his book, the author seems to pause a minute, as if he were pondering whether it were wise to let the truth out' (150–1). The uncanny effect of this kind of faithful representation, within the narrative itself, of our experience of reading it, is one which Banville achieves with his own *mise en abyme* contrivances. In *Ghosts*, for instance, Freddie makes a remark about Vaublin's *Le monde d'or* which expresses precisely the kinds of perplexity which mark our reading of the novel:

> I look at this picture, I cannot help it, in a spirit of shamefaced interrogation, asking, What does it mean, what are they doing, these enigmatic figures forever frozen on the point of departure, what is this atmosphere of portentousness without apparent portent? [...] In this picture there seems to be a kind of valour in operation, a kind of tight-lipped, admirable fortitude, as if the painter knows something that he will not divulge, whether to deprive us or to spare us is uncertain. (Banville, 1993a: 95)

What Banville has inherited from Gide and from Nabokov is a method whereby the fiction can narcissistically contemplate its own reflection. The *mise en abyme*, by continually drawing attention to the fabricated status of the narrative in which it is embedded, makes it impossible for us to forget about the figure of its fabricator. In this sense, it is an example of what Hutcheon terms 'overt linguistic narcissism': a device by which a work shifts focus 'from the "fiction" to the "narration" by either making the "narration" into the very substance of the novel's content, or by undermining the traditional coherence of the "fiction" itself' (Hutcheon, 1984: 28). In Banville's work, such a strategy allows the novels to address themselves, without as it were breaking their own narrative frames, to the matter of their own internal processes and effects. What is perhaps finally most important about Banville's use of *mise en abyme*, however, is not that it allows him to reflect – and reflect upon – his own writing, but that it forces us as readers to reflect upon our own reading. The representations of fictions within the fictions themselves – the strange spectacle of a character in a fiction struggling to interpret a work of art in a way which reflects our own struggles to interpret that fiction – brings us ultimately to a consciousness of our own role as readers, and to a recognition of the importance of the acts of reading and fiction-making in everyday life. Banville uses the *mise en abyme*, in other words, to set up a fictional hall of mirrors in which the reflections of the author, the reader and the narrator become artfully confused. In this way, the self-reflexivity of Banville's novels takes the central concern with narcissism beyond the confines of psychology – with how the characters interact with themselves and others – and into the realm of our experience of the fiction. The author's self-involved engagement with his own writing becomes, of necessity, the reader's narcissistic encounter with his or her own reading.

7
The Paradox of Empathy

In the period between the completion and the publication of *The Infinities*, Banville gave an interview with *The Paris Review* in which he spoke about his initial attempts to write his previous novel, *The Sea*, in the third person. Despite working on this version for 18 months, he claimed, his efforts to break out of his accustomed narrative mode proved unsuccessful. 'I suspect that the reason I don't really believe in the third-person mode,' he said, 'is due to the fact that I'm such an egomaniac. Unless it's me speaking, it's not convincing – to me, that is' (Banville, 2009a: 147–8). Although allowances should be made for a certain amount of self-ironisation, the comment nonetheless deserves to be taken seriously as a writer's appraisal of his own tendencies. Until *The Infinities*, each of Banville's novels since *Kepler* had (with occasional deviations) taken the form of the first-person confessional narrative. Where his novels switch to a third-person perspective – much of *Ghosts*, parts of *Shroud*, most of *The Infinities* – the narration becomes highly problematic, and is always revealed to be an effort on the part of a first-person narrator to recount a story from a point of view other than his own. These forays out of the accustomed perspective of the self into that of third-person omniscience might be viewed as imaginative attempts by these narrators to transcend their own obsessive self-regard, to move beyond their own narcissistic encounters with the world.

There is, for example, an extremely powerful passage in the closing pages of *The Book of Evidence* in which Freddie Montgomery comes to the conclusion that the reason he was able to murder Josie Bell was that she was never fully real for him:

> That is the worst, the essential sin, I think, the one for which there will be no forgiveness: that I never imagined her vividly enough, that I never made her be there sufficiently, that I did not make her live. Yes, that failure of imagination is my real crime, the one that made the others possible. What I told that policeman is true – I killed her because I could kill her, and I could kill her because for me she was not alive. (Banville, 1989a: 215)

What Freddie is guilty of, in other words, is a narcissism so extreme as to be a complete denial of the independent reality of this other person. The explicit view of human relations here is that in order to transcend this kind of pathological narcissism, it is necessary to 'imagine' the other person into being. His primary transgression – his original sin, as it were, 'for which there will be no forgiveness' – is one of omission rather than commission: he fails to engage in this imaginative act of empathy. For much of the rest of the Art Trilogy, and in *Ghosts* in particular, Freddie is concerned with imagining the inner lives of others, and thereby seeking some kind of atonement for his murder of Josie Bell. This latter novel is greatly exercised by the difficulties and complexities attending the relationship between an author and his creations (his 'creatures'), and with the odd parallels that exist between that relationship and those between people generally. What I want to bring to light in this final chapter are the ways in which these problematic attempts at third-person narration are instrumental in the narrators' efforts to transcend their narcissism and advance towards a more empathic, less self-centred position in relation to others.

Although the Freddie we encounter in *The Book of Evidence* is an extreme case, the distinction between him and Banville's other protagonists is one of degree rather than kind. These men tend to be characterised by a bewildered scepticisim about the inner lives of others; they are, in a sense, reluctant solipsists. This position is outlined in the early pages of *The Infinities* when one of the characters watches a young boy through the window of a stalled train and considers the apparent self-contradiction of the existence of other selves. 'How can he be a self and others others since the others too are selves, to themselves?' he asks, before concluding that the whole problem is simply a matter of perspective, a kind of existential optical trick. 'The eye, he tells himself, the eye makes the horizon [...] The child on the train was a sort of horizon to him and he a sort of horizon to the child only because each considered himself to be at the centre of something – to be, indeed, that centre itself – and that is the simple solution to the so-called mystery. And yet' (Banville, 2009b: 9).

The argument of this chapter is that when we encounter these third-person narratives in Banville's work, what we are essentially encountering is an attempt to solve this 'so-called mystery' by addressing the problem of perspective, of illusory horizons. Before setting out this argument in relation to the novels themselves, however, it will be helpful to briefly address the idea of empathy, in particular its relationship to narcissism and to the concept of narrative itself.

Along with narcissism, empathy is one of the psychoanalytical concepts with which Kohut engages most extensively in his writing. He categorises it, in fact, as one of what he calls the 'transformations' of narcissism – as one aspect of 'the ego's capacity to tame narcissistic cathexes and to employ them for its higher aims' (Kohut, 1966: 85). He links the capacity for empathy with the stage Freud outlined as primary narcissism, in which the relationship between an infant and a mother – the original 'selfobject', in Kohut's terminology – takes the form of a kind of psychic merging.

> The groundwork for our ability to obtain access to another person's mind is laid by the fact that in our earliest mental organisation the feelings, actions, and behaviour of the mother had been included in our self. This *primary empathy* with the mother prepares us for the recognition that, to a large extent, the basic inner experience of people remain similar to our own. Our first perception of the manifestation of another person's feelings, wishes, and thoughts occurred within the framework of a narcissistic conception of the world; the capacity for empathy belongs, therefore, to the innate equipment of the human psyche and remains to some extent associated with the primary process. (Kohut, 1966: 78 [emphasis in original])

Empathy, for Kohut, is therefore the ability to psychically place oneself in another person's mind – to perform a trick of perspective – and this is an ability that must grow out of an initial narcissism. The apparent paradox in this position is resolved in the image of the infant who sees no distinction between itself and its mother. Just as such a merger is inherently narcissistic (in that the mother's face is a reflection of the infant's inner state of exultation or distress), it is also a profoundly empathic one. Without a barrier between self and other, that is, the affective interchange moves in both directions.

Kohut most lucidly defined empathy as 'the capacity to think and feel oneself into the inner life of another person', as 'our lifelong ability to experience what another person experiences' (Kohut, 1984: 82). As such, empathy involves an imaginative leap akin to the work of the novelist. To ask what it might be like to be another person is, in a sense, to create a character, just as the creation of a character necessarily involves asking what it might be like to be that particular (imagined) person. Kohut is not alone in seeing this as less an analogy than an identity. The American philosopher Martha Nussbaum, for instance, has written extensively on the centrality of imagination to empathy, and on the vital connections between the reading and writing of fiction and the ability to understand and share the feelings of real others. She distinguishes empathy from compassion by stressing that it has no moral content per se: it is, as she puts it, 'simply an imaginative reconstruction of another person's experience, whether that experience is happy or sad, pleasant or painful or neutral' (Nussbaum, 2003: 302). Empathy is, in other words, a necessary but not a sufficient condition for compassion, and it is for just that reason that it is important: 'If I allow my mind to be formed into the shape of your experience, even in a playful way and even without concern for you, I am still in a very basic way acknowledging your reality and humanity' (333). It is through our engagement with fictions that we increase our capacity to engage empathically with other human beings. Tragedies in particular, she argues, promote empathy by provoking us to consider the possibility that we may find ourselves in similar situations. The arts in general, and the narrative arts in particular, provide a foil to the perils of pathological narcissism: 'The tragic spectator, as long as she plays that role in the way that the drama constructs it for her, will not be afflicted by pathological narcissism or a paralysing shame at her failure to be omnipotent [...] Nietzsche's idea was that this experience helps people to embrace their own lives. Sophocles' (closely related) idea – and my own – is that it helps them to embrace the lives of others' (353). This is, perhaps unsurprisingly, a view frequently shared by novelists, many of whom have explicitly linked the practice of their art with the crucial human quality of empathy. George Eliot, in her essay on German realism, explicitly outlined the idea that art can jolt us out of our selfish complacency and into a deeper sense of the actual experiences and sufferings of others. 'The greatest benefit we owe to the artist,' she wrote, 'whether painter, poet, or novelist, is the extension of our sympathies. Appeals founded on generalisations and statistics require a sympathy ready-made, a moral sentiment already in activity; but a picture of human life such as a great artist can give, surprises even the trivial and the selfish into that attention to what is apart from themselves, which may be called the raw material of moral sentiment' (G. Eliot, 1967: 270–1). Likewise Virginia Woolf, with a typical combination of arrogance and insight, wrote in her journals that 'the reason why it is easy to kill another person must be that one's imagination is too sluggish to conceive what his life means to him' (Woolf, 1977: 186). More recently, in J. M. Coetzee's *Elizabeth Costello*, the eponymous novelist asserts that the true horror of the Nazi death camps was the refusal of the murderers – and of those German citizens who ignored their crimes – to think themselves into the place of their victims. Coetzee/Costello's view of the Holocaust is like a version of Freddie Montgomery's crime on a massive scale: millions of people refusing to make the suffering of millions of others into a reality for themselves; failing to make these others real by failing to imagine them:

> They said, 'It is *they* in those cattle cars rattling past.' They did not say, 'How would it be if it were I in that cattle car?' They did not say, 'It is I who am in that cattle car.' They said, 'It must be the dead who are being burned today, making the air stink and falling in ash on my cabbages.' They did not say, 'How would it be if I were burning?' They did not say, 'I am burning. I am falling in ash.' (Coetzee, 2003: 79)

What unites these authors is the conviction that art and empathy are indivisible. Eliot's high Victorian 'moral sentiment' and Coetzee's post-Holocaust emphasis upon the ethical importance of translating 'they' into 'I', though very different in their modes of expression, essentially articulate this same conviction. If we can imagine the inner lives of others, then we are more likely to feel an important connection with them and are therefore less likely to do harm to them.

Banville is even less of a straightforward moralist than Coetzee, and any discussion of such matters as they relate to his fiction has to take into account the ambivalence with which they are handled. His public persona is (more often than not) that of the unapologetic aesthete, and he has repeatedly given short shrift to the notion that literature may have any social function. He is fond of repeating Wilde's famous pronouncement that 'all art is perfectly useless', with the emphasis as strongly on the concept of perfection as on that of uselessness. Here is how he put it in a 2003 interview with the American writer Ben Ehrenreich:

> I'm rather inclined to agree with Auden, that poetry – all art – makes nothing happen. Real art is perfectly useless, if by useful we are thinking of politics, morals, social issues, etc. Cyril Connolly put it well and simply when he declared that the only business of an artist is to make masterpieces. (Banville, 2005a: 51)

He is clearly unwilling to be read as an author with any kind of moral purpose; his artistic aims are descriptive rather than prescriptive. But there is a crucial sense in which the descriptive project can have moral ramifications, and this is something at which Banville hints later in the same interview:

> You ask me what a work of literature must do in order to be worthy of the name. I suppose I would say it must have a quality of the transcendent. I do not mean metaphysical transcendence, but a kind of heightening. In the work of art, the world is made for a moment radiant, more than itself while at the same time remaining absolutely, fundamentally, mundanely, utterly itself. So the artistic act is almost like the sexual act: in the glare of its attention, the Other, in a sudden access of self-awareness, takes on a transcendent glow. High talk, I know, but we are, I take it, talking of high art. (Banville, 2005a: 51)

Part of the definition of literature for Banville is its acute attention to what is outside of the self, to the capitalised 'Other'. It is worth recalling at this point that Freddie Montgomery's crime is represented as one of *inattention* to the other: he never makes his victim 'be there sufficiently' (1989a: 215). He recognises in himself a need 'to pay more attention to people', and is surprised that, when he really tries, he is 'afforded a glimpse into what seems a new world, but which I realise has been there all along, without my noticing' (213). Similarly in *Shroud*, when Vander comes to realise the nature of his mistreatment of Cass Cleave, he traces its roots to the same source. 'It was plain inattention,' he confesses. 'The object of my true regard was not her, the so-called loved one, but myself, the one who loved, so-called' (2002: 210). And so the difference between attentiveness and inattentiveness has profound moral ramifications; it is the difference between narcissism and empathy. The sin for which Ovid's Narcissus is punished, after all, is essentially that of inattention. He is blithely uninterested in everything and everyone outside of himself. As counterintuitive as it may seem to say, there is a sense in which fiction writing, for Banville, is a way out of, or a way through, narcissism. That this claim is not quite as at odds with the fiction as it appears to be – or with the view of it I have so far been advancing – is something that will become clear in the pages that follow.

At the conclusion of *The Book of Evidence*, Freddie resolves somehow to atone for his murder of Josie Bell. His task, as he puts it, is 'to bring her back to life'. He is unsure what it is he might mean by this, but the notion strikes him nonetheless 'with the force of an unavoidable imperative' (1989a: 215–16). This is, by definition, an unachievable project, but the implication seems to be that he might somehow be able to do this by 'inventing' her anew, by creating her as a writer would a character. 'How am I to make it come about, this act of parturition? Must I imagine her from the start,' he wonders, 'from infancy? I am puzzled, and not a little fearful, and yet there is something stirring in me, and I am strangely excited. I seem to have taken on a new weight and density. I feel gay and at the same time wonderfully serious. I am big with possibilities. I am living for two' (216). The language here explicitly links the process of gestation with the process of literary creation, hinting at, if not an equivalence, then a correlation between the two. Freddie is leading himself (and the reader) to believe that he has the power to create life, that were he to just 'imagine' Josie Bell as he failed to do when he killed her, he might somehow put things right. The absurdity of this idea is self-evident, though it is by no means apparent that Freddie is being disingenuous. It would, nonetheless, be unwise to take his claims at face value. It may be less painful for him to claim that he killed Josie Bell because she was not 'really there' than to admit that he saw her clearly enough, apprehended her in her otherness, and yet still killed her. Freddie's description of her in the moments before the murder echoes Banville's statement about how, in the glare of art's attention, the world is made 'for a moment radiant, more than itself while at the same time remaining absolutely, fundamentally, mundanely, utterly itself':

> I could not speak, I was filled with a kind of wonder. I had never felt another's presence so immediately and with such raw force. I saw her now, really saw her, for the first time, her mousy hair and bad skin, that bruised look around her eyes. She was quite ordinary, and yet, somehow, I don't know – somehow radiant. (Banville, 1989a: 113)

Banville evidently wants the reader to think about the parallels and the differences between Freddie's response to the woman depicted in the portrait he has just stolen and his response to Josie. Freddie is struck by the way in which the woman in the painting seems to look at him, by the 'querulous, mute insistence of her eyes.' He squirms, he tells us, 'in the grasp of her gaze. She requires of me some great effort, some tremendous feat of scrutiny and attention, of which I do not think I am capable. It is as if she were asking me to let her live' (105). He goes on to honour that request by inventing a detailed third-person narrative about the woman, imagining her life and, in particular, the days on which she sat for the portrait. The painting's penetrating gaze seems to mirror not just Freddie's last glimpse of the living Josie, but Banville's ideas about art's almost sexual glare of attention, in which 'the Other, in a sudden access of self-awareness, takes on a transcendent glow'. The artist fixes his eyes upon her with 'a kind of impersonal intensity, and she flinches, as if caught in a burst of strong light. No one has ever looked at her like this before. So this is what it is to be known. It is almost indecent' (106–7).

The fact we cannot disregard is that Freddie is moved by the gaze of the woman in the painting to imagine a life for her, while his vision of Josie as 'ordinary and yet [...] somehow radiant' immediately precedes his killing her. Elke D'hoker rightly points out a strong resemblance between Freddie's language and that of Emmanuel Lévinas, in whose philosophy the face of the other is a challenge to the self to respect that other's absolute autonomy and difference, and to forego all exercise of power and violence. 'Whether or not Banville consciously used Lévinasian diction to describe the irreducible responsibility Freddie owes the work of art,' writes D'hoker, 'his description installs an analogy between the encounter with a work of art and an interpersonal encounter, which has become a commonplace in contemporary literary theory' (D'hoker, 2004a: 148). D'hoker rejects Nussbaum's 'all too optimistic hopes of an easy transference of imaginative identification from the realm of art into the real world' and her 'confidence in the moral value of the imagination' (169). In her Lévinasian reading of *The Book of Evidence*, to imagine the inner life of another – as opposed to respecting that other's absolute strangeness and separateness – is somehow to expropriate that person's selfhood and assimilate it to one's own mental categories. The imagination, she claims, is marked by a 'destructiveness' and by an 'authoritarian tendency to deny difference and recuperate the other to the same' (169).

D'hoker's anti-Nussbaumian argument suggests that Freddie's imaginative identification with the woman in the portrait is really just a narcissistic form of self-identification. When Freddie turns toward the portrait, she points out, he sees himself turning, and when he stares at the portrait, 'he finds himself being stared at in return. The properties thereby ascribed to the portrait are not so much those of a painting,' she concludes, 'but look suspiciously like those of a mirror, suggesting – even if still only tentatively – that what Freddie encounters in the portrait is perhaps only a mirror image of himself' (153). Though it is worth observing that one's own reflected face is not the only face that returns one's stare, D'hoker's reading is still compelling. Freddie's engagement with art, like that of all Banville's protagonists, is deeply narcissistic. She fails, however, to establish precisely how Freddie's identification with the woman in the portrait is at the root of the failure 'to respond adequately to the ethical call of the other in Lévinas' terms' that leads him to murder Josie Bell.[1] The crucial point she ignores is that, while Freddie does engage imaginatively with the portrait, he never does so with Josie. If anything, the epiphanic face-to-face confrontation in the car before he murders her is much closer to the Lévinasian ethical encounter than to Nussbaum's or Kohut's ideas of imaginative identification. For Lévinas, 'the face of the other in its precariousness and defence-lessness is for me at once the temptation to kill and the call to peace, the "You shall not kill"' (Lévinas, 1996: 167). Above all else, what haunts Freddie is the fact that he has had such a face-to-face encounter and succumbed to the temptation rather than the interdiction. In *Ghosts*, Freddie's third-person retelling of the murder registers this sense of moral bewilderment:

> He recalls with fascination and a kind of swooning wonderment the moments before he struck the first blow, when he looked into his victim's eyes and knew that he had never known any creature – not wife, child, not anyone – so intimately, so invasively, to such indecent depths, as he did just then this woman whom he was about to bludgeon to death [...] How, with such knowledge could he have gone ahead and killed? How, having seen straight down through those sky-blue, transparent eyes into the depths of what for want of a better word I shall call her soul, how could he destroy her? (Banville, 1993a: 85–6)

It is not that Freddie fails to *see* her then, so much as that he fails to engage imaginatively with what he sees. If he had given life to the real image of Josie Bell in the way that he gave life to the artistic vision of the woman in the portrait, he would most likely not have killed her. D'hoker is right to characterise Freddie's identification with the portrait as a narcissistic one, but that narcissism is more complex than she allows for. This complexity is captured in a phrase with which Kohut attempted to define empathy: 'vicarious intro-spection'. The term, in its apparent self-contradiction, encapsulates the way in which empathy is, from his psychoanalytical point of view, dependent on a fundamental, primary narcissism. Kohut sees empathy as 'the capacity to think and feel oneself into the inner life of another person', and the subject in that formulation is every bit as important as the object.

Banville himself would in fact appear to be more aligned with the Kohut/Nussbaum school of thought than with Lévinas. In a

2000 interview, he acknowledged both an ethical dimension and an unintended allegorical theme to the book:

> I realized many years after I had written it that *The Book of Evidence* was, in many ways, about Ireland because it was about the failure of the imagination and the failure to imagine other people into existence. You can only plant a bomb in Omagh main street if the people walking around in the street are not really human. And what happened in Ireland in the last 30 years was a great failure of the imagination. (Banville, 2000d: 15)

And so if *The Book of Evidence* is, as Banville puts it, about the failure to imagine other people into existence, *Ghosts* is about the attempt to redress that failure. One of the major frustrations this attempt meets is Freddie's uncertainty about his own identity, his seeming inability to be 'simple, candid, natural [...] to be *honest*'. His essential difficulty is the narcissistic problem of self-identity. 'How then,' he asks at the outset of his narrative, 'was I to be expected to know what others are, to imagine them so vividly as to make them quicken into a sort of life?' (1993a: 27).

Given the centrality of this question, it is perhaps inevitable that there are moments at which *Ghosts* feels like little more than a very elaborate and skilfully executed creative writing exercise. It is as though Freddie, the narcissistic 'little god' of his fictional world, were trying to train the direction of his gaze outward through the application of the literary imagination. It often seems to be this outwardness itself – the direction of the gaze rather than its object – that matters. So the narrative is characterised by a kind of languor and aimlessness, as though Freddie were simply making up the whole thing. At one point, for instance, after describing the lounge of the house in which he is living, his attention is drawn, for no obvious reason, towards tea and the drinking of it. 'Tea. Talk about tea', he directs his writing self. He discourses eloquently for a third of a page about various blends and drinking vessels before outlining, in fine novelistic detail, a scene brought to his mind by the drinking of tea:

> Tea tastes of other lives. I close my eyes and see the picker bending on the green hillsides, their saffron robes and slender, leaf-brown hands; I see the teeming docks where half-starved fellows with

legs like knobkerries sticking out of ragged shorts heave stencilled wooden chests and call to each other in parrot shrieks; I even see the pottery works where this cup was spun out of cloud-white clay one late-nineteenth-century summer afternoon by an indentured apprentice with a harelip and a blind sister waiting for him in their hovel up a pestilential back lane. Lives, other lives! a myriad of them, distilled into this thimbleful of perfumed pleasure. (Banville, 1993a: 54)

A similar impression of spontaneity is conveyed by the way in which Freddie's third-person narration flits between his various 'creatures'. 'Croke now, try Croke,' he proposes to himself before embarking on an account of Croke's ramble in the woods around the house (118). Shortly after Croke suffers what appears to be a minor heart attack – or shortly after Freddie imagines him doing so – Freddie suddenly breaks off the narrative and returns to himself. He feels a pain in his own chest, and reflects that he may be 'the one who is dying of his heart' (126). This sense of the permeability of the boundaries between Freddie's own mind and those he is attempting to inhabit with his narration is one of the most intriguing and frustrating elements of *Ghosts*. It reflects the equivalent porousness of the boundary between fact and fiction, in that we never know whether Freddie is imagining the inner lives of actually existing others, or whether these others are entirely his own inventions. As a narrator, Freddie is unreliable in the extreme. Rüdiger Imhof's recommendation on how to view this radical indeterminacy seems, at first, a sensible one to follow. 'Perhaps,' he suggests, 'it is best to suppose that the whole is a product of Freddie's imagination, albeit based on fictional "fact". Freddie may be on the island, and when one day that group of shipwrecked pleasure trippers comes to the house, he experiences other lives and takes occasion to fill these with his imaginings for a particular purpose: the restitution of a life' (Imhof, 1997: 198–9).

And yet, as so often with Banville, an apparent truth is challenged by an apparent counter-truth. The notion of a distinction between the real and imagined is always undermined. There is an enigmatic moment close to the end of the novel where Freddie speaks of how 'one day' he would 'look out the window and see that little band of castaways toiling up the road to the house and a door would open into another world'. What follows seems to suggest that Freddie is in fact still confined to his prison cell, and that the entirety of his narrative – both the first-person account of his own experience and the third-person accounts of others' – has been an invention:

> And out there in that new place I would lose myself, would fade and become one of them, would be another person, not what I had been – or even, perhaps, would cease altogether. Not to be, not to be: the old cry. Or to be as they, rather: real and yet mere fancy, the necessary dreams of one lying on a narrow bed watching barred light move on a grey wall and imagining fields, oaks, gulls, moving figures, a peopled world. (Banville, 1993a: 221)

What this rather vague and ethereal passage hints at is a conception of 'self' and 'other' as hazily delineated categories. The 'they' to whom Freddie refers, the 'moving figures' in his 'peopled world', are like ghosts, neither wholly exterior nor wholly interior to the self. Just as when we read this passage we come to realise the likelihood that Freddie's entire narrative has been an invention, we are also implicitly encouraged to think about other people as 'real and yet mere fancy', about how they are always 'necessary dreams'. Whether Freddie is in a cell or whether he is on an island may be finally (in both senses of the word) immaterial. What ultimately matters is the isolation and solitude inherent in both positions, and the imaginative leap of faith that is necessary for him to leave that isolation, to come to the 'new place' outside of his narcissistic seclusion.

One of the implications we might take from this is the necessity of a kind of soft – as opposed to hard – solipsism. The self must imagine the other in order for that other to have any reality for the self. The (perhaps illusory) barrier between self and other has to come down in order for an empathic connection to take place. As an idea, this resonates with Kohut's notion of empathy as a 'capacity to think and feel oneself into the inner life of another person', a capacity fundamentally rooted in an original narcissistic conception of the world.

As D'hoker has pointed out, *Ghosts* is filled with depictions of characters standing in door frames, suspended in shadow between one space and another (D'hoker, 2004a: 160–1). Licht 'hovered in the dimness of the doorway'; Flora 'shimmered in the doorway'; Mrs Vanden is seen 'rising up suddenly in the dim doorway'; Croke's 'shadow fell in the doorway'; while Freddie even depicts himself as 'a half figure, a figure half-seen, standing in the doorway' (Banville, 1993a: 15; 40; 43; 75; 130). This neither-here-nor-thereness of the characters is central to the philosophical substance of *Ghosts*. Others are neither entirely illusory nor entirely real – existing like ghosts in neither one ontological space nor another – and it is the medium-like agency of the imagination which can bring them across the threshold of the self into a state of full (subjective) reality. Others must be brought into focus by the imagination. Banville's claim that 'the world is not real for me until it has been pushed through the mesh of language' would appear to be a way of phrasing this kind of soft solipsism (2009a: 135). The artistic imagination, and specifically the medium of narrative, must be brought to bear on the world in order for the self truly to connect with it.

Such attempts at connection are at the heart of *Shroud*. Axel Vander tries and ultimately fails to solve the enigma of Cass Cleave by means of a free indirect narrative which represents the events of the novel from her point of view. As with *Ghosts*, there is a crucial link between the process of third-person narration and the desire to atone for the sin of 'inattention', but there is little to suggest that Cass might be an invented character, at least in the literal sense. It is her unknowability as a woman that constitutes an intractable moral and emotional problem for Vander. He is, as he puts it, 'dazzled by the otherness of her' (2002: 214). This language of awed incomprehension, particularly as it relates to the opposite sex, is a major feature of Banville's work; the other, in his novels, is almost always the female other.[2] In *Athena*, for example, Freddie admits to a similarly thorough incomprehension of women. 'I do not understand women,' he admits. 'I mean I understand them even less than the rest of my sex seems to do. There are times when I think this failure of comprehension is the prime underlying fact of my life, a blank region of unknowing which in others is a lighted, well-signposted place' (1995: 46).

One of the more disturbing aspects of *Shroud*, however, is the way in which Vander equates his desire to understand Cass with a longing to possess her, to take occupancy of her body and mind. In an unforgettably gruesome series of images, Vander represents his sexual attraction to her as a furious desire for absolute penetration. 'Even her nakedness would not be enough,' he says, 'I would open up her flesh itself like a coat, unzip her from instep to sternum and climb bodily into her, feel her shocked heart gulp and skip, her lungs shuddering, clasp her blood-wet bones in my hands' (2002: 68). He does not want simply, in the vernacular of desire, to 'possess' her, but to occupy her, to usurp her. There is a striking correspondence here between this expression of aggressive sexual longing and the idea of the author who longs to 'inhabit' – to *get inside* – his character. The sections of the novel in which Cass's experience is narrated from the third-person perspective are those in which Vander attempts this authorial infiltration of the other. Again and again, these creative and sexual aims are conflated in a manner that obstructs any attempt to make a direct connection between narrative and empathy. Vander is attempting to 'think and feel himself' into the inner life of Cass, but his designs upon her are as much about possession as vicarious introspection.

This is not to imply that Vander is incapable of empathic feelings for Cass, or that his third-person narration is purely a bid for imaginative occupancy. *Shroud* is a particularly complicated novel, even within the context of a particularly complicated *oeuvre*. Vander's desires and motives are obscure even to himself, and there are no plain moral distinctions in his narrative. Perhaps the most that can confidently be said on the subject of Vander's empathy for Cass is that the matter is radically obscured by desire. At one point, as he watches her reflection in a hotel room mirror, he is completely overwhelmed by her otherness and by his own desire not simply to grasp it, but to infiltrate it:

> Who was she, what was she, this unknowable creature, sitting there so plausibly in that deep box of mirrored space? Yet it was that very she, in all the impenetrable mysteriousness of her being entirely other, that I suddenly desired, with an intensity that made my heart constrict. I am not speaking of the flesh, I do not mean that kind of desire. What I lusted after and longed to bury myself in up to the hilt was the fact of her being her own being, of her being, for me, unreachably beyond. Do you see? Deep down it is all I have ever wanted, really, to step out of myself and clamber bodily into someone else. (Banville, 2002: 214)

This passage exhibits an elaborate network of associations. There is, first of all, the familiarly metafictional usage of 'creature' and 'plausibly'. Then there is the conflation of the penetrative imagery of sex and violence ('bury myself in up to the hilt'), and the notion of clambering bodily into another which is suggestive of authorial desire to 'inhabit' a character, as well as of Vander's own appropriated identity. The complications and contradictions surrounding the notion of empathy are inescapable here. Vander's obsession with the otherness of his lover has more to do with himself than with her. He admits as much, acknowledging that he 'used' her 'as a test of my authentic being', that he 'seized her to be my authenticity itself'. 'That was what I was rooting in her for,' he tells us, 'not pleasure or youth or the last few crumbs of life's grand feast, nothing so frivolous; she was my last chance to be me' (210).

His failure to connect with her is figured in terms of an analogous authorial failure – a failure, as it were, to capture her consciousness. 'I tried, I tried to know her,' he laments. 'I tried to see her plain and clear. I tried to put myself into her inner world, but [...] I came only to an immemorial, childhood place, exclusive haunt of the third-person. She would not be known; there was not a unified, singular presence to know' (212). As an account of a frustrated attempt at interpersonal connection, it is difficult to read this passage as anything other than a veiled allusion to the author's own difficulties with third-person narrative.

And yet what is so often striking, despite Vander's insistence upon the ultimate failure of his narrative experiment, is just how convincing (or, to use his preferred term, 'plausible') he manages to make those sections of the novel which he narrates from Cass's point of view. Vander, though he is almost always present as an object of Cass's thoughts and perceptions, is almost always invisible as an authorial presence. It is (when he wants it to be) a remarkably persuasive act of literary ventriloquism. He has done his research; he has, as he puts it, 'been looking into' the condition from which she suffers (202). When Cass is introduced in the first of these third-person sections, she is sitting in the lobby of Vander's hotel waiting for him to come down from his room to meet her. Her mental instability is instantly apparent in the way in which her neurosis and paranoia seem to cripple her ability to engage in even the most superficial of social transactions. When the receptionist asks her whether she would like tea or coffee while she waits, she feels compelled to decline. She does not know, we are told, 'what the procedure for paying would be'; she imagines herself 'offering him money only to be met with an offended stare'. She feels certain that he knows she is not a guest, and that his manner of ironic condescension towards her is a consequence of this. She considers a very strange explanation for how he might have come to know this about her: 'Perhaps everyone checking in was photographed in secret,' she speculates, 'and the pictures were kept in a file under the desk, and he had gone through it and not found hers' (55).

This may or may not be a faithful representation of the way in which Cass's damaged mind works; the reader cannot know either way. But what seems certain is that it is not Vander's way of thinking; when he imagines her here, he imagines her as thoroughly strange, thoroughly other. There is a sense here of real empathy. One possible explanation for Vander's use of the third- rather than first-person form in his representations of Cass is that it allows for a certain respectful distance. From this narrative vantage point, he can try to know her without fully occupying her. She retains her separateness, her strangeness; in this way, her suffering is rendered as uniquely hers. 'To pity another's woes,' as Rousseau puts it 'we must indeed know them, but we need not feel them' (Rousseau, 1979: 190).

One of the most intriguing aspects of *Shroud*, and a major factor in its seemingly endless ambivalence, is the apparent impossibility of ascertaining just how noble an endeavour Vander's narrative exercise actually is. Though *Ghosts* and *The Infinities* are, in their different ways, highly subtle and complex novels, the 'moral sentiment' which motivates their narrators' explorations of others' inner lives seems much clearer. It is in *Shroud* that Banville most starkly presents his bleak view of intersubjectivity, of the complex of desires and compulsions that is at once oversimplified and hopelessly obscured by the word 'love'. When Vander is questioned as to whether he loves Cass, his answer discloses the severity, and the fundamental narcissism, of this attitude: 'I said that of course I loved her, but love is only an urge to isolate and be in total possession of another human being' (Banville, 2002: 234). Love, in this sense, looks more like greed than affection, more like the desire for mastery than for intimacy. This is no less reductive and shallow than the more conventional and sentimental view; it is also no less legitimate, no less true. Vander's entire relationship with Cass might be seen as, amongst other things, a reminder of the fact that the Latin word for love or desire, *cupido*, is the root of both 'Cupid' and 'cupidity'.

The attitude (or perhaps the pose) of the novel's early pages is one of contrition. There is a strong sense that the text itself, which is nominally addressed to Cass, is a kind of bid for moral salvation. 'I am going to explain myself, to myself, and to you, my dear, for if you can talk to me then surely you can hear me, too,' writes Vander. 'Calmly, quietly, eschewing my accustomed gaudiness of tone and gesture, I shall speak only of what I can vouch for' (4–5). He is haunted, he reveals, by the notion of his 'being given one last chance to redeem something of myself', and it occurs to him that this 'might have been your real purpose, not to expose me and make a name for yourself at all, but rather to offer me the possibility of redemption' (5). And towards the end of the novel, when Vander finds out that Cass is pregnant with his child, it is to the prospect of redemption that his thoughts immediately turn. This conception – which Cass's suicide ensures will never come to fruition – is viewed as a 'saving grace':

> Let me be clear; it was not I who would be saved. For once, it was others I was thinking of. Growing already inside this girl was the enfolded bud of what would be a world reclaimed [...] My gentle mother, my melancholy father, my siblings put to summary death before they had lived, all would find their tiny share in this new life. Oh, fond old man! How could I have thought this world would allow for such redemption? (Banville, 2002: 240)

Vander's thoughts about the prospect of fatherhood echo Freddie Montgomery's thoughts about the prospect of authorhood at the end of *The Book of Evidence*, where he feels he has 'taken on a new weight and density', that he is 'big with possibilities' (1989a: 216).[3] Neither man can help himself from believing that there might yet be some hope for redemption of past sins. Though Vander insists it is not his own salvation he is thinking of here, the claim seems somewhat dubious. His bad conscience about the fate of his family is as much the guilt of the betrayer as of the survivor; his narrative is an attempt to recover the lost prospect of redemption Cass's pregnancy seemed to offer.

It is only after Cass's death, after all, that Vander begins to write his narrative (and hers), and it is only then that he begins to care for the dying Kristina Kovacs. There is undoubtedly a causal connection between Cass's death and Vander's uncharacteristic empathy towards Kristina (who, until this late stage, has been disdained as little more than a past sexual conquest and a present annoyance). But there is something strangely disturbing in his tendency to collapse the distinctions between the women he has wronged and survived. The deceased Magda becomes the living Cass, and the deceased Cass becomes the dying Kristina. It is as though his narcissistic callousness has led him to sin against some abstract platonic category ('woman'), as opposed to – more mundanely and more significantly – against actual individual women. Vander repeatedly conflates Magda and Cass in his imagination, and his guilt about the former undergoes a dramatic transference onto his feelings about the latter. He ignored his wife while she was alive, and now he cannot help seeing her in Cass:

> While she was alive I could hardly be said to have given her a second thought, while now she was constantly on my mind, if only as a shadow, the solitary spectator sitting in the benches above the spotlit ring where the gaudy and increasingly chaotic performance of who and what I am pretending to be is carried on without interval [...] Only in death has she begun to live fully, for me. (Banville, 2002: 35–6)

Significantly, it is only when Vander is first struck by a resemblance between Cass and Magda that he begins to feel something other than contempt for her. Watching her walk down the stairs of the house once occupied by Nietzsche, he admits, 'I thought, jarringly, of Magda'. He embraces her and, as they kiss, he has a vision of himself sitting opposite Magda in their home, feeding her the tablets which killed her. The kiss ends, he releases Cass, and she stares at him with 'Magda's very gaze' (70–1). We later learn that during their subsequent love-making Vander whispers his dead wife's name in Cass's ear (103).

Shroud is a novel about, amongst other things, the breaking down of boundaries between people. Vander crosses a moral and psychological boundary to usurp the identity of his friend; Cass and Magda merge in Vander's imagination; and his imagination, in turn, attempts to break down the boundary between himself and Cass through narrative invention. But just as such boundary-crossings can, and do, lead to increased empathic engagements with others, they can also lead to a position whereby the distinctions between individual others are lost, to where the self is the only real subject. Vander's attempts at imaginative occupation of Cass's mind are also an attempt to atone for his mistreatment of Magda, just as his caring for Kristina Kovacs in her last days is an attempt to atone for his failure to care for Cass in hers. One of Vander's critics, he recalls, once claimed that 'moral shiftiness was the most striking characteristic of every line that I wrote' (65). It is precisely this moral shiftiness that characterises every line of *Shroud*. It is almost always impossible to tell whether Vander is facing up to or evading the moral magnitude of his wrongs, whether his narrative is an atonement or an artful equivocation. The reader must constantly question the truth of what he or she is being told, and must constantly ask who is doing the telling, 'who speaks'. Plausibility, as always, is a key concept, and Vander's overwhelming difficulty is that he is not plausible to himself. The problem that confronts Vander, then, may be a more extreme version of the problem that confronts Banville himself as an author. To say, as he has, that one doesn't really 'believe' in the third-person mode, is to say more than that one has certain difficulties with the technical or aesthetic aspects of a given narrative approach. It is not so much a statement of preference, in other words, as a statement of belief. As a writer, his faith in the third-person mode is subject to the same kind of crisis as his narrators' faith in the possibility of knowing other people, in the possibility of representing otherness through narrative. The self is the central problem, which must be solved before the mystery of the other can be addressed, but it is a problem without a solution. This is the question that so torments Vander. How is he to know someone else, to know who that other is, when he is so irredeemably other to himself? This same question torments Freddie in *Ghosts*, and it is one which has yet to be resolved fully in Banville's *oeuvre*. It is in *The Infinities*, however, that he comes closest to reaching some form of accommodation with the problems of intersubjectivity and empathy.

Although very different in tone and published 16 years apart, there are many respects in which *Ghosts* and *The Infinities* might be viewed as counterpart works within the context of Banville's *oeuvre*. The events of both novels take place over the course of a single day and are confined in both cases to the setting of a large rural house. Both are unusual in that they focus not on a single male protagonist but on a group of disparate figures brought together through unfortunate circumstances – the cruise ship running aground in *Ghosts* and, in *The Infinities*, the serious illness and imminent death of Adam Godley (called 'old Adam', as much to distinguish him from his son as to associate him with the first man of Christian mythology). In both books the reader is addressed directly by a voice which claims the status of divinity – the 'little god' who speaks in *Ghosts* and the narrator presenting himself as the Greek god Hermes in *The Infinities*. In each novel, there is furthermore a point at which the reader begins to realise that the events being related may in fact be taking place not in 'reality' but in the narrator's head. In the passage quoted above, Freddie appears to reveal himself as conjuring the narrative of *Ghosts* out of thin air as he lies in his prison cell. Similarly, there are several points in *The Infinities* at which it becomes apparent that the voice that has all along been identifying itself as Hermes is in fact that of old Adam, who is lying in a coma and cannot possibly have the intimate knowledge he claims of others' inner lives. There is, with each novel, a point of epiphanic disclosure at which we realise that the narrative that has actually been unfolding is very different to the one we thought we were following; where the things we have been reading about are revealed to have been the inventions of a man alone in a room with his imagination.

In each case, there are hints quite early on that the narrated events may be the result of such cryptic fabulism. Freddie, attempting to imagine the horrors of the famine of the 1840s, remarks that such grief and suffering is 'unimaginable', before deciding this is not the case: 'No, that's not right. I can imagine it. I can imagine anything' (1993a: 31). Our first direct introduction to old Adam in *The Infinities* is in the third-person mode, though the voice – ostensibly that of Hermes – insinuates that what we are reading may be the product of Adam's own imagination. The phrasing is markedly similar to the corresponding passage in *Ghosts*:

> And look, here he is, old Adam, the dying progenitor himself. Dying, yet he cannot conceive of a world from which he will have departed. No, that is not right. He could conceive of it. He can conceive of anything. Conception of impossible things is what he does best. He was ever pregnable by the world. (Banville, 2009b: 30)

As with the passage in *The Book of Evidence* in which Freddie wonders what 'act of parturition' will be necessary to create the murdered Josie Bell anew, the language here exploits the dual senses – creative and procreative – of terms like 'progenitor', 'conceive' and 'pregnable'. Old Adam, like his biblical namesake, is the progenitor figure in this story, the fatally ill father around whom the other characters are gathered. He is also, in a sense which has not yet become apparent, the progenitor *of* the story itself. Old Adam, who is locked inside the world of his own head, represents an extreme instance of a problem which has, to some degree or other, characterised almost all of Banville's protagonists. Where this would be true figuratively of Freddie Montgomery or Axel Vander, it is true both figuratively and literally of old Adam. He is not, that is to say, just a solipsist; he is a solipsist in a coma. Like Malone in Beckett's *Malone Dies*, he is telling himself stories as he waits for the end. The difference here would seem to be that he is not inventing characters, but imagining the thoughts and interactions of real people. He is attempting to transcend his narcissism by projecting himself into the minds of the people closest to him, by exercising what Kohut calls 'the capacity to think and feel oneself into the inner life of another person'.

Lying immobilised in bed, he tries to think about his daughter-in-law Helen, asleep elsewhere in the house, and comes up against what seems to be a kind of logical conflict:

> He tries to grasp with his mind the reality of her, asleep or waking, being there where he is not. Before the autonomous existence of others he shares his son's doubt and wonderment [...] He asks, how can people go on being fully real when they are elsewhere, out of his ken? He is not such a solipsist – he is a solipsist, but not such a one – that he imagines it is proximity to him that confers their essential realness on people. Of course others exist beyond his presence, billions of others, but they are not part of the mystery proper since he knows nothing of them, cares nothing for them. The truly mysterious ones are the ones who are most familiar to him, his sad wife, his neglected offspring, his desired daughter-in-law. (Banville, 2009b: 34–5)

The use in this context of words like 'doubt', 'wonderment', and 'mystery', is expressive of a particular existential orientation – or disorientation – that is essential to Banville's art. Banville, as we have seen, has claimed that bafflement is his 'strongest artistic sensation'; the process of writing is, for his narrators, a means of attempting to address this bafflement (Banville, 2006b: 206). With *The Infinities*, as with *Ghosts* and *Shroud*, the act of narrating is a means of confronting a specific source of this kind of bafflement: the enigma of other minds. In those parts of the novel supposedly narrated by Hermes, the god's-eye-view is an attempt to see through the impenetrable opacity of otherness. The fictive device of the Hermes persona allows old Adam (as well as Banville) to inhabit various characters, and to view the world through their eyes. Hermes is an appropriate choice for this task. In Greek mythology, he is not only the messenger god and the guide to the underworld, but also the god of boundaries and of those who cross them.[4]

The Infinities can be seen as a novel concerned with the crossing of two sorts of boundary: that between life and death, and that between self and other. Hermes (who it is worth noting also serves as god of invention and lies) allows Adam to cross the border not just between this world and whatever comes after it, but also the border between himself and those around him. He allows him to transcend the solipsism which has characterised his world view; he enables him to think and feel himself into the lives of others. Hermes, from whose name the term hermeneutics derives, is a method by which sense can be made of other minds.

There is, of course, an artistically appealing (and quintessentially Banvillean) irony in all of this, which is that in order to achieve this transformation of narcissism into empathy, Adam imagines himself a deity. Hermes, the messenger god, serves as a visionary medium between himself and the people closest to him. For this great physicist, whose discoveries have changed the quasi-mythical world in which the novel is set, and whose solipsism and remoteness align him with the Science Tetralogy's 'high, cold heroes who renounced the world', this imaginative transformation – this apotheosis – might be seen as the literalisation of a figurative truth (see *The Newton Letter* (Banville, 1982: 50)).

At one point, old Adam speaks of having been greatly unnerved by the 'incontrovertible otherness' of his infant children, his 'conjured creatures', as he calls them (2009b: 229). Their strangeness and disconnection from him was, he insists, of a more extreme form than that of either of his two wives, because with the latter there was always 'a passionate cleaving to me that gave at least the illusion of getting over that gap, the gap of otherness' (230). The strange mutability of the novel's narrative voices and perspectives, its elisions of the first- and third-person modes and its contraction of the spaces between individual positions, all represent a closure of this gap of otherness. The comatose Adam has, we are told, achieved 'the apotheosis he has always hankered after' and has become 'pure mind' (31).[5] His own consciousness, his own self, has become strangely diffuse. An unbodied presence in his own world, his relationship with those around him is suggestive not just of that between god and mortal, but of that between author and character. In old Adam's mind, as in the novel itself, the phenomenological boundaries have come down; past and present, self and other, are no longer stable and distinct categories. 'Everything blurs around its edges,' we are told, 'everything seeps into everything else. Nothing is separate' (71). It is signalled at one point, for instance, that the child looking at the house through the window of a stalled train in the novel's early pages – the child by whom young Adam is prompted to think about the paradox of other minds – might well have been an apparition of his father's younger self. We are informed that, as a child, old Adam was taken by his mother to the city for 'a Christmas treat' and bought 'a ten shilling watch':

> Even in those days the train used to stop here for no reason, in the middle of nowhere, and he would press his face to the window and look longingly at this house standing in a shroud of frost-smoke – this very house, if he is not mistaken and he believes he is not – and dream of living here, of being what his disparaging mother would have called a big fellow, with money and a motor car and a camel-hair overcoat. (Banville, 2009b: 32)

This irruption of the past into the present is even more remarkable when we consider that it also doubles as an authorial interpolation. In a television interview around the time of *The Infinities'* publication, Banville spoke about the novel's genesis:

> When I was a child I was taken on my birthday every year to Dublin for a treat. We bought a watch in Clery's. And the train

used to stop, somewhere near Gorey I think, every morning. It was a very early morning train, and the dawn was coming up, and I used to look across the field at a house there, and I used to try to imagine what lives were going on inside it. You know, there's something about a house standing on its own in a field. And that I suppose was the germ. (Banville, 2009c)

There are two distinct senses, therefore, in which the entire novel is the work of the staring boy's imagination. He is both Banville and Godley, and *The Infinities* is the space in which their imaginings are brought to life. The reality of the novel, then, is one in which Godley's theory about 'our existing in the midst of multiple, inter-twined worlds' holds (2009b: 35). The boy on the train occupies a liminal space between the past and the present and between the realms of fiction and reality. The profound irony of his brief appear-ance in the story is that, although when young Adam sees him he reflects upon the absolute separateness and unknowability of others, he in fact operates as an image of the *lack* of such distinct boundaries between selves. Narrative – the writing of fiction and the imagining of others' inner lives – is the medium through which such bounda-ries may be broken down.

One of the ways, then, in which *The Infinities* can be understood as representing an effort to transcend narcissism and move towards a position of empathy or other-directedness is this sense that all the characters are united by the fluid medium of the novel's narration. There is a seeming paradox here in that this breakdown of the bound-ary between self and other can just as easily be seen as solipsism. This paradox, which resonates strongly with Kohut's understanding of empathy as growing out of a fundamental narcissism, is what gives the novel much of its intellectual vitality and mystery. It seems, fur-thermore, to encapsulate something essential about Banville's view of human relationships in all their enigmatic contradictions. Towards the end of his narrative, Hermes/Adam seems to lose track of his shifting personae. 'Who am I now?' he asks. 'Enough, enough, I am one, and all – Proteus is not the only protean one amongst us' (244). This admission on the part of a profoundly unreliable narrator echoes a similar admission by Banville himself, who has said of the characters in the novel that they are 'all me, they're all versions of me. They have to be – I'm the only material I have to work with' (2009c).

One of the elemental ironies of *The Infinities* is that, while old Adam is a rather cold and remote figure – a narcissist with, we are told, an odd aversion to addressing people by their names – the 'Hermes' persona is (certainly by the standards of Banville narrators) an unusually warm and empathic narrative voice. He is mischievous and playful, to be sure, but his covert interactions with, and observations of, the novel's cast of characters are marked by an unusually high degree of imaginative identification. It is as though, in his suspended state between life and death, old Adam were being given a chance to atone for his lifelong narcissism through a radical opening-out of perspective. The insuperable division which had seemed to exist between himself and the world is now no longer, and he is able to feel with and *for* others. 'How all things hang together,' observes Adam/Hermes, 'when one has the perspective from which to view them' (2009b: 241).

It is through the third-person perspective, through the god's eye view of 'Hermes', that the dying Adam becomes a more benign and empathic figure than he ever was in life. He seems to want – the novel itself seems to want – happiness for his loved ones, for his 'characters'. Most of Hermes' interventions into the mortals' world are aimed at making things better for them, at bringing them together and making their lives more tolerable. As the novel draws to a close, we begin to realise that old Adam is telling himself stories about the happy lives his loved ones (his alcoholic wife, his self-harming daughter, his unhappily married son) will live after he is gone, and that he knows these stories for the fictions they are:

> They shall be happy, all of them. Ursula will drink no more, she and her son will go down and ceremonially empty the laurel hedge of its burden of bottles and the rats will come out and frolic like lambs. Adam and Helen will move here to Arden to live, Adam will delve and till as his originary namesake did, while Helen will wear a bonnet and carry a pail, like Marie Antoinette at the Petit Hameau. Petra will put away the razor and wound herself no more. (Banville, 2009b: 299)

The transparency of these fantasies is what makes them so affecting. These are, presumably, the final moments of Adam's life, but we are not hearing about Adam; we are hearing about his family, and about his wishes for their happiness. They are gathered around him in his final moments, and in this sense he is the centre of the narrative. He is not, however, that narrative's focus. On the threshold of death, he becomes, in every sense of the term, selfless. Like his Hermes persona, he is 'one, and all'.

The Infinities, for all its extravagant conceits and ludic involutions, presents us with a starkly paradoxical conception of intersubjectivity. We never know the extent to which the events we are reading about are 'real' events, and this is more than just a by-product of the way the novel is written – it is, in many respects, its most important feature. In order to get beyond his steadfast narcissism, old Adam has to imagine the inner lives of others; in order to make people real, in other words, he has to make them up. Freddie Montgomery's recognition in *The Book of Evidence* that his essential sin was 'a failure of imagination' is, in this sense, a pivotal moment in Banville's *oeuvre*, because it identifies a problem which has characterised so much of the moral content of the fiction. Though it is a problem which is never fully resolved, it is *The Infinities* which, in its elliptical way, comes closest. Through the process of narration old Adam manages to transcend his self-absorption, and this redirection of attention away from the subject and towards the object is reflected in the atypical warmth and lightness of the novel itself. The fact that this outwardness and empathy is indivisible from the narrator's fundamental solipsism – the fact that, enclosed, so to speak, hermetically in his coma, he invents the inner lives of those around him – attests to the great richness of irony and complexity that characterises Banville's view of the selfhood and intersubjectivity.

8
Conclusion

In attempting to account for his devotion to the first-person narrative form, Banville has spoken of a 'monotonous murmur' in his head, and of how he feels he must translate this murmur into prose 'over and over again' in order to do it justice, to 'get it right' (Banville, 2006b: 201; 203). It is this murmur, he says, which is the source of his fiction: 'I'm not interested in politics, I'm not interested in society, I'm not interested in Man. I seem to be just interested in this voice that goes on and on and on in my head' (201). Banville's avowed lack of artistic concern with the world outside of his own consciousness is not so much a restriction upon the scope of his vision as an intensification of its focus. His work, as this book has explored, is concerned with the narcissistic character, and is likewise narcissistic in its forms and techniques. His style is a highly self-conscious one; just as his narrators are obsessively inward-directed, his language is always acutely concerned with its own elegance, its own ambiguities and evasions. The result is a radically self-enclosed body of work. As he put it in an *Irish Times* article following the death of Samuel Beckett: 'All literary artists in their heart want to write about nothing, to make an autonomous art, independent of circumstance' (Banville, 1989b: 18). Banville no doubt errs on the side of generalisation here, but what is not necessarily true of all literary artists is certainly true of him. His art, like his narcissistic narrators, aspires to the condition of absolute autonomy. Its mood of total, often oppressive interiority is a function of this narcissistic rejection of context: the voice – the 'monotonous murmur' of consciousness – is everything.

Ideas of selfhood and identity have long been recognised as central to Banville's fiction. The individual's encounter with and representation of the world has emerged as a dominant theme in the ever-growing body of scholarship on his work. The complexity of Banville's engagement with these issues can be seen in the centrality of contradiction and paradox to his fictional imagination. His prose is vivid and composed, yet it is frequently ambiguous, shrouded and enigmatic. His characters are overwhelmingly concerned with self-display, and yet they are tormented by anxieties about exposure, about being laid bare to the scrutiny of others. They frequently create grandiose self-images and exhibit a deeply arrogant attitude towards the world, and yet are afflicted with shame about themselves and their origins. They are obsessed with finding a degree of authenticity, with locating some kernel of truth about themselves, yet are rigorously sceptical about the very notions of selfhood and truth.

The forms of isolation with which these novels are concerned – remoteness from others and alienation from the self – are mirrored in the literary forms through which they are represented. Banville's preferred narrative style, the first-person confessional, is also marked by a central contradiction. Its apparent aims are self-revelatory, but it lends itself more than any other style of narration to the kinds of obfuscation and circumvention that are so characteristic of these novels. The narcissists behind these first-person accounts are scarcely more convincing to themselves than they are to the reader. They are too fragmented within their psyches and too subjective in their engagements with the world to present a coherent and intelligible totality. They do not conform to the patterns of 'realistic' characterisation, but it is their lack of realism in the literary sense that ensures their psychological verisimilitude. They are unreliable not just as narrators, but as selves: the term 'reliable' derives from the Latin word *religare*, meaning 'to bind together forcefully.' Like Narcissus, who fails to achieve a union with himself, these unreliable narrators, despite their attempts at narrative self-composition, fail to bind themselves together. Like Narcissus, they are attentive almost exclusively to their own reflections, but are always misled (and misleading) as to the reality of themselves. And if psychoanalysis could be said to have a single identifiable aim, it would be the scrutiny of people's narratives of selfhood, the exposure of their inventions and misconceptions about themselves.

Moreover, his work's concern with its own fictionality and its shrewd manipulations of the uneasy relationship between the real and the imagined are inseparable from the psychological complexities of the narcissistic character. The narrators' doubts about their own authenticity and about the reality of others are mirrored, that is, by the metafictional ambiguities of the novels they narrate. There is, in this sense, an integrity to Banville's work, a correspondence of form and content, which might not be apparent from a casual reading, and which I have been endeavouring to bring to light here. The fiction's most powerful challenges to the tradition of novelistic realism are posed in its repeated inquiries into the issue of voice and its origins, its endless reformulations of the question 'who speaks?' Banville's nebulous vision of the narrating 'I', and of the subject who may or may not lie behind it, is rooted in a narcissistic sense of the self as primary and ultimate, as all there is, and at the same time strangely spectral – endlessly obscure and possibly immaterial.

The self-enclosure of the fiction – its endless self-reflections and narrative involutions and its representation of relentlessly inward-directed minds – is its most important characteristic. Narcissism, as both technique and theme, is so profoundly engrained in these texts that it makes sense to think of them as a series of fictional meditations on, and formal experimentations with, the concept. It is ever-present, manifesting itself again and again in various guises. The recurring motif of twins and doubles is a symbolic rendering of the psychological divisions of narcissism, of its complex of powerful attractions and compulsions. The pervasive concern throughout the *oeuvre* with shame, and with rejection of the family in favour of an idealised self-conception, becomes comprehensible when seen as an aspect of the characters' narcissism.

Narcissism manifests itself everywhere as both an ontological and epistemological problem, as a pervasive question of being and knowing, encapsulated in Freddie's confusion about how, when he is so uncertain as to his own identity and reality, he can possibly 'know what others are' or 'imagine them so vividly as to make them quicken into a sort of life' (Banville, 1993: 27). And this, crucially, is also the moral question at the heart of Banville's fiction, the central ethical difficulty which makes it so much deeper and more demanding an artistic venture than the mere exercise in formal and aesthetic mastery many critics have dismissed it as being. Narcissism is a core concern of Banville's *oeuvre*, a crucial feature of its content and its composition, and it is the psychological stalemate which his protagonists must attempt to transcend in order to begin to live fully and authentically. It is, for Banville, the ultimate truth of the self and its troubled relationship with the world.

Notes

1 Introduction

1. There is a degree of uniformity to these characters, their situations and their mindsets, that allows us to speak of a typical Banville protagonist with as much legitimacy as we may speak of a typical Beckett or Kafka protagonist. There is an undeniable continuity – much more pronounced than mere fictional family resemblance – between all of Banville's protagonists, stretching arguably from *Nightspawn*'s Ben White, but certainly from Freddie Montgomery in *The Book of Evidence*, to *The Sea*'s Max Morden.

2. Freud's first use of the term 'narcissism' appears in a footnote added in 1910 to his 'Three Essays on the Theory of Sexuality', to denote a phase in the development of male homosexuality. His interpretation of the classical myth is, in this sense, quite a literal one.

2 Banville's Narcissists

1. This article of faith is one which character and creator evidently hold in common. In the essay 'Making Little Monsters Walk', Banville delivers the following series of excessively lofty aphoristic paradoxes: 'Nietzsche was the first to recognize that the true depth of a thing is in its surface. Art is shallow, and therein lies its deeps. The face is all, and, in front of the face, the mask.' (Banville, 1993c: 108).

2. Kleist and *Amphitryon* have proven enduring inspirations for Banville. *The Infinities* is plainly based on the story, and contains a number of metafictional allusions not just to the story itself, but to Banville's own, not particularly successful, stage adaptation of it. One of the novel's central characters, the actress Helen, is preparing for her role as Amphitryon's wife Alcemene in the play. The version in question is clearly Banville's own adaptation, as she mentions it 'all takes place round Vinegar Hill, at the time of the Rebellion' (Banville, 2009b: 192).

3. A passage such as this one from *Lolita* – particularly with respect to the comic vainglory of its tone – imparts a strong sense of Cleave's literary bloodline: 'Let me repeat with quiet force: I was, and still am, despite *mes malheurs*, an exceptionally handsome male; slow-moving, tall, with soft dark hair and a gloomy but all the more seductive cast of demeanor. Exceptional virility often reflects in the subject's displayable features a sullen and congested something that pertains to what he has to conceal. And this was my case. Well did I know, alas, that I could obtain at the snap of my fingers any adult female I chose' (Nabokov, 1959: 27).

4. It is very likely significant that Lydia's real, or given, name is Leah: in the Book of Genesis, Leah is the first of Jacob's wives and the mother of six of the twelve tribes of Israel.

5. This aspect of Vander's character is modelled on the life of Paul de Man, who was posthumously revealed to have contributed almost 200 articles to the Nazi-controlled Belgian collaborationist newspaper *Le Soir* between 1940 and 1942. Much of the language and detail of Vander's pronouncements is evidently appropriated from de Man's 1941 piece 'The Jews in Contemporary Literature', in which he argues that Western civilisation has remained healthy only insofar as it has resisted 'the Semitic infiltration of all aspects of European life' and concludes that banishing the Jews to an island colony remote from Europe would lead to absolutely no 'deplorable consequences for literature' (Hamacher et al., 1998: 45). Banville also acknowledges a debt to Louis Althusser's posthumously published autobiography, *The Future Lasts a Long Time*, in which he discusses his killing of his wife. Readers might also catch fleeting glimpses of Nabokov's public persona in Vander's high patrician arrogance. When, after a guest lecture in Turin, he is asked what his view of the current state of cultural criticism is, Vander replies that it is '"Very fine, from this elevation, thank you"' (Banville, 2002: 97). The quip is a paraphrase of one of Nabokov's more notoriously arrogant interview performances, in which he was asked about his position in the world of letters and replied that he had a 'jolly good view from up here' (Nabokov, 1990: 181).

6. In this respect, *Shroud's* opening powerfully recalls that of *The Book of Evidence*, where Freddie, as we shall see, is concerned first and foremost with recording impressions of himself as he imagines others to receive them.

7. This view of love and sexuality is prevalent throughout Banville's work. In *The Infinities*, for instance, the narrator, ostensibly the god Hermes, characterises love among mortals as self-regard projected outward: 'Show me a pair of them at it and I will show you two mirrors, rose-tinted, flatteringly distorted, locked in an embrace of mutual incomprehension. They love so they may see their pirouetting selves marvellously reflected in the loved one's eyes' (Banville, 2009b: 74).

8. The allusion appears to be to the events of 'Bloody Thursday', 15 May 1969, when the then California governor Ronald Reagan sent 2700 National Guard troops into People's Park (a formerly empty lot on the Berkeley campus expropriated and turned into a public park by students and other radicals) to forcibly remove a group of peaceful protesters. The events, in which over 100 people were hospitalised, with one fatally shot and one blinded, came to be seen as a pivotal moment in the tensions between radicals and the establishment which characterise the late 1960s. This is the context to which Banville is alluding. Freddie, however, is merely alluding to the smell of tear-gas: his interest in such things goes no further. It is, it should be noted, merely 'a faint whiff'.

3 Missing Twins

1. These celestial associations are also present in *The Sea*, where the surname Grace is given to the twins Chloe and Myles.
2. For a comprehensive discussion of Banville's use of Faustian structure and motifs, see the chapter on *Mefisto* in Rüdiger Imhof's *John Banville: a Critical Introduction* (1997).
3. Felix also repeatedly addresses Gabriel Swan as 'bird-boy'. This is principally a Dioscurean allusion, linking him to the twins born of Zeus's rape (in swan form) of Leda. It might also, however, be interpreted as suggestive of Pinocchio's long, beak-like nose.
4. In Klein's developmental model of the human psyche, the infant is incapable of reconciling the mother towards whom it feels anger and hatred – the mother, that is to say, who seems to gratuitously withhold the breast – with the mother it loves and desires. Neither is it capable of reconciling its own painful feelings of distress, frustration and dread with its pleasant feelings of contentment and gratification. This leads to a 'splitting' process, whereby the child creates a 'good' and 'bad' mother, a 'good' and 'bad' breast, and a 'good' and 'bad' self. It is only after the child is weaned that it begins to integrate, albeit imperfectly, these previously 'split off' aspects of self and other and thereby reaches what Klein refers to as the 'depressive position'. It is worth noting the resemblance between Klein's notion of the internalised good object and Kohut's idealised selfobject, as well as the correspondence between her 'depressive position' and his notion of optimal frustration, as outlined in this book's introduction.
5. See Lacan's *The Four Fundamental Concepts of Psychoanalysis* (1997).
6. Elke D'hoker suggests that this Kleinian model 'proves particularly interesting in the context of Banville's complementary female figures because the very first instantiation of an oppositional female pair can be found in the split mother figure of *Birchwood*' (D'hoker, 2004a: 142).
7. The return home of a twin brother in the guise of a cousin seems to point towards Nabokov's *Ada*, a novel which exhaustively explores the narcissistic personality, incestuous twin relationships, and the connections between them. *Ada*'s narrator Van Veen is perhaps the most narcissistic of all Nabokov's protagonists. His self-infatuation and his erotic obsession with his twin sister Ada, whom he originally believes to be his cousin, are of a piece. The fact that one of the twins in the circus is named Ada might also be taken as a nod toward Nabokov's novel.
8. In Gnostic mythology the name Sophia is that which is given to the final and, along with Christ, lowest manifestation of God. In most of the Gnostic cosmologies, it is Sophia who gives birth to the demiurge and is thus responsible for the creation of the material universe. She calls the being *Ildabaoth*, meaning 'child of chaos'. Sophia, then, is both wisdom and chaos. 'Chance' is both the first and the last word of *Mefisto*, a novel about the failure to impose even a superficial order upon the original

chaos of the universe. Whether Banville has this Gnostic sense of the name Sophia in mind is difficult to say with any certainty, but its implications do seem relevant to the novel's themes of knowledge and chaos.

9. Interestingly, Banville repeats this formulation almost word for word in *Athena*. In his description of a fictional portrait of his lover, Freddie notes that 'a crease runs athwart it like a bloodless vein'. The next sentence – 'Everything is changed and yet the same' – might well be read as an oblique allusion to the recurrence in a slightly altered form of a sentence from a previous work (Banville, 1995: 232).

10. This description of Gabriel's defaced condition is suggestive of the bird-like mask worn by doctors in continental Europe during the time of the plague. The eyeholes of the mask were covered with netting or glass ('dead eye sockets') and the long, beak-like protrusion ('hawk nose') was filled with pungent herbs and cotton soaked in camphor. Essentially an early version of the gas mask, it became popular as a Venetian carnival mask in the years after the plague and was frequently used in *commedia dell'arte* performances. This association links *Mefisto* to a later novel similarly concerned with the mutability of identity, defacement and masks, and featuring *commedia dell'arte* motifs: *Shroud*.

11. Imhof is referring here primarily to the opening and closing words of *Birchwood*: 'I am therefore I think' and 'whereof I cannot speak, thereof I must be silent'. The first is an inversion of Descartes' famous 'Cogito ergo sum', the second a paraphrase of proposition 7 of Wittgenstein's *Tractatus Logico Philosophicus*, 'whereof one cannot speak, thereof one must be silent'.

4   The False Self

1. There is an obvious link here to Lacan's notion of the mirror phase, and Winnicott acknowledges this influence at the beginning of his paper.

2. See Leibniz (1992: 67–90).

3. For a thorough discussion of *Tempest* associations in *Ghosts*, see Hedwig Schwall's essay 'Banville's Caliban as a Prestidigitator'. Schwall sees Freddie as combining 'the roles of Caliban, Ariel, Prospero and Ferdinand' and reads *Ghosts* as a whole as a re-imagining of *The Tempest* (Schwall, 1997: 292).

4. This image seems deliberately to evoke the elegiac early sentences of *Lolita*: 'She was Lo, plain Lo, in the morning, standing four feet ten in one sock' (Nabokov, 1959: 7).

5. She also claims to be the 'survivor of a pair of twins', her 'double' having 'come out dead', and suggests that perhaps Freddie too 'had a twin that died, and they didn't tell you'. Although Freddie recognises this for the 'outlandish claim' that it is, it retains for him 'even still a distinct tinge of authenticity [...] even if the details were shaky' (Banville, 1995: 123). This notion links A. to the surviving twins of *Mefisto* and *Birchwood*.

5   Shame

1. Axel Vander also describes the friend from whom he appropriates his identity in a similar way: 'He was one of those people, the beautiful, the vivid ones, whose sense of themselves must be preserved above everything else, so that the rest of us shall not be undone, in ways we cannot quite specify [...] content if only something of his luminence should reflect on us' (Banville, 2002: 134). In a similar way, Chloe Grace is a kind of narcissistic selfobject for Max Morden: 'If her sense of herself were tainted,' he writes, 'by doubt or feelings of foolishness or of lack of perspicacity, my regard for her would itself be tainted' (2005a: 167).

2. In *The Book of Evidence*, Freddie's return home after many years abroad is marked by similar impressions, rendered in similar terms. He invokes the 'humble, drab, brownish smell' of the house in which he grew up (Banville, 1989a: 43).

3. We first encounter this exact situation (and locution) in *Kepler*, where the astronomer, now a great success, returns home to his family after years abroad. He is stricken by what he calls 'a sudden faint disgust at the spectacle of family resemblance, the little legs and hollow chests and pale pinched faces, botched prototypes of his own, if not lovely, at least completed parts' (92).

4. The town of Ballyless is evidently based on Rosslare Strand in County Wexford. Banville published a short biographical piece in the *Irish Times* in 1989 in which he writes about his childhood summers in Rosslare. Sufficient details from *The Sea* are recognisable in the piece to warrant speculation about the novel's having strongly autobiographical elements. There is a boy, like Myles Grace, with webbed toes. There is a dairyman named Cormie Duggan – 'a decent, gentle man' – from whom the young John Banville was sent to collect cans of milk, as Max Morden is sent to collect milk from Christy Duignan. The Banvilles stayed, like the Mordens, in a small wooden chalet or 'hut'. Their hut was distinct from the others in the field in being a wooden railway carriage with its wheels removed, and Banville recollects being asked by a girl 'with a curled-up lip if I belonged to that family who couldn't afford to rent a *real* hut and had to make do with that awful train thing'. He speculates that this may have been his 'first taste of social ignominy' (Banville, 1989b: 11). In a 2005 online interview with the novelist Mark Sarvas, Banville speaks about the biographical elements of the novel: '[*The Sea*'s] childhood scenes are obviously based on my own [...] we used to spend our summers in Rosslare Strand, which is about fourteen miles south of Wexford'. He goes on to mention a childhood romance: 'I had a girlfriend, she used to come and stay at Rosslare Strand from her home in Liverpool. She'd come with her family. In fact, she stayed in a house that was very near the house that The Cedars is modeled on in *The Sea*, which is a house I used to go to with a friend of mine. So I've kind of conflated the two. But she would come every summer and we were just crazy about each other from the age of nine or ten' (Banville, 2005b).

5. The name Morden itself, the infinitive form of the German verb 'to kill' as Rüdiger Imhof points out, is as suggestive of mortality as the name Grace is of divinity (Imhof, 2006: 174).

6 Narrative Narcissism

1. One of the characteristics of metafiction identified by Waugh is 'a parodic, playful, excessive or deceptively naïve style of writing' (1984: 2). There is another sense in which the writing can be identified as distinctly metafictional: its obvious evocation of the opening pages of Joyce's *A Portrait of the Artist as a Young Man*.
2. Brian McHale identifies Banville's work as representative of the importance of the tension between historical fact and fiction in the postmodern historical novel: 'Where the classical historical novel sought to ease the ontological tension between historical fact and fictional invention,' he writes, 'and to camouflage if possible the seam along which fact and fiction meet, postmodernist historical fictions such as those written by Pynchon, Barthes, Fowles, Coover [...] John Banville [...] and others, aim to exacerbate this tension and expose the seam. They do this, for instance, by contradicting familiar historical fact, by mingling the realistic and fantastic modes, and by flaunting anachronism' (McHale, 1992: 152). Each of these strategies has been conspicuous in Banville's work from as early as *Birchwood*, with its contemporaneous telephones and potato famines, and as recently as *The Infinities*, with its steam trains and water-powered cars.
3. Source identified by John Kenny in *John Banville* (2009: 46).
4. The narrator of *Shroud* refers to himself as Axel Vander throughout the novel, although this is eventually revealed to be a stolen identity.
5. He takes Imhof to task, for instance, for his self-confessed inability to fathom any sense in which the book might be satirical: 'He is unable to do so because of his persistent disregard for considering Banville as having anything to say about the Irish condition' (Hand, 2002: 42–3).
6. For a fuller discussion of the ways in which *The Newton Letter* is indebted to these works, see Imhof's *John Banville: a Critical Introduction* (1997: 145–50).
7. The use of the name in both *Birchwood* and *The Newton Letter* may also be a reference to the Anglo-Irish writer Emily Lawless, whose fiction, biography and poetry dealt with the experience of the ascendancy class.
8. In an interview with *The Paris Review*, Banville was asked what it was that attracted him to novel writing. His answer was as follows: 'Language. Words. The world is not real for me until it has been pushed through the mesh of language' (Banville, 2009a: 135). In this respect, these sentiments recall those of Gide's autobiographical novelist-within-a-novel in *The Counterfeiters*, who describes his journal – and the narrative's *mise*

en abyme – as his 'pocket mirror', and claims that 'I cannot feel that anything that happens to me has any real existence until I see it reflected there' (Gide, 1966: 142).

9. It is worth noting that in *The Sea*, Max Morden informs us that his daughter has abandoned a long-term research project on 'Vaublin and the fête galante style' (Banville, 2005c: 63).

10. Banville has himself dabbled in film. He wrote the screenplay for the 1999 adaptation of Elizabeth Bowen's *The Last September* and, with Glenn Close, co-wrote *Albert Nobbs*, based on a short story by George Moore.

7 The Paradox of Empathy

1. Brendan McNamee dissents from D'hoker's view of Freddie's crime as 'ethical rather than imaginative', rejecting the notion of such a binary. In Banville's work, he claims, 'ethics and imagination are the same thing; the failure of one is the failure of the other (in both senses of the word "other")' (McNamee, 2005: 83n). The terms, he claims, are effectively synonymous: 'True imagination, seeing things *as they are*, is realising that "something other than one's self is real", and, as Iris Murdoch has it, it is a form of love' (81).

2. This tendency to idealise and essentialise women has been noted, and even condemned, by a number of critics. See, for example, Patricia Coughlan's essay 'Banville, the Feminine and the Scenes of Eros' and John Kenny's discussion of Banville's female characters in his book *John Banville* (Kenny, 2009: 152–63).

3. Anja Müller, in an essay exploring representations of women in the Art Trilogy, identifies what she calls 'the myth of a solipsistic parturition' as a common element of *Ghosts* and *Athena* (Müller, 2004: 198).

4. In *Shroud*, the letter that Cass Cleave sends to Vander informing him of her discoveries about his background is delivered by a 'helmed and goggled Hermes on a bike' (Banville, 2002: 5). The message has to do with Vander's crossing of boundaries of identity in the past; it also represents, in this sense, a crossing of the boundary between past and present. Vander himself articulates it as the crossing of an internal boundary, a partition between one and another version of the self. 'I had the certain sense,' he writes, 'of having crossed, of having been forced to cross, an invisible frontier, and of being in a state that forever more would be post-something, would be forever an afterwards. That letter, of course, was the crossing point. Now I was cloven in two more thoroughly than ever, I who was always more than myself' (7).

5. There is a particularly vivid irony to this notion of Adam as a divinely unbodied presence. The stroke which led to his coma was caused, after all, by his straining too forcefully on the toilet. As so often with Banville, the juxtaposition of the idealised divine and the ignobly corporeal is a

rich source of bathos. It is worth noting here that in the manuscript of *The Infinities*, though not in the published novel, Banville uses as an epigraph Emerson's line 'A man is a god in ruins'. See the reproduction of the opening pages of the manuscript that illustrate the *Paris Review* interview 'John Banville: the Art of Fiction No. 200' (Banville, 2009a: 136).

Bibliography

American Psychiatric Association. 1980. *Diagnostic and Statistical Manual of Mental Disorders*. Third edition. Washington, DC: American Psychiatric Association.

Banville, John. 1971. *Nightspawn*. London: Secker & Warburg.

——. 1973. *Birchwood*. London: Secker & Warburg.

——. 1976. *Doctor Copernicus*. London: Secker & Warburg.

——. 1981a. 'An Interview with John Banville.' Interview by Rüdiger Imhof. *Irish University Review* 11.1 (Spring 1981): 5–12.

——. 1981b. 'A Talk.' *Irish University Review* 11.1 (1981): 13–17.

——. 1981c. *Kepler*. London: Secker & Warburg.

——. 1981d. 'My Readers, That Small Band, Deserve a Rest.' *Irish University Review* 11.1 (John Banville Special Issue, Spring 1981): 5–12.

——. 1982. *The Newton Letter: An Interlude*. London: Secker & Warburg.

——. 1986a. *Mefisto*. London: Secker & Warburg.

——. 1986b. Out of Chaos Comes Order. John Banville Interviewed by Ciaran Carty.' *Sunday Tribune* 14 September 1986: 18.

——. 1987. 'Q. and A. with John Banville. Interview by Rüdiger Imhof.' *Irish Literary Supplement* (Spring): 13.

——. 1989a. *The Book of Evidence*. London: Secker & Warburg.

——. 1989b. 'Lupins and Moth-laden Nights in Rosslare.' *The Irish Times* 18 July 1989: 11.

——. 1989c. 'Samuel Beckett Dies in Paris, Aged 83.' *The Irish Times* 25 December 1989: 18.

——. 1993a. *Ghosts*. London: Secker & Warburg.

——. 1993b. *South Bank Show*, interview with Melvyn Bragg. LWT/Ulster Television.

——. 1993c. 'Making Little Monsters Walk.' In Clare Boylan (ed.), *The Agony and the Ego: the Art and Strategy of Fiction Writing Explored*. London: Penguin.

——. 1995. *Athena*. London: Secker & Warburg.

——. 1997a. 'An Interview with John Banville.' Interview by Hedwig Schwall. *The European English Messenger* 6.1: 13–19.

——. 1997b. *The Untouchable*. London: Picador.

——. 2000a. *Eclipse*. London: Picador.

——. 2000b. 'Freud and Scrambled Egos.' *The Irish Times* 18 November 2000: 53. Print.

——. 2000c. 'John Banville.' Interview by Joe Jackson. *Hot Press* 8 November 2000: 58–61.

——. 2000d. 'Oblique Dreamer: Interview with John Banville.' *Observer* 17 September 2000: 15. Print.

——. 2002. *Shroud*. New York: Knopf.

——. 2005a. 'John Banville.' Interview by Ben Ehrenreich, in Vendela Vida (ed.), *The Believer Book of Writers Talking to Writers*. San Francisco: Believer Books: 43–58.

——. 2005b. 'The John Banville Interview.' Interview by Mark Sarvas. *The Elegant Variation* (blog) 26 September 2005. *http://marksarvas.blogs.com/ elegvar/2005/09/the_longawaited.html*. Website accessed on 18 December 2008.

——. 2005c. *The Sea*. London: Picador.

——. 2006a. 'Curing Our Hatred of the New.' *The Irish Times* 16 August 2006, Weekend Review: 11. Print.

——. 2006b. 'John Banville and Derek Hand in Conversation.' Irish University Review 36.1 (Special Issue: Spring/Summer 2006): 200–15.

——. 2007. 'John Banville Confronts Benjamin Black.' http://www. benjaminblackbooks.com/BBworld.htm. Website accessed on 13 January 2008.

——. 2009a. 'The Art of Fiction No. 200.' Interview by Belinda McKeon. *The Paris Review* 51.188 (Spring 2009): 132–53.

——. 2009b. *The Infinities*. London: Picador.

——. 2009c. *The View*. Interview. RTE. Broadcast 29 September 2009.

——. 2009d. 'John Banville.' Interview by Beth Jones. *Untitled Books* (website). 7 September 2009. http://untitledbooks.com/features/interviews/john-banville/. Website accessed on 29 March 2010.

——. 2009e. 'Writing for a Living: a Joy or a Chore: Nine Authors Give Their Views.' *The Guardian* 3 March 2009: 11. Print.

——. 2012. *Ancient Light*. London: Penguin.

Barthes, Roland. 1977. *Image-Music-Text*. Transl. Stephen Heath. New York: Noonday.

Beauvoir, Simone de. 1997. *The Second Sex*. Ed. and transl. H. M. Parshley. London: Vintage.

Beckett, Samuel. 1983. *Disjecta: Miscellaneous Writings and a Dramatic Fragment*. London: Calder.

Bersani, Leo, and Adam Phillips. 2008. *Intimacies*. University of Chicago Press.

Borges, Jorge Luis. 2001. *The Total Library*. London: Penguin.

Boyd, Brian. 1993. *Vladimir Nabokov: the American Years*. London: Vintage.

Cameron, Katherine. 1996. 'Winnicott and Lacan: selfhood versus subject-hood.' In Val Richards and Gillian Wilce (eds), *The Person Who is Me: Contemporary Perspectives on the True and False Self*. London: Karnac: 37–45.

Coetzee, J. M. 2003. *Elizabeth Costello*. London: Vintage.

Cooper, Arnold M. 1986. 'Narcissism.' In Andrew P. Morrison (ed.), *Essential Papers on Narcissism*. New York University Press: 112–43.

Dallenbach, Lucien. 1989. *The Mirror in the Text*. Transl. Jeremy Whiteley and Emma Hughes. Cambridge: Polity Press.

Derrida, Jacques. 2004. *Dissemination*. London: Continuum.

D'hoker, Elke. 2004a. *Visions of Alterity: Representation in the Works of John Banville*. Amsterdam: Rodopi.

——. 2004b. '"What Then Would Life Be But Despair?": Skepticism and Romanticism in John Banville's Doctor Copernicus.' *Contemporary Literature* 45.1: 49–78.

Eliot, George. 1967. *Essays of George Eliot*. Ed. Thomas Pinney. London: Routledge.

Eliot, T. S. 1974. *Collected Poems 1909–1962*. London: Faber.

Fayek, A. 1981. 'Narcissism and the Death Instinct.' *International Journal of Psycho-Analysis* 62: 309–22.

Freud, Sigmund. 1963. *A General Introduction to Psychoanalysis*. New York: Liveright.

——. 1986. 'On Narcissism: An Introduction.' In Andrew P. Morrison (ed.), *Essential Papers on Narcissism*. New York University Press: 17–43.

——. 1995. 'Three Essays on the Theory of Sexuality.' In Peter Gay (ed.), *The Freud Reader*. London: Vintage.

——. 2008. *The Future of an Illusion*. Transl. J.A. Underwood and Shaun Whiteside. London: Penguin.

Friburg, Hedda. 2006. '"[P]assing Through Ourselves and Finding Ourselves in the Beyond": the Rites of Passage of Cass Cleave in John Banville's *Eclipse* and *Shroud*.' *Irish University Review* 36.1 (Spring/Summer 2006): 151–64.

Gide, André. 1966. *The Counterfeiters*. Transl. Dorothy Bussy. London: Penguin.

——. 1978. *Journals 1889–1949*. Transl. and ed. Justin O'Brien. London: Penguin.

Hamacher, Werner, Neil Herz, and Thomas Keenan. 1988. *Responses: On Paul de Man's Wartime Journalism*. Lincoln, NE: University of Nebraska Press.

Hand, Derek. 2002. *John Banville: Exploring Fictions*. Contemporary Irish Writers. Dublin: Liffey Press.

Heaney, Seamus. 1998. *Opened Ground: Poems 1966–1996*. London: Faber and Faber.

Holmes, Jeremy. 2001. *Narcissism*. Cambridge: Icon.

Hutcheon, Linda. 1984. *Narcissistic Narrative: the Metafictional Paradox*. New York and London: Methuen.

——. 1988. *A Poetics of Postmodernism*. London: Routledge.

Imhof, Rüdiger. 1981. 'John Banville's Supreme Fiction.' *Irish University Review* 11.1: 52–86.

——. 1987. 'Swan's Way; or Goethe, Einstein, Banville – the Eternal Recurrence.' *Etudes Irlandaises* 12.2: 113–29.

——. 1997. *John Banville: a Critical Introduction*. Dublin: Wolfhound.

——. 2006. 'The Sea: "Was't Well Done?"' *Irish University Review* 36.1: 165–81.

Jones, Ernest. 1955. *The Life and Works of Sigmund Freud*. Vol. 2. New York: Basic Books.

Kenny, John. 2009. *John Banville*. Dublin; Portland, OR: Irish Academic Press.

Kermode, Frank. 1967. *The Sense of an Ending*. New York: OUP, 1967.

Kernberg, Otto F. 1986. 'Factors in the Psychoanalytic Treatment of Narcissistic Personalities.' In Andrew P. Morrison (ed.), *Essential Papers on Narcissism*. New York University Press: 213–44.

Kilroy, Thomas. 1993. 'The Isle is Full of Noises.' *The Irish Times* 27 March 1993: 36. Print.

Klein, Melanie. 1988. *Envy and Gratitude: And Other Works 1946–1963*. London: Virago.

Kleist, Heinrich von. 1997. *Selected Writings*. Transl. David Constantine. Oxford: Dent.

Kohut, Heinz. 1966. 'Forms and Transformations of Narcissism.' In Andrew P. Morrison (ed.), *Essential Papers on Narcissism*. New York University Press: 61–87.

——. 1971. *The Analysis of the Self: a Systematic Approach to the Psychoanalytic Treatment of Narcissistic Personality Disorders*. Madison, Connecticut: International Universities Press.

——. 1972. 'Thoughts on Narcissism and Narcissistic Rage.' *The Psychoanalytic Study of the Child* 27 (1972): 360–400.

——. 1984. *How Does Analysis Cure?* University of Chicago Press, 1984.

Kohut, Heinz, and P. Seitz. 1963. *The Evolution of Self Psychology: Progress in Self Psychology*. Hillsdale, New York: Analytic Press.

Lacan, Jacques. 2006. 'The Mirror Stage as Formative of the *I* Function as Revealed in Psychoanalytic Experience.' In Jacques Lacan, *Ecrits*. Transl. Bruce Fink. New York, London: Norton.

——. 1977. *The Four Fundamental Concepts of Psycho-analysis*. Transl. Jacques-Alain Miller and ed. Alan Sheridan. London: Institute of Psycho-analysis, 1977.

Laertius, Diogenes. 2006. *The Lives and Opinions of Eminent Philosophers*. Transl. C. D. Yonge. Whitefish, MT: Kessinger, 2006.

Lasch, Christopher. 1980. *The Culture of Narcissism: American Life in an Age of Diminishing Expectations*. London: Abacus Press.

Leibniz, G. W. 1992. *Discourse on Metaphysics and the Monadology*. Transl. George R. Montgomery. Amherst, NY: Prometheus.

Lévinas, Emmanuel. 1996. *Basic Philosophical Writings*. Ed. Adriaan T. Peperzak, Simon Critchley, and Robert Bernasconi. Bloomington, IN: Indiana University Press.

Lewin, Vivienne. 2004. *The Twin in the Transference*. London: Whurr.

Lynd, Helen M. 1958. *On Shame and the Search for Identity*. New York: Harcourt Brace.

McHale, Brian. 1992. *Constructing Postmodernism*. London: Routledge.

McMinn, Joseph. 1991. *John Banville: a Critical Study*. Dublin: Gill & Macmillan.

——. 1999. *The Supreme Fictions of John Banville*. Manchester University Press.

McNamee, Brendan. 2005. 'The Human Moment: Self, Other and Suspension in Banville's Ghosts.' *Miscelánea* 32 (2005): 69–85.

Mollon, Phil. 1993. *The Fragile Self: the Structure of Narcissistic Disturbance*. London: Whurr.

Morrison, Andrew P. 1989. *Shame: the Underside of Narcissism*. Hillsdale, New Jersey: Analytic Press.

Müller, Anja. 2004. '"You Have Been Framed": the Function of Ekphrasis for the Representation of Women in John Banville's Trilogy (*The Book of Evidence, Ghosts, Athena*).' *Studies in the Novel* 36.2 (Summer 2004): 185–205.

Nabokov, Vladimir. 1959. *Lolita*. London: Penguin, 1959.

——. 1990. *Strong Opinions*. New York, Vintage.

——. 2001. *The Real Life of Sebastian Knight*. London: Penguin; New York, Cambridge University Press.

Nussbaum, Martha. 2003. *Upheavals of Thought: the Intelligence of Emotions*. Cambridge University Press.

O'Leary, John, and Fred White. 1986. 'Shame and Gender Issues in Pathological Narcissism.' *Psychoanalytic Psychology* 3.4: 327–39.

Ovid. *Metamorphoses*. 1986. Transl. A. D. Melville. Oxford University Press.

Pausanias. 1918. *Description of Greece*. Transl. W. H. S. Jones. London: Heinemann.

Phillips, Adam. 1995. *Terrors and Experts*. London: Faber and Faber.

Phillips, Adam. 1988. *Winnicott*. London: Fontana.

Plato. 1997. *Complete Works*. Ed. John M. Cooper. Indianapolis, IN: Hackett.

Rank, Otto. 1911. 'Ein Beitrag zum Narzissismus.' *Jahrbuch für Psychoanalytische und Psychopathologische Forschungen* 3: 401–26.

Reich, Annie. 1986. 'Pathologic Forms of Self-Esteem Regulation.' In Andrew P. Morrison (ed.), *Essential Papers on Narcissism*. New York University Press: 44–60.

Ricoeur, Paul. 1988. *Time and Narrative Vol. 3*. Transl. Kathleen Blamey and David Pellauer. Chicago, London: University of Chicago Press.

Roth, Philip. 1990. *Deception*. London: Cape, 1990.

Rousseau, Jean-Jacques. 1979. *Emile: Or, On Education*. New York: Basic Books.

Russell, Bertrand. 1966. *Philosophical Essays*. London: Allen & Unwin; also London, Longman (1910).

Sartre, Jean Paul. 1943. *Being and Nothingness*. London: Methuen.

Schwall, Hedwig. 1997. 'Banville's Caliban as a Prestidigitator.' In Nadia Lie and Theo D'haen (eds), *Constellation Caliban: Figurations of a Character*. Amsterdam: Rodopi.

Sennett, Richard.1977. *The Fall of Public Man*. Cambridge University Press.

Stolorow, Robert D. 1986. 'Toward a Functional Definition of Narcissism.' In Andrew P. Morrison (ed.), *Essential Papers on Narcissism*. New York University Press: 197–209.

Trivers, Robert. 1985. *Social Evolution*. Menlo Park, CA: Benjamin Cummings.

Walshe, Eibhear. 2006. '"A Lout's Game": Espionage, Irishness, and Sexuality in the Untouchable.' *Irish University Review* 36.1: 102–15.

Warner, Marina. 2006. *Phantasmagoria: Spirit Visions, Metaphors, and Media into the Twenty-first Century*. Oxford: OUP.

Waugh, Patricia. 1984. *Metafiction: the Theory and Practice of Self-Conscious Fiction*. London: Methuen.

Wilde, Oscar. 2000. *The Picture of Dorian Gray*. London: Penguin.

Winnicott, D. W. 1965. *The Family and Individual Development*. London: Tavistock Publications.

———. 1990. 'Communicating and Not Communicating Leading to a Study of Certain Opposites.' In D. W. Winnicott, *The Maturational Processes and the Facilitating Environment*. London: Karnac: 179–92.

———. 1996. 'Ego Distortion in Terms of True and False Self.' In Val Richards and Gillian Wilce (eds), *The Person Who is Me: Contemporary Perspectives on the True and False Self*. London: Karnac: 7–22.

———. 2005. *Playing and Reality*. London: Routledge.

Woolf, Virginia. 1977. *The Diary of Virginia Woolf. Vol. 1, 1915–1919*. Ed. Anne Olivier Bell. London: Hogarth Press.

Yeats, W. B. 2001. *Major Works*. Oxford: OUP.

Žižek, Slavoj. 1992. *Everything You Always Wanted to Know About Lacan But Were Afraid to Ask Hitchcock*. London: Verso.

Index